"No d   for her ears alone.

Cecily's heart thudded.

"Be calm," he murmured, and swiftly, so swiftly that Cecily
had no notion of what he was about, he released her and
reached up. Deftly unpinning her veil, he cast it aside.
Stunned beyond movement, for no man had ever touched her
clothing so intimately, Cecily swallowed and stood meek as a
lamb, while quick fingers reached behind her to release the
tie of her wimple, and then that, too, followed her veil into a
corner. Reaching past her neck, he found her plait and drew
it forward, so that it draped over her shoulder.

For all that the brightest of flags must have been flying on
her cheeks, Cecily shivered, shamefully aware that it was
not with distaste.

She had eyes and ears only for the man in front of her, the
man whose green eyes even now were caressing her hair.
He no longer touched her anywhere, yet she could scarcely
breathe.

"No dowry," he repeated softly, still gazing at her hair. "But
there is gold enough here for any man."

* * *

The Novice Bride
Harlequin® Historical #217—August 2007

CAROL TOWNEND

has been making up stories since she was a child. Whenever she comes across a tumbledown building, be it castle or cottage, she can't help conjuring up the lives of the people who once lived there. Her Yorkshire forebears were friendly with the Brontë sisters. Perhaps their influence lingers….

Carol's love of ancient and medieval history took her to London University, where she read history, and her first novel (published by Mills & Boon) won the Romantic Novelists' Association's New Writers' Award. Currently she lives near Kew Gardens with her husband and daughter. Visit her Web site at www.caroltownend.co.uk.

CAROL TOWNEND

The Novice Bride

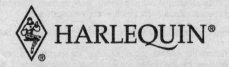

HARLEQUIN®

TORONTO • NEW YORK • LONDON
AMSTERDAM • PARIS • SYDNEY • HAMBURG
STOCKHOLM • ATHENS • TOKYO • MILAN • MADRID
PRAGUE • WARSAW • BUDAPEST • AUCKLAND

ISBN-13: 978-0-373-30526-1
ISBN-10:   0-373-30526-5

THE NOVICE BRIDE

www.eHarlequin.com

Printed in U.S.A.

Author Note

England at the time of the Norman Conquest—what an extraordinary period of history! It is all there in the clash of two cultures, the civilized Anglo-Saxons and the ruthless Norman invaders. The English population are desperate to hang on to their way of life, while the incoming Franks are out for what they can get. The possibilities for dramatic stories are endless.

In *The Novice Bride,* a young Anglo-Saxon novice finds herself accepting marriage with a total stranger— a Breton knight in William of Normandy's train. The knight, Sir Adam Wymark, is a man of experience, whereas his bride, novice Cecily, is all innocence. The contrast between the two fascinated me. I went to a Yorkshire convent school, but can't say whether that influenced me in choosing my heroine. Cecily sprang into my mind fully formed; she was not consciously created.

Here are three books that give a flavor of the period:

The Bayeux Tapestry by Wolfgang Grape, Prestel, 1994

1066: The Hidden History of the Bayeux Tapestry by Andrew Bridgeford, Harper Perennial, 2004

The Year 1000 by Robert Lacey and Danny Danziger, Abacus, 2003

Of course, there are many other inspirational books, and I hope to use some of them to write more romances set in the early Norman period.

For Granny

With thanks to John, my first reader,
Den for the Breton Hero,
and Claude at *Les Chênes* who helped me finish.

Chapter One

Novice Cecily was on her knees in St Anne's chapel when the shouting began outside. According to the candle clock it was almost noon, and Cecily—who in her former life had been called Lady Cecily Fulford—was in retreat. She had sworn not to speak a word to anyone till after the nuns had broken their fasts the next morning. A small figure in a threadbare grey habit and veil, alone at her *prie-dieu*, Cecily had about eighteen hours of silence to go, and was determined that this time her retreat would not be broken.

Lamps glowed softly in wall sconces, and above the altar a little November daylight was filtering through the narrow unshuttered window. Ignoring the chill seeping up from the stone flags, Cecily bent her veiled head over her prayer beads. 'Hail Mary, full of grace, blessed art thou amongst women and blessed is—'

A thud on the chapel door had her swinging round. Another harder one had the thick oak door bouncing on its hinges.

'Cecily! *Cecily!* Are you in there? You *must* let me speak to you! It's—'

The woman's voice was cut off abruptly, but Cecily's prayers were quite forgotten. For though the voice did not belong to any of the nuns, it seemed vaguely familiar. She strained to hear more.

Two voices, arguing, and none too quietly. One belonged to

Sister Judith, the convent portress. The other voice, the outsider's, went up a notch in pitch, touched on hysteria...

Part curious, part anxious, Cecily scrambled to her feet. Not more bad news, surely? Hadn't the loss of both her father and brother at Hastings been enough...?

She was halfway up the aisle when the door burst open. Lamps flickered, and her blood sister, the Lady Emma Fulford, threw off the restraining arms of the portress and hurtled into the chapel.

One year Cecily's senior, seventeen year-old Emma was a vision in flowing pink robes and a burgundy velvet cloak. Dropping a riding crop and a pair of cream kid gloves onto the flagstones, she flung herself at Cecily.

'Cecily! Oh, Cecily, you *must* speak to me. You must!'

Finding herself enveloped in a fierce embrace that bordered on the desperate, Cecily fought free of silks and velvets and the scent of roses so that she could study her sister's face. One look had her abandoning her vow of silence. 'Of course I'll speak to you.'

Emma gave an unladylike sniff. 'She—' a jerk of her head at Sister Judith set her long silken veil aquiver '—said you were in retreat, not to be disturbed. That you may at last be going to take your vows.'

'That is so.' Emma had been crying, and not just in the past few minutes either, for her fine complexion was blotched and puffy and her eyes were rimmed with shadows. In the four years since Cecily had been brought to the convent she and her elder sister had become strangers, but her sister's delicate beauty had lived on in her mind. This distraught, haggard Emma made her blood run cold.

Sister Judith shut the chapel door with a thump and stood just inside the threshold. Folding her arms, she shook her head at Cecily, the novice who once again had failed to keep her retreat.

Cecily took Emma's hand. Her fingers were like ice. 'Something else has happened, hasn't it? Something dreadful.'

Emma's eyes filled and she gave a shuddering sob. 'Oh, Cecily, it's Maman…'

'Maman? What? What's happened to Maman?' But Cecily had no need to wait for an answer, for she could read it in Emma's expression.

Their mother was dead.

Knees buckling, Cecily gripped Emma's arms and the sisters clung to each other.

'Not Maman,' Cecily choked. 'Emma, please, not Maman too…'

Emma nodded, tears flooding openly down her cheeks.

'Wh…when?'

'Three days since.'

'How? Was it…was it the babe?' It had to be that. Their mother, Philippa of Fulford, had been thirty-seven—not young—and she had been seven months pregnant at the time of the battle at Hastings. Of Norman extraction herself, she had found the great battle especially hard to cope with. Cecily knew her mother would have taken great pains to hide her emotions, but the deaths of her Anglo Saxon husband and her firstborn son would have been too much to bear.

Many women died in childbed, and at her mother's age, and in her state of grief…

Emma dashed away her tears and nodded. 'Aye. Her time came early, her labour was long and hard, and afterwards… Oh, Cecily, there was so much blood. We could do nothing to stem the flow. Would that you had been there. Your time at Sister Mathilda's elbow has taught you so much about healing, whereas I…' Her voice trailed off.

Cecily shook her head. It was true that she had greedily taken in all that Sister Mathilda had chosen to teach her, but she also knew that not everyone could be saved. 'Emma, listen. Maman's death was not your fault. Once bleeding starts inside it's nigh impossible to stop…and besides, it's possible she simply lost the will to live after father and Cenwulf were killed.'

Emma sniffed. 'Aye. We were going to send for you. Wilf was ready to mount up. But by the time we realised the dangers it…it was too late.' Emma gripped Cecily's hands.

'It was not your fault.'

'Nobody'd trained me! Oh, Cecily, if you could have seen her after the messenger came from Hastings. She could not eat or sleep. She wandered round the Hall like a ghost. It was as though, with Father dead, a light went out within her. Father was not an easy man, and Maman was not one to wear her affections openly—'

'"Displays of sentiment are vulgar, and not suited to a lady,"' Cecily murmured, repeating a well-worn phrase of her mother's.

'Quite so. But she loved him. If any doubted that—' Emma gave Cecily a penetrating look, knowing that Cecily and her father, Thane Edgar, had crossed swords on more matters than the delaying of her profession. 'If any doubted that, this last month would have set them right. And Cenwulf.' Emma's gaze brimmed with sympathy. 'I realise you did adore him too.'

'Maman's heart was broken.'

Emma gulped. 'Aye. And twisted.'

'Because her own countrymen were the invaders?'

Emma squeezed Cecily's hand. 'I knew you'd understand.'

'Lady Emma…' Sister Judith's voice cut in, reminding the girls of the portress's presence by the chapel door.

It was Sister Judith's duty to give or deny permission for outsiders to enter the convent. Since the order was not an enclosed one, permission was granted more often than not, but *never* when a nun or novice was on retreat. Hands folded at her girdle, silver cross winking at her breast, the nun regarded Emma sternly, but not unkindly. She had been moved, Cecily saw, by what she had heard.

'Lady Emma, since you have seen fit to break your sister's retreat by this conference, may I suggest that you continue in the portress's lodge? The Angelus bell is about to strike, and the rest of the community will be needing the chapel.'

'Of course, Sister Judith. Our apologies,' Cecily said.

Bending to retrieve Emma's riding crop and gloves, Cecily took her sister's hand and led her out of the chapel.

A chill winter wind was tossing straw about the yard. Wood-smoke gusted out of the cookhouse, and their breath made white vapour which was no sooner formed than it was snatched away.

Emma drew the burgundy velvet cloak more tightly about her shoulders.

Cecily, who had not touched a cloak of such quality since entering the convent, and in any case was not wearing even a thin one since she was within the confines of the convent, shivered, and ushered her sister swiftly across the yard towards the south gate.

The portress's lodge, a thatched wooden hut, sagged against the palisade. Abutting the lodge at its eastern end was the convent's guest house, a slightly larger, marginally more inviting building; Cecily led her sister inside.

Even though the door was thrown wide the room was full of shadows, for the wooden walls were planked tight, with only a shuttered slit or two to let in the light. Since no guests had been looked for, there was no fire in the central hearth, only a pile of dead ashes. November marked the beginning of the dark months, but Cecily knew better than to incur Mother Aethelflaeda's wrath by lighting a precious candle. If she added the sin of wasting a candle in daylight to the sin of her broken retreat, she'd be doing penance till Christmas ten years hence.

Dropping Emma's riding crop and gloves on the trestle along with her rosary, Cecily wrenched the shutters open. The cold and ensuing draughts would have to be borne. Emma paced up and down. Her pink gown, Cecily now had time to notice, was liberally spattered with mud about the hem, her silken veil was awry, and the chaplet that secured it was crooked.

'You rode fast to bring me this sad news,' Cecily said slowly, as her sister strode back and forth. Now that the first shock was passing, her mind was beginning to work, and she had questions. 'And yet…if Maman died three days since, you must have delayed your ride to me. There is more, isn't there?'

Emma stopped her pacing. 'Yes. The babe lives. A boy.'

Cecily gaped. 'A boy? And he lives? Oh, it's a miracle—new life after so much death!' Her face fell. 'But so early? Emma, he *cannot* survive.'

'So I thought. He *is* small. I took the liberty of having him christened Philip, in case…in case—'

Emma broke off with a choking sound, but she had no need to add more. Having lived in the convent for four years, Cecily knew the Church's view as well as any. If the babe did die, better that he died christened into the faith. For if he died outside it, he would be for eternity a lost soul.

'Philip,' Cecily murmured. 'Maman would have liked that.'

'Aye. And it's not a Saxon name, so if he survives…I thought his chances better if he bore a Norman name.'

'It is a good thought to stress Maman's lineage rather than Father's,' Cecily replied. The son of a Saxon thane could not thrive if in truth England was to become Norman, but the son of a Norman lady…

Emma drew close, touched Cecily's arm, and again Cecily became conscious of the incongruous fragrance of roses in November, of the softness of her sister's gown, of the whiteness of her hands, of her unbroken lady's nails. All the mud in England couldn't obscure either the quality of Emma's clothing or her high status.

She brushed awkwardly at her own coarse skirts in a vain attempt to shake out some dust and creases, and hide the hole at the knee where she'd torn the fabric grubbing up fennel roots in the herb garden. There were so many holes in the cloth it was nigh impossible to darn.

'I would have come at once to tell you, Cecily, if I had not had my hands full caring for our new brother.'

'You were right to put Philip first. Do you think he may thrive?'

'I pray so. I left him with Gudrun. She was brought to bed a few months since herself, with a girl, and she is acting at his wet nurse.' The restless pacing resumed. 'He would not feed at first, but Gudrun persevered, and now…and now…' A faint smile lit Emma's eyes. 'I think he may thrive, after all.'

'That at least is good news.'

'Aye.' Emma turned, picked up her riding crop from the trestle and tapped it against her side. She stood with her back to Cecily, facing the door, and stared at the cookhouse smoke swirling in the yard. 'Cecily…I…I confess I didn't really come to tell you about Philip…'

'No? What, then?' Cecily made as if to move towards Emma, but a sharp hand movement from her sister stilled her. 'Emma?'

'I…I've come to bid you farewell.'

Thinking she had not heard properly, Cecily frowned. 'What?'

'I'm going north.' Emma began to speak quickly, her back unyielding. 'More messengers came, after Maman…after Philip was born. Messengers from Duke William.'

'Normans? At Fulford Hall?'

A jerky nod. 'They'll be there by now.'

Cecily touched Emma's arm to make her turn, but Emma resisted Cecily's urging and kept staring at the door. 'The carrion crows are come already,' Emma said bitterly. 'They are efficient, at least, and have not wasted any time seizing our lands. The Duke knows that our father and Cenwulf are dead. In a convoluted message that spoke of King Harold's perfidy as an oath-breaker, I was informed that I, Thane Edgar's daughter, have been made a ward of Duke William, and I am to be given in marriage to one of his knights. And not even a man with proper Norman blood in him, like Maman, but some Breton clod with no breeding at all!'

Emma swung round. Her eyes were wild and hard, and the

riding crop smacked against her thigh. 'Cecily, I won't. I can't—
I *won't* do it!'

Cecily caught Emma's hands between hers. 'Have you met him?'

Emma heaved in a shuddering breath. 'The Breton? No. Duke
William's messenger said he would follow shortly, so I left as soon
as I might. Cecily, I *can't* marry him, so don't talk to me of duty!'

'Who am I to do that when I have delayed committing myself
to God for so many years?' Cecily said gently.

Emma's expression softened. 'I know. You never asked to be a
nun. You follow our father's will in that. I have often thought it unfair
that simply because I was born first I should be the one expected
to marry while you, the younger girl, were sacrificed to the Church
and a life of contemplation even though you had no vocation.'

'We both know it was a matter of riches. The Church accepted
me with a far smaller dower than any thane or knight ever would.
Father could not afford to marry us both well.'

Emma brightened. 'Think, Cecily. Father is gone; the Church has
had your dower, such as it was—what is to prevent your leaving?'

'Emma!'

'You were not made to be a nun. I know Father promised you
to the Church, but what promise did *you* ever make?'

'I swore to try and do his will.'

'Yes, and that you have done. Four years mewed up in a convent. And look at you.' Emma's lip curled as she plucked at the
stuff of Cecily's habit. 'This grey sackcloth does not become you.
I'll warrant it itches like a plague of lice…'

'It does, but mortification of the flesh encourages humility—'

'Rot! You don't believe that! And look at the state of your
hands. Peasant hands—'

'From gardening.' Cecily lifted her chin. 'I work in the herb
garden. It's useful and I enjoy it.'

'Peasant hands, as I said.' Emma lowered her voice. 'Cecily, be
bold. You *can* leave this place.'

Cecily made an exasperated sound. 'Where would I go? Back to Fulford, to your Breton knight? Be realistic, Emma, what use has this world for a dowerless novice?' She smiled. 'Besides, I'm wise to you. You only suggest this as a sop to your conscience.'

Emma stiffened. 'What do you mean?'

'Like it or not, Emma, your duty is at Fulford. You are, as you say, the eldest daughter, born to wed. The people at Fulford need you. Who else will speak for them? And what of our new brother? I'll warrant Duke William doesn't even know of his existence. How do you think his knight will react when he finds that Fulford has a *male* heir after all? No, Emma, your duty is plain and you cannot shirk it. You must return to Fulford and wait for the knight Duke William has chosen for you.'

Emma was very pale; her mouth became a thin line. 'No.'

'Yes!'

'No!'

Cecily shook her head, thinking how little she knew her sister now. Emma was more concerned to avoid marriage with the Duke's man than she was about her baby brother. 'Emma, please think of our people, and of Philip. What chance does that tiny baby have when his identity becomes known? One of us should be near, to guard him from harm.'

A pleat formed on Emma's brow, and her eyes lost their warmth. 'Save your breath for your prayers. I will not submit to a lowborn Breton, especially one whose hands may be stained with our family's blood. And even if all the saints in heaven were to plead alongside you, I would not move on this.'

'Not even for Philip's sake?' At Emma's blank look, Cecily sighed. 'You *must* marry this knight. Run away, and at best you condemn Philip to a false life as Gudrun's son. At worst…' Cecily let the silence spin out, but she could see her words were having little effect. She looked down at the ashes in the hearth, and poked at a charred log with her boot. 'What would Father wish, Emma?

And Maman? Would she have wished her son to lead the life of a
house-serf? Besides, where would you run to?' She looked up as
a new possibility dawned on her. 'You have a sweetheart, don't
you? Someone you—'

'Don't be ridiculous!' Emma clenched her jaw. 'Since you are
so hot to see our brother safe, then you may return—yes, *you*! Get
you back in the real world and see how you like it. Go to Fulford
yourself. Marry the Duke's precious knight. Then *you* can see that
Philip is safe. You are as much his sister as I.'

Stunned, Cecily stared. Her sister's suggestion that she, a novice, should consider leaving the convent to marry was shocking
indeed. And yet…if she were honest…shock warred with a curl
of excitement.

What did he look like, this Breton knight?

'No…*no*.' Cecily's cheeks burned. 'I…I could not.'

Emma raised an eyebrow, and a small smile appeared, as though
she knew that Cecily was tempted.

'Emma, I couldn't. What do I know of men and their ways?'
Cecily waved a hand to encompass the convent. 'Since I was
twelve years old all I have known is the company of women.
Prayers, chanting, fasting, growing herbs, healing, doing penance
for my sins.' She gave a wry smile. 'These things I know. But life
outside these walls—it's a mystery.'

Emma shrugged. 'You are not entirely ignorant. You must remember something of life at Fulford before you came here. You've
seen the stallion put to our mares…'

Cheeks aflame, Cecily bit her lip and shook her head. 'Does…
does he have a name, this knight Duke William has chosen for
you?'

Emma frowned, wearily rubbing her face. 'Yes, but I forget. No,
wait…it's Wymark, I think. Sir Adam Wymark… And I give him
to you, Cecily, for I do not want him.'

Chapter Two

As soon as they were clear of the forest, Sir Adam Wymark reined in his chestnut warhorse, Flame. They were a couple of hundred yards short of St Anne's Convent. Though he'd not come this way before he knew it at once, thanks to the cross that topped the tower of the only stone building in the vicinity. Somewhere, a cock crowed.

With a swirl of blue, Adam tossed his cloak over his shoulder and waved his troop—a dozen mounted men—to a halt behind him. Flame snorted and sidled, churning up the mud. Harness clinked. 'This must be the place,' he said, addressing his friend, Sir Richard of Asculf.

Richard grunted assent, and both men took a moment to absorb the lie of the land, eyes narrowed while they assessed the likelihood of the troop being attacked. True, they were armed and mounted to a man, but they were the hated invaders here, and they could not afford to relax their guard for a moment—even if, as now, there was not a soul in sight.

Of the men, only Richard and Adam, the two knights, wore hauberks—mail coats—under their cloaks. As for the troopers, the cost of a mail coat put such an item far beyond their reach. Had Adam been a rich lord he would have equipped them with chainmail himself, but he was not rich. However, he did not want to lose anyone, and he had done his best for them, managing to ensure they had more than the basics. Under their cloaks each man wore a thickly padded leather tunic; they each had a conical helmet with a noseguard; they all carried good swords and long, leaf-shaped shields.

The nunnery was surrounded by a wooden palisade and tucked into a loop of the river near where it snaked into the forest. The river was swollen, its water cloudy and brown. Cheek by jowl with the convent, on the same spit of land, stood a small village. It was little more than a hotch-potch of humble wooden cottages. Adam wondered which had come first—the village or the convent. He'd put his money on the convent. It was probably filled to the seams with unwanted noblewomen, and the village had sprung up around it to provide them with servants.

As far as he could see, the cottages were roofed with wooden shingles. A clutch of scrawny chickens pecked in the mud in between two of the houses; a pig was scratching its hindquarters on the stake to which it was tied, grunting softly. A dog came out of one of the houses, saw them, and loosed a volley of barks. Other than these animals the place looked deserted, but he was not fooled. The villagers were likely keeping their heads down—he would do the same in their place.

It had stopped raining some half-hour since, while Adam and his troop had been picking their way through the trees. The sky remained overcast, and the wind—a northerly—nipped at cheeks and lips.

Cheek and lips were the only parts of Adam's head that were exposed to the elements, for his dark hair was hidden by his helm, and the noseguard obscured his features. Under his chainmail Adam wore the usual leather soldier's gambeson—a padded one— in addition to his linen shirt and undergarments. His boots and gloves were also of leather, his breeches and hose of finespun wool, his cross-gartering blue braid. For this day's work Adam had elected to wear his short mail coat, leaving his legs largely unprotected, much to Richard's disgust. Adam was ready to build bridges with the Saxon population, but Richard, a Norman, had a distrust of them that went bone deep, and thus was mailed top to toe.

The rain-soft dirt of the road which bypassed the convent had been ploughed into a series of untidy ridges and furrows, like a slovenly peasant's field strips.

'A fair amount of traffic's been this way,' Adam said. He frowned, and wondered if his scout had been right in declaring that his intended bride, Lady Emma Fulford, had come this way too. It was possible that she had kin here—a sister, a cousin. In the aftermath of Hastings confusion had reigned, and his information was sketchy.

The soldier in Adam took in at a glance the fact that the wooden palisade around the convent would offer little resistance to anyone seriously desirous of entering. His scowl deepened as he wondered if Lady Emma was still at St Anne's. He misliked today's errand; forcing an unwilling woman to be his wife left him with a sour taste in his mouth. But he was ambitious, and Duke William had commanded him to do what he may to hold these lands. Since that included a marriage alliance with a local noblewoman in order to bolster his claim, then he would at least meet the girl. The good Lord knew he had little reason to return to Brittany. Adam was grimly aware that here in Wessex the people had more cause to hate Duke William's men than most, for the Saxon usurper, Harold, had been their Earl for well over a decade before he'd snatched the crown promised to Duke William. Local loyalties ran deep. Adam's task—to hold the peace in this corner of Wessex for Duke William—would not be easy. But he'd do it. With or without Lady Emma's help.

Misliking the absence of villagers, Adam was torn between fear of a Saxon ambush and the desire not to approach the convent and his intended bride in the guise of robber baron. He signalled to his men to pull back deeper into the meagre cover offered by the leafless trees and shrubs. There were enough of his countrymen using the excuse of uncertain times to plunder at will, and that was one accusation he was not about to have levelled at him. With Brittany no longer holding any attraction for him, he intended to settle here, make it his home. Making war on helpless women and alienating the local population was not part of his plan.

Pulling off his helmet, and hanging it by its strap from the pommel of his saddle, Adam shoved back his mail coif. His black hair was streaked with sweat and plastered to his skull. Grimacing, he ran a hand through it. 'I'd give my eye teeth for a bath. I'm not fit to present myself to ladies.'

'Give me some food, rather.' Richard grinned back. 'Or a full night's sleep. I swear we've neither eaten nor slept properly since leaving Normandy.'

'Too true.' Ruefully, Adam rubbed his chin. He'd managed to find time to shave that morning, but that had been the extent of his toilet.

'You look fine, man.' Richard's grin broadened. 'Fine enough to impress Lady Emma, at any rate.'

Adam gave his friend a sceptical look, and flushed. 'Oh, aye. She's so impressed she's taken to her heels rather than set eyes on me.' He swung from his horse and held Richard's gaze over the saddle. 'As you know, there's been no formal proposal as yet. Notwithstanding Duke William's wishes, I've a mind to see if we'd suit first. I wouldn't marry the Duchess herself if we didn't make a match.'

Richard stared blankly at him for a moment before saying, 'Admit it, Adam, you want to impress this Saxon lady.'

'If she's not here, it would seem impressing her will not be easy.'

An unholy light entered Richard's eyes. 'Ah, but think, Adam. If you do get her safely wed you can *impress* her all you will.'

Adam scowled and turned away, muttering. He pulled on Flame's saddle girth to loosen it.

'Don't tell me, Adam,' Richard went on quietly, 'that you hope to find love again. You always were soft with women…'

Silently Adam turned, and led Flame under cover of the trees at the edge of the chase. He threw the reins over a branch. Richard followed on horseback.

'Stop your prodding, man, and do something useful,' Adam said after a moment. 'Help me with my mail.'

Not above squiring for his friend, Richard dismounted. Dead leaves shifted under their feet. 'You do, don't you?' Hands at his hips, Richard continued to needle him. 'Not content with Gwenn, you still want to marry for love…'

'My parents wrangled through my childhood,' Adam said simply, as he unbuckled his sword and tossed it over. 'I'd hoped for better.'

'Be realistic, man. You and I know we come to add teeth to William's legitimate claim to the English throne. What Saxon heiress would take you or me willingly? They're more like to name us murderers—of their fathers, brothers, sweethearts…'

Adam shrugged. 'Nevertheless, I had hoped to win some regard.'

Richard shook his head, watching, amused, as Adam struggled to do the impossible—get himself out of his hauberk unaided. 'You've turned dreamer. That knock on the head you took when we first arrived has addled your brain. And why in the name of all that's holy do you want to take that off? Those pious ladies in there—' Richard jerked a thumb in the direction of St Anne's '—those sweet Saxon ladies you so want to impress, would as soon stick a knife between your ribs as parley with the Duke's man. Especially if they knew you were the knight who rallied his fellow Bretons when their line broke…'

'Nevertheless,' Adam repeated, 'Emma Fulford may be in there, and I do not choose to meet my lady mailed for battle.' He stopped wrestling with his chainmail and gave Richard a lopsided grin. 'And, since it was your testimony that won me Fulford Hall, you can damn well help me. Get me out of this thing, will you?'

'Oh, I'll squire you, but don't blame me if you end up on a Saxon skewer.'

Adam raised his arms above his head and bent. Richard gripped his mail coat and heaved, and the mail slithered off, leaving Adam in his brown leather gambeson, marked black in places where the metal rings had chafed. Breathing a sigh of relief, Adam straightened and rolled his shoulders.

'You'll keep on your gambeson?' Richard advised.

'Aye, I'm not that much of an optimist.'

Without his helm and mail coat, Adam looked more approachable. Instead of a hulking metalled warrior who kept his face hidden from the world, there was a broad-shouldered, slim-hipped young man, with long limbs and unruly dark hair. With his open countenance and striking green eyes he made a stark contrast to Richard in his full mail and helm. Reaching for his sword belt, Adam refastened it. His fingers were long and slender, but crisscrossed with scars, and his right palm was callused from long bouts of swordplay.

'Glad to see you've kept some sense.'

'Enough to know we can't afford to alienate these women more than they are already. The Lady Emma *must* consent to marry me. Remember, Richard, we need a translator, if nothing else. Neither of us knows more than a dozen words of English.' Adam smiled at his fellow knight. 'You'll await me?'

'Of course.'

'Keep the men and the horses out of sight while I scout around. There may be no-one abroad now, but that's not surprising. It's possible the villagers got wind of our arrival and have hidden. I'll shout if I need you.'

Face sobering, Richard nodded. 'At the least sign of trouble, mind.'

'Aye.' Saluting, Adam twisted his blue cloak about his shoulders and strode purposefully out of the trees and onto the path that led into the village.

The road between the houses was a mess of muddy ridges. Old straw and animal bedding had been strewn across it, but had not yet been trampled in—proving, if proof were needed, that the village was not utterly deserted; earlier that day someone had tried to make the path less of a quagmire.

A rook cawed overhead and flew towards the forest. Adam glanced up at the clouds and drew his cloak more securely about him, thankful for the fur lining. More rain was on the way. Cautious, aware that his lack of English would betray him if he was challenged, he paused at the edge of the village. The tracker in him noted the line of hoofprints that he and his men had left at the edge of the woodland. Where he and Richard had dismounted their destriers had sidled, and their great iron hoofs had obliterated other tracks, which had also come from the direction of the wood.

Attention sharpening, Adam retraced his steps along the road. Yes—there, leading out from under the tracks he and Richard and his troop had made. Two *other* sets of hoofprints. Smaller horses. Ponies, not destriers. Animals such as an Anglo-Saxon lady and her groom might ride…

The tracks led straight as an arrow to the convent gate and vanished. No tracks came out, implying that unless there was another gate his lady would seem to be still at the convent…

Just then, a bolt was drawn back and the convent gates shifted. Adam darted behind the wall of the nearest house. The door in the palisade yawned wide, and out slipped a nun. Peering round the wall, Adam caught a glimpse of a dark habit, a short veil and a ragged cloak. The nun, who was carrying a willow basket covered with a cloth, headed for the village, hastening to one of the wood-framed houses. Behind her, the convent gate clicked shut and bolts were shot home.

By skirting the dwellings at the margin of the wood Adam was able to keep the nun in sight, and when the slight figure knocked at a cottage door he was in position himself behind the same cottage. It was a matter of moments to find a crack in the planking where the daub had fallen away...

Inside, the cottage was similar in style to many peasants' dwellings in Adam's native Brittany: namely one large room with a fire in a central hearth. The smoke wound upwards, and found its way out through a hole in the roof. To one side of the fire a hanging lamp illuminated the scene. A string of onions and some dried mushrooms dangled from the rafters. By twisting his head, Adam could just make out a rough curtain that hung across one end of the room. The curtain was made out of sackcloth, crudely stitched together. Behind the curtain someone—a woman, if Adam was any judge—cried out in pain.

At the nun's knocking there was a scrape of curtain rings, and out strode a lanky young man with a back bent like a bow and a face that was creased into a worried frown. On seeing his visitor, the young man's brow cleared as if by magic. 'Lady Cecily, thank God you got my message!'

That much Adam *could* understand, though the young man's accent was thick.

The nun moved to set her basket down on the earthen floor and stretched her hands out to the fire for a moment, flexing her fingers as though they were chilled to the bone—which they well might be, since she had no gloves. 'Is all well with Bertha, Ulf?'

Whoever lay behind the curtain—presumably Bertha—gave another, more urgent groan, and two small children, a girl and a boy, came out of the shadows to stand at the young man's side.

'My apologies for not coming at once,' the nun said, moving calmly towards the recess.

'Lady Cecily, please...' The lanky young man took her unceremoniously by the hand to hurry her along, proving by his mode of address and familiarity that St Anne's Convent was no enclosed order.

Odd though, Adam thought, that the nun should be addressed

as 'Lady'. Doubtless old habits died hard, particularly if this man had known her before her profession and had been her vassal.

A series of panting groans had Lady Cecily whisking out of Adam's line of sight, deep into the curtained area. 'Bertha, my dear, how goes it?' he heard.

A murmured response. Another groan.

Then the nun again, her voice soft, reassuring, but surprisingly strong. Adam made out the words 'Ulf' and 'light', and another word he did not know, but which he soon guessed when Ulf left the recess and hunted out a tallow candle from a box by the wall. Then the Saxon for 'water', which he knew.

Ulf dispatched the girl and boy with a pail, returned to the curtain, and was gently but firmly thrust away, back into the central room. The curtain closed, and the young man took out a stool and sat down, hands clasped before him so tightly Adam could see the gleam of white knuckles. Ulf fixed his gaze on the closed curtain and chewed his lips. Each time a groan came forth from behind the curtain he flinched.

Despite the gulf that yawned between them, Adam knew a pang of fellow feeling for the man. Had his Gwenn not died early on in her pregnancy this would no doubt have been his lot, to sit on a stool tearing his hair out, waiting for her travail to be ended. Well, he was spared that now. His pain was over. Richard might tease him about wanting to find love in his new bride, but Adam was not so ambitious. Affection, yes. Respect, by all means. Lust—why not? Lust at least could be kept in its place. But love?

Ulf had started chewing on his nails, a look of helpless desperation in his eyes as he kept glancing towards the recess.

Love? Adam shook his head. Never again. He had had enough pain to last him several lifetimes…

The hour wore on. More groans. Panting. A sharp cry. A soft murmur. And so it continued. Ulf twisted his hands.

The girl and the boy returned with a pail of water and were directed to set it in a pot by the fire.

More groans. More panting.

Adam was on the point of withdrawing to fetch Richard and seek entry to St Anne's when a new sound snared his attention. The cry of a newborn baby.

'Ulf!'

The nun Cecily appeared at the curtain, all smiles. In her role as midwife she had discarded cloak, veil and wimple, and had rolled up her sleeves. For the first time Adam had a good look at her face.

She was uncommonly pretty, with large eyes, rosy cheeks and regular features, but it was her hair that made him catch his breath. The nun Cecily had long fair hair which brightened to gold in the light of the fire and the hanging lamp. Nuns' hair was usually cropped, but not this one's. A thick, bright, glossy braid hung down one shoulder. Unbound, he guessed it would reach well below her waist.

A feeling of pure longing swept through Adam, and he frowned, disconcerted that a nun should have such a powerful attraction for him. But attract him she did, in no uncertain terms.

Impatiently, almost as if she knew Adam's gaze was upon it, the nun Cecily tossed her braid back over her shoulder and held her hand out. Adam had no difficulty in guessing the meaning of her next words.

'Come, Ulf. Come and greet your new son.'

Face transfigured with relief, Ulf all but staggered through the gap in the curtains and pulled it closed behind him.

The golden-haired nun—God, but she was a beauty, especially when, as now, she was smiling—spoke to the children by the hearth. She must have asked something about food for the elder, the girl, nodded and showed her a loaf and a pot of some broth-like substance.

The nun smiled again and, taking up her wimple and veil, set about re-ordering her appearance. Adam watched, biting down a protest as she set about hiding all that golden glory from the world.

By the time she had finished, and had flung her flimsy cloak about her shoulders, Adam had turned away, irritated by his reaction to her. Picking his way along the narrow track behind the wooden houses, he headed back to his troop.

He had learned nothing about the whereabouts of his errant fiancée, the Lady Emma Fulford, but more about his need to master the English tongue. Best he think on that—for a fine lord would he be if he couldn't even converse with his people. As Adam approached the margin of the forest, he shook his head, as if to clear from his mind the persistent image of a slender nun with a glorious golden fall of hair.

Chapter Three

A grey dusk was beginning to fall when at length Adam and Richard rode openly to the convent gate. Mentally cursing the short November day that meant he and his men would likely have to beg a night's refuge at the convent, Adam raised a dark eyebrow at his friend.

His heart was thudding more loudly than it had when they'd waited for the battle cry to go up before Caldbec Hill, though he'd die before admitting as much. A man of action, Adam had been trained to fling himself into battle. This foray into the domain of high-born ladies was beyond his experience, for his own background was humble and his Gwenn had been a simple merchant's daughter. He was unnerved, yet he knew his future in Wessex hung on the outcome of what happened here as much as it had when he had rallied his fellow Bretons at Hastings.

'I can't persuade you to doff your mail, Richard?' Adam asked. He was still clad only in his leather gambeson and blue fur-lined cloak. 'You've no need to fear a knife in your ribs. This is holy ground. There's sanctuary of a sort.'

Richard shook his head.

'You will terrify the ladies…'

'I doubt that,' Richard said, dismounting. 'Nuns can be fear-some harpies—as I know to my cost.'

Adam banged on the portal. 'How so?'

Richard shrugged. 'My mother. When my father set her aside to marry Eleanor, Mother moved herself and her household to a nunnery back home. Took my sister Elizabeth with her. When I visited them, Elizabeth told me the whole. Believe you me, Adam, ungodly things go on in holy places.'

Momentarily distracted, Adam would have asked more, but just then the window shutter slid back, and he found himself gazing at the wizened face and brown eyes of the portress. The nun's face was framed with a wimple that even in this fading light Adam could see was none too clean.

'Yes?' she said, eyeing him with such blatant misgiving that Adam felt as though he must have sprouted two heads.

'Do you speak French, Sister?'

'A little.'

'I've come on the Duke's business. I need to speak with your Prioress.'

The brown eyes held his. 'When you say Duke, do you mean the Norman bastard?'

Adam drew in a breath. It was true that William of Normandy *was* a bastard, his mother being a tanner's daughter who had caught the eye of the old Duke, but few dared hold his birth against him these days. It was shocking to hear such a word fall so casually from a nun's lips. He shot a look at Richard.

'Told you,' Richard muttered. 'There'll be little holiness here, and little courtesy either. They hate us. The whole damn country hates us.'

Adam set his jaw. The Duke had charged him with seeing to it that the peace was kept in this corner of England, and, hard though that might be, he would do his utmost not to let him down. 'We'll see. It was their high-born King Harold who was the oath-breaker, not our lord, bastard though he may be.' He gave the nun a straight look. 'Duke William is my liege lord, and I must speak with your lady Prioress.'

The brown eyes shifted towards the clouds in the west, behind which the sun was lowering fast. 'It's almost time for Vespers. Mother Aethelflaeda will be busy.'

'Nevertheless, Sister—' Adam made his voice hard '—I will speak with the Prioress at once. I'm looking for my Lady of Fulford, and reports have it she rode towards St Anne's.'

The face vanished, the portal slid shut, a bolt was drawn back. Slowly, reluctantly, the door swung open.

'This way, good lords,' the nun said, and even though she mangled the French tongue her voice dripped with irony.

Adam and Richard were ushered into a small, dark, cheerless room, and left to kick their heels for some minutes. There was no welcoming fire, and they were offered no refreshment.

'As I feared,' Richard said, with a wry grin. 'Sweet sisters in Christ—harpies all.'

The winter chill seeped up through the earthen floor, and a solitary candle, unlit, stood on the trestle next to a small handbell. Adam grimaced, and knew a pang of pity for the nuns who must spend their lives here. If most of the convent was appointed like this, it was dank and miserable.

With a rustle of skirts, a large, big-bellied nun came into the room, hands tucked into the wide sleeves of her habit. This woman's wimple was clean, and the stuff of her habit was thick and rich, of a dark violet rather than Benedictine black. The cross that winked on her breast was gold, and set with coloured gems. Clearly not all were made to live penitentially among these grim buildings. This woman, by her garb, hailed from a noble Saxon family, and did not appear to stint herself.

Adam stepped forwards. 'Mother Aethelflaeda?'

'My lords,' the Prioress replied stiffly in the Saxon tongue, barely inclining her head. Her smile was tight and forced, her face the colour of whey.

'My name is Wymark,' Adam said, 'and I've come to fetch Lady Emma of Fulford. Reports say she came here. I'm to escort her back to Fulford Hall.'

Mother Aethelflaeda's gaze shifted from Adam to Richard and flickered briefly over his chainmail before returning to Adam. She nodded. The strained smile twitched wider, but she did not speak.

'Lady Emma of Fulford?' Adam repeated patiently. 'Is she here?'

He was wasting his breath. It was as if the Prioress couldn't hear him. Though she continued to nod and smile, her stance was too rigid, her smile was fixed and her eyes—which appeared glazed—were pinned on Richard once more. A woman in whom disdain and fear were equally mixed.

'She's afraid,' Adam said.

'Aye,' came Richard's complacent reply.

'Shame on you, to scare the wits from her. I told you, Richard, they'd not like you mailed.'

Unrepentant, Richard grinned through his helm.

The Prioress gave a strangled sound and moved back a pace.

'She doesn't understand a word you're saying either, man,' Richard said.

Adam swore under his breath, drawing the gaze of the Prioress. A small furrow had appeared between her brows. 'I'm not so sure,' he murmured. 'It may be she seeks to obstruct us.' He took a step closer to the nun. 'The Lady Emma of Fulford—is she here?'

Mother Aethelflaeda stared at Adam for a moment, took up the handbell and shook it. Immediately, the portress appeared in the doorway, so swiftly that Adam had little doubt that she had been listening and waiting for the summons.

There followed a brief exchange in the English tongue which Adam could not follow, save that he thought he caught the name

'Cecily'. An image of a slight figure with a long golden braid shining in the firelight sprang into his mind. Firmly, he dismissed it.

The portress hurried out, leaving the three of them—Adam, Richard and the Prioress—to stand awkwardly looking at each other. The gloom deepened.

Quick footsteps sounded on the flags outside the lodge, the door was hurriedly pushed open, and the light strengthened as a young nun who was little more than a girl swiftly entered the room. She held a lantern in delicate work-worn hands…

Adam's stomach muscles clenched.

Cecily.

Next to the richly gowned Prioress, her faded grey habit was no more than a thin rag, and her cross was not bright yellow gold, but simple unvarnished wood. However, the nun Cecily's bearing would see her accepted anywhere, be it castle or byre. Her body was straight-backed and slender, and her head was held high, without hint of disdain.

Close to, Adam could see how very young she was, and that even her hideous wimple and veil could not disguise that she was more than pretty. Such fine features: arched brows; a small, retroussé nose; lips that curved like a bow. Thick lashes swept down over eyes that were an arresting blue…

Breathlessly, Cecily hurried into the room.

Though she misliked the Prioress, she always jumped to do her bidding—for Mother Aethelflaeda had an uncertain temper, and her power over those under her was absolute. Giving her a brief obeisance, Cecily turned to look at the two men. One of these must be the Breton knight Emma had spoken of. The thought that these men might have had a hand in the deaths of her father and brother made her belly quake. So much emotion rolled within her they must surely see it. She strove for control.

Her eyes widened as she took in the mailed knight lounging

with his shoulders against the wall, his legs crossed. A cold sweat broke out between her shoulderblades. With his great metal helm, the knight's features were all but hidden, and she was unable to read his expression. He looked confident and very much at his ease. This must be Sir Adam Wymark.

Willing her hands not to shake, Cecily curbed the urge to turn on her heel and placed the lantern on the table. A swift glance at the knight's companion and she had him pegged for his squire. Yes, definitely his squire. For though he was dressed in a leather soldier's tunic, he wore no armour.

The squire was as tall as his knight, and darkly handsome. Polite, too, for the moment their eyes met, he bowed. His murmured 'Lady Cecily' surprised her, for only the villagers, like Ulf, named her by her old title. Inside these walls she was 'Novice' or simply 'Cecily'. Mother Aethelflaeda judged that it was misplaced pride for anyone but herself to be styled 'my lady'.

'Cecily, be pleased to translate for me,' Mother Aethelflaeda said in English, her tone less imperious than usual. 'These…' the brief hesitation was a clear insult '…men are the Norman Duke's, and they are come on his business.'

It was on the tip of Cecily's tongue to protest, for Mother Aethelflaeda spoke French almost as well as she did. Like her, Mother Aethelflaeda came from a noble family, and while Mother Aethelflaeda might not have had a Norman mother like Cecily, Norman French was commonly understood by most of the Anglo-Saxon aristocracy.

Calm, Cecily, calm, she told herself. Think of baby Philip, who needs your help. These men are the means by which you may reach him. Put fear aside, put anger aside, put thoughts of revenge aside. By hook or by crook, you *must* get these men to help you care for little Philip. That is all that matters…

'As you will, Mother Aethelflaeda.' Cecily laced her fingers together and forced herself to smile at the mailed knight.

His squire stepped into her line of vision. 'Lady…that is, Sister Cecily…we are looking for one Emma of Fulford. My scouts tell me she came here. I'd like to speak to her.'

The squire came yet closer as he spoke. Cecily, who for four years had had scant contact with strange men, apart from villagers like Ulf with whom she was familiar, found his physical presence overpowering. His eyes were green, and once they had met hers it was hard to look away. His face, with its strong, dark features, was pleasing, yet somehow unsettling. His black hair was cropped short and, again in the Norman fashion, he was clean-shaven. Most of her countrymen wore their hair and beards long and flowing. Cecily blinked. She had thought it would make a man look like a little boy to be so close shaved, but there was nothing of the little boy about this one. There were wide shoulders under that cloak. And his mouth…what was she doing looking at his mouth?

Becoming aware that they were staring at each other, and that he had been studying her with the same intensity with which she had been studying him, Cecily blushed. It's as though I am a book and he is learning me. He is not polite after all, this squire. He is too bold.

'Emma Fulford?' Cecily said slowly. 'I am afraid you are too late.'

'Hell and damnation!'

Mother Aethelflaeda bristled, and Cecily bit her lip, waiting for the rebuke that must follow the squire's cursing, but Mother Aethelflaeda subsided, managing—just—to adhere to her pretence of not speaking French.

The squire's sharp eyes were focused on the Prioress, and Cecily realised that he knew as well as she that the Prioress did speak French, and that she affected not to speak it merely to hinder them. The knight remained in the background, leaning against the wooden planking, apparently content for his squire to act for him.

'Did Lady Emma say where she was going?' the squire asked.

'No.' The lie came easily. Cecily would do penance for it later. She'd do any amount of penance to keep that mailed knight from finding her sister. Would that she could do something to ensure her baby brother's safety too…

The squire frowned. 'You have no idea? Lady Emma must have told someone. I thought perhaps she might have kin here. Who was she visiting? I'd like to speak to them.'

Cecily looked directly into those disturbing eyes. 'She was visiting me.'

His expression was blank. 'How so?'

'Because Lady Emma of Fulford is my sister, and—'

A lean-fingered hand shot out to catch her by the wrist. 'Your sister? But… I…' He looked uneasy. 'We were not certain she had a sister.'

Trying unsuccessfully to pull free of his hold, Cecily shot a look of dislike at the knight lounging against the wall, looking for all the world as though these proceedings had nothing to do with him. 'Is it so surprising that your Duke has an imperfect knowledge of the lands he has invaded and its people?' she replied sharply. She bit her lip, only too aware that if she were to find a way to help her new brother she must not antagonise these men. She moderated her tone. 'Emma had a brother too. Until Hastings. We both did.' She looked pointedly at the fingers circling her wrist. 'You bruise me.'

Stepping back, the squire released her. 'My apologies.' His eyes held hers. 'And I am sorry for your brother's death.'

Cecily felt a flash of grief so bitter she all but choked. 'And my father's—are you sorry for that too?'

'Aye—every good man's death is a waste. I heard your father and brother were good, loyal men. Since they died at Caldbec Hill, defending their overlord when the shield wall broke, there's no doubt of that.'

'Oh, they were loyal,' Cecily said, and try as she might she could not keep the bitterness from her tone. 'But what price loyalty when they are dead?' Tears pricked her eyes, and she turned away and struggled for composure.

'Perhaps,' the squire said softly, 'you should more fairly lay the blame for what happened at Hastings on Harold of Wessex? It was he who swore solemn oath to Duke William that the crown of England should go to Normandy. It was he who went back on his word. It was his dishonour. What followed lies at the usurper Harold's door rather than my lord William's.'

Because Mother Aethelflaeda was in the habit of hugging what little news that filtered through the convent walls to herself, Cecily's knowledge of goings-on in the world was limited. Her years in the novitiate meant she scarcely understood what the squire was saying.

A movement caught her eye as the knight—what had Emma called him? Sir Adam Wymark?—uncrossed his legs and pushed away from the wall. After stripping off his gauntlets, he lifted his helm. When he brushed back his mail coif to reveal a tumble of thick brown hair, and smiled across the room at her, the foreign warlord responsible for her family's troubles vanished and a vigorous, personable man stood before her. Like his squire, he was young—not so handsome as the squire, but by no means ill-favoured…

Cecily fiddled with the rope of her girdle while she considered this sudden transformation, and an idea began to take shape in her mind—an idea that Emma had half jokingly presented to her. It was not an idea she had any great liking for—particularly since, given a choice between the two men before her, she would choose the squire.

Emma's alarming parting shot: 'Sir Adam Wymark…I give him to you, for I do not want him' still echoed in her mind. Could she do it? For herself, no, Cecily thought, staring at the mailed knight. But for her brother and her father's people? She straightened her shoulders.

She'd do it. For her brother…she *must* do it…

Mother Aethelflaeda shifted. 'Hurry them up, Cecily,' she said in English, in a curt tone which told Cecily she was fast recovering her *sang-froid*. 'The sooner these Norman vermin are out of our hair, the better.'

'Yes, Mother,' Cecily said, deceptively meek, but in no hurry herself—for every minute they spent talking was giving Emma more time to get away.

The squire's green eyes captured hers. He was frowning. 'Your sister said nothing to you of her destination?'

'No.'

'You'd swear that on the Bible?'

Cecily lifted her chin and forced the lie through her teeth—not for honour, which was a cold and dead thing, a man's obsession, but for her sister's sake. Emma had been so desperate to escape. 'On my father's grave.' She steadied herself to make what she knew all present would condemn as an improper and an absurdly forward suggestion. But just then the squire turned and sent a lop-sided smile to his knight.

'It would seem, Richard, my friend,' he said, 'that my lady has well and truly flown.'

Cecily caught her breath and blinked at the mailed figure by the wall. 'You…you're not Sir Adam?'

'Not I.' The knight jerked his head at the man Cecily had mistaken for his squire. 'Sir Adam Wymark stands beside you, Sister Cecily. I am Richard—Sir Richard of Asculf.'

'Oh.' Cecily swallowed. Face hot, she quickly rethought her impetuous plan. Her heart began to beat in thick, heavy strokes, as it had not done when she had considered it with Sir Richard in mind. 'M-my apologies, S-sir Adam. I mistook you…'

A dark eyebrow lifted.

'I…I thought Sir Richard was you, being mailed, and you…you…'

Sir Richard gave a bark of laughter. 'By God, Adam, that'll teach you to doff your armour. She mistook you for my squire!'

Cecily's cheeks were on fire, but she did not bother to deny it.

This was not a good start in view of her proposal. 'M-my apologies, my lord.' If only the ground would open up and swallow her. Cecily lifted her eyes to Sir Adam's, noting with relief and not a little surprise that he seemed more amused than angry. Most men, in her limited experience, would view her misunderstanding as a slight. Her father certainly would have done.

'"Sir" will suffice, my lady.' He smiled. 'Duke William has not yet made us lords.'

Emboldened, Cecily rushed on before she could change her mind, thoughts crowding confusedly in her mind. Think of baby Philip, she reminded herself, now Maman is…no more. Imagine him being brought up by strangers with little love for Saxons, let alone for Saxon *heirs*. Think of Gudrun and Wilf, and Edmund and…

Step by step.

She hauled in a breath, bracing herself for step one. 'Sir Adam, I have a suggestion…'

'Yes?'

Cecily twined her fingers together and lowered her head, affecting a humility she did not feel to hide her feelings. Those green eyes were too keen, and the thought that she might be an open book to him was unsettling. 'I…I wonder…' She cleared her throat 'Y-you will need an interpreter, since my sister is not at home. Not many will speak your tongue…and my mother—my late mother—was Norman born.'

Sir Adam folded his arms across his chest.

'I…I wondered…' She shot a look at Mother Aethelflaeda. 'If you would consider taking me? I know the people of Fulford, and they trust me. I could mediate…'

The man her sister had rejected kept silent, while his eyes travelled over her face in the intent way that she found so unnerving. 'Mother Aethelflaeda would permit this? What of your vows? Your duties to the convent?'

'I have taken no final vows yet, sir. I am but a novice.'

His gaze sharpened. 'A novice?'

'Yes, sir. See—my habit is grey, not black, my veil is short, and my girdle is not yet knotted to symbolise the three vows.'

'The three vows?'

'Poverty, chastity and obedience, sir.'

His hand came out, covered hers, and once more those strong fingers wrapped round her wrist. 'And you would return to Fulford Hall to interpret for me?'

'If Mother Aethelflaeda will permit.'

Adam Wymark smiled, and a strange tension made itself felt in Cecily's stomach. Hunger—that must be the cause of it. She had missed the noonday meal doing penance for her missed retreat, and then with Ulf's wife there had been no time. She was hungry.

'Mother Aethelflaeda will permit,' he said, with the easy confidence of a male used to his commands being obeyed.

Not fully satisfied with their agreement, Cecily took another steadying breath. She thought of these warriors terrifying the villagers at home, discovering little Philip. With her parents dead and Emma gone, who else was left to protect them? Fear and stress drove her on.

Now for step two—the steepest step. 'One thing more, sir…'

'Yes?'

'Since my sister has fl—' swiftly she corrected herself. 'Has gone, I was wondering…I was wondering…' Her cheeks flamed. Cecily was about to shock even herself, and for a moment she was unable to continue.

'Yes?'

Really, those green eyes were most unnerving. 'I…I…that is, sir, I was w-wondering if you'd take m-me instead.'

'Instead?' His brow creased, his grip on her wrist eased.

Cecily tore her eyes from his and studied the floor as though her life depended on it. 'Y-yes. Sir Adam, I was wondering if you'd be p-pleased to take me to wife in Emma's stead.'

A moment's appalled silence held the occupants of the lodge.

Mother Aethelflaeda, shocked out of her pretence that she could not speak French, stirred first. 'Cecily! For shame!'

Sir Richard gave a bark of laughter.

Adam Wymark loosed her wrist completely and stepped back, slack-jawed, and Cecily was left in no doubt that, whatever he had been expecting her to say, he had *not* been expecting a proposal of marriage.

For a long moment his eyes held hers—Sir Richard and Mother Aethelflaeda were forgotten. She fought the impulse to cool her cheeks with the back of her hand, fought too the impulse to stare at the floor, the table—anywhere but into those penetrating green eyes. So briefly she must have imagined it his face seemed to soften, then he inclined his head and regained his hold of her wrist.

'Mother Aethelflaeda,' he said, turning to the Prioress, who was still spluttering at Cecily's audacity. 'I have need of this girl. And, since she has not taken her vows, I take it there can be no objection?'

He had made no mention of Mother Aethelflaeda's attempt at obstruction. It was beneath him, Cecily supposed. She looked down at the long, sword-callused fingers holding her to his side. Her heart was pounding as though she'd run all the way back to Fulford, and she was painfully aware that Adam Wymark had not deigned to respond to her rash proposal. That, too, was probably beneath him. A man like this—a conqueror who came in the train of the Duke, and was confident enough not to noise his consequence about by lording it over strangers in his chainmail—would not dignify her boldness with a response.

He would not wed her.

He glanced down at her. 'You are certain about returning with us as interpreter, my lady?'

'Yes, sir.' And that was about as much a reply as she was like to get from him, she realised. He wanted her to be his translator.

His lips softened into a smile, and that hard grip slackened. 'It is well.'

A queer triumph easing her mind and heart, for at the least she would be able to look to her brother, Cecily managed to return his smile.

Mother Aethelflaeda's bosom heaved, and her jewelled cross winked in the lantern light. 'Novice Cecily! Have you no decorum? That you, a youngest daughter—a *dowerless* daughter—one who has spent four years preparing to become a Bride of Christ—that you should brazenly offer yourself…for shame!' All but choking, the Prioress glared at the knight at Cecily's side. 'Sir Adam, forgive her her impertinence. I can only say she is young still. We have all tried to curb Cecily Fulford's exuberant nature, and I had thought some progress had been made, but…' Imperiously, Mother Aethelflaeda waved a dismissal at Cecily. 'You may leave us, Novice. And you had best do penance for your impertinence to Sir Adam on your knees. Repeat the *Ave Maria* twenty times, and be sure to take no fish this Friday. You'll fast on bread and water till you repent you of your hasty tongue.'

Long years had ingrained the habit of obedience into Cecily, and she made shift to go—but Adam Wymark had not released her wrist.

'Sir…' Cecily attempted to pull away.

'A moment,' he said, but his hold was not hard.

Mother Aethelflaeda gestured impatiently. 'The girl has no dowry, sir.'

Pride stiffened Cecily's spine. 'I did have. I distinctly remember my father entrusting a chest of silver pennies to your keeping.'

Mother Aethelflaeda's lips thinned. 'All spent on improvements to the chapel, and to the palisade that was intended to keep out foreign upstarts.' The last two words were laced with venom. 'Much good it did us.'

'And the altar cross,' Cecily added. 'Father donated that too.' Raising her head, she gave the Prioress back glare for glare. For a woman of her birth to be labelled completely dowerless was shame indeed, and though it might have been unladylike of her to offer herself as wife to Sir Adam, she would *not* be so shamed before these men.

Sir Adam's grip shifted as he moved to face her. He held her gently, only by her fingertips. 'No dowry, eh?' he said softly, for her ears alone.

Cecily's heart thudded.

'Be calm,' he murmured, and swiftly, so swiftly that Cecily had no notion of what he was about, he released her and reached up. Deftly unpinning her veil, he cast it aside. Stunned beyond movement, for no man had ever touched her clothing so intimately, Cecily swallowed and stood meek as a lamb while quick fingers reached behind her to release the tie of her wimple, and then that, too, followed her veil into a corner. Reaching past her neck, he found her plait and drew it forward, so it draped over her shoulder.

For all that the brightest of flags must be flying on her cheeks, Cecily shivered, shamefully aware that it was not with distaste.

Mother Aethelflaeda spluttered with outrage, and even Sir Richard was moved to protest. 'I say, Adam…'

But Cecily had eyes and ears only for the man in front of her—the man whose green eyes even now were caressing her hair. He no longer touched her anywhere, yet she could scarcely breathe.

'No dowry,' he repeated softly, still gazing at her hair. 'But there is gold enough here for any man.'

'Sir Adam!' Mother Aethelflaeda surged forwards. 'Enough of this unseemly jesting. Unhand my novice this instant!'

He lifted his hands to indicate that he was not constraining Cecily, his eyes never shifting from hers.

For a moment, despite herself, Cecily's heart warmed to him—a Breton knight, an invader. It was beyond her comprehension that any man of standing should consider taking a woman for herself alone. Such a man should expect his marriage to increase his holdings.

And how on earth had he known about her fair hair? True, many Saxon girls were blonde, but not all by any means. As she stared at him, his lips quirked briefly into a lopsided smile, and then he stepped back and Cecily could breathe again.

The Prioress had a scowl that would scare the Devil. She was using it now, but for once Cecily did not care. She did not know exactly what was going to happen to her, but she read in Adam Wymark's eyes that he would take her back with him to Fulford.

She was going home!

Not only would she be in a better position to see her new brother was cared for, but she would see Fulford again. The lodge was lost in a watery blur. Without her family Fulford Hall would not be the same, but she would see Gudrun and Wilf—there'd be Edmund and Wat—and was her father's old greyhound, Loki, still alive? And what of her pony, Cloud—what had happened to her?

The longing to stand in her father's hall once more, to be free to roam the fields and woods where she and Emma and Cenwulf had played as children, was all at once a sharp pain in her breast. Blinking rapidly, hoping the Breton knight and his companion had not seen her weakness, Cecily held herself meekly at his side.

'How soon may you be ready to leave?' he was asking. He shot a swift look at the Prioress before adding, 'As my interpreter.'

'But, Sir Adam.' Mother Aethelflaeda glanced through the door at the murk in the yard outside. 'The sun has set. Will you ride through the night?'

A swift smile lit his dark features. 'Why, Mother Aethelflaeda, are you offering me and my men hospitality? I own it is too over-cast to make good riding tonight…'

'Why, no—I mean, yes—yes, of course.'

Rarely had Cecily seen Mother Aethelflaeda so discomposed. She bit down a smile.

'I've brought a dozen men at arms, including Sir Richard and myself.'

'You are welcome to bed down in this lodge, sir,' the Prioress said curtly. 'Cecily?'

Even now, when she was about to leave her authority, possibly for ever, Mother Aethelflaeda did not dignify her with her full title. 'Yes, Mother?'

'See to their needs.' The look the Prioress sent Cecily would have frozen fire. 'And make sure that your party is gone by the time the bell for Prime has rung on the morrow. This is a convent, not a hostelry. Sir Adam, you may leave your offering in the offertory box in the chapel.'

It was customary for travellers who stayed overnight in monastery and convent guest houses to leave a contribution to cover the cost of their stay, but so common was this practice that Mother Aethelflaeda's reminder was pure insult.

Twitching the skirts of her violet habit aside, as though she feared contamination, the Prioress swept from the room.

'Holy God, what a besom!' Sir Richard said, grimacing as he set his helmet on the table next to the lamp. 'As if we'd abide in this dank hole any longer than we must.'

Sir Adam ran his hand through his hair. 'Aye. But we'd be better bedded down here for the night than taking our chance on a dark road with no moon.'

Cecily stooped to gather up her veil and wimple and, overcome with shyness, edged towards the door. 'I'll see some wood is brought in for a fire, sir, and order supper for you and your men.'

And with that Cecily ducked out of the room, before Sir Adam could stay her. She had never met his like before—but then, cloistered in St Anne's, she had not met many men. As she latched the door behind her, to keep draughts out of the lodge, her thoughts raced on.

By the morning she would be free of this place! Her heart lifted. She would be free to care for her brother and, with any luck, free to distract the man in the lodge from tracking her sister. Recalling his fierce grip, she rubbed at her wrist and frowned. Sir

Adam Wymark was not a man who would let go easily, but she hoped for her sister's sake he would forget about Emma so she would have plenty of time to make good her escape.

Chapter Four

Veil and wimple safely back where they should be, on her head, Cecily took another lantern from the storeroom and lit it with hands that were far from steady. Then she hastened—not to the cookhouse, but to the stables. If challenged, she would say she was seeing to the comfort of their guests' horses, but in reality she wanted to ensure that Emma had left no tell-tale signs of her visit—particularly no tracks that might be followed. She might not approve of Emma's desertion of their brother and their father's people, but she was not about to betray her sister's destination to these foreign knights.

Two hulking warhorses, a chestnut and a grey, dwarfed Mother Aethelflaeda's pony. Both carried chevalier's or knight's saddles, with high pommels and backs. Bulky leatherbound packs were strapped behind the saddles. Draped over one of the stalls was the mail body armour of a knight of Duke William's company, gleaming like fishscales in the light of her lamp. A pointed metal helm shone dully from a nearby wall hook, and a leaf-shaped shield and sheathed sword leaned against the planking. Sir Richard had been wearing his sword and helm in the lodge, so these must be Sir Adam's.

Staring at the sword, Cecily swallowed and thrust aside the image of it in Sir Adam's hand, being wielded against the people of Wessex.

The chestnut destrier stamped a hoof, straining at its reins as it turned its head to look at her. Cecily had never seen its like before. It was much larger boned than a Saxon horse. Giving the chestnut's huge iron-shod hoofs a wide berth, for they were deadly weapons in themselves, she edged past to the end stall, where Emma and her groom had briefly stabled their ponies.

Straw rustled. The chestnut snickered, an incongruously gentle sound from such a huge beast, which put her in mind of Cloud, the pony her parents had given her as a child. Tears pricked at the back of her eyes. Maman!

Blinking hard, Cecily lifted the lantern so it cast its light in the end stall and fell on more scuffled straw and some fresh dung. These were of little import, since the Breton knight knew already that Emma had fled to St Anne's.

Warily retracing her steps past the knights' destriers, Cecily went back into a night that was pitch-black, with no moon. The wind whistled into the compound, and bit at her fingers and nose. Shrinking deeper into her thin habit, intending to destroy any betraying hoofprints at the north gate, Cecily was halfway towards it when behind her the *south* gate creaked open. She turned and froze.

In the flickering torchlight by the portress's lodge Sir Adam Wymark was overseeing the opening of the gate, his cloak plastered against his long body by the wind. Outside the compound, a mounted troop of horse-soldiers shifted in the darkness—a shadowy, bristling monster that had no place entering a convent. Metal helms pointed skywards; pointed shields angled down.

Sir Adam's voice rang clear over the wind. 'This way, men. There's only stabling for a couple more, but at least the others will be safer in the palisade.'

A murmur of agreement. One of the horse-soldiers tossed a joke at his fellow, and the troop plodded into the yard in disciplined single file, despite the cold.

Out of the corner of her eye Cecily glimpsed movement in the chapel and in the cookhouse doorway—the flutter of a veil, heads swiftly ducking out of sight. She was not the only one in the convent to be watching England's conquerors.

A nervous giggle, quickly stifled, escaped from the cookhouse. It was followed by the unmistakable sound of a sharp slap. The cook-house door slammed shut. The joker in the troop made another comment, which Cecily could not make out, but, since it elicited guffaws of ribald laughter, doubtless it was made at the nuns' expense.

A brisk word from Sir Adam and the laughing stopped abruptly.

Inside the yard, the men began to dismount and disarm, and as they did so the sense that Sir Adam's troop was a bristling monster lost its force. They were soldiers, yes—strange, beardless soldiers, with shorn hair—but with their helms off most were revealed to be little more than boys, not much older than she. They were tired, nervous, hungry, and many miles from home. Cecily frowned. Boys they might be, but she could not forget they were boys who nonetheless had been trained to kill.

Sir Adam's dark head turned in her direction, and she saw him mouth her name—'Lady Cecily.' Her heart missed a beat.

'Look to Flame's saddle, will you, Maurice? And bed him down,' Sir Adam said, addressing one of the men. 'And persuade the portress to light us a fire in the guest house. We're not about to sleep in an ice-box.'

'Aye, sir.'

And then he was striding across the yard towards her, throwing commands over his shoulder. 'We'll maintain a watch tonight, as ever, Maurice.'

'Even in this place, sir?'

'Even here. Four-hour watches. We all need sleep.'

'Aye, sir.'

Reaching Cecily, he gave her a little bow. Uncertain whether he was mocking her or not, Cecily stood her ground, lantern at her side. Really, this knight from Brittany had the most unsettling effect on her senses—again she felt oddly breathless, as she had done in the guest-house, again her heart was fluttering. It must be fear. It must be hate. Or could it be that she was unused to the company of men?

He looked past her to the north gate, a crease between his brows.

Quickly Cecily shifted her lantern, so the light was not directed towards the hoofprints that *must* be visible. 'Sir?'

'You will not say where your sister has gone?'

'I...no!'

His face went hard. 'You do her a disservice.'

'How so?'

'If by refusing me and fleeing she thinks to ally herself with the Saxon resistance, it will go badly for her when she is captured. And captured she will be, in the end. For what Duke William holds, he holds hard.'

As do you, Cecily thought, recalling that firm grip on her wrist. She raised her chin. 'Sir, it is true that my sister came to St Anne's, and it is true that she has fled, but she did not tell me where she was going.'

'Would that I could believe you.' Folding his arms across his chest, he glanced speculatively at the north gate. 'If I were determined to flee, I'd head north, since our forces already have London and the south reasonably secure. What think you, Lady Cecily? Is my guess a reasonable one?'

Cecily shrugged, affecting a nonchalance she did not feel. Here was a man who would not take kindly to being deceived, and that was exactly what she was trying to do—to deceive him. How would her father have reacted in Adam Wymark's shoes? The answer was quick in coming—her hot-tempered, proud, impatient father, rest his soul, would have beaten the truth out of her.

Would Adam Wymark beat her? She stared up at him, a tall, broad-shouldered silhouette with the torchlight behind him, but his expression was lost in the half-light and she could not read him. *Had* he seen the hoofprints? He was certainly looking in that direction…

To distract him she burst into speech. 'In truth, sir, I know little of such matters. And you may beat me, if you like, but I'll know no more afterwards than I do now.'

'Beat you?' His tone was startled. 'I don't beat women.'

Cecily snorted. Most men beat women. Her father certainly had. He had loved her, and yet he hadn't hesitated to take a switch to her on a number of occasions—most notably when she had at first refused to enter the convent. Beatings had been part of her life for as long as she could remember, and even at the convent they continued. To Mother Aethelflaeda, physical chastisement—'mortification of sinful flesh'—was a means of enforcing discipline and instilling the necessary penitence and humility in the nuns in her care.

'I don't beat women,' he repeated softly.

Cecily bit her lip. He sounded as if he meant it. 'Not even when they cross you?'

'Not even then.'

His gaze went briefly to her mouth, lingering long enough for Cecily, despite her lack of experience, to realise that he was thinking about kissing her. As his particular form of chastisement? she wondered. Or mere curiosity on his part? Or—more unsettling, this—would he think it a pleasure to kiss her? And would it pleasure *her* to kiss him? She had never kissed a man, and had often wondered what it would feel like.

Shocked at the carnal direction of her thoughts, Cecily took a couple of hasty steps back. 'Be careful, my lord—'

'Sir,' he reminded her. 'I told you, I am but a mere knight…'

'Sir Adam, if you seek to rule my father's hold, you'll find velvet gloves may not be enough.' She frowned. 'What would you do to my sister, if she were to return?' Surely then he must see

Emma chastised? By rejecting his suit so publicly, her sister had shamed Fulford's new knight before his tenants. Might he want revenge? On the other hand, perhaps he had heard of Emma's beauty—perhaps he still wanted to marry her? Her confusion deepened as she discovered that this last thought held no appeal. How strange...

Sir Adam was her enemy. Of course—that must be it. What kind of a sister would she be to wish an enemy on her sister?

He had tucked his thumbs into his belt, and was looking at her consideringly. 'What would I do with your sister? That, my Lady Cecily, would depend.'

'On...on what?'

He took his time replying. From the direction of the stable came the clinking of chainmail and the odd snatch of conversation as his men settled their warhorses for the night. The wind cut through Cecily's clothes, chilling her to the bone, and despite herself she shivered. Adam Wymark glanced at the north gate, and Cecily thought he was smiling, but in the poor light she could not be certain.

'On a number of things,' he murmured.

And with that the Breton knight Cecily's sister had rejected gave her one of his mocking bows and a moment later was stalking back to the stable.

'Tihell!' he called.

One of the men broke away from the group in the yard. 'Sir?'

'Don't get too comfortable, Félix. I've a commission for you,' Sir Adam said.

His voice gradually faded as he and his subordinate moved away. 'I want you to rustle up a couple of sharp-eyed volunteers...'

Wishing she had more time to get used to the day's turn of events, for her head was spinning, Cecily stumbled towards the cookhouse. Lifting the wooden latch, she was instantly enveloped in a comforting warmth.

Yellow flames flickered in the cooking hearth, and grey smoke wound up to the roof-ridge. A fire-blackened cauldron was hanging over the centre of the fire on a long chain suspended from a cross beam. At the hearthside, a three-legged water pot was balanced in the embers, bubbling quietly. Some chickens were roasting on a spit. Cecily inhaled deeply. Roast chicken and rosemary. The chickens were not destined for the novitiate, but that didn't prevent her mouth from watering.

Two novices were in charge of that evening's meal—Maude, Cecily's only true friend at the convent, and Alice. With one hand Maude was stirring the contents of the cauldron, and with the other she steadied it with the aid of a thick cloth. Her skirts and apron were kilted up about her knees, to keep them clear of the flames, while her short leather boots—serviceable ones, like Cecily's—protected her feet from straying embers. As was Cecily's habit when working, Maude had rolled up her sleeves and discarded her veil and wimple. A thick brown plait hung down her back, out of the way. Dear Maude.

Alice was kneading dough at a table, shaping it into the round loaves Mother Aethelflaeda so liked. Alice's loaves would be left to rise overnight, and in the morning they would be glazed with milk and finished with a scattering of poppy seeds.

It was part of a novice's training to learn all aspects of life in the convent, and Cecily knew how to make the loaves, as well as the many varieties of pottage that the nuns ate. Pottage was the usual fare, unless it was a saint's day—or, Cecily thought ruefully, one was fasting or doing penance. This evening the aroma coming from the stockpot was not one of Cecily's favourites, yet on this shocking, disturbing, distressing evening it was strangely reassuring to observe the familiar routine.

Here, in the cookhouse, all seemed blessedly normal. So normal it was hard to believe that a troop from Duke William's army had just invaded St Anne's.

'Turnip and barley?' Cecily asked, wrinkling her nose.

Maude nodded. 'Aye—for us. There's roast chicken for Mother Aethelflaeda and the senior sisters.'

'We've guests,' Cecily told her. 'They'll want more than barley soup.'

'I know. So I saw.' Maude grinned and ruefully indicated a reddened cheek that bore the clear imprint of Mother Aethelflaeda's hand. Wiping her forehead with the pot cloth, she continued, 'Mother beat you to it, and she made a point of insisting that the foreign soldiers were to have the same as us novices. Oh, except they can have some of that casked cheese…'

'Not that stuff we found at the back of the storehouse?'

Maude's grin widened. 'The same.'

'Maude, we can't. Is there none better?' Cecily and Maude had found the casket of cheese, crumbling and musty with mould, when clearing out the storehouse earlier in the week. It looked old enough to date back to the time of King Alfred.

Maude winced and touched the pot cloth to her slapped cheek. 'Not worth it, Cecily. She'll check. And think how many *Ave Marias* and fast days she'd impose upon you then…'

'No, she won't. I'm leaving.'

And while Maude and Alice turned from their work to goggle at her, Cecily quickly told them about her sister Emma and her sad news; about Emma's proposed marriage to Sir Adam and her subsequent flight; about the reason for Sir Adam's arrival at St Anne's; and finally—she blushed over the telling of this—about her indecorous proposition to a Breton knight she'd only set eyes on moments earlier.

'So you see, Maude,' she finished on a rush, 'we must say our goodbyes this night, for I'll be leaving with these knights in the morning—before Prime. I'm returning to Fulford.'

While Maude still gaped at her, Cecily turned for the door. 'Mind that pottage, Maude. You've not stirred it in an age.'

* * *

Cecily snatched a few moments in the chilly gloom of the chapel to try and calm herself and come to terms with her new circumstances. It was not easy. She was about to leave a quiet, ordered, *feminine* world of prayer and contemplation and re-enter the world that she had left behind—her father's world. She shivered. Her father's world was a warrior's world, a noisy, messy, intemperate world, where real battles were fought and blood was spilled.

And that, she reminded herself, as she stared at the altar cross shining in the light of a single candle, was why she was returning. Someone had to look out for her baby brother and her father's people. It had been a wrench to leave the world outside the convent walls and, though she had no great love for life at St Anne's, she did not expect her transition back into it would be easy.

In the way of warriors, one warrior in particular—one from across the sea—kept pushing his way to the forefront of her mind. Wincing, she recalled her proposition to him—worse, she recalled that he had ignored it. Something about Sir Adam disordered her thoughts. But she was going to have to overcome her fear of that if she was to be of use to Philip and the people of Fulford.

Cecily's thoughts remained tangled, and all too soon she was interrupted by Maude, come to tell her that it was time they served the convent's unlooked-for guests with their evening meal.

The soldiers—about a dozen—sat round a hastily erected trestle in the guest house. The instant Cecily walked through the door she registered that Sir Adam was sitting next to Sir Richard, on a bench at the other end of the table. Deliberately, she kept her gaze elsewhere.

Tallow candles had been hunted out of storage and stuck in the wall sconces. They guttered constantly, and cast strange shadows on the men's faces—elongating a nose here, the depth of an eye socket there. A sullen fire hissed in the central hearth, and clouds of smoke gusted up to the vent in the roof, but several weeks of rain had seeped into both thatch and daub. It would take more than one night's fire to chase away the damp.

The men were talking easily to one another and laughing, seemingly perfectly at ease having found some shelter in their new country. Their voices, masculine voices, sounded strangely in Cecily's ears after years of being attuned only to women. Her hands were not quite steady. A fish out of water, she did not know what to expect. It was most unsettling. Shooting them subtle sideways glances, she tried not to stare at the shaved cheeks and short hair which made boys of them all. But some of them were young in truth—and surely too young to shave? She wondered how much of their manner was simply bravado.

Moving about the table as unobtrusively as possible, Cecily set out tankards of the ale that was usually served with meals. It was too chancy to drink water straight from the well. She continued to avoid Sir Adam's gaze.

More than anyone else at the convent, she had no good reason to welcome him and his troop, but Mother Aethelflaeda's parsimony was shaming. Did he set his poor welcome at *her* door? She hoped not, because she dared not court his dislike—not when she was reliant on him to take her to Fulford.

The sisters had beeswax candles aplenty in the chapel—why couldn't they have brought out some of those? Beeswax candles burned more evenly, and gave off a pleasant scent that was a world away from the rank stink of tallow. It wouldn't have hurt to be more hospitable. Tallow candles were used mainly by the peasantry; they were cheap, and they spat and sputtered and gave off cloying black smoke. The room was full of it. To make matters worse, the Prioress had had all the dry wood bundled into the sisters' solar and had insisted they used green wood for the guest house fire. The result was inevitable: a spitting fire and yet more smoke.

Sir Richard coughed and waved his hand in front of his face.

'It's worse than the Devil's pit in here,' he said. He spoke no less than the truth.

Cecily shot a covert look across the trestle at Sir Adam. He was leaning on his elbow, quietly observing her. He murmured non-committally to his friend, his eyes never leaving her.

Flushing, she ducked her head and hurried over to the cauldron of pottage. She concentrated on ladling out the broth into shallow wooden bowls and tried, unsuccessfully, to ignore him. To think that she had proposed marriage to him… What must he think of her?

'Where's Tihell?' Sir Richard murmured.

Intent on her ladling, Cecily missed Sir Adam's swift head-shake. 'Oh, just a small errand.'

Sir Richard lowered his voice further, and Cecily thought she heard her sister's name. She strained to hear more, but Sir Adam's response was inaudible, and out of the corner of her eye Cecily thought he briefly touched his forefinger to his lips.

Maude slapped the mouldering cheese and several loaves of that morning's baking on the trestle.

Sir Richard took a sip of his ale and grimaced. 'Saxon swill,' he muttered. 'Never wine. Even mead would be better than this.'

Aside from Sir Richard's comments about the lack of wine, Cecily heard no other complaints. But when she put a steaming bowl of broth before Adam Wymark she distinctly heard his stomach growl. Acutely aware of the lack of meat in the pottage, and the fact that they had been ordered to offer novice's portions, which would not fill *her* stomach, let alone that of a tall, active man like Sir Adam, Cecily finally met his gaze.

'Mother Aethelflaeda's generosity knows no bounds,' he said dryly, breaking off a hunk of bread and dipping it into his bowl.

'Mother Aethelflaeda bade me tell you that our order has been impoverished by the warring,' Cecily said. 'She conveys her apologies for the simplicity of our food.'

'I'll lay odds she also said that since we are God-fearing men we will not mind Lenten fare instead of a meal.'

Sir Adam's assessment was so close to the truth that Cecily was hard put not to smile. Demurely, she nodded. 'Aye, sir. Mother Aethelflaeda also said that in the case of you and your men such fare would be especially apt, as every man who fought at Hastings should do a hundred and twenty days' penance for each man that he has killed.'

He stared at her, chewing slowly; Sir Richard choked on his ale; a man-at-arms guffawed.

A dark eyebrow lifted. 'Did you know that His Holiness the Pope did bless our cause over that of your Earl Harold the oath-breaker?' Sir Adam asked.

'I did not.'

'No, I thought your Prioress would keep that interesting titbit to herself.' He reached for the cheese platter, and eyed the cheese for a moment before sliding it away, untouched. 'Tell me, Lady Cecily, do all the nuns eat this…this…fare?'

'We novices do, sir—save for the cheese.'

'You call this *cheese*?'

'Yes, sir.'

Unexpectedly, a grin transformed his face. 'You save that for special guests, eh?'

Cecily hid a smile. 'Yes, sir.'

'Do all in your order eat like this?'

Thinking of Mother Aethelflaeda's chickens, roasting on the spit, Cecily was careful to avoid Maude's eye, but her burning cheeks betrayed her.

'Aye,' he murmured. 'A proud Saxon lady that one. One who would deny us what she may. I could swear I smelt chicken earlier.'

Cecily shot him a sharp look, but he met her gaze blandly.

Mumbling a reply, Cecily beat a hasty retreat and returned with relief to ladling out the pottage.

By insisting that Maude hand out the remaining platters she managed to avoid talking to Sir Adam for the rest of the meal. Out of the corner of her eye she watched him converse with Sir Richard. Not long after that, as soon as she decently could, Cecily murmured her excuses and left the new Lord of Fulford to bed down for the night. She had a few hours left in which to accustom herself to the idea of placing herself at the mercy of the man who had come to take her father's lands. She prayed that it would be long enough.

What *had* she done?

Chapter Five

Next morning, Adam woke when the day was but a faint streak of light in the east. The guest house floor was unforgiving, and the cold had seeped through to his bones. Grimacing, he stretched, noted that his squire Maurice Espinay was up before him, and that the tantalising smell of fresh baked bread was floating in from the cookhouse.

His stomach grumbled. Hunger had been his constant companion since Hastings—the more so because he did not permit his men to ravage the countryside. Most Norman commanders saw it as their right, but Adam could not see the sense in looting and pillaging a village if one ever planned to rule it. Hopefully, when he and his men were settled, they could leave hunger behind.

As Adam unwound himself from his cloak, he saw in his mind's eye the lively dark eyes and the smiling mouth of Gwenn, his dead wife and his love. He thought about her most on waking. In the early days of his grief he had tried to discipline himself not to think of her, but as a strategy that had proved useless. Grief was a sneaky opponent. On the rare mornings he had succeeded in pushing Gwenn's memory away, the grief had simply bided its time and crept up on him later, when he had not been braced for it. So, sighing, Adam had given himself permission to think about Gwenn first thing, since that was when he woke expecting to find her at his side.

Some mornings were more bearable than others. Even though it was two years since Gwenn had been laid to rest in the graveyard at Quimperlé, there were times when the grief was as fresh as though she had died but the day before; times when it was impossible to believe that never again would he look into those smiling, loving eyes. Ah, Gwenn, he thought, relieved that this looked as though it was going to be one of the more bearable mornings. Today he was going to be able to think of her sadly, to be sure, but without the lance of pain that had so crippled him in the weeks immediately following her death.

Briskly, Adam rubbed his arms to get his circulation going. His stomach growled a second time and his lips curved into a twisted smile. Gwenn was spared further suffering—she was safe beyond cold, beyond hunger—but he most definitely was not. Wryly he wondered what crumbs Mother Aethelflaeda would throw them for breakfast.

Shivering, he washed in the icy brackish water Maurice carried into the guest house in an ewer. Then, after eating a meagre nuns' breakfast of bread and honey, washed down with small ale of a bitter brewing, he left the lodge with Richard to arm himself for the ride to Winchester and thence to Fulford. His stomach still rumbled. The poppyseed bread had been mouthwateringly good—fragrant and warm from the oven, not the crumbs he had feared being given—but there had not been enough of it. Not nearly enough.

Daylight was strengthening by the minute, and a light frost rimmed the horse trough white. As the two knights walked towards the stable their breath huffed out like mist in front of them. Glancing skywards, Adam noted some low-lying cloud, but thankfully the rain was holding off. Rain played havoc with chainmail, and his was in sore need of an oiling. It was not Maurice's fault. Emma Fulford's precipitous flight had left them with no time to pause for such niceties.

Where *was* Cecily Fulford? he wondered. She should have put in an appearance by now. Prime could not be far off. He conjured up her image in his mind and her blue eyes swam before him, her lips pink and kissable as no novice's had any right to be—except that she was always worrying at them with those small white teeth. Worrying, worrying. Where had she slept? In a cell on her own? Or in a dormitory full of other novices? Had she been as cold as he? Had she broken her fast with fresh poppyseed bread?

'We can't afford to take any risks going through Winchester,' Adam said, once Maurice had him armed. Their helms dangled from wooden pegs and their long shields were stacked with several others against a partition. 'I don't want a seax in my ribs.'

With his mail coif heavy about his neck, he leaned against a stall and watched Richard's squire, Geoffrey of Leon, do the honours with his friend's chainmail.

Straw rustled underfoot. 'Nor I,' Richard mumbled, emerging red-faced through the neck of the chainmail.

Maurice led the destriers out. Their hoofbeats initially rang loud on the stone flags in the stable, but when they reached the beaten earth in the yard the hoofbeats changed, became muted.

'Maurice?' Adam leaned through the stable door. 'Commandeer a pillion saddle from the Prioress.'

'Yes, sir.'

'And don't take no for an answer.'

'No, sir.'

'Put the saddle on Flame, when you find it. Oh, and Maurice—?'

'Sir?'

'Charge Le Blanc with guarding our rear on the road, will you? You can keep watch ahead. If anyone attacks, it's possible they'll do it in Winchester.'

He ducked back into the stable. Lady Cecily Fulford. He was glad she was to accompany them. Her presence would be invaluable—and not just for her help with the language. Where *was* the girl? Impatient with himself for letting musings on Cecily Fulford's whereabouts distract him from the business at hand, Adam rolled his shoulders so his chainmail sat more comfortably. He trusted that she had not changed her mind about going with them…he *wanted* her to go with them, he realised. Purely as an interpreter—nothing more, naturally. She would be most useful.

Richard reached for his sword belt. 'I agree we should keep a sharp lookout, Adam, but I disagree about Winchester being a point of possible ambush. The Duke's men already have it garrisoned. And the streets are far too narrow—any fighting would mean the certain death of women and children, not to mention damage to property. I don't think the Saxons would risk that—'

Adam shook his head. 'You're forgetting, Richard—Winchester's the heart of Wessex. Harold and his kin have made it their capital for decades: there's a great cathedral, royal palaces—loyalty will be at its strongest in the city. No, we'll watch our backs most diligently when we pass through there.'

Richard grunted and buckled on his sword. 'You're the one in command.'

Adam smiled and clapped Richard on the shoulder. 'My thanks for your support, my friend. Without it I… Suffice it to say I'll not forget it.'

'Heavens, man, you're the hero who rallied the Breton cavalry. All I did was inform the Duke of your actions.' He shrugged. 'Besides, I have plenty of lands in Normandy already. My time here will come. I'd as lief support you as anyone.'

'My thanks.' Adam frowned out into the courtyard. 'Any sign of my lady Cecily?'

'Your lady, is she?' Richard grinned. 'Will you wed her in her sister's place?'

'If I can't track down the sister I just might.'

'I suppose one Fulford wench is as good as another?'

'This one may be better, since she has offered herself to me.'

'Adam, you don't have to wed either of them if they don't please. The Duke gifted Fulford Hall and the lands to you uncon- ditionally. All you had to do was swear fealty to him. *You* hold title to them now.' He tilted his head to one side and looked thought- fully at Adam. 'In fact, you might do better to look elsewhere, since the novice has no dower. Marrying her won't fill empty coffers.'

Adam nodded. 'That's true. But it would help my cause at Fulford if I were to wed one of Thane Edgar's daughters.'

'Then take the little novice, Adam, since she has offered. I can see that she appeals…'

Aye, damn her, she more than appeals, Adam thought as he went to find her and hurry her along. He could wish that she didn't appeal—he needed to keep his heart whole. He had given his heart once before, to his beautiful dark-eyed Gwenn. Pain sliced through him, hitting him off-guard. Never again. Never would he put his happiness in the hands of one woman.

Speaking of women—where *had* that novice got to? If they were to reach Winchester by noon, as he had planned, they must leave at once. He had urgent despatches for the Duke, and he did not think Novice Cecily would enjoy it if they had to gallop the entire way to the city.

The herb garden behind the chapel was reached via an arch through a high wattle fence, and it was there that Adam found her. He paused under the arch, watching her slight form as she made her way up one of the turf paths between the beds. Lady Cecily Fulford, Saxon noblewoman. Her footprints left tracks in the melting frost.

How tiny she was. He'd noticed yesterday that she barely reached his shoulder, but today, in the garden, she looked smaller still. She was clad in her novice's habit and veil, and that thin cloak. Perhaps that was all she had—but it wasn't much considering she was a thane's daughter, an aristocrat. What would she think, he wondered, if she knew that he did not have a drop of noble blood in his veins? Would she turn tail, as her sister had done? Would she lift that little nose of hers and…? Certainly she would not have made that impetuous proposal if she knew of his humble origins. But… Impatiently, he shook his head. Such thoughts were pointless.

Being the end of the year, nothing in the herb garden was growing: the twiggy remnants of some herb poked out of the ground here; brown, frost-scorched root-tops wilted there. Adam was no gardener, but he could see that this garden had been carefully laid out and tended. In the centre stood a gnarled and leafless apple tree. A small bundle lay at its foot.

Lady Cecily had yet to see him. Hardly breaking step, she bent to pull some red hips off a straggling briar and tucked them absently into the folded-back sleeve of her habit. It was a nun-like gesture. She moved on; she straightened a stake.

Watching how she gazed at the sleeping plants, Adam saw love for the garden in every line of her body, in the caressing way her fingers trailed over a rosemary bush, a bay tree… He shifted his stance against the fencing, struck with an uncomfortable thought. Was his desire to take this woman with him as his interpreter pure selfishness? Was he standing in the way of a true vocation? Watching her in this garden he had second thoughts, but yesterday—yesterday in the lodge—he had not gained that impression.

No, he was not doing wrong to take her. There was no love lost between Cecily Fulford and the Prioress, and no sign of a great vocation either. Cecily Fulford might love this garden, but she did not love the convent. She had *asked* to go with him, which in itself was something of a mystery. There would be other gardens. For his part, he must be on his guard, lest his attraction to her person made him forget that she must have her reasons for suggesting she married him. And not for one moment would he forget the pain that loving could bring—that aching void after Gwenn had died. Not even for beauty such as Lady Cecily's would he go courting that a second time. He would wed Cecily Fulford if she agreed, with gladness, but this time he would think of it as a business transaction. He would keep his heart out of it.

A robin landed on a branch of the apple tree. Pushing himself away from the arch, Adam cleared his throat and called her by her secular name—her *true* name. 'Lady Cecily?'

The robin took flight; she turned and, seeing him, took a hasty pace back. His chainmail—she misliked it. He had been right to remove it yesterday.

Her cheeks were white as alabaster. He saw her swallow. 'Y-you are ready to leave, Sir Adam?'

'Aye.'

'I also am ready. I said my farewells yesterday.' She came towards him via the apple tree, resting her hand on the bark as she retrieved the bundle.

He took it from her, noting that she was careful to avoid contact with his fingers. 'This is everything?'

She nodded, eyes wary, still absorbing his changed appearance. Did she fear him? Or, worse, hate him? Adam wanted her to think kindly of him, but since he had arrived in her life as a conqueror he acknowledged the difficulties. No, he was not so naïve as to think that Cecily Fulford had proposed because she liked the look of him. She must have some ulterior motive in mind. Seeing Fulford Hall again? Caring for her father's people? Escaping from the convent?

He glanced at her mouth, at the rosy lips turned up to him, and wondered at a world that would see such beauty wither unseen behind high convent walls. Madness—it was nothing less than madness. Those lips were made for kissing, and he—out of the blue a shocking thought took his breath—he wanted to be the one doing the kissing…

Abruptly, he looked away. What was happening here? One moment he was missing Gwenn, and the next… His mind raced. Perhaps he should *not* have kept himself faithful to Gwenn's memory. Richard had warned him that celibacy turned men's minds. Perhaps Richard was right.

This girl was a novice, for pity's sake, an innocent. He *must* control himself. He might be aware of her in a carnal sense, and she might have asked him to marry her, but he would be damned if he would accept until he had discovered her true motives.

'You haven't the weight to handle one of our horses on your own,' he said in commendably cool tones. 'Would you be content to ride pillion behind one of the men? Our saddles are fashioned for battle, but if we can't find a pillion saddle I am sure we can put something together.'

'Oh, no,' Cecily said. She felt her cheeks grow hot. 'That is… I couldn't…'

Before entering the novitiate Cecily had been taught to ride pillion, as all ladies were. But it had been over four years since she had ridden—pillion or otherwise—and she did not think she still had the knack. Would she be riding astride? Or side saddle? Either way filled her with alarm. To ride astride behind one of these…these invaders would surely be seen as unseemly—and yet if she rode side saddle she'd be in the mud in no time…

His dark brows came together. 'You do not like horses?'

'Oh, no—I do like them. But I am woefully out of practice. And yours are so large. Could I take Mother Aethelflaeda's pony?'

'I asked, but she refused to lend it.' Briefly his green eyes lit up. 'No doubt she thinks I'll mince it and feed it to the dogs.'

'But, sir—'

He turned and, brushing her protests aside, ducked under the arch. 'We'll find something suitable.'

With a scowl, Cecily followed, her eyes fixed on Adam's mail-clad back. Ride pillion behind one of his men? No, no, *no*. It was one thing to race across the downs with her brother Cenwulf as a child, but then she had been riding her own gentle Cloud, not clinging to one of Sir Adam's men astride a hulking great warhorse. And she would certainly not—her cheeks positively flamed—perch behind *him*, the strange Breton knight who had come to lay claim to her father's lands.

The yard was a mill of armed and mounted men. Harness jingled as the destriers tossed their heads and stamped great dints in the earth. With their helms on, Cecily could not recognise any of the men and boys from the previous night. All were terrifying alien beings, with loud voices and metal weapons that gleamed in the morning light. They looked prepared for anything.

Her heart thumped. Was she really going with these foreigners? She must be mad. For a moment the coward in her had the louder voice, urging her to remain safely in the convent. What if her countrymen attacked them? Of all in their party she would be the only one with no chainmail or gambeson to keep her safe, and it would take but one arrow from a Saxon bow to put an end to her. A cold lump settled in her belly, like yesterday's porridge.

'Cecily! *Cecily!*' Maude's voice cut across the general clamour, and then her friend was beside her, hugging her, eyeing Sir Adam and his men askance. 'Are you sure this is wise?' Maude hissed, veil quivering.

Adam Wymark turned his head—he had not yet mounted. His mail coif was pulled up, but Cecily knew that he could hear them. She thought of her newborn brother, an orphan with no other family to fend for him, and she nodded.

'Don't they frighten you?' Maude whispered, pressing a small sacking-wrapped bundle into Cecily's hands.

Stiffening her spine, Cecily ignored the question and glanced at the sacking. 'What's this?'

'Healing herbs. I took them from the infirmary—horehound, poppyseeds, woundwort and suchlike... You grew them, dried them—I thought you should have them. I knew you'd never take them, but you don't know how your mother's store cupboard stands.'

Cecily's eyes widened. 'Maude, you shouldn't have. What if Mother finds out? She'll beat you for stealing.'

'Who's to tell? I certainly won't, and since you won't be here…'

Cecily shook her head, smiling. 'My thanks. I may well need them.'

Adam Wymark threw his mount's reins at a man and strode towards them. His black hair was no longer visible under the mail coif, but his green eyes remained the same—not harsh or mean, but enquiring—and with a lurch in her belly Cecily realised she did not hate him. Of all the men the Norman Duke could have sent to Fulford, he was probably the least offensive. Why, the good Lord knew how harsh and unreasoning her own father had been at times. It seemed possible that Sir Adam was more temperate—she would watch and reserve her judgement.

With a wave of his hand, Sir Adam indicated his troop. 'My men are at your disposal, my lady. With whom do you ride?'

'W-with whom?' Cecily bit her lip as all eyes turned on her. What was more unsettling? The thought of riding pressed against Sir Adam, or the thought of riding with one of his men? 'S-sir, I…I…'

Maude, who spoke French, had watched this exchange. She stepped forward, a stubborn set to her jaw that Cecily recognised from one of the many times she had seen Maude wilfully disobey one of their order's rules. 'Lady Cecily should not be riding with a common soldier, sir.'

Afraid for her friend, Cecily caught Maude's sleeve. 'Maude, no!'

Sir Adam looked thoughtfully down at Maude, and said with pleasant deliberation. 'You are in the right—though my men would no doubt not thank you for naming them "common"…' He sighed heavily. 'And here I was thinking that, in God's eyes at least, all men are equal.'

'They are, sir,' Maude said, hastily backing down. 'Indeed they are.'

'Ah, well, that is good. Because I am a common man, and Lady Cecily is to ride with me.'

Catching sight of a suspicious gleam in his eyes, a twitch of his lips, Cecily frowned. To be sure there was an edge to his voice, but he was laughing—the wretch was making fun of them...

'Say your farewells,' he said, and stood aside to allow Maude and Cecily to embrace.

Then, taking her by the wrist as he had done the previous evening, he led her to where a man—no, he was a boy—was holding his destrier, the magnificent chestnut. Cecily bit her lip. She'd never ridden anything half that size.

'Don't fear him.'

'I...I don't.'

'Here...' He drew her level with the horse's head. 'His name is Flame. Let him see you, smell you. He won't hurt you if he knows you're with me. You can touch him. I've never known him bite a woman.'

She shot Adam Wymark a startled look, but it was impossible to tell whether he was teasing or not. 'He bites men, then, sir?' In battle, she supposed, this destrier would do anything its master asked of it. It was a sobering thought.

'Go on—stroke him.'

Tentatively, Cecily reached out and patted the great arched neck, murmuring softly, as though the warhorse were one of her father's ponies. Thus she had petted her own Cloud before coming to St Anne's. Cloud had gone back with her father to Fulford as novices were not allowed ponies. What had happened to her? This horse's chestnut muzzle, she discovered, was just as soft as Cloud's had been.

'Warm velvet,' she murmured.

'That's it—let him know you're not afraid,' said the man at her side. He still had a firm grip on her wrist.

'I'm *not* afraid,' Cecily said, pulling away from the fingers on her wrist.

A brief smile lit those disturbing eyes and he released her, turning away to reach something down from behind the saddle— a saddle which was not the chevalier's saddle she had noticed the day before. Somehow he had contrived to find one suitable for carrying a lady pillion.

She frowned. 'You planned to have me behind you all along…'

Ignoring her remark, he handed a blue bundle to her. 'Here— you'd best borrow this.'

His cloak, and the finest Cecily had held in an age. Of rich blue worsted, lined with fur. Carefully, so as not to startle the chestnut, Cecily unfolded it. So heavy, so warm, so sinfully sensual. You could bury your face in it and….

Momentarily speechless at such thoughtfulness, she blinked up at him, confused by the contradictions he presented. A foreign knight who had come to take her father's lands and yet who considered her comfort.

He shrugged and turned away to pull something else from his pack, the faintest colour staining his cheekbones. 'My mother would have had that thing you're wearing for dish-clouts years ago,' he said gruffly. 'You'd best borrow these too. They'll be overlarge for you, but better than the nothing that the convent has seen fit to provide you with.'

Gloves. A warrior's pair, to be sure, but again of the best quality, carefully cut, the stitching perfect, lined with sheepskin.

'B-but, sir—what of you?'

'My gambeson is padded, Lady Cecily. Your need is greater.'

Cecily draped the cloak about her, almost moaning in delight as its warmth settled about her shoulders. The fabric held within its folds an elusive fragrance: sandalwood, mixed with a scent particular to the man to whom it belonged. Tentatively, Cecily inhaled. Her cheeks grew warm, and under cover of tugging on his gloves she ducked her head to escape his gaze.

He clapped on his helm and with a clinking of harness and

chainmail, and a creaking of leather, mounted. 'Help Lady Cecily, will you, Maurice?' With the reins in one hand, he held out the other towards her.

Maurice—the lad was clearly his squire—bent and cupped his hands. Cecily stepped up, took Sir Adam's hand, and a moment later was seated behind him. Astride.

Too high. It was far too high. And her legs were showing almost to her knees, revealing her pathetically over-darned grey stockings. Wondering if one could die of mortification, Cecily clutched at Sir Adam's pack, at her own meagre bundle which was strapped next to his, at the side of the saddle—anywhere but at the mailed knight who shared the saddle with her. With one hand she snatched at the skirts of her habit, trying to pull it down over her legs.

He nudged the horse with his heels and they turned towards the gate. Almost unseated, she squeaked a protest.

The helmed head twisted round. 'My lady, it will not kill you to hold onto me, but it may well kill you if you don't. You must get proper purchase.'

He was right. But Cecily had never in her life sat so close to a man who was not related to her. Thanking God for the chainmail that would surely keep him from feeling the press of her body against him, and thankful that his men seemed to be ignoring the shocking sight of her legs, she surrendered to the inevitable and gripped his sword belt firmly—a shocking intimacy that would have had Mother Aethelflaeda in a swoon.

'That's it, my lady.' He waved his troop on and they trotted through the gate and onto the high road, just as the chapel bell began summoning the nuns to Prime.

Jostled and juddering on the back of Adam Wymark's destrier, Cecily looked down at the ground passing beneath them and hung on desperately. Craning her neck to look through the troop of horse-soldiers following them, she could make out Maude, waving by the gate. Cecily had no hand spare to wave back, but she found a smile and hoped that Maude would see it.

'Fare thee well, Maude.'

The convent bell rang out. Maude glanced over her shoulder, spoke briefly to someone behind her in the convent yard, leaned her weight into the great doors and pushed them shut, nipping inside herself at the last moment.

Cecily did not know why, but she kept her eyes fixed on those closed gates for as long as she could, finally losing sight of them when they clattered over the bridge and took the road that led into the forest.

The ride to Winchester from St Anne's could have been accomplished in two hours at full stretch, but Adam, conscious of the tension in the girl perched behind him on the saddle, didn't push it. True, he wanted his despatches to reach Duke William in London as soon as possible, but wording them would not be easy, and he could use the time to compose his thoughts and justify the decision he had made.

The horses forged on through a dense, largely leafless woodland. Overhead, twisted branches formed a black latticework against the grey backcloth of the sky. The rain held off. On the ground, leaf-litter muffled their hoofbeats; briars curled like coiled springs by the wayside. Glossy rosehips and stale blackberries hung from spindly twigs.

Keeping a wary eye out for Saxon rebels, they passed a series of holly bushes, bright with red berries. They had dark leaves in abundance—good cover for those preparing an ambush. Glancing at Le Blanc, Adam saw he was already alert to the dangers as he waved two men out of line—one to watch the right hand, one the left.

They rode on.

Aware that ahead of them lay a barren stretch of downland before they gained the city, Adam found himself wondering not about how Tihell, his captain, was faring on his mission to find the missing Lady Emma, not about rebellious Saxons, not even about the wording of the letters he intended to send from Winchester, but about Cecily Fulford herself. What was going through her mind?

He couldn't begin to imagine what her life had been like in the convent, but of one thing he was certain: it would have been restricted in the extreme. She might once have been a horsewoman, but it did not appear that the Prioress gave leave for any of the novices to exercise the pony in the stable. Any riding skills that Cecily Fulford had once possessed had to be rusty. For the first mile or so through the forest her demeanour confirmed this. She held herself stiffly, jouncing up and down behind him like a sack of wheat.

Then Adam realised his mistake—it wasn't lack of expertise that kept her so lumpen, she was intent on avoiding bodily contact with him. Whether that was because she was unused to men, or whether it was because she mistrusted and misliked him, he couldn't tell. She must think of him as the enemy.

Suffice it to say here she was, a lone Saxon girl who had put herself into the hands of her conquerors, willingly, without duress, while her sister had fled. Cecily Fulford might be lacking in worldly experience, but she did not lack courage.

What Adam had yet to fathom was why she had offered to go with them, and why she had asked to take her sister's place. He could only think that she sought to distract him from following the Lady Emma. He smiled wryly at such innocence. Distract him she certainly did, but not in the way she sought. And little did she know that he had sent Tihell after Emma Fulford, notwithstanding. Those hoofprints that left St Anne's by the north gate simply could not be ignored.

Acutely conscious of the slight body held so stiffly behind him, of the small hands that were clinging to his sword belt, Adam held his peace as the miles passed. He simply urged Flame steadily on and willed the girl behind him to relax.

This should not matter to me, he told himself. But it did. He wanted Cecily Fulford to feel at ease in his company—although this was, as Richard had been swift to point out, something of an impossibility. Not only was he the invader of her father's land, but class lay between them too. Maude had known that instinctively. Cecily Fulford—*Lady* Cecily Fulford—was highborn, while he... Impatient with himself, Adam snapped the thread of his thought. This should not matter. This did not matter. Especially given that he had sworn off emotional entanglements.

Adam and his troop ploughed on, and the wording for his dispatches continued to elude him. The trees thinned. The wind rose, chilling Adam's ungloved hands, turning them red. His men's breath and the breath of the horses turned to smoke in the air about them. Woodland gave way to downland, and the track was a chalky mire which sucked at the horses' hoofs.

Adam tightened his grip on the reins. Overhead, a buzzard circled.

As they crested a treacherous rise Flame stumbled. Adam almost dislodged his shield when he thrust an arm behind him to keep Cecily safe. Simultaneously she flung both arms round his waist. Flame regained his footing. Through his mailcoat Adam felt Cecily press herself against his back. His heart lightened. At last.

Again Flame skidded as he picked his way down the incline.

When they reached the bottom Cecily shifted in the saddle behind him, bringing her thighs and body closer yet. She did not let go of his waist.

Yes, Adam thought. *Yes.*

And thus it was that as they covered the final miles towards the capital of Wessex Adam found the wording of his despatches came more easily than he would have dreamed possible.

Chapter Six

From time to time Cecily rested her head against Adam Wymark's broad back, pillowing her cheek with the fur-lined hood of his cloak. His leather jacket was visible through the links of his hauberk.

Fulford's new lord was right-handed, so his shield was slung on his left. Whenever Flame broke into a trot it banged her thigh—she would have a bruise there for certain—but that was the least of her worries. Every muscle in her body was shrieking so loudly it was a wonder the whole troop couldn't hear; every bone ached. Biting her lip to stifle her moans, Cecily clung to Sir Adam, and prayed that St Christopher, Patron Saint of all travellers, would keep her glued to Flame's back. Once, riding had been a pleasure, today it had to be endured.

Circling thoughts had had her tossing and turning the night through, but one night's loss of sleep was not the sole cause of her exhaustion. Rather, it was the series of night vigils that Mother Aethelflaeda had imposed on her in the week before Emma had run to the convent. That, and being permanently put on a fast. Fasting might be good for the soul, but it certainly weakened the body. Surreptitiously shifting her position, Cecily held down another groan. For all that she had rested her face against Adam Wymark's cloak, by now it must bear the imprint of his chainmail. She was beyond caring.

At a moss-covered milestone which announced they had reached the outskirts of Winchester, they joined a steady stream of knights and pilgrims heading for the heart of the city. She was struck by how many *men* there were.

Ill at ease, she pushed herself upright. For the most part the men looked hairy and unwashed. Rough, and not a little frightening. Her convent eyes were to blame for this perception, no doubt. But they all looked so…so vigorous—though not quite as vigorous as the man sitting before her. They looked more alarming, however. More alarming than Duke William's knight? Cecily puzzled over this for a moment, for the men were Saxons, like herself. But there was not one within sight that she would care to run into on a dark night, and she did not think the knight would hurt her. She caught her breath. She *trusted* him? That was not possible, Adam Wymark was her *enemy*.

Setting her jaw, telling herself she must keep her wits about her, Cecily glanced about. She had only entered the capital of Wessex once before, on the day her father had brought her to the convent, and that day had been so coloured by anger and grief and, yes, bitterness at being sent away from home that she had taken in little.

Winchester was circled by ancient Roman walls, and successive Saxon Kings from Alfred down to Harold had kept them in good repair. Wondering if the Normans had breached the walls in taking the city, Cecily craned her neck, but for the most part they looked intact, a solid line of grey stone which followed the course of the River Itchen. The river was wide and in full spate, and it flowed along just outside the walls. They would have to cross the river to enter the city.

Ahead of them was Eastgate and the bridge. The road filled with traffic. Dozens—no, hundreds of men here: bearded Saxons with shaggy manes of hair, clean-shaven foreigners. She saw Saxon women too, carrying babies on their backs, a priest on a mule, two dogs fighting—it was a stomach-churning contrast to the peace and quiet of the convent. One could so easily get lost if separated from one's companions. Unconsciously, she tightened her grip on Adam Wymark's belt.

He turned towards her, resting a hand on her knee. 'We're almost at the garrison,' he said. 'Can you last a little longer?'

The pressure of his hand was gentle, but Cecily felt it like a brand through her worn habit. She shot a look at the long, strong fingers, tinged red with cold because she had taken his gloves. His knuckles were grazed, his fingernails bitten down to the quick. Too human, those bitten nails. Better that she had not noticed them…

'I'm fine, thank you,' she said, though her muscles screamed that she'd be stiff for a sennight.

Duke William's knight nodded, removed his hand from her knee and faced forwards, leaving Cecily blinking at a row of burnt-out dwellings that lined the route.

War damage? Some of the houses had been left without roofs, others were skeletons, with charred timbers that clawed at the sky. The smell of smoke was eye-wateringly strong. A lump closed her throat. Neither the Roman walls nor the River Itchen had been able to do much to save the buildings clustered on the outskirts of the old Saxon capital. The recent fighting had destroyed all but the most sturdy.

Moving with careful desperation in the debris, sifting through the wreckage, ragged figures picked through the pitiful remnants like crows at a carcase. It mattered not whether they were dispossessed householders or looters, it came to one thing—here on the outskirts of Winchester people had been reduced to penury. Cecily's heart ached. Dear God, let Fulford not have suffered like this. Let the villagers be whole.

A troop of Norman horse-soldiers trotted smartly out of Eastgate and across the bridge, cutting a swathe through the pilgrims. When the troop drew level with Sir Adam, the leading knight saluted. 'Wymark!'

'*Holà*, Gervais!' Turning his mailed head, Adam smiled over his shoulder. 'Hang on, Lady Cecily, a few minutes more.'

She avoided his gaze. Adam Wymark might talk righteously about oaths sworn between kings, and of oaths broken, but what did the poor, ordinary folk know of that? No, this knight and his kind had caused too much suffering. The loan of a cloak and a pair of gloves and a few kind words could not begin to atone for what Duke William's warriors had done to her homeland…

It was painfully clear that the Duke's forces had been more than thorough in their attempts to stamp out any resistance. Since Winchester was the traditional heartland of the Earls of Wessex, she supposed it was logical that the Normans should scour the hinterland for rebels, but she did not have to like it.

One of the town mills, half consumed by fire, had collapsed into the river, its blackened debris forming a rickety raft. Ducks waddled across sodden, flame-scorched timber and planking. As one launched itself into the swift-flowing water, Cecily's eyes filled. They edged past a Saxon pilgrim swinging himself along on crutches. His straggling brown hair was tied back with a piece of string and he had one foot, but despite this he was moving at a fair pace…

Another lame man, one bent leg encased in bandages…

And another, flat out on a hurdle. There were so many sick and wounded; there was so much suffering.

He had doubtless played his part. She shut her eyes to close out the sight of a young boy of about ten years of age who had lost his arm above the elbow, and a tear ran hot down her cheek. Loosening her grip on Adam Wymark's belt, Cecily tried to shift back, away from him.

Old Minster—the Saxon Cathedral—had for centuries been renowned as a place of healing. These poor people were heading there, to the tomb of St Swithun, as they had always done in troubled times. They hoped for a miracle, and Cecily prayed they found it.

At the gate, a blind man held out his hand for alms. Fulford's new lord dug into a small pouch and a silver farthing arced through the air, to land with a clink in the begging bowl.

Cecily frowned. The man was a mass of contradictions. What should she make of him? One minute he was William of Normandy's loyal knight—a man capable of killing her countrymen—and the next he was giving succour to Saxon beggars.

A girl limped along on crutches, her clothes scarcely better than sacking. A young woman with a hen tucked under her arm took one look at their troop and spat pointedly in their direction. Fearful for the woman, Cecily went rigid. Her hot-tempered father would have leapt from his horse and taken his crop to her for such insolence. Sir Adam's hands merely tightened on the reins and they pressed on steadily.

The bridge rang hollow under the horse's hoofs. A heartbeat later and the stone arch of Eastgate was a cool shadow over their heads, and then the light strengthened as they emerged into the city proper.

Inside the walls, there was little damage. Her heart lifted as the horses' hoofs beat a sharp tattoo on the cobblestones. Passing lines of wooden houses—*intact* wooden houses—they entered the market square.

Saxons were selling eggs alongside cabbages, vending bread and new-baked pies, hawking ale alongside holy relics. Voices flew to and fro across the street like shuttles on a loom: speaking English, speaking French, speaking Latin—so many tongues that Cecily could not attune herself to all of them. It was a far cry from the peace and quiet of St Anne's. And then, just as she thought she could take in no more, a voice she recognised cut right across the cacophony…a male voice.

'Meet me in the Cathedral an hour from now.'

Ahead of her! No, on her right…

Tightening her grip on Sir Adam's belt, Cecily turned swiftly to either side, her gaze sweeping the square. No—no, it could not be! But that voice…*that voice*…where was he?

'Meet me in the Cathedral an hour from now.' Yes, that was what he had said, clear as day. Judhael! One of her father's men! It could not be he…and yet surely that voice was his? And who had he been talking to?

The crowd milled around them. Wildly, with her heart in her mouth, Cecily peered this way and that but could see no one she knew. And certainly there was no sign of Judhael, who had been her father's most promising housecarl and her brother Cenwulf's best friend…

Her head was spinning.

Had she *dreamed* hearing Judhael's voice among the crowd? A faint moan escaped her, and she sagged against Adam Wymark's broad back. Her mind was playing tricks. She was exhausted and near sick with worry, and it was hard to credit that her father's hearth troops were probably all dead. She *wanted* them to have lived, and she was just conjuring up Judhael's voice. Sister Mathilda had told her that the mind could play tricks, and Sister Mathilda was very wise—for hadn't another sister, Sister Beatrice, regaled the nuns with the visions she'd had after a particularly penitential Lenten fast…

The Breton knight reached back and touched her knee. 'Lady Cecily? What's amiss?'

Dear Lord, the man didn't miss a thing, Cecily thought, hastily straightening. 'It…it's nothing—a momentary dizziness, that's all.' And then she wished she'd said something—anything—else, for his grip shifted and he pulled her close to his mailed body.

'Hold hard, my lady.'

Her fingers were already clinging so tightly to Adam Wymark's sword belt she wondered if she'd ever pry them loose. Giving an inarticulate murmur, Cecily gazed steadfastly at the market stalls.

Anything rather than meet the disconcerting green eyes of Duke William's knight.

Meet me in the Cathedral an hour from now.

Judhael—if that really had been him—must have meant the Old Saxon Cathedral, St Swithun's, not the New Minster which stood next to it.

An hour from now...an hour from now...

Somehow, within the next hour, she must free herself from Adam Wymark and make her way to the Cathedral. Judhael might well be with his Maker, but if she wasn't in St Swithun's to make certain that she had dreamed his voice she would *never* forgive herself.

A brace of clean-shaven Norman guards were stationed at each corner of the market square. Their hair was cropped in like manner to Sir Adam and his men. Each guard was fully armed in the costly chainmail, so they must either be knights or in the Duke's personal entourage. She caught glimpses of several pointed shields, like the one which hung at Adam Wymark's saddle and was bruising her thigh.

A woman threw a bowl of slops under Flame's feet. The destrier didn't miss a step. They clopped over the cobbles, the rhythm of the hoofbeat tattoo unbroken.

I have to get to the Cathedral, I have to, she vowed, as she jounced past the market cross and several squawking chickens in cages. Head in a whirl, she felt a pang for the peace and solitude of the convent herb garden. Her lips twisted. For years she had longed to be part of just such a bustle and rush, but now she was in the thick of it it made her dizzy and she could not think.

Think, think. How to get to the Cathedral unobserved...?

Adam Wymark wheeled his chestnut into an alley and they entered the Cathedral Close. At once, as though a curtain had been drawn shut behind them, the bustle and rush and noise of the market fell away.

Peace. Thank the Lord, Cecily thought, ruefully acknowledging that there must be more of the nun in her nature than she had realised.

They drew rein outside the long stone building that once had housed the Saxon royal family, the Palace of the Kings. A stone arch framed the thick oak of the palace doorway, impressively carved with leaves and fruit. A flight of steps ran up the outside of the wall, leading, Cecily surmised, to a second floor and the private apartments of her father's liege lord, the late Harold of Wessex.

Today the Palace of the Kings—the *Saxon* Kings of Wessex— was bursting at the seams with what looked like the whole of Duke William's invasion force. Despite her borrowed cloak, Cecily's blood chilled, and the voice she'd imagined hearing in the market was pushed from her mind.

Was nothing sacred?

Two mailed Norman guards flanked the central doorway. Another pair were stationed on the landing at the top of the outside stairway. And in front of the Palace, on the flagstones, piles of weapons were being sorted by more of the Duke's men—swords, spears, bows—the booty of war? A distant hammering told her that nearby a smith was hard at work.

Adam Wymark dismounted, stretched, and offered her his hand. His helmed head turned in the direction of her gaze. 'Not what you'd expected?'

Cecily swallowed, and sought to express the confusion of emotions warring within her. 'Yes… No…' She tried again. 'It's just that it…it's our Royal Palace.'

'Last month it was,' he said, eyes half hidden by his noseguard. He reached up to help her down. 'Today it is our headquarters.'

'So I see.' His hands, without his gloves, were red with cold. They rested briefly on her waist to steady her, and for a moment there was not enough air in the courtyard. She stared stolidly at his mailed chest, all too conscious of Adam Wymark's superior height, of the lithe straightness and strength of the body under the chainmail, of the width of his shoulders. 'Thank you, sir.' His proximity was most disturbing.

'I would think it an honour if you would call me by my Christian name,' he said softly, for her ears alone.

Astonished, Cecily raised her eyes. He dragged off his helm and pushed back his coif, apparently waiting for her response, apparently meek. Not fooled for a moment, for this man was a conqueror, she swallowed. 'But, sir, th-that would not be seemly.'

His lips curved, his eyes danced, a hand briefly touched hers. 'Not seemly? You did propose marriage to me, did you not, Lady Cecily?'

'I…I…'

His expression sobered. 'Have you changed your mind?'

Cecily bit her lip. He had made his voice carefully neutral, had posed the question as casually as he would if he had been discussing the weather, so why was he watching her like a hawk? Because that was his way.

'I…no, I have not changed my mind.'

If only he would not stare like that. It made her hot and uncomfortable. Had he taken her hasty offer of marriage seriously? She had not thought so, yet there was a tension about him, as if her response mattered to him. She could not think why that should be so. She had no dowry and he was *already* in possession of her father's lands.

What was the nature of the knight she had offered to marry? Undoubtedly he was physically attractive, but what of his character? What *was* Sir Adam Wymark? A ruthless conqueror or an honest man upon whom she could rely? Whatever his nature she *must* agree to marry him if she was to be certain of accompanying him to Fulford. Her newborn brother needed her help if he was to thrive—as did her father's people, if a repetition of what had happened outside these city walls were to be avoided. Since Emma had refused him, Cecily was left with no choice. With baby Philip and innocent villagers to care for, she was needed at Fulford. Marry him she must. Her heart pounded. Why was there no air?

Around them, the Breton's men were dismounting and leading

their horses round to the back of the palace towards what had been the Kings' Mews. The squire Maurice took Flame's reins, and his knight's helm, and followed the others.

Adam Wymark was looking at her lips. She could not think why he would be doing that unless that was what men did when they were thinking about kissing a woman. Was he? To her horror, Cecily's eyes seemed to develop a will of their own, and she found herself examining his. They were well shaped and, oddly, looking at them made her pulse quicken. Slowly, they curved into a smile.

A guilty glance back up. Amusement was glittering in the green eyes.

Heat scorched Cecily's face, and just as swiftly she ducked her head.

'Lady Cecily, I have business in the garrison, despatches to send, so I must hunt out a scribe. If you would care for refreshment, Sir Richard will attend you until my return.' He raised her hand, pushed back the hem of the glove with his thumb and pressed a swift kiss to her wrist. Her heart jumped.

'Th-thank you, sir,' Cecily murmured, staring at the cobbles as though they were runes that held the secret of eternal life.

'Adam—my name is Adam.'

Cecily peeped up in time to catch that swift smile before he bowed and marched towards the sentries at the palace doorway. Her mind raced as she watched him go. Think, *think*. He is the enemy, and he cannot write. Remember that. It might be useful. He cannot write. Cecily could write—her mother had seen to it that both Emma and Cecily were lettered—and in the convent Mother Aethelflaeda had been quick to make use of Cecily's talent in copying out and illustrating missals for the nuns. But she would not call him back and offer to be his scribe—not when she must go to the Cathedral without him. His eyes were too keen, and if by some miracle she did find Judhael in St Swithun's she did not think that she could hide it from him.

Sir Adam spoke briefly to the guards by the arched doorway and vanished into the Palace of the Kings. Suddenly cold, Cecily pulled her—his—cloak more tightly about her.

'My lady?'

She started. Sir Richard was at her elbow.

'You are thirsty?'

She nodded.

'Follow me, and we'll see what the storemaster has to offer.'

It was easier than she had dared hope to escape alone into the Cathedral. Having refreshed herself, she simply asked leave of Sir Richard to visit St Swithun's tomb, saying she wanted to pray for her family. She said she hoped to find some peace. Neither of these remarks were lies, and she would not think about sins of omission...

Thus it was that an hour later Cecily was walking with Sir Richard across the Close, past New Minster, to the porch of Old Minster. She left him leaning irreverently on a crooked tombstone that dated back to a time before King Alfred.

'Take as long as you need,' Sir Richard said.

Inside, the cool dimness of the great Cathedral surrounded her.

Oddly, the large interior was made small by lack of light and the press of an army of pilgrims. It would be hard to pray. And as for peace—why, the Norman garrison was more orderly than St Swithun's Cathedral. The air was smoky with incense; walking sticks and crutches tap, tap, tapped against the floor tiles; priests chanted a Latin psalm. A bell rang. One young woman had her arm entwined about her young man's waist, and was giggling at his whispered witticisms, another hissed none too quietly to her deaf grandmother, and a small dog—a *dog*?—yelped as a pilgrim tripped over it...

But no sign of Judhael. No sign at all. Buffeted and knocked by those behind her, keeping an eye out for Judhael, Cecily was pushed slowly and inexorably into the shadowy nave. A couple of hundred people, maybe more, were queueing to file past St Swithun's tomb. Mother Aethelflaeda would be shocked at the lack of decorum and respect.

'A candle, sister?' asked a priest, thrusting one under her nose in a businesslike manner. 'To help your prayers fly to God.'

Cecily shook her head as she squeezed past him. 'I…I'm sorry, I have no coin.' God would have to heed her prayers without a candle, she thought ruefully. If she'd had coin she would have bought three candles: one each for her mother and father, and one for her brother, Cenwulf.

The line of pilgrims pressed on, and Cecily was carried with them, like a straw in a flood, to the foot of St Swithun's tomb.

Hanging-lamps and candleholders dangled from the lofty roof overhead. Bathed in a pool of candlelight, the tomb itself was, ironically, almost buried beneath dozens of crutches and sticks and cripples' stools that had been nailed onto the cover by grateful pilgrims. Even the great round pillars nearest the tomb had hooks hammered into them, and each was also hung about with yet more crutches, more sticks and more stools. The limewash behind the pilgrims' offerings was almost invisible, and lead tokens bearing the Saint's image lay scattered across the floor like autumn leaves.

So many miracles must have been wrought here, Cecily thought. Surely God will heed my prayers? And thus, for the few rushed seconds that she found herself before St Swithun's tomb, she prayed. Not for the family that she had lost, but for the family that remained: for her sister Emma, that she might find peace and happiness wherever she had gone, and for her new brother, Philip, that he might grow safely to manhood, and finally that her brother's friend Judhael might perhaps be alive and well and not simply exist in her imaginings.

Then the pilgrims behind her pressed forward, and she had passed the tomb. No Judhael. Not ready to return to the alien place that the Palace of the Kings had become, she broke free of the queue that was pushing her to the north door. Perhaps it would be quieter in the east end.

Near the transept, a rampantly carved wooden screen kept the great mass of people separate from the bishops and priests and their choir. Knowing better than to pass into the hallowed precincts beyond the screen, Cecily walked up to it and sank to her knees before a section carved with swirling acanthus leaves. Closing her eyes, she folded her hands in an attitude of prayer and sought to reconcile her mind to the revolutions in her life.

Whatever lay before her, she must do her utmost to ensure that no more evil befell Philip or the people of Fulford. Whether she could best serve as mediator for Adam Wymark, or as his wife, she could not say. In time, God would no doubt reveal His plans for her…

Placing herself in God's hands, Cecily was preparing to rise when she became aware of a furtive argument on the other side of the rood screen.

'No, I'm sorry. I found I could not!'

A woman in the priest's stalls? A woman whose voice was an exact match for her sister Emma? Impossible. Heart in her mouth, convinced that she must be mistaken, for Emma had clearly stated that she was heading north, Cecily strained to hear more. It was hard to be certain, for the woman's voice was distorted by anger and muffled both by the screen and the noise of the pilgrims in the nave.

'You are a fool!' A second voice, harsh and uncompromising and much easier to hear. Male—it was definitely male. Her pulse quickened. Judhael?

'It was not possible.' Emma—that *had* to be Emma…

'You are weak.'

'Compassionate, rather.'

For a space the man made no reply, and Cecily heard only the pilgrims at prayer; the tapping of crutches; the chanting of priests. She thought quickly. Back in the market square her mind had *not* being playing tricks on her—she *had* heard Judhael. Once his voice had been as familiar to her as her father's or her brother's. Judhael was *alive*! One of her father's housecarls, and Cenwulf's close friend, Cecily had assumed he had been killed at Hastings. She wanted to look, to see for herself, but fear of causing a commotion and bringing the Normans down upon them kept her on her knees.

Judhael's voice softened. 'Perhaps you do not trust me.'

'I want to trust you,' Emma murmured. 'But there is more than trust at issue here. It could have been his death, and what good would that do anyone? He is an innocent.'

What were they talking about? Clumsily, Cecily clambered to her feet. She rested a hand—it was shaking—against an acanthus leaf and peered through the tracery.

Yes! Praise the Lord, it *was* Judhael who faced her—a tall man with his long fair hair tied back at his neck, Saxon fashion. Hands on his hips, he was scowling at her sister. Cecily could only see Emma's back, but there was no doubt that it was she. That burgundy cloak was confirmation, if confirmation were needed. Emma had worn that cloak when visiting Cecily in the convent.

Emma had *not* gone north. Emma had lied to her. Why? And what was she doing in Winchester, meeting secretly with Judhael?

'You should have brought him,' Judhael said.

Cecily's stomach lurched. God in Heaven, the man was wearing his seax—his short sword—in the Cathedral!

'You broke your oath to me,' he went on, white about the mouth. As a child, Cecily had never seen Judhael look like this, furiously, uncompromisingly angry. But she knew that look. Her father had worn it often enough.

'My loyalty was torn…' Emma gave a little sob, and her head sank. 'Judhael, you are too harsh.'

Something about Emma's tone of voice, meek, yet unashamedly emotional, caught Cecily's attention. Back at the convent she had asked Emma if she had a sweetheart, now she realised with a jolt that matters had progressed far beyond that. Judhael was her sister's lover. Emma's next words confirmed this.

'Judhael, my love—'

Just then Judhael looked past Emma, towards the rood screen. Cecily fell to her knees, clutching an acanthus leaf. If she revealed herself, she risked drawing Richard of Asculf down on them. She glanced over her shoulder. There was no sign of him in the shuffling press of pilgrims around the tomb, but he could not be relied upon to wait her pleasure in the Close. He might come looking for her at any moment.

What would happen if Judhael and Emma were discovered here? She did not know what they were doing, but their discovery by Sir Adam or one of his men could only lead to their capture. And with Judhael in this mood, and armed as he was, it could well lead to bloodshed…

'I see only a woman whom I cannot trust.' Judhael's tone was icy.

Another little sob from Emma. 'And I see a man who…'

The rest of Emma's words were lost under the sound of brisk footsteps coming towards Cecily from behind. Turning her head towards the main body of the Cathedral, she felt her heart turn to stone.

Sir Adam Wymark had stepped out of the crowd and was marching purposefully towards her.

Chapter Seven

'S-Sir Adam!'

With her hood up, her features were partly shadowed, but
even so the frozen expression on the little novice's face brought
Adam to an abrupt halt a few feet away from her. He frowned.
He was not wearing the mail coat he was certain she hated, having put it off to enter the Cathedral, and Richard was guarding
his sword outside, so why that look of absolute horror the
moment her eyes lit on him? He had hoped she was beginning
to trust him. Given his recent decision, and the letter he had despatched to Duke William, it was *essential* that she trusted him.

White as whey, she was scrambling to her feet, almost trip-
ping over her threadbare habit in her haste to get round him, to
reach the door.

Heart sinking, Adam caught at her wrist, and she stilled in mid-
step, looking back at him. No, she would not even meet his eyes.
She was looking past him at a naked Eve on the carved rood
screen, eyes wide and full of fear.

'Sir Adam! I…I'm sorry if I kept you. I…I thought you were
still at the Palace.' She tugged against his hold, edging them both
back into the stream of pilgrims pouring out into the relative
brightness of the Close.

Refusing to release her, Adam did, however, surrender to the desperation in her eyes and allowed himself to be drawn along. They emerged, blinking, in the cobbled forecourt, where a feeble November sun was struggling to get through the cloud. Free of incense and candle-smoke, the fresh air raised goosebumps on his neck.

Richard was lounging against the wall where he'd left him, paring his nails with his dagger. On seeing them, he straightened and made to bring Adam his sword. Adam caught his eye and shook his head.

Cecily continued to draw him away from the Cathedral entrance, away from the pilgrims and the crush in the porch, and gradually her momentum slackened. Her eyes remained wide, but her cheeks had regained some of their colour, thank God. She tipped her head back to look up at him, and the hood of the cloak he had lent her fell back to reveal the grim novice's wimple, the short grey veil.

Her eyes were as blue as forget-me-nots, her lashes long and dark. Her lips were trembling—rosy, kissable lips. Adam's stomach clenched. *Forgive me, Gwenn.* This girl's colouring was the opposite of Gwenn's—Cecily of Fulford was tiny and fair, whereas Gwenn had been tall and dark. And until yesterday Gwenn's dark colouring had been Adam's model of beauty. But today…today…

Confused by his reaction to her, Adam looked down at Cecily Fulford and hoped she could not read his mind. He did not want her to know the extent to which her delicate beauty moved him. He would not grant her that much power. Why, even with the girl dressed like this, in a beggarly novice's habit, he desired her. Perhaps he might begin by caressing her cheeks, by testing their softness…no, he would start by kissing those lips…

Hell's teeth—how could he hope to court her when she regarded him in this manner? He might think her the prettiest girl in Wessex, but his Duke's ambition and her family's destruction lay between them. He must tread softly if he was to win her. And win her he would. He rubbed his forehead, wondering briefly how his mind had altered in the past few hours. When the little novice had first offered him her hand in exchange for her sister's he had vowed to tread warily. He had thought to refuse her until he knew more of her character and her motives in offering to accompany them back to Fulford. But now—Adam gazed into the largest blue eyes he had ever seen and his mind was in ferment.

Forgive me, Gwenn.

'My lady, you did ask to wed me,' he reminded her. 'Yet you regard me as though I were a monster. You did not regard me so in the convent. What have I done?'

She bit her lip, stared intently at the great door of the Cathedral, at the pilgrims filing out, and gave him no answer. Her bosom heaved as she dragged in a breath.

Adam set his jaw. Perhaps she had considered further and thought the gulf between them was impassable. Yes, that might be the sum of it. He did not only have to contend with the fact that he was an invader in her eyes; she had realised that she was gently born while he came from humble stock. Gripping her wrist more firmly, he tried again. 'My lady…Cecily…I give you notice I have decided to accept your proposition—*both* your propositions, that is. I *will* marry you.'

His answer seemed to rouse her, for she stopped staring at the Cathedral entrance long enough to dart him a quick sideways look. 'Aye, sir, as you wish.' And with that her gaze returned to the door.

He shook his head. He was eternally grateful that his heart was not involved in this betrothal, but it was galling to have a woman hardly react when a man agreed to wed her. What *was* going on?

'You make me very happy,' he said dryly. 'I must inform you that I have had a scribe write to the Duke saying formally that you will take your sister's place. I will *not* change my mind. Do you think there can at least be amity between us?'

A swift nod, a cursory glance, and once again her eyes slid away from his, back to the great door.

Adam sighed and determinedly walked her round the outer

wall of the north transept. She came meekly enough. In the lee of the wall they were, as he had hoped, shielded completely from watchful eyes and the noise and bustle of the forecourt. At the heart of Winchester, they had for a few moments a world to themselves—albeit a small one—bounded on one side by the wall of the Cathedral and on the other by a wooden fence the height of a man.

White teeth were worrying away at her bottom lip.

With careful determination, Adam manoeuvred her against the wall. When she offered no resistance, some of the tension began to leave him. And when he saw that the panic was dying from her eyes, he relaxed further, reaching up to touch her mouth, fingers as gentle as he could make them. She was so tiny. Next to her he felt huge and ungainly. 'No need to eat yourself up with anxiety,' he murmured, voice suddenly husky. 'I know you are innocent, a maid. When we wed I will be gentle, take care of you.'

Her eyes were huge and fastened on his. He felt her tremble. *Forgive me, Gwenn.* Telling himself that Gwenn was not here, while this girl most definitely was, he slid his fingers across her cheek—so soft—and under the starched edge of her wimple. He held her head steady, keeping his touch light, and slowly, so she could have no doubt what he was about and could break free if she wished, he lowered his lips to hers.

Warm. Her lips were warm and sweet.

Adam wanted to linger, but he knew better. Pure—she is pure. Easing back after the lightest of kisses, careful to keep the rest of his body away from her, he looked into her face. Her expression was startled; her colour had risen; her breath was coming faster. But there was no fear—not of him. He'd wager Flame on that.

He smiled. 'Lady Cecily, I make you this promise. I will marry you, but I will never force you. We shall wait to consummate our marriage until you are ready.'

'I…I thank you, but I was not always in the convent. My mother explained something of the duties of a wife to me. Our marriage will not be a true one unless it is consummated. I will not refuse you, sir.'

More reassured by her words than he cared to admit, Adam stroked her cheek with the backs of his fingers, and was startled to realise that his heartbeat was not as steady as it should be. Which was odd, given that she was the one lacking in experience, not he. 'Adam—my name is Adam,' he reminded her once again. 'And, since you are my betrothed, it is not unseemly for you to address me by it.'

'Adam.'

Her cheeks had gone the colour of wild roses. She lowered her gaze, but Adam would have none of that. He looked at her mouth, aching for another, deeper kiss. This was just lust, he told himself. It had been an age since he had loved his Gwenn. The tender feeling he had for this girl was not dawning love, it was mere lust. He wanted to kiss her and he would kiss her. It did not mean anything—not as it had done with Gwenn. He could kiss Cecily Fulford without putting his heart at risk. He tipped her chin up. 'Kiss me again, little Cecily.'

'If you would free me, S…Adam.'

Belatedly Adam remembered his hold on her wrist. He opened his fingers. 'My apologies. I did not mean to constrain you.'

Shyly, she smiled and looked at his mouth.

Their lips met. This kiss began innocently, as the first one had, with no more than their lips touching. Adam withdrew, then kissed her again. And again. Light kiss after light kiss. Another, another.

Cecily stood passive under his measured onslaught, and then, when Adam felt his control was about to snap—for he burned to sweep her into his arms and press her against the wall with his body—he felt the touch of a hand on his. Their fingers entwined. A small response, but one that had a jolt of sensation sweeping through him to his groin.

Startled, he pulled back. He had never been profligate. Gwenn had always been the world to him. His response to Cecily's delicate touch caught him unawares. It was hot. Urgent. Her eyes were closed, her long lashes rested against her cheeks, her lips were trustfully lifted to his. He fought down a groan. Such innocence, it could tear a man apart.

Experimentally, Adam touched his tongue to the fullness of her lower lip. He heard her indrawn breath. Her eyes remained shut. He repeated the gesture with her top lip. She leaned towards him. He took her other hand and moved closer, so they stood a mere inch apart, fingers clinging. Adam wanted to press his body close, so he could feel her breasts against his chest, but she was wearing his cloak and he his padded leather gambeson—and besides, it was full day, and they were in the middle of the old Saxon capital behind St Swithun's Cathedral, and he was Duke William's knight and a grown man, and he ought to know better…

It was so innocent, this gentle kissing. He was likely the first to kiss her. She did not know how to respond to a man, and had yet to open her mouth, but Adam had never felt so aroused in his life. Making certain he kept his lower body clear of her, for fear his ardour would frighten her, he rubbed his cheek against hers, pressing kisses against her neck, absorbing her scent.

She gave a soft moan. He nudged her headdress aside and managed to kiss her ear, nipping softly at the lobe. Another little moan. And when he next nuzzled her neck she turned her face into his, and he was almost certain…yes, it was only the most fleeting of touches, but she kissed his neck back.

He worked his way back to her mouth, gradually, oh, so gradually, increasing the pressure of his lips against hers. Kissing, kissing, kissing, hungry for a stronger response from her…

'Cecily,' he groaned. 'Sweet Mother, open your mouth.'

Dazed blue eyes met his. 'Wh…what?'

He dropped her hands and took her face in his. 'Relax your jaw, sweetheart. Let me in. Like this…'

She jolted in his hands when his tongue first pushed past her teeth. She quivered, but she did not draw back. He took his time, letting her grow accustomed. And then, all at once, it was as though his kiss had brought her to life. Her arms slid up and around his neck and she held his head to hers, even altering the angle of her head to grant him better access. Her tongue flickered over his in a tentative response.

Yes! Smiling, Adam tried to raise his head, but with a murmur she held him close, and then it was she who was covering his face with kisses, it was she who was kissing, kissing, kissing…

Her fingers tunnelled into his hair. She was stroking and petting his head so much his ears burned. If this was a taste of what was to come in their marriage bed, Cecily Fulford might bring him great joy.

Closing his eyes, Adam held still while untutored fingertips explored his eyebrows, his cheekbones, the shape of his lips. Still smiling—he could not seem to stop—he gently trapped her forefinger in his teeth.

She gave a little laugh and his eyes flew open.

A curl of long yellow hair peeped out from under her wimple. Idly, still using every ounce of control not to pounce on her and devour her as he wished, he wound it round his fingers. With her cheeks flushed, her lips red with his kisses and her bosom heaving, she was temptation incarnate.

The Cathedral bell tolled.

'Oh!' In a trice, the dreamy expression vanished from her eyes and she stepped back, muttering, 'Th-the Angelus bell.'

She made as if to cross herself, noticed he had her hair wound round his finger, and tugged it free. 'I…I must tidy myself, sir.' Hastily she pushed the curl back under the wimple and drew his cloak more closely about her.

The bell tolled on.

She continued to fuss with the sackcloth that passed as her clothing, straightening her veil, her wimple.

Adam grinned. 'Be calm, Cecily. You are not in the convent now.'

'I know. It's just that it…it's the first time I've missed the Angelus in four years. It feels wrong—like a sin.'

Shaking his head, he took her hand, kissed it. 'It's no sin if you are my betrothed. You were not made to be a nun. What age are you?'

'Sixteen.' Her blue eyes regarded him gravely. 'And you, sir, what age are you?'

'Twenty-two.' He bent to murmur in her ear. 'And you called me Adam a moment ago.'

'Adam.' She whispered his name and blushed, but would no longer meet his eyes. The Cathedral bell had reminded her of who she was, and who he was. Cecily had reverted, and was once again the shy Saxon novice he had taken from St Anne's, and he was a Breton knight, Duke William's man. Their tryst was ended.

Gently, Adam took her hand again and cleared his throat. 'We ride for Fulford in half an hour, in order to make the most of the light.' He eyed her wimple and grey veil with distaste, remembering how far Fulford was from Winchester's market. 'But first, if there is anything you need to buy here, I have some silver.'

She blinked. 'I thank you, S…Adam. But until I see what state my parents'…that is…*your* holding is in, I cannot say what provision we may need.'

'I'd have you better gowned. My wife will not walk around in rags.'

Cecily looked down at her skirts as though seeing them for the first time. 'Oh.'

He tugged at her wrist. 'Come—there's bound to be a mercer's stall at the market.'

She hung back, shaking her head.

'Cecily?'

'I would not waste your money. My mother used to keep bolts of fabric in a chest. There should be enough stuff for a gown for me.'

He bit back a smile. 'I see I am marrying a thrifty soul.'

'It's the convent, Sir—'

'Adam—remember?'

'Adam. The convent made me so. The Rule of Holy Benedict…'

Raising her hand to his lips, Adam took pleasure in the colour that washed into her cheeks. 'Tomorrow,' he said softly.

'Sir?'

'We'll get to Fulford tonight, and tomorrow we'll wed.'

'S-so soon?'

Leaning forwards, he pressed a kiss on the part of her brow not hidden by her wimple. 'I see no reason to delay. Once at Fulford Hall you will have time to renew old acquaintance and—' he flicked at the wimple with a grimace of distaste '—set a maid to see to your clothing. And then we'll marry.'

Leading her back round the north wall of the transept, Adam marched to the Cathedral forecourt, where Richard was waiting. As he buckled on his sword he intercepted one of Cecily's shy smiles. His heart felt lighter than it had in years.

Adam had not known what to expect when he had first gone to Normandy to uphold Duke William's claim to the English throne. Setting out from Brittany, he had hoped for land and favours, for a new life away from the places where Gwenn's ghost haunted him at every turn. He had thought he might win himself a new wife, but he'd never dared hope for one as lovely as this. One who might, if he were not on guard, tempt him into losing his heart again. He'd certainly not reckoned on an innocent novice for a bride either, but that was of no matter. Her smile alone was worth the crossing of several seas.

He was, he realised with baffled astonishment, feeling an emotion that was too complicated to be expressed as happiness, but it came close—damn close. And for that Cecily Fulford was entirely responsible.

His lightheartedness lasted as long as it took to walk back to the Saxon Palace, where the troop was stationed. The guards jumped to attention as they entered the main hall.

Cecily kept close, white teeth still nibbling at her lip. That pretty flush was gone. 'You've been here before?' he asked.

She swallowed. 'Once, years ago. With my father—with Thane Edgar.'

Adam nodded. This must be hard for her, and he had no words to make it easy. In her place he would be counting the differences between now and then.

He had not seen the Palace of the Kings when the Duke's men had first entered the city, but he'd heard about beautiful wall-hangings ripped from the walls—even now the hooks and rods on which they had hung were still visible, bent awry by careless hands. He'd heard about antique arms that had hung proudly over the main dais where the Royal family of Wessex had taken their seats to break bread. Telltale white marks on the smoke-blackened limewash were all that remained of them. He'd heard about costly silver plate—looted, most likely, from the self-same sideboard that Cecily was gazing at. One of the sideboard doors hung askew on one hinge, and one of its legs was broken. He'd heard of a great shield, emblazoned with the dragon of Wessex. There was no sign of that, either. No, Adam decided ruefully, nothing he could say would make this easy.

His captain, Félix Tihell, was back, talking to Maurice on the other side of the central fire. Adam steered his betrothed to a bench by the wall. 'Wait here,' he said, and left her gazing up at the gallery constructed at one end of the hall, on the first-floor landing, well away from the central fire. The room on the gallery had served as a private solar for the Earls of Wessex. The garrison commander had taken it over.

It was warm by the central fire, which was a proper roaring fire, piled with dry logs, not like the sulky affair at the convent guest house. Tihell had his helm under his arm, and he was out of breath, with a light sheen of sweat coating his forehead as though he had been running. He broke off at Adam's approach.

'Sir Adam.' Tihell saluted. 'In your absence, I was about to give Maurice my report.'

'Give it to me direct,' Adam said, waving his squire away. 'Don't tell me the trail went cold?'

'No, sir,' Tihell said, chest heaving as he caught his breath. 'I followed the pony tracks from the convent, out of the north gates as you directed, but they did not continue north, as we expected. Instead they circled round to the west in a wide loop. Lady Emma stayed overnight with her groom at a tavern called the Green Man, and the next day they continued, eventually hitting the road to Winchester.'

Adam tensed. 'Winchester? She came here? Lady Emma came here *today*?'

His captain nodded. 'Aye. We made good time, and I managed to catch up with her. Actually, I came through Hyde Gate behind her. Followed her straight to the Cathedral.'

Feeling as though he'd been kicked in the gut, Adam's eyes went involuntarily to Cecily, sitting demurely on the bench on the other side of the fire, with her hands folded nun-fashion in her lap. Smoke and flames curled between them, but she intercepted his gaze and sent a shy smile across the hall. When he did not return it, her smile faltered. Something within him twisted. 'The Cathedral?' he repeated slowly. 'Which one? Old Minster or New Minster?'

'The one which holds their saint's relics.'

'Old Minster. Hell, I should have known,' Adam said, closing his eyes as Cecily's reaction when she had caught sight of him flashed into his mind. That sudden pallor…that frantic scramble for the Cathedral door.

Cecily had known her sister was in the Minster and was playing him for a fool. Had she met secretly with Emma? Were they hatching a plot between them to see to his downfall? He shoved his hand through his hair and braced himself to turn back to Félix, to confirm the worst. 'You're stating that Emma Fulford definitely entered St Swithun's Cathedral today?'

'Yes, sir.'

His belly was full of cold stones.

When Adam remained silent, Tihell added, 'A couple of the lads are keeping watch on her, but I'd best not stay long. They're young and untried, and I don't want to lose her. Unless…unless you want me to bring her in, sir?'

Adam's gaze was drawn back to the girl on the bench. So pure. So innocent. Or so he had thought. His jaw tightened. Those kisses— had they meant something to her? Or had they been a blind—a cover to hide the fact that she had been meeting with her sister? His eyes narrowed. He had let a woman close before, and her death had all but torn his heart to shreds. Grimly, he wondered which was worse: the death of a loved one, or betrayal by a loved one.

Not that that was about to happen here. Thane Edgar's youngest daughter was nothing to him. *Nothing.* His hands curled into fists. Sitting there so pale and so pretty, so *demure*, Cecily Fulford did not look as though she had any guile in her. But she was Saxon, and he must not forget that. He had hoped she was warming to him, but he'd clearly been blinded by his attraction to her person. He had quite forgotten that to her he would always be Duke William's man, a conqueror.

'Sir Adam? Is…have I done wrong?' Tihell asked, shifting his helm to his other arm.

Adam forced a smile. 'Nothing's wrong but the times we live in.'

'Yes, sir.' Tihell paused. 'Sir?'

Adam tore his gaze from Cecily. 'Mmm?'

'Do I continue my surveillance of Emma Fulford, or do I bring her in?'

'Continue to watch her. Take careful note of everywhere she goes, of everyone she meets. I'm to marry the younger sister—' he jerked his thumb towards the small figure on the bench and his lips twisted '—and I want to know most especially of any communication between the two of them.'

'Aye, sir.'

Félix Tihell snapped his heels together and clapped on his helm, leaving Adam to stare through the smoke at his betrothed and wonder what he was marrying. A sweet novice bride with whom he might build a new world? Or a scheming Saxon witch who would thrust a seax in his back the first time it was turned?

Abandoned to her own devices in the great hall while Adam stalked into the upstairs chamber, presumably to confer with the garrison commander, Cecily had never felt so alone. Of course she was not really alone. How could she be when she was surrounded by so many of Duke William's men? Men. Life at the convent had left her unused to their company. She would have been uncomfortable even among men of her own people, but as for these…these invaders: her skin crawled; her mouth was dry.

The Saxon Palace was alive with hulking Franks in chainmail who thundered in and out, who charged up and down the stairs, oblivious of the graves over which they trampled. On her bench, Cecily held herself as still as a mouse in the presence of several cats, trying not to draw attention to herself. She was not afraid. She was *not*.

She was the only woman present. Had they murdered all the other women? A wave of nausea swept through her and she buried her face in her hands.

'Don't be sad, *chérie*,' a strange voice said. It was full of false sympathy and something else—something dark and unknown that had Cecily shuddering behind her hands and her blood running cold. She refused to lift her head. 'Come here, *chérie*. I will warm you.'

Covertly, she peered through her fingers. A brace of Norman knights who had been hugging the fire were winking and gesturing in her direction. She sat very straight. They would not *do* anything. She was betrothed to one of their number, so she would be safe, wouldn't she? But where were Sir Adam's men? Not one of them was in sight…

'*Chérie…*'

One of the knights was rising to his feet. Cecily closed her eyes—she felt sick, she actually felt sick. That edge in the man's voice had visions of assault—rape—running rampant in her mind. If he touched her she would vomit. She—

'My lady?'

Adam's squire, Maurice Espinay, was at her elbow, and Cecily all but slumped in relief. Politely, he offered her his arm and escorted her to a bench at the far end of the hall. Others of Adam's troop had staked a claim there, she realised, for men she recognised were dicing on an upturned packing crate. Warriors from another land, to be sure, but ones who answered to Sir Adam. More of her tension ebbed away.

With another bow, Maurice turned and marched back to the Normans at the fire. She could not catch what he said to them, but it proved effective, for afterwards they did not so much as glance her way.

Returning to her side with her bundle, Maurice dropped it at her feet and remained nearby, rooting through a saddlebag that must belong to Sir Adam. Adam must have asked him to watch over her, but whether that was for her safety or because he did not trust her she could not say. Whatever his reason, Cecily was grateful. Being taken from the convent with so little warning was hard enough. She had no experience of fending off foreign knights.

Was she really going to marry one of them? It did not seem possible. Adam Wymark's acceptance of her wild proposal seemed to have knocked the sense from her head. She glanced towards the fire, frowning at the two knights as she took a moment to absorb the implications of marrying Sir Adam. Like them, Adam Wymark was her enemy. She chewed her lip. She had offered to take her sister's place on impulse. A foolhardy move, perhaps, but she had not been certain that volunteering to be Adam's interpreter would be enough to convince him to take her with him. One thought had been clear: her brother and the people of Fulford must *not* be abandoned to the enemy. In order to be certain to get home she would have offered to marry the devil himself.

And now he had accepted her. The devil—the foreign devil who had sailed with Duke William and stolen her father's land. By rights she should fear him as she feared those Norman knights. Yet she felt safe at this end of the hall, in the company of his men. How could that be when only moments ago she had looked at his fellow Franks and had feared…?

'Sir Adam said to tell you that his plans have changed,' Maurice said. 'We will not be returning to Fulford till tomorrow at the soonest.'

'Oh?' She was uncertain whether to be relieved or dismayed. It would mean her wedding to Adam Wymark would be delayed, but it would also mean not meeting her baby brother for another day. Thank the Lord that Fulford's new lord did not fill her with revulsion, as those other knights had done. How curious. Adam Wymark had come with the Normans, and yet he did not revolt her or fill her with fear. He was not like those others. How strange.

Maurice was industriously hauling bedding from a heap at the far end of the hall. More soldiers tramped in. Normans, Bretons… invaders.

'Maurice, where will I sleep?'

Being in the Palace of the Kings in these circumstances was hideously unsettling, with reminders of how life had changed at every turn. By the Minster, in those few brief moments when she had been alone with Adam, when they had kissed, she had been able to forget about the changes. Adam had seemed a different person then—handsome, smiling and *approachable*, someone who would take note of her feelings and show genuine concern for her.

By the Minster it had seemed that a small miracle had taken place, and that everything might yet turn out well, but the moment they had crossed the Palace threshold Adam's demeanour had altered. One word with his captain and his smile had gone. He had glowered, positively glowered across the fire at her.

Were military matters so pressing that they drove all finer feelings from his mind? Or, worse, had he somehow found out about Emma and Judhael's presence in the city? She prayed not. For if Adam Wymark—Adam—were to challenge her on that subject, she did not know how she would answer him.

The key point, though, and the one she must hold fast to, was that she should get to Fulford to see to her brother's safety. She must also keep an eye on her father's people.

Were they the only things that mattered? a little voice wondered as she recalled the warmth of Adam's smile after they had kissed. A genuine warmth, she would swear. And yet, set that next to the way he had scowled and glowered at her only a few moments ago. But, scowl and glower though he may, she did not fear him. She sighed. Life might have been bleak in the convent, but it had been so much simpler.

'Maurice, where will I sleep?' she repeated, inwardly praying there was a ladies' bower. Given that she was the only woman in the hall, it seemed a faint hope.

Maurice spread his hands. 'Sir Adam didn't say. You'd best ask him at supper.'

She rose from her bench. 'Is there anything I can do?'

The squire shot her a startled look. 'Do, my lady?'

'I'm not used to being idle. I'd rather *do* something.'

'Such as?'

She shrugged. 'Anything. Is there an infirmary? I could help there. Or I might be of use in the cookhouse…'

Maurice looked shocked. 'No, my lady. Sir Adam wouldn't want you wandering off. Besides…' He rolled his eyes towards the knights hogging the central fire. 'There's plenty more like them roving the city. You'd do best to keep your head down, if you see my meaning. You'll be safe enough here, among Sir Adam's troop.'

Shifting the bench nearer to the men who were dicing, Maurice indicated that she should take her seat.

Sighing, Cecily settled in for a long afternoon. With something of a jolt she realised she would feel happier if Adam was here in person. While she was still uncertain of what to make of him, she did prefer it when he was around, even if all he did was glower at her.

Chapter Eight

By the time Adam returned to the Royal mead hall night had long since fallen. Torches chased the shadows away, candles glowed in beaten metal wall sconces, the central fire crackled and spat. The room was filled with the gentle buzz of conversation, the occasional roar of laughter.

Adam's hair was damp from recent washing, and he was wearing his dark blue tunic, belted at the waist with a chased leather sword belt, and a serviceable brown wool cloak bought from the garrison's quartermaster. His leather gambeson dangled from his fingers. Slinging it over one shoulder, he rested his other hand on his sword hilt and paused just inside the threshold, searching for Richard and his men and…

No sign of that petite figure in her drab veil and gown. He'd left her alone deliberately, to see what she might do. Where the devil was she? His stomach tightened into several knots. That night's rations were to blame—not the fact that he didn't know where she was. He had eaten with the Duke's commanders in the upstairs solar. Food had been plentiful, but too much bread and ale and oversalted pork after weeks of hunger was not good for a man's digestion.

He grimaced. Who was he fooling? *She* was the cause of his indigestion; he wanted to think the best of her. Damn it, how could that have happened already? He'd not known the woman more than a few hours…

Groups of men were clustered in the various pools of light made by the torches. Laughter floated out from under the nearest torch, where men were drinking and dicing. Farther down the hall came the rhythmic scrape, scrape, scrape of a whetstone on steel. A blue spark flashed—a squire sharpening his knight's sword. From under another torch came a quiet muttering as friends simply talked.

There—there she was. Perched on a bench at the wall at the far end, in an oval pool of light. Brian Herfu, the youngest in his troop, sat next to her, and she was turned towards him, veil quivering as she listened to what he was saying. A string of rosary beads was wrapped round her wrist, and a missal lay on top of her small bundle of belongings. A missal? She could *read*? Wondering if Cecily could write—that would be a rare and wonderful accomplishment in a wife—Adam started towards them.

Brian had lost his older brother shortly after Hastings, and when Adam saw that the lad's eyes were glistening with tears he had little doubt but that they were discussing Henry's death.

Cecily touched Brian's arm. The movement made the rosary swing gently to and fro. 'How did Henry die?' she was asking.

Brian's dark head bent towards Cecily's. 'Blood loss, my lady. A leg wound. He—'

Not needing to hear the rest, Adam turned away. He had been beside Brian at Henry's deathbed, and did not begrudge him any comfort that Cecily might give him. Catching Maurice's eyes, he motioned him over.

'You've eaten, sir?' Maurice asked.

'Aye. And the men?'

Maurice nodded.

'And my lady? You saw to it that she was well fed?'

'Yes, sir. It was plain fare, but good. She seemed very hungry. I think they must have rationed her at the convent.'

'Likely you're right,' Adam said, glancing across at the slight figure by the wall. Cecily had turned towards Brian and was holding his hand in both of hers. He saw Brian clutch convulsively at the sympathy she offered. 'Where's Sir Richard?'

Maurice tried, unsuccessfully, to smother a grin. 'Went out earlier. Not back yet. He mumbled something about trying to find a *proper* bathhouse.'

Adam rolled his eyes, the distinction not lost on him. There was nothing wrong with the wash-house next to the palace. In the main the Saxons had clearly used it for doing the royal laundry, but one could bathe there if one had a mind. He had done so, and doubtless countless Saxon princes and lords had also done so before him. Since it was a Royal Palace there were bathtubs. Richard must have other activities in mind.

'He might not find much favour with Saxon women,' Adam said.

'He will if he pays enough,' came the dry response.

'Enough, Maurice! You are not his peer, to speak about him with such familiarity.'

'My apologies, sir.'

Adam looked pointedly at Cecily. 'You watched her close?'

'Aye, sir. She hasn't stirred all evening—except for a visit to the latrines and the wash-house.'

Adam narrowed his eyes. 'You accompanied her?'

'Of course. But I didn't go into the latrine with her, if that's what you mean. I simply escorted her to the privy and back.'

'And she met no one?'

'No one.'

'And what about the wash-house? Anyone there when she went in?' Since Adam had paid a visit to the wash-house himself, he knew first-hand how there was room enough for anyone intent on a clandestine meeting to hide behind the great cauldrons or the washtubs.

'No.' Maurice looked affronted. 'I checked the place was empty before she went in.'

Adam started to chew a fingernail, and checked himself. 'You are certain?'

'Aye. She went to wash and change her habit, nothing more.'

'Very good, Maurice.' Some of the groups under the torches were starting to break up. Men were rolling into their cloaks, eager to bag places close to the fire. 'We'll bed down shortly. Who's watching the horses?'

'Charles, sir, followed by George.'

'Good. Stow this and get yourself settled.' He tossed Maurice his gambeson. 'I won't need you again tonight.'

'My thanks, sir.'

Adam found a blanket in his pack and took it over to where Cecily was sitting. She was so pretty, with those delicate features and huge dark-lashed blue eyes. Gut-twistingly pretty. If only he could be sure she would not betray him...

At his approach, Brian coloured and tugged his hands free. 'Excuse me, my lady,' he said. Bowing, he made himself scarce.

'You will need this,' Adam said, handing Cecily the blanket. He pointed at the wall. 'May I suggest you lie there? It's farthest from the fire, I'm afraid, but you'll be safer beringed by my men.'

Her cheeks flamed. 'Is there no ladies' bower, sir?'

'We cannot afford such refinements. This is a garrison. You'll have to bed down by me.'

A guffaw, quickly suppressed, came from one of Adam's men.

'B-by you, sir?'

'I know this cannot be easy, my lady,' Adam said, deliberately using her title as a means of demonstrating to his men that he wanted them to use courtesy in their dealings with her, 'but you truly will be safer by me.'

Rising swiftly, Cecily set about ordering her bed. Absurdly self-conscious, she hoped no one could see how her hands were shaking. Within moments she had made a place for herself near the wall, and had removed her veil and wimple. Her heart pounded. Though she kept her back to Sir Adam, she could feel his gaze on her as clearly as she would a caress—on her shoulderblades, her hair. Burrowing into the luxurious fur-lined cloak, she fixed her eyes on the rough wall plaster, focussing on a crack in the render. A shiny black beetle was scuttling into the crack. Though she could not see Adam, she could hear him moving about behind her.

From the sounds she judged that he must be quite near, but she did not like to look. A knight had come in with his wife at suppertime, but apart from that single woman she had seen no other all afternoon. She was adrift in a man's world, and the rules were very different from those of the convent. Usually Cecily slept on her other side, but that would mean facing Adam, and she felt too vulnerable to face him while she slept, too exposed.

An amused whisper reached her. 'Do you always sleep with your hair so tightly braided? Gwenn used to loose hers—'

She risked a glance over her shoulder. 'Gwenn?' He was crouching on his haunches, scarcely two feet away, dragging another blanket from his pack.

'My wife.'

Cecily blinked. 'You have a wife, sir? But…but—'

'I have no wife now.' His lips twisted. 'Rest assured, little Cecily, you do not marry a bigamist.'

Cecily turned back to the wall and the beetle while she digested this new piece of information about the Breton knight who had agreed to marry her. He had already been married. She sighed, shamefully aware of a bitter taste in her mouth as she wondered if Adam Wymark's wife had liked his kisses as much as she had done when he had kissed her by the Cathedral. Those kisses had been a revelation to her—those little darts of pleasure shooting along her skin, his ability to make her bones feel as though they were melting, the urge to touch, to stroke, to *be* stroked—was this what others felt when they kissed? When Ulf and his wife… She bit her lip. No. *No*. It was shameful, what Adam Wymark had made her feel. He was her *enemy*.

His wife's name had been Gwenn. Had he loved her? What had she looked like? And what had happened to her? Had she died or had he put her aside?

In England it was easy for a man to repudiate a woman—even one to whom he was married. It was common practice in Wessex, and there was no reason to suppose matters were arranged any differently in Brittany. A man could have any number of reasons for setting a woman aside—failure to provide the promised dowry, non-consummation of the marriage, for not producing the required male heir.

She sighed. Would Adam Wymark set her aside if she did not please? If she did not provide him with a male heir? Lord knew she was not providing him with a dowry.

Racking her brains, she could not recall any instances of a *woman* setting a *man* aside. Truly, the world was not made for women.

The palace floor tiles were cold, and harder than the straw pallet she had slept on in the convent. As Cecily wriggled deeper into his cloak and tried to get comfortable, she numbered the reasons for making a success of this marriage. There were the villagers and inhabitants of Fulford, and there was Philip, not to mention the pressing need to distract Adam from searching for Emma…

She could like Adam for himself, given half a chance. How much better it would be if she only had that to think about—if the strongest reason for marrying him could be the fact that she actually had a liking for this Breton knight and found him personally attractive. Instead, their dealings must be confused by politics and by her concern for what was left of her family. It was such a tangle.

In her mind's eye she could see his green eyes gazing into hers, as they had done outside the Cathedral…darkening, softening. She could feel the warmth of his fingers as they had twined with hers, the light touch of his lips; she could hear the huskiness in his voice as he had called her sweetheart and asked her to open her mouth to his…

So much weighed in his favour. If only he had not come to England with Duke William to win lands for himself—if only those lands had not belonged to her father.

Turning her shoulder, she gave him a swift glance. He was shaking out another blanket, making a bed near enough that he could reach her. Near enough and yet not too near. No one can come between us, she realised with a jolt.

He caught her eye and gave her a crooked smile. 'If you need me, you only have to say.'

Cecily gave him what she hoped was a haughty look to cover a peculiar increase in her heart-rate—why was it he had this effect on her? It was most unsettling. She turned to face him properly. Not because her eyes were hungry for him—most certainly not! No, one simply could not converse peering over one's shoulder. ''Tis not seemly to lie so close.'

In a trice he was at her side. Drawing one of her hands out of its hiding place in the blue cloak, he brought it to his lips and a *frisson* of awareness ran all the way up her arm. How did he do that? And why did her body react in such an unpredictable way whenever he came near?

'My lady, you are my betrothed.' He gestured around the hall. 'But if you would prefer some other protector you only have to say the word. I bid you recall that my right to Fulford Hall rests on Duke William's gift, and is in no wise connected to any union with you.'

She stared past him, her face as wooden as she could make it. The only protector she wanted was looking right into her eyes, but she could not bring herself to admit it. *He is your enemy…your enemy.* Unaware that her fingers had tightened momentarily on his, she darted a fearful glance towards the fire, towards the knight who had tried to solicit her attention, but he was no longer there.

Her eyes met Adam's, and for all his hard words she found gentleness in their expression. His pupils were darkening, his smile softening, and she sensed he was waiting for her response. He had washed his hair, she noticed irrelevantly. It was wet and neatly combed, save for one dark lock which fell over his eye. But what could she, a Saxon, say to him, one of Duke William's knights?

Abruptly, he released her, and pushed his hair back. Jaw tight, he turned away and shifted his belongings a little farther off.

Cecily felt the loss of him like an icy draught. He was only a yard away—the seemly distance she had asked for—yet now he had retreated, perversely she wanted him closer. She did not face the wall again. It was comforting to be able to see him in the gloom. And now was not the time to wonder why this should be so, any more than it was the time to wonder about the extraordinary effect he had on her senses. Later she would think about these things, when she had slept…

The floortiles grew harder, and colder. Fingers and toes were turning into icicles, goosebumps rose on the back of her neck. Cecily shrank deeper into his cloak.

The hall was quietening. One by one torches were doused, save a couple by the door and a lantern or two hanging from the rafters. Shadowy figures hunched around the hearth, faces shiny in the firelight. The knight who had so discomposed her might have gone, but her unease remained, and a low murmur of voices ran on, broken occasionally by a crack of laughter. Male laughter, *predatory* male laughter. Duke William's men.

Cecily's eyelids closed, but her nerves were stretched tight as a bowstring. She had had four years in the convent, with scarcely a glimpse of a man, and suddenly she was sleeping with a roomful. What penance would Mother Aethelflaeda impose for that?

A mild commotion near the door had her eyes snapping open. A drunk staggered in, held upright by two companions. Drawing in a shaky breath, she stole another look in Adam's direction. He was lying on his side, head on his hand, watching her. His face was in shadow, but she thought his eyes were cool.

'Be at peace, Cecily,' he said softly. 'If you mean to make me a good wife, you will want for nothing.'

His long, sword-callused fingers lay relaxed on his blanket a few feet away. Never had so short a distance seemed so large.

'I want…'

'Yes?'

'Don't leave me here alone,' she whispered. 'Tonight—that's all I want.' Tentatively, she reached across the ravine.

Warm fingers closed on hers. 'Be loyal to me and I will never leave you. But fail me…' His voice trailed off.

A cold knot made itself felt in Cecily's stomach even as she clung to his hand. Did he know about Emma?

But the contact must have soothed her, for very soon after that her eyelids closed of their own accord and sleep took her.

Some time later, she stirred and came slowly back to consciousness.

Warm. *Warm.*

What a delightful, impossible dream. She had not been warm at night in winter since entering the nunnery. Giving a comfortable little moan, she wriggled closer to the source of that warmth. Willing the dream to continue, she tried to slide back into sleep, but instead came more awake.

Her breath caught. Adam. It was he who was giving her his warmth. She was lying next to—no, her head was pillowed on Adam's bicep, and her nose was pressed into the warmth of his ribcage. His scent surrounded her: alien, male, seductive. And until yesterday absolutely forbidden. She had her arm over his chest, which rose and fell gently under her palm.

Warm, so warm.

Fully awake, she readied herself to pull away if he made the slightest movement. Lying in a man's arms like this was so far beyond unseemly that Mother Aetheflaeda would have had her drummed out of the convent for even imagining such a thing.

Carefully, she lifted her head. Yes, he was asleep. She allowed herself to relax. His arms were linked loosely about her, and at some point he must have wrapped the blankets round them both. The warmth—oh, dear God, the warmth. One could marry a man for the warmth alone, she thought with a wry smile.

In the dim light of a glass hanging-lamp that had miraculously survived the Normans' depredations, she studied his face. He was a joy to look upon—particularly now, when he was unconscious of her gaze. Usually she felt too shy. Dark eyelashes lay thick on his cheek. She gazed at the high cheekbones and the straight nose and frowned, for she longed to touch, to stroke, but such longings were surely sinful—and in any case she did not want to wake him.

Staring at him like this was a secret, private pleasure. She had not been outside the convent a day, but already she was learning that other men did not draw her gaze in the same way. Adam Wymark muddled her thoughts; he muddled her senses. He disturbed her, but it was by no means unpleasant…

A dark shadow was forming on the strong jawline, telling her that Adam's beard, were he to grow one, would be thick and dark as his hair. How often did he have to shave to keep his cheeks smooth, in the Norman fashion? His lips were parted slightly in sleep—beautifully shaped, firm lips—lips that could…

He stirred, turning his head and nuzzling her. That stray lock of hair fell across his face.

Repressing an impulse to nuzzle him back, Cecily lifted her palm from his chest and lightly stroked his hair out of the way. Then she replaced her hand on his broad chest and slowly lowered her head back onto that warm bicep. Softly.

It might be sinful, but they had come together thus in sleep. His warmth, and the long, strong length of him next to her was so delicious she did not care if it was a sin. And in truth it did not feel wicked or depraved, which surely sin always did? It was comforting to lie thus with Adam. It was…cosy. The palace floortiles might be hard, but she would lie on nails if it meant she could awaken again like this.

Someone coughed. Belatedly, Cecily was reminded of the others in the Old Palace. Normans for the most part—men who had used Duke William's disagreement with King Harold as an excuse to come to England to plunder in the wake of the Duke's conquest, men whom Cecily had cause to fear. Adam Wymark had come with them. This she could not deny. But now, lying at the side of the hall, wrapped in his arms, she felt safer than she had ever felt. The irony was not lost on her.

Snuggling closer, safe in the arms of the enemy, breathing in the comfort of his forbidden, alien scent, Cecily slid back into sleep.

Some time before dawn someone slipped stealthily into the hall and found a place among Adam's men. Stirring in Adam's arms, so full of sleep that she didn't realise he was still holding her, Cecily lifted her head from his chest.

Sir Richard. Returning from whatever business had kept him last eve. With a sigh, she let her head fall back, and sleep took her again.

At cock crow, gentle fingers were playing in her hair, loosening her braid. Green eyes smiled into hers. 'Good morning, betrothed,' he murmured.

'G-good morning.' Cheeks hot, Cecily steeled herself to ignore the dark warmth of his gaze. He was looking at her lips, with no trace of the coldness of manner that she had noticed on their arrival at the palace. Her chest constricted, and she thought of the kisses they had shared outside the Cathedral. Breathless. His look made her breathless.

Catching her braid, Adam gave a small tug and realigned her

body against his. 'A good-morning kiss,' he whispered. His lips met hers, warm and soft. Lazily, his tongue outlined her mouth.

For a moment, hazy with sleep, Cecily let the disordering pleasure wind through her—then she stiffened. What was she doing? She had to keep her wits about her.

'What's the matter?'

'For shame, Sir Adam. Remember where we are! And in any case we are not wed that we should lie this close.'

Eyes laughing, he pulled her tight against him, so she could feel the length of his strong, lean body from breast to thigh. Despite herself, she gloried in it—she actually *ached* with wanting to press even closer. He seemed to sense it, for under cover of the cloak and blankets his hand ran lightly down her back and came to rest possessively over one of her buttocks.

She gasped. Never had she been touched so intimately.

'Damn the conventions,' he said with a grin. 'No one knows what we're about. They can't see.'

Cecily's loins felt as though they were melting. She longed to run her hand over that broad chest and discover the feel of his skin. Biting her lip, she strove to hide such a sinful reaction. Did Judhael make Emma feel this way? If so, she was beginning to understand why her sister might take Judhael as a lover—even though it was a sin and she risked giving birth out of wedlock.

Adam's touch filled her with wanton longings. He was yet a stranger to her, so she could not fathom why her senses swam when he kissed her, but swim they did. Why, she could almost believe the man would turn Mother Aethelflaeda wanton! The image of Adam with the Prioress was so ludicrous a gurgle of laughter escaped her.

'What now?'

She shook her head. 'Nothing—I…I was just thinking of you and Mother Aethelflaeda.'

A dark eyebrow twitched. 'Me and Mother Aethelflaeda?'

Shaking his head, not understanding, he ran his hand back up her spine and loosed a shiver of delight through her body. He pushed his fingers into the hair at the base of her plait. 'One more kiss,' he muttered, tipping her face to his.

'Remember where we are…'

'That's Mother Aethelflaeda speaking, not you.' Smiling, he pressed a firm, all too brief kiss on her mouth. 'But have no fear, little Cecily, you'll not lose your maidenhood in a room full of soldiers.'

'Adam!' She thumped at his chest with her fist. 'Someone will hear!'

He caught her hand, toying with her fingers. When he caressed her palm with his thumb, the tingle raced to her toes. 'Relax, sweetheart. I've better plans for you—if you will be my true and faithful wife.'

His reference to her being a true and faithful wife gave her pause. Hadn't he said something similar last night?

'Sir…?'

'Mmm?' Idly he ran a finger down her cheek and throat to the neck of her gown.

When his fingers lingered, her pulse raced. She wanted to run. She wanted to stay. She struggled to keep her mind clear. 'Your wife—Gwenn…?'

His hand stilled. An arrested look came into his eyes, as though for a moment he could not recall having had a wife. 'Mmm?'

The questions were piling up in her head. What had happened to Gwenn? Had he had her set aside? Did he have children? The questions were burning into her soul, for the answers would reveal much about his nature.

Was she marrying a man who would set his wife aside the first time she crossed him? Clearly Adam Wymark could charm the finches from the trees if he had a mind, but how would he react if he found out about her newborn brother? How would he react if he knew she had concealed the fact that she had seen Emma yesterday? How would he react if he knew Cecily had seen her with one of her father's housecarls in the Minster and—?

A cold fist gripped her heart. She *knew* where Emma and Judhael had gone! Why had she not realised before?

Hastily lowering her eyes, for Adam's keen gaze was on her, and he seemed to possess an uncanny ability to read her mind, she let her thoughts run on. Judhael's sister, Evie, had married one of Winchester's goldsmiths—Leofwine. Judhael would take Emma to his sister's house, to Evie and Leofwine...

This was yet another secret to keep from Adam. She hid a groan. *Another* secret—as if she were not already the keeper of more secrets than anyone in Christendom.

If Adam discovered any of them, how would he react? So far he had shown her only his gentle side, but he was the Duke's man. Would he reject her out of hand? His trust would certainly be forfeit.

Taking in a breath, Cecily raised her eyes and forced a smile. She would have to be very circumspect if he was not to find her out. She could not risk being set aside—not if she was to succeed in her aims.

'What happened to Gwenn?' she asked, and immediately wished she hadn't, because his face became hard.

'I do not wish to speak of her.'

Easing himself back, Adam rolled away and out from under the blankets. Cecily was left to follow him with her eyes as he stretched his long body and combed his dark hair with his fingers. Then, without so much as a backward glance, he snatched up a cloak and strode towards the morning light that was creeping through the main door of the hall. It was as though, Cecily thought with a pang, they had never spent the night in each other's arms; it was as though they had never kissed, had never agreed to marry.

Adam Wymark, my betrothed. A Breton knight, the Duke's man. He was once married to a woman named Gwenn, of whom he will not speak. What will he do if he discovers the secrets I am hiding from him? Will he ever love me? And why, Cecily thought with a grimace, should I be so concerned about *that*?

Breakfast was taken in the Old Palace hall. Small ale, warm bread and a creamy white cheese that—luxury of luxuries—showed no sign of mould.

Afterwards, Cecily picked up the blue fur-lined cloak and draped it over her arm. She had not seen Adam since he had left at cock crow.

'Maurice?'

'My lady?' Maurice was sitting cross-legged on the floor, to all intents and purposes occupied in restitching a saddlebag.

'Where is Sir Adam?'

'He is…elsewhere in the city, on the Duke's business.'

She fiddled with the girdle of her habit. 'Did he say when he will return?' Not for some hours, she hoped.

'No, lady.'

'I'm going to the Minster. If he asks after me, please tell him.'

Maurice glanced up. 'You won't go farther, my lady?'

'No…no.' *Liar. Liar.*

Maurice's brown eyes searched hers and then, apparently satisfied with what they saw, bent back over the saddlebag. 'Good, because Sir Adam would string me up if anything happened to you.'

'Oh. Yes. I…I shall only be in the Minster. At prayer.'

'Very good, my lady.'

Swinging the cloak about her shoulders, Cecily hurried outside, praying that Maurice had believed her, and praying also that he didn't have instructions to follow her.

It was bright, if chill in the Palace courtyard. The sky was patchy with cloud, and a low winter sun was throwing long shadows through them. A couple of Duke William's knights were putting their horses through their paces, ready to turn the courtyard into a tiltyard as they wheeled their mounts and prepared to charge. Lance-tips gleamed. The horses' breath hung in the air, and their hooves struck sparks on the cobblestones as they champed at their bits, impatient for the signal.

Scurrying swiftly past, Cecily almost jumped out of her skin as someone barked out, 'Roderick, get that beast out of here!' The garrison commander. 'If you must play at tourneying—' the commander's face was suffused with anger '—get round to the practice field. I'll have no mêlée in the garrison forecourt.'

Glancing over her shoulder at the door of the Palace—no sign of Maurice, thank the Lord—Cecily quickened her pace. In a moment she was through the Palace yard and out of the gates, staring up at the two Minsters.

So, Adam's whereabouts that morning was a mystery. No matter. She had no wish to see him, for she had business of her own to attend to.

Family business—*Saxon* business—and he would definitely not approve.

Chapter Nine

A rush of tears for her father, her brother and her mother blinded her, and the entrance to New Minster hove into view all blurry. Cecily blinked hard. Glancing over her shoulder to ensure that Adam's squire hadn't followed her, she ducked her head and, instead of following a straggle of pilgrims into the dark interior, took a couple of quick steps sideways, darting round between the two massive church buildings.

So far, so good. No sign of Maurice.

Emma and Judhael *must* have gone to Golde Street, and if they were still there it was vital she spoke to them. But it was equally vital she got there unseen by Adam or any of his troop…

Cecily had been but a child at the time of her last visit to Winchester, and her memory of the city's layout was sketchy. As far as she could recall Golde Street, where Judhael's sister Evie lived with her goldsmith husband, was sited in the western quarter, in the lee of the city walls. From Market Street she would try going up the hill towards Westgate.

Pulling the hood of Adam's cloak up over her veil and wimple, and fastening it tight to obscure her face, Cecily dived into the shade between the two Minsters and turned left.

Quickly, quickly, through the graveyard. Rows and rows of gravestones.

No Maurice. No one following her.

Oh, sweet Lord, she thought, her breath coming fast. Adam must not find out about this. Quickly, quickly, on into Market Street, Another left turn. People setting up stalls, hawkers grabbing her arm…

'Silk ribbons! Silk ribbons!'

'Fresh loaves! Baked this morning!'

Shaking herself free, Cecily ploughed on. Up past Staple Street. The crisp air was filled with the bleating of sheep as shepherds with crooks led a flock to the slaughter pens. It's November, she realised, with something of a jolt. They kill the animals that can't be over-wintered in November. It felt oddly like an affront to see such a normal everyday sight so soon after the killing of England's King and the loss of so many men. But the year turned regardless of the falling of kings and men. Everyday life must resume, and the meat would certainly be needed in the cold months to come. A butcher, wearing a sackcloth apron that was dark with blood, stepped out in front of her, and a metallic smell rose to her nostrils. All but gagging, Cecily pressed on.

Sweat breaking out on her brow, she glanced back and caught her boot on a loose cobble. No Maurice, no Adam, and no sign of any of his troops, thank God.

A stone was digging into the ball of her foot; her boot had a hole. Pausing to shake the stone free, she skirted round some night soil a householder had tipped into the gutter in the centre of the street and went on. And then Westgate reared up in front of her, gates yawning wide to let people bound for market into the city. Practically running, Cecily turned into a street that hugged the old Roman walls. Wooden houses, some thatched, others tiled with wooden shingles.

The morning sun was a low dazzle before her. She paused to

catch her breath. Golde Street had to be near here: a few yards more, a little further. *There!* Golde Street. She shaded her eyes against the glare. The street was not as she remembered it when her father had brought her here. The shops had been open for business then, and bustling with trade. Now it looked like the Sabbath. The shopfronts had wooden bars nailed across the shutters, giving the impression that the shopkeepers had no intention of opening this side of the Day of Judgement. Where was everyone? Had trading ceased since Duke William's invasion?

A girl sat on a threshold, suckling a baby. An old woman hobbled towards her, coming from the well with a bucket in hand, water slopping over the rim. A dog lifted its leg on the corner of a house. But where were the goldsmiths, the merchants, the customers?

And there, at the end of the street by the well, what was happening there? A group of men—Normans, to judge by their attire and by their priest-like shaved heads—were clustered round a barrel, staring at a scroll of parchment that was weighed down with stones. One man was leaning on a stick—no, it was a measuring rod. A measure? What *was* going on? Surely there was no room for more houses?

White stone markers had been laid out at intervals along the street, but Cecily could see no rhyme or reason in their placing. Half a dozen men wearing leather aprons and toolbelts that named them builders and carpenters stood close by. Their long hair proclaimed them to be Saxon, and their sullen, slouching posture told her they were to labour unwillingly.

Cecily hurried on—on past a wheelbarrow spilling ropes and tackle onto the ground. Leofwine's house had been about here…

Yes—this was it! Leofwine's shop was barred, like the others, but, undeterred, she banged on the door. At the southern end of the street there was a rumble of wheels and four yoked oxen rounded the corner. They were hauled to a halt. A plough team? In Golde Street? The world had run mad.

'Leofwine! Evie!'

A bolt shot back with a snap, the door opened a crack. 'Yes?'

'Leofwine, you might not remember me—' she began in English. 'Your wife's brother, Judhael—'

A hand shot out, caught the sleeve of her habit and hauled her unceremoniously into an ill-lit room. The door slammed, the bolt snapped back and she was shoved against the wall with such force that her head cracked against an oak upright. For a few seconds the workshop whirled about her.

Hand hard on her chest, Leofwine held her immobile. A seax winked in his other hand, and she felt the cold prick of steel at her throat.

'L-Leofwine?'

'Who the hell are you?'

Leofwine's eyes were like ice. Cecily would never have known him for the carefree goldsmith who had married Judhael's sister Evie five years earlier. 'It's Cecily—Cecily Fulford. Leofwine, don't you remember me?'

'Can't say as I do.'

Cecily's eyes were adjusting to the gloomy interior. Behind Leofwine a three-legged stool stood before a scarred workbench, the surface of which glittered with flecks of silver and gold. Fine chisels and pliers were lined up in racks on the wall, there were delicate hammers and tweezers, and to one side a miniature anvil. It looked as though it had been some time since Leofwine had been at work. A crucible lay on its side in the far corner, next to a small brick furnace. Several sets of long metal tongs hung from hooks on the adjoining wall.

A skirt swished, and something dark moved at the back of the workshop, by the door that led to the private family chamber. A white face appeared. 'Evie!' Cecily cried, almost choking as Leofwine pressed the point of his blade into her throat. 'Come out! Please, speak for me!'

Skirts rustled. Leofwine slackened his grip and scowled over his shoulder. 'Well, Evie? Is this yet another Fulford woman come to put us in peril?'

Cecily looked an appeal at Evie. There were tight lines around the girl's eyes, and she clutched protectively at her belly, her *large* belly, with both hands. Evie was heavy with child.

'Evie, *you* remember me, don't you? It's Cecily—Cenwulf's sister.'

More rustling of skirts as Evie came to stand close. She tipped her head to one side, examining Cecily's profile, raising her hand to draw back the edge of the novice's veil. Slipping her fingers under Cecily's wimple, Evie extracted a long strand of yellow hair. Then she nodded and stepped back.

'Aye.' Her sigh was heavy. 'It is Cecily Fulford. The likeness to Cenwulf is remarkable. If you think back, Leo, Cecily was the sister they sent to the convent…' Briefly, Evie touched the wooden cross at Cecily's breast. 'Both this and her habit attest that she speaks true. This can be none other than Cecily of Fulford.'

Leofwine's seax vanished. Taking Cecily by both arms, he shook her so her teeth rattled.

'Listen, Cecily of Fulford, I don't know why you have come visiting, and to be frank I do not care. I want you to leave. Evie and I have enough to contend with without your family stirring things up for us.'

Manhandling Cecily to the door, he reached for the latch.

'A moment, please.' Cecily bit her lip and gestured apologetically at Evie. 'I…I'm sorry, but I saw my sister Emma at the Cathedral yesterday, talking to Judhael. I thought they might have come here.'

Evie and Leofwine gazed blankly at her.

'Did they?'

Leofwine set his teeth, unlatched the door, and attempted to shove Cecily into the street.

'Did they? Evie?' Resisting Leofwine with all her might, Cecily felt the words tumble out. 'I would have talked to them if I could, but it…it was not possible. I only want to know Emma is well…that she is not alone. Do you think she's with Judhael, Evie?'

Evie turned her head away, chewing her lower lip.

'Evie? Please…'

Evie spun back, and with little more than a swift headshake stopped Leofwine ejecting Cecily into the street. 'Cecily…my lady…in the past your family were more than good to mine. Would that we could help you…' again her hand rested upon her belly '…but we have our own family to consider—'

'Aye,' Leofwine all but growled. 'Years without her quickening, then now, of all times, when the saints have deserted us and the world is in turmoil…'

'Babies choose their own times,' Cecily murmured, and sent Evie a warm smile. 'I am happy for you.'

Evie inclined her head. 'I thank you. But you must see how difficult it is for us. I will tell you what I told Emma—'

'So she *did* come here. I knew it!'

'Evie—' Leofwine's face darkened '—be wary.'

Evie placed a hand on her husband's arm. 'Think, love. Since Judhael told us less than nothing of his plans, there's not much we can tell. But we can at least put her mind to rest on one score. Emma is with Judhael, Lady Cecily.'

'They have left Winchester?'

'I believe so.'

'But you don't know where they've gone?'

'No—and we will have no part in any scheme of yours. As we will have no part in any of Judhael's. I told both him and your sister as much. We are ordinary working people, my lady, and even at the best of times we walk a tightrope. Now—' she lifted her shoulders '—we have to tread even more carefully.'

Cecily's shoulders drooped, and she scrubbed wearily at her

forehead. 'I'm sorry. Perhaps I shouldn't have come. I'd hoped to see Emma—to convince her that flight is not the only road open to her, to persuade her to come back to Fulford with me.'

'She'll never do that. Not while a Norman is suing for her hand.'

Cecily met Evie's gaze, thankful that the poor light hid the hot colour that rushed into her cheeks. 'Adam Wymark is from Brittany, not Normandy.'

Evie shrugged. 'What's the difference? Breton, Norman—marauders all. Your sister will have none of them.'

Cecily swallowed. She had heard similar words from Emma's own lips. And if Judhael was Emma's lover, Emma's flight was all the more understandable. 'Emma need have no fear of Adam Wymark. Not now,' she said. 'Evie, if you should see her again, I'd like to leave a message—'

'No,' Leofwine broke in curtly. 'No messages.'

'A few words only—should you chance to meet her.' Suddenly it was vital that Emma knew of Cecily's betrothal to Adam. 'Please tell her that the Breton knight has agreed to marry me in her stead.'

Evie's jaw dropped. '*You*, my lady? You'd *marry* one of them?'

Cecily lifted her head. 'Aye. I am returning to Fulford. Please tell her.'

'You're mad. Being cooped up in that convent's sent you mad.'

'You may have something there,' Cecily said quietly. 'I loathed it.'

Evie's face softened, and impulsively she took Cecily by the hand. 'You poor thing. It must have been bad to make marrying one of them a better choice.'

'Adam Wymark is not an evil man,' Cecily said, knowing it to be the truth, but wondering how she knew this.

'No?' Evie patted her hand, her face the image of disbelief. 'You poor thing.'

'He's not!'

Another pat. 'I'm sure he is not.'

But Cecily intercepted the look Evie sent her husband, and she knew that Evie did not believe her. In Evie's mind all the Duke's men had souls as black as pitch. But life was not that simple. It would be easier if it were, for then she would not feel so guilty. It was as if, merely by talking to Leofwine and Evie, she was somehow betraying Adam. But there was no time to examine her guilt—which was misplaced anyway—she had a newborn brother and the villagers of Fulford to look to: They must come first.

'If you please, I will leave now.'

Leofwine gave her a mocking bow and pushed open the door. A stream of sunlight rushed into the room. Momentarily blinded, Cecily picked up her skirts and stepped over the threshold.

'Don't fear for your sister, Lady Cecily,' Evie called. 'Judhael will look after her.'

Cecily nodded, though she had to push aside a nagging memory of the cold, almost callous expression on Judhael's face when he had been talking to Emma in the Minster.

'He will—I swear it.' Evie smiled through the doorway and opened her mouth to say more, but Leofwine swung the door shut and cut off her words. The bolt scraped home.

Hunching into her cloak, Cecily glanced swiftly to left and right. At the southern end of Golde Street the sullen workmen were receiving their orders from a crop-headed Norman overseer in a scarlet tunic. The overseer's shoulders were wrapped in a purple velvet cloak the emperor of Byzantium would have been proud to call his own. The booty of war, perhaps? By comparison the Saxon workmen were dull, in their brown and grey homespun. At their backs, the oxen were being roped to a series of metal grappling hooks that glinted menacingly in the sun.

Not that way. Turning on her heel, Cecily retraced her steps, hoping to be back before any of Adam Wymark's company marked her absence. If questioned, she had a story ready, may the Lord forgive her for the lie: she would say she had been visiting Nunnaminster, the nunnery founded by King Alfred's Queen Ealhswith.

In the sunless alley running along one side of Leofwine Smith's workshop, Adam Wymark and his captain exchanged glances. They were standing under the eaves, two men who had stood still and silent for some time, cloaks firmly wrapped about them to ward off the chill.

'My apologies, Tihell, I should not have doubted you,' Adam murmured, a grim set to his jaw. Since Félix Tihell, like him, came from Brittany, he was speaking in his native Breton. 'Emma Fulford must have come here. You say you saw her leave the city afterwards?'

'Aye, sir. She left by the Hyde Gate—the one that bypasses the abbey.'

An overwhelming surge of emotion was building inside Adam. It had been building from the moment he had heard Cecily in the workshop. Struggling to contain it, for a cool head was needed here, he lifted a brow. 'So the Lady Emma does go north?' He was furious: he wanted to tear the workshop apart plank by plank; he wanted it never to have existed. Cecily Fulford had come here. Cecily Fulford was a devious, lying witch. Damn her—damn her and her betraying blue eyes—damn her to hell.

'So I believe.'

Adam's hands were curled into fists. He forced them to relax. 'I wonder… We thought that before and were wrong. Was Lady Emma on her own or did she have an escort?'

'One Saxon man accompanies her—a groom, I think. I've a man tracking them. Told him to send word back to the garrison from her next stopping place.'

'Good lad.' Adam scowled at the workshop's rough wooden planking. It was green with damp. 'You say that the man who lives here is a goldsmith?'

'Yes, sir.'

'Why should both Fulford ladies come here? What is the connection?'

'As yet, I don't know,' Tihell said. 'Could you make out what they were saying?'

'No, damn it. My English is not yet up to it. Yours?'

'Sorry, sir. Mine is no better. I caught a name or two—Emma, Judhael, your Lady Cecily…'

'My Lady Cecily.' Adam's tone was bleak.

'What will you do, sir?'

'Do?'

Tihell peered round the corner of the workshop and looked meaningfully down the street, the way Cecily had gone. 'About her. I doubt she was exchanging recipes for pancakes.'

Adam's mouth twisted. 'Hell's teeth, Tihell—'

'Will you report her to the garrison commander?'

Adam stepped out into the street and stood, hands on hips, staring towards Westgate, but in truth he saw nothing. 'Hell's teeth,' he repeated. 'One minute I'd swear she was the sweetest girl in Christendom, and the next I wonder if I've contracted to marry a viper.'

Tihell was eyeing the shuttered window and the closed door of the workshop. He leaned a broad shoulder testingly on the wood. 'You want to see inside, sir?'

Adam held up a hand. 'No—no need for that as yet. It would give the game away.'

'Sir?'

'You and I know that the Fulford ladies have been here, but I don't want our knowledge proclaimed from the rooftops.'

'Sir?'

Lowering his voice, tamping down the irrational anger that was burning inside him, Adam leaned closer. 'We play a waiting game, Tihell. Watch, pretend to know less than nothing, and we may draw them out. Don't mention Lady Cecily's visit here to the men, will you?'

'No, sir.'

Clenching his teeth against the pitying look his captain sent him, Adam started off up the street.

Tihell kept pace alongside. 'On the other hand, sir,' he said thoughtfully, 'it may not be as bad as it looks.'

'Rebels *are* known to be in the area,' Adam said curtly.

'Yes, sir, I know. But Lady Cecily is not necessarily—'

Adam checked. 'You seek to advise me? Out of your great wisdom?'

'No, of course not. It's just that I… Will you report her to the commander?'

'Since we didn't understand above a word of what was said, we've no proof of what she's up to either way. Anyway, what's it to you if I do report her?'

His captain shrugged. 'Nothing. But she does have a way with her.'

'Oh?'

'No need to look daggers at me, sir, but she *does* have a way with her, and you can't deny it. I've seen you watch her. And young Herfu told me that last night you and she—'

'Tihell, you're on thin ice. An old friendship can only be tested so far.'

'Yes, sir.'

They continued in silence for a pace or two.

'Sir?'

Adam sighed. 'Captain?'

'Herfu likes her. And Maurice. Already.'

'And I. That's the hell of it,' Adam said softly.

'She seems kind—genuinely kind,' Tihell went on, as they reached Westgate and started down the hill behind a man rolling a barrel towards the market. 'No foolish airs and graces. Will you hand her over to the commander?'

Adam made a dismissive movement. 'Damn it, man, can't you sing another tune?'

His captain flushed. 'My apologies, sir.'

'Listen, Tihell—listen carefully. Rather than see Lady Cecily put in some dank cell when we've no solid proof of her disloyalty, I intend to take her back to Fulford. I can keep better watch over her there—if she is in contact with the Saxon resistance, she will act as bait.'

'You intend to use her?'

'I do indeed. Lady Cecily will draw them out. If I handed her over to the garrison commander Duke William's cause would not be advanced one whit. Watch her and we may uncover an entire nest of vipers—'

'But, sir, there is another possibility…'

'Something warns me that you're about to tell me what that might be.'

Tihell gave him an earnest nod. 'There might be a perfectly innocent reason for Lady Cecily's visit to Golde Street.'

Adam stared. 'It seems that Herfu and Maurice are not her only conquests. You also seek to be her champion.'

Tihell kicked a chicken bone into the gutter and would not meet his eyes. 'Don't rush to judgement, sir, that's all,' he muttered. 'If she is disloyal, time will tell.'

'We're all fools,' Adam said slowly.

'Sir?'

'Have done, man, have done. I've a mind of my own and have already decided on Lady Cecily's fate.'

'Aye, sir.'

Adam smiled. 'Perhaps another commission will put a stop to your philosophizing?'

'Sir?'

'When the troop leaves for Fulford I want you to stay behind. Wait for your man to send word, and then get on Lady Emma's trail yourself.'

'Yes, sir.'

'And be wary, Tihell. I don't want to lose you.'

'Sir.'

'Then, regardless of what you discover, we shall *rendezvous* in three days' time, at the garrison. Noon. You can give me your report then.'

'Yes, sir.'

Chapter Ten

He caught up with the little novice before he had worked out what he was going to say to her. There was a flash of blue ahead of him—his cloak—moving swiftly along the path through the cemetery. At least she is not running off, like her sister, he thought, and some of the tension he had been carrying fell away. He did not want to lose her.

Hell, that was not right. He did not want to lose the chance of using her. Give her some rope and she would help flush out resistance to Duke William's rule. Yes, that was it: he was planning to use her...

Adam shook his head at the chaos an innocent-looking face was bringing to his normally orderly mind, and began closing the distance between them. That hideous veil was lost beneath the hood of his cloak. A strategist by nature, Adam fought to compose his thoughts. He misliked entering a field of battle in disarray.

Was that was this was? A battle? Damn it, a couple of hours ago he had woken with the girl in his arms, soft and pliant from sleep. Her morning kisses had tasted of welcome; they had seemed to hint that they might deal well together, had seemed to promise affection, if not love itself, given time. Hah! The little novice might well have been moved by love this morning, when she had visited the goldsmith's house, but it was not love for him. No. He must strive to remember that.

But, with his eyes fixed on that diminutive cloaked figure, his thoughts refused to get back into line. The touch of her…the smell of her…somehow she had driven out his longing for Gwenn. Temporarily, of course, but it had been a first to awaken and not ache for Gwenn. That should have alerted him. The little novice was not as harmless as she appeared. He was treading on treacherous ground.

His lips curved into a self-deprecating smile. Wonderful. He had no clear strategy; he did not have the lie of the land; he was about to engage with the enemy. Bloody wonderful.

Cursing himself for the worst kind of fool, Adam stared at that slender back and narrowed the distance between them. If only he could read minds. She was hoping, no doubt, that her visit to Golde Street had gone unobserved. Gritting his teeth, ignoring a bitter taste in his mouth, he waved his captain on with a muttered, 'Look to the horses, man, and get the troop in order. We're leaving for Fulford in half an hour.'

'Yes, sir.'

He strode up to the little novice and caught her by the shoulder. 'Lady Cecily?'

'Sir Adam!' She practically leapt out of her skin. 'I…I was just wondering where you were.'

I'll bet you were, Adam thought, missing neither the nervous smile nor the guilty flush. For his part, he was wondering what lies she would feed him. 'Where have you been?'

'I…I…thought I would take a look round the town. It's been so long since I was last here.'

Taking her hand, placing it carefully on his arm, he urged her towards the garrison. 'Where is Maurice? He should have escorted you.'

Her eyes were wide, her expression earnest. 'I did not think I would go far,' she said. 'I told him I was only going to the Cathedral, but then I...I thought I would like to see the convent at Nunnaminster.'

Liar, liar, Adam thought, fighting to school his expression to one of polite interest. 'What was it like?'

'The nunnery?'

'What else?' A tendril of hair was curling out under the edge of her wimple, gleaming gold in the sun. He tore his gaze away and reminded himself of what he must do. Nothing. He must do *nothing* because this was a waiting game. Give her some rope and see what she does with it.

It would be easier, cleaner, quicker—an end to this torment, this polite fencing that left so much unsaid—to shake the truth out of her once and for all. He grimaced. Direct confrontation might put an end to the ache that was not knowing whether he could trust her or not, but it would not advance Duke William's cause. No, he must play the waiting game. It should not be hard. A pretty Saxon face and a soft, warm body would not distract him from his duty to his lord.

'I...I could not find the convent,' she was saying. 'I l-lost my way at the top of Market Street and came straight back.'

She was the most terrible liar. No, it was more than just that. She did not like lying to him. Unaccountably Adam's heart lifted. Nodding at her almost cheerfully, he covered her hand with his and they proceeded towards the Old Palace, outwardly a Breton knight, with his lady at his side. And inwardly? Her fingers were trembling under his and she would not meet his gaze. Adam might be deluding himself, but he did not consider that all was lost if she disliked feeding him lies.

Adam had borrowed a horse from the garrison for Cecily to ride home. It was a wreck rather than a horse. Gripping the reins, Cecily glared at the back of the animal's head and, using her heels, tried vainly to urge it into a trot. She was riding astride, no ladies' saddle being available at the Palace stables, and today that was a blessing. Had she been riding sidesaddle she doubted she would have been able to get the wreck to do more than shuffle, and she was lagging behind as it was. Astride, there was some measure of control, or so she liked to imagine. The wreck was spavined and flea-bitten—not fit even to be a packhorse.

Struggling with her mount left Cecily with no energy to worry about displaying darned stockings or watching their route. It left her with little energy for worrying about the disturbing conversation she had had with Adam outside the Palace walls. She could not put her finger on why the conversation had disturbed her, but she could not set it behind her. Nothing overt had been said, and yet dark undertones had been present. Of course she did not know Adam Wymark well enough to know his every mood. He might have a nature as volatile as her father's, but she did not think so. Outside the Palace she had sensed…she had sensed…

Had Adam found out about her visit to Leofwine's house? It was certainly possible, but he had not said as much. Throughout his manner had been polite, watchful—yes, very watchful—and ever so slightly off. He must know more than he was saying.

She glanced over the ears of the wreck she was riding. She had no idea how far they had gone. Apart from Maurice, who rode silently at her side, everyone else in Adam's troop, including Adam himself, was several hundred yards in front of them. Sighing, Cecily reapplied her heels to the wreck's ribs.

The road was bordered by spindly hawthorn bushes that were peppered with berries. Old man's beard snarled in the leafless branches of blackthorn bushes and tangled in thin, red-stemmed dogwoods.

As their party rounded the next turn they came to a crossroads, where the way was scarred with deep ruts, white with the chalk that told her they were nearing the downlands—sheep-farming country. In the summer the downs were a haze of bees and blue butterflies, and as for the skylarks... But this was November, Cecily reminded herself. The downs would be quiet. There would be no skylarks spiralling in the heavens—the downs would be resting, like the convent herb garden.

They passed a moss-covered milestone with the name 'Fulford' carved deep into its surface and she realised with a jolt that they were almost home.

Home. Perhaps it had been a mercy that for the past few miles her mind had been occupied, for now they were almost there her stomach began to churn. What would she find at Fulford? Was there anyone left who would recognise her? Would she be able to keep her brother safe?

Cecily dug in her heels and the horse's ears flickered, but the beast must have a hide of iron and the will of a mule, for its pace was unalterable. Slow, slow, slow.

Ahead of them, Adam shoved his cloak back over one shoulder and leaned a hand on the cantle of his saddle. 'Maurice, take Lady Cecily's reins, will you? She's obviously in difficulties, and it's dangerous to be strung out along the road like this.'

Without waiting for any response, he about-faced, pulling his cloak back into place.

Since returning with her to the Palace, the man she had agreed to marry had not spared her so much as a glance. He *must* know about her visit to Golde Street. The warm, considerate, handsome man who had kissed her that morning had been transformed into a harsh, glacial-eyed warrior. Were they one and the same person? First thing this morning Adam had seemed kind—almost sweet, if a man could be sweet. But after she had returned to the Old Palace he had been cold and distant. Unapproachable.

And now he was bent on humiliating her in front of his squire. She huffed out a breath. She was not in difficulties. It was the pitiful shambles of a horse she'd been given. Poor bony nag, it could barely stand. Her father would never have mounted her on such a beast; he would have deemed it only fit for dog meat.

Maurice reached down and took her reins.

'It's *not* me,' Cecily muttered, glaring at Adam's broad back.

Maurice urged his own destrier on, and its sheer size and strength forced the wreck to keep up. 'I know,' Maurice said. Behind the nose-guard of his helm, his dark eyes were smiling. 'And so does Sir Adam.'

'Then why did he choose such a horse for me?'

'Sir Adam was lucky to get a horse at all. It was the last in the stables.'

'The last? I wonder why? I should have thought the Duke's men would have fought to the death over it.'

'Quite so, my lady.' Maurice's lips twitched. 'But it must be better than sharing Sir Adam's.'

'Oh, yes, Maurice. At least I've been spared that.'

Trotting along with Maurice, several yards behind Flame, Cecily ignored the sharp look that Adam's squire gave her and concentrated instead on keeping the horse moving.

The Wessex countryside slid by, becoming more and more familiar with every step. The road ran up a rise and down the other side, beginning a gentle descent into a lightly wooded valley that sliced a long bite out of the downland. Flocks of sheep moved placidly over the downs, and below, on the floor of the valley, the River Fulford flowed slowly on. It would eventually reach the Narrow Sea. Generations of Cecily's family had lived near the River Fulford. Its waters had ground their corn, kept their fish fresh in the fish pond, helped them grow cress…

In no time Cecily was looking at strips of farmland that had been cut out of the woodland. Ahead, Adam reined in, and allowed them to draw level with him.

'Familiar, my lady?' Maurice asked.

'Aye. Fulford Hall.' She cleared her throat. 'It's very close.'

'I'll take it from here, Maurice,' Adam said, taking her reins from his squire. He pulled off his helm, looped the strap round the pommel of his saddle and pushed back his coif. 'See to the horses, will you?'

'Aye, sir.' Maurice spurred on ahead.

Adam's profile was stern. And then he looked at her and smiled. But it seemed Cecily was getting to know him. His smile was false.

'Sir?'

'Be my guide, will you? When we took possession we were hard pushed to make out a word that was said to us, and I would know the name and station of everyone on this holding—down to the last soul. You swore to be my guide, remember? And I want you to teach me English.'

When we took possession. Cecily swallowed and nodded, lowering her gaze to hide a flash of anger. She did not know what she had expected to feel at her homecoming, but she had not thought to feel anger. Could he not allow her a few moments to come to terms with the changes—parents and brother gone, sister fled? Callous, cold, *insensitive* brute.

But then, surprisingly, anger was pushed aside, for their horses were walking past the peasants' field strips on the outskirts of Fulford village, and there was too much she wanted to see.

The woods had been cut back in the four years she had been away, and two whole new fields had been made. Each peasant's strip was clearly marked out from his neighbours—ridge, furrow, ridge, furrow, ridge, furrow. As expected, the wheat field had been harvested, and several pigs were tethered there, rooting about in the stubble, digging, manuring, turning all to mud. The fallow field had turned into a sheep-pen, and the frost-scorched grasses and clover had been nibbled down to the bare earth.

Cecily frowned.

'What is it? What's wrong?' Adam asked.

'Too many animals,' she told him, her frown deepening. The thatch on one farmer's cottage needed repair; another had a door falling off its hinges. 'Far too many. And the winter feed has not been cut.'

'Explain, please?'

Cecily sent him a sharp look, wondering how deep his interest went. Did he intend to strip Fulford of what riches it possessed, leaving it so impoverished that it would no longer be able to sustain itself? Or was he intending to husband her father's land carefully? Was Adam Wymark a locust, or a good steward?

'I need to know,' he said, his expression earnest. 'I'm a soldier, not a farmer. I was brought up in a town; there's much I must learn.'

She nodded, prepared—for the moment—to give him the benefit of the doubt. 'It's November,' she said. 'Hard enough to keep more than a handful of animals alive through the turn of the year, even with plenty of winter feed—but that lot is far too many. They'll starve, and the breeding stock will be weakened. They should have chosen the best animals to keep, and the rest should have gone to slaughter.' Seeing she had his attention, she continued, waving at the cottages. 'Look at those houses. People will be freezing come January. It's in no one's interests if half the village succumbs to lung fever.'

Adam gave her a lop-sided smile, and this time it did reach his eyes. 'Cecily, I can work that one out for myself.'

'I can't think what Godwin's about—'

'Godwin?'

'The reeve—at least he was reeve four years ago. He was old then. Perhaps he's ill.' She scowled meaningfully at him. 'Or maybe he's dead too.'

His smile fell away. 'Who lives in that cottage?'

'The one that's lost most of its thatch? Oswin and May.'

'And that one?'

'Alfred. Poor Alfred lost his wife when his son Wat was born. Wat is my age.' And Wat is simple, she thought, damaged at birth. She said nothing of this to Adam. Alfred's cottage looked abandoned. What had happened to him? As a farmer, Alfred had not been one of her father's housecarls, but perhaps he had formed part of the local levy, and had been drummed up to go to Hastings with billhook or pitchfork. If something had happened to Alfred, who was caring for Wat?

They drew level with the mill. Its wheel was larger than a tall man. Water gushed noisily into the channel, machinery clanked and banged, wooden cogs creaked and rattled. The hoist shutters on the upper floor were closed to keep out the November chill, and no one came to the door to watch their passing—but then the sound of their horse's hooves was no doubt muffled by the mill workings.

'How do you call this in English?'

'It's a mill.'

'Mill,' Adam said carefully, trying the word out. 'Mill.'

Did he really intend to learn English? Covertly, hungrily, Cecily examined his profile, baffled by a most powerful need to lock every last detail of him safely in her mind—from the precise colour of his dark hair, so like the wing of a blackbird, to the perfect straightness of his nose. She was gazing with something that felt oddly like longing at the compelling curve of his lips when he glanced across at her. Hurriedly, she dropped her gaze and lurched into speech.

'The miller's name is Gilbert. He's married to Bertha, and when I left they had a girl called Matty, and two boys, Harold and Carl. Matty should be about fourteen and the boys would be eleven and twelve by my reckoning.'

Adam nodded. 'Mill,' he repeated.

They rode on. The noise of the mill diminished as the village church, a simple thatched building with a cross on the roof ridge, rose up in front of them.

'And this building? What is the English word?'

'The word is church.'

'Church,' Adam murmured. 'Church.' He reverted to Norman

French. 'It's wooden, like the cottages and the mill. There are no stone buildings in Fulford. At my home in Brittany it is the same; in the main only great lords' castles and cathedrals are built in stone.'

Absently, Cecily nodded. Her eyes were drawn to the glebeland next to the church, to the graveyard. And there, through the split-rail fence, she found what she was looking for—a wreath of ever-greens someone had placed on some freshly turned earth. Her mother's grave?

Her hands jerked on the reins; her eyes filled. Quickly averting her head, she forced her gaze past the cemetery, on to the priest's house and Fulford Hall, which stood facing each other on opposite sides of the village green.

Tears ran hot down her cheeks once again, and the sheep-nibbled grass of the village green, trampled and muddied as it was by many horses' hoofs, blurred and wavered like a field of green barley in a March wind. Swallowing down the lump in her throat, Cecily tried to speak normally. 'As you may guess, the cottage next to the glebeland belongs to the priest. He lives off the tithes everyone brings him. Father Aelfric—'

Adam gave a snort of laughter. 'I've met Father Aelfric. *And* his wife.'

Forgetful of the tears drying on her cheeks, Cecily whipped her head round. 'I...I did not know that Father Aelfric had taken a wife.'

As Adam's green eyes met hers his expression sobered. 'Ah, Cecily, what a fool I am.' He reached across and gently traced a tear-track with his finger. 'Your mother...my apologies.'

Fiercely Cecily shook her head and batted away his hand. 'Don't. Please. Not here. Not now.' She would break down if he offered sympathy, and she would not be so shamed—not in front of his men and the whole village. She was her mother's daughter.

Adam took up the reins again, and perhaps he understood her need for distraction, for he went on conversationally, 'Father Aelfric has two small children.'

Cecily dashed away her tears with her sleeve. 'Oh?'

'Is it common in England for priests to have wives?' Adam asked, and she realised that, yes, he was giving her time to compose herself before they reached the Hall. He was not a complete boor.

'Sometimes they do.'

'Duke William does not approve of such practices.'

Cecily shrugged. Monks, nuns and priests all took the vow of chastity, but priests, and even bishops, did sometimes make their housekeepers their 'wives'. She wondered who Aelfric had 'married'. He had always been fond of Sigrida, and she of him…

Fulford Hall. Finally she was home.

The Hall overlooked the village green. It was a long building, taller and wider than any for miles. On either side of the door unglazed windows with sliding wooden shutters stared across the green towards the church opposite. The thatch was weathered, grey in parts, mossy in others—in short it looked to be in no better condition than the thatch on many of the serfs' cottages. Smoke made a charcoal smudge in the sky above the roof. Ordinarily, Cecily's heart would have lifted to see it, but today…

They drew rein by the door. Maurice and Geoffrey were leading their horses towards the stables, swapping jokes. Inside, by the fire, Sir Richard was tossing his cloak at one of the men, laughing with another. Shadowy silhouettes moving about in her father's hall. Normans. Bretons. *Conquerors.*

She could hear the murmur of conversation, the snicker of a horse, the honking of geese. Where was Philip? Where was her brother? Gripped by a sense of unreality, Cecily focused on the wooden carvings around the doorframe of the Hall, on the snake winding up its length, at the trailing vine, the flowers and twisting patterns she had traced with her fingers so many times, and she felt…she felt nothing. Her father's hall was in the hands of a stranger from Brittany and she felt empty, scoured of emotion.

The stranger was looking her village over with a proprietorial eye. In the middle of the green, under the branches of an oak that had been ancient when her father had been born, stood the village stocks and the pillory post. The stranger, the *invader*, frowned and pointed at the stocks. 'We have these in Quimperlé. What are they called in English?'

'The stocks.'

'And the other? Is it the whipping post?'

'That is a pillory. Sometimes my father used it as a whipping post.'

He repeated the words under his breath as he dismounted, and Cecily watched his mailed figure, wondering whether he would be as stern a judge as her father had been. Thane Edgar had once removed a serf's hand for stealing. He had occasionally used the branding iron, and both the stocks and the pillory had seen regular use. The stocks and the pillory, however, were usually effective enough as deterrents.

But Philip...where was baby Philip? Her gaze glided over Godwin the reeve's house, on past the sheep-pens, the piggery, over the cook-house. Someone was swinging towards them on crutches, scattering hens before him, silver bracelets chinking on his wrists. 'Edmund!'

The same age as Judhael, Edmund had been another companion of her brother Cenwulf, and a housecarl of her father's. The bracelets would have been gifts from her father to a favoured warrior, in return for loyal service. He looked thin and haggard. His light brown hair hung lankly about his shoulders, and his grey eyes seemed to have sunk into his sockets.

'Cecily?'

Cecily dismounted and flung herself at her brother's friend, almost unbalancing him. 'Oh, Edmund, I'm so glad to see you! I feared that you too might be gone.'

Edmund grunted, adjusted his crutches, and glanced coldly at Adam. 'Have a care, Cecily,' he said in English. 'You'll have me over.'

'Speak French, will you?' Fulford's new lord asked, frowning.

'He can't. My apologies. Oh, Edmund, it is so good to see you.' She drew back, smiling, for the moment ignoring the man she had agreed to marry. Adam stood slightly to the side, his horse's reins in hand, and that watchful look in his green eyes.

The hose of Edmund's left leg, instead of being bound with braid, had been slit, and his leg was in a splint. He looked as though he'd not slept in a month, but he was alive. 'What happened to your leg?'

Leaning on his crutches, Edmund lifted his shoulders. 'Fell from my horse. Bad break, or so your mother said. Otherwise I'd have been at Hastings with your father. Every housecarl went but me.' He let out a bitter laugh. 'Even Alfred went.'

'As home guard?'

'Yes.' He paused. 'None returned.'

Unable to speak for the knot clogging her throat, Cecily nodded.

'Gudrun splinted my leg for me.'

'Gudrun?'

'Under your mother's supervision.' Edmund met her gaze directly. 'Cecily, I'm so sorry about Lady Philippa. We all are. The day she died—'

Swiftly, lest Edmund let fall anything about her brother that Adam might understand, Cecily leaned forward and pressed a kiss on his mouth. Placing a hand over his, she squeezed it meaningfully and ignored Adam's gaze boring into her back. 'We will talk later. We have much to catch up on. But I am more than glad to see you whole.' She turned towards the hall. 'Gudrun?'

Edmund's grey eyes met hers. 'Within. With your...with the new babe. You know about that?'

'Emma told me the news.'

Edmund shifted on his crutches, moving his splinted leg so it was bearing more of his weight. He winced, and immediately repositioned himself. 'Holy God! It's not healing as it should.'

'I'll look at it before supper,' Cecily promised. 'Before we lose daylight.'

'My thanks. I hear you're as skilled as your mother was.'

Glancing uncertainly at Adam—his expression was quite definitely stormy—Cecily swept past him into the hall.

Inside, Cecily had no thoughts for Breton knights who could not speak English. She only had eyes for Gudrun. She found her sitting on a wall bench, partially screened by the looped-back sleeping curtain. The veil that covered Gudrun's brown hair was drawn forward round her shoulders for modesty as her gown was unlaced at the front. She was discreetly suckling a newborn baby.

Philip! Cecily hurried over, trying to disguise her eagerness. Philip was smaller than she had imagined, with a wrinkled face and an astonishing crest of thick dark hair. One tiny hand was splayed out on Gudrun's breast, and his eyes were shut, but he was feeding strongly. Her brother. The rightful heir to Fulford Hall.

'Lady Cecily!' Gudrun's gasp quickly turned into a smile of relief and welcome. 'This is Philip.'

Cecily dropped to her knees on the rushes and reached out to stroke the tiny head. 'Oh, Gudrun. He's beautiful.'

Gudrun's expression softened. 'Isn't he?'

Another baby, a plump, rosy-cheeked bundle, was asleep in a reed basket by Gudrun's feet. Gently, Cecily stroked a chubby little foot that was sticking out of its coverlet. 'And this? Who is this?' She tucked the cover back in place.

Gudrun smiled. 'That is my Agatha.'

'Agatha. She is lovely too.'

Cecily's gaze was drawn back to her brother. And while she struggled with yet more tears Gudrun lowered her voice. 'I'm right glad you are come, my lady. Wilf and I have been afraid with these—' she jerked her eyes in the direction of Richard and his companions by the central hearth '—come here. Afraid of what they might do. Not knowing what would be best for this little one— whether to stay, or go like your sister. But with you home…you will know what to do. You will stay, won't you, my lady?'

'Yes, I'm to marry Sir Adam.'

Gudrun's eyes widened, and she looked at Cecily's habit, at the wooden cross on her breast. 'You, dear?'

Cecily had to smile. Gudrun had not changed, thank the Lord. Sometimes she would remember, and call Cecily by her title, but more often a simple 'dear' would suffice. Cecily would have had it no other way.

A shadow fell across the entrance. Adam. He'd removed his chainmail and sword, and a plain green tunic covered those broad shoulders; a belt with a silver buckle encircled that slim waist. As Cecily had observed in the convent, he appeared slighter without his armour. His shape pleased her eyes. He was her enemy but, unlikely as it seemed, she *liked* looking at him. It was most disorientating. He marched to the fire, holding his hands out to the blaze. Nail-bitten fingers, she recalled. Sir Richard addressed him and Adam answered, even as his eyes roamed the room and came to rest on her.

He always does that when he enters a room and I am already there. He looks for me. He *watches* me. And I do not think it is because *I* please *his* eyes—no, he is suspicious of me. I must be on my guard, for Philip's sake.

'Well, I don't know,' Gudrun was saying. 'I thought you were promised to God. But, since your sister would have none of him, perhaps it's for the best.'

'Yes. I…I think so. Tell me how things stand at Fulford.'

Gudrun rattled on, bringing Cecily up to date: Lufu the cook had vanished; they were short of butchered meat; Gudrun and her husband Wilf needed help with running the household as Marie, her mother's maidservant, had been worse than useless since Lady Philippa's death…

While Gudrun talked, Cecily searched for changes in the Hall itself. The whitewashed walls, blackened by smoke from the central hearth, the lofty roof space, criss-crossed with dark oak beams—all were blessedly familiar. As was the curtained recess used as sleeping quarters by married couples in the Thane's household since her grandfather's time. Around the recess, the walls were dotted with storage chests and people's bundles. Cloaks hung from wall pegs. Her mother's tapestry brightened the south wall.

Nothing was obviously out of place. Nothing appeared damaged. The world had been turned on its head in the past month, and the only fault that Cecily could find was that the clay floor was covered with rushes that smelt as though they had needed freshening weeks ago.

'Gudrun?' Cecily interrupted the flow of talk.

'Yes, dear?'

'No looting seems to have gone on.'

Gudrun's brow creased, 'No,' she agreed, her voice puzzled. 'That's true. I feared it might happen, but he—' she looked past the fire at Adam '—keeps his men in order.'

'What about my father's wolfhounds? Where are they? Did Lightning and Greedy go with him to Hastings? And is Loki still with us?'

'No, dear, Loki died last winter. But Thane Edgar left Lightning and Greedy behind to keep your mother safe. And they would have done so too, if she'd still been with us. You should have seen them when these foreigners rode in. I learnt then how a wolfhound can turn into a wolf.'

Cecily caught her breath. 'The dogs weren't killed?'

'No, dear. The new lord had them chained in the yard out back, by the stables.' Gudrun gave a reminiscent grin. 'Right carry-on there was—snarling, snapping. They'd have torn his throat out, given half a chance.'

Glancing at the men by the fire, Cecily rose. 'I'd better see to their needs.'

Gudrun's lips twitched. 'Whose needs, dear? The men or the hounds?'

'Both,' Cecily said, on a laugh such as she'd not expected to make this day. 'Oh, Gudrun, it is good to see you.'

Gudrun's veil quivered as she nodded agreement. 'Aye, dear, so it is. Now be off with you—before yon lord wonders why a mere servant so commands your attention. Best keep them sweet. And our secret safe.'

'Aye. No one has brought them refreshment yet. Where is Wilf? If Lufu is not to be found, he can give me a hand.'

'Oh, no, dear. A wheel on the cart was wobbling, so Wilf took it to the smithy. He should be back any time.'

'Marie, then. Surely she can help?'

Gudrun made an impatient sound. 'I've not seen her. Try the church. Since your mother went, rest her soul, Marie's all but moved in there.' She winked. 'I expect Sigrida would be glad if you prised her out of there.'

'Gudrun?'

'Yes, dear?'

'My pony…Cloud…?'

Gudrun smiled. 'Still here. Your father was thinking of selling her, but your mother wouldn't hear of it. You'll find her in the paddock.'

Chapter Eleven

Fearful that Adam might confront her directly over her visit to Leofwine's house, Cecily spent the next few hours avoiding him. Initially that was not hard: there were old friendships to rekindle; there were rushes in need of replacing; there was Cloud and her father's wolfhounds to look to…

When she entered the cookhouse to take stock, the importance of keeping Adam and his troop well fed was large in her mind. Her contact with men might been scant of late, but she would never forget how ill-tempered her father had become if he'd missed a meal. It followed that Adam and his men were more likely to deal even-handedly with the villagers if they had full stomachs. Enemies of the Saxon people though they might be, it was in everyone's interests that she gave them good meals.

As Gudrun had warned her, there was no sign of Lufu, and the cookhouse was deserted. Golden strings of onions dangled from nails in the roof-plate. Good—plenty of those. Next to the onions hung bundles of herbs—parsley and sage and bay. Bunches of chives. The way the herbs were knotted told Cecily they had been dried by her mother in the summer just past. Damping down a rush of emotion, Cecily forced herself to continue with her review. Adam and his men *must* be fed…

Above the main cooking fire and slightly to one side of it the hook on which a smoked ham usually dangled was empty. She sighed. A cooking vessel sat empty on the coals, the water having boiled away hours ago. Reaching for a cloth, Cecily took the pot from the fire and set it on a flat stone to cool. Filthy, unwashed pots lay everywhere. Dirty serving dishes were piled high on the table. Used knives and spoons had been thrown down beside them. The sour stench of unwashed pot-cloths filled the air.

It got worse. The bread oven was so cold it could not have been fired in days. The fire under the washtub was also out. If her father had been alive he would have had Lufu in the stocks for such slovenliness…

Afraid that the state of the cookhouse was the least of Lufu's negligence, Cecily picked up her skirts and climbed the short flight of stairs which led to the storeroom. The door swung open at a touch when it should have been locked.

Gripped by a growing sense of urgency, she tapped one of the barrels where the salt meat should be stored. It rang hollow. She tapped another—that too was empty. And another. Again, empty. The costly sacks of salt were there, ready for use, but as she had feared the killing and salting had yet to be done. If it wasn't done soon the salt would grow damp and spoil. Adam would have to be told of the state of the storeroom, and the thought filled her with dread. In like circumstances, her father would have gone beserk.

Someone had made a start with the apples, though. Neat rows of green cookers and lines of rosy russets filled two of the shelves, but the apples should be up in the apple loft by this time, packed away in straw. There were three casks of ale and a couple of wine. Several sacks of grain. A heap of turnips. Half a dozen rounds of cheese, wrapped in sacking. Preparations for winter had begun, but not enough had been done—not nearly enough. The meat was the worst of it, for without it everyone would be tightening their belts in weeks, if not days. Tempers would start to get frayed, as if there wasn't enough to worry about…

Cecily needed no seer to tell her that her mother, great with the child that she had been too old to be bearing, and weighed down with grief on learning of the deaths of her husband and her son at Hastings, must have lost heart.

Where *was* Lufu? The girl's short-sighted laziness would see everyone suffering this winter. And Godwin? In her mother's absence, the reeve too must share the responsibility for what had not been done here. Sins of omission, as Mother Aethelflaeda would say.

A movement in the cookhouse had her whirling around as a tall streak of a boy shuffled into the storeroom. He stooped his head as he passed under the doorframe. Cecily half recognised him. Of about her own age, he wore a coarse brown peasant's tunic that was torn at the shoulder and in dire need of a wash. The bindings of his chausses were unravelling. He looked a shambles, but his face was alight with honest pleasure. 'C…C…Cec?' he said. '*Yes!* Cec!'

'Wat? Oh, Wat, I am glad to see you well.' It was Alfred's motherless son. He was in need of a scrubbing, but hale, thank the Lord. Apparently, he was just about coping without his father.

Wat grinned and nodded. 'Cec, Cec.' He had always liked Cecily, though he had never managed her full name. He reached for her hand. 'Cec!' he repeated, and, still grinning, clumsily raised her fingers to his lips. 'Cec come home!'

'Yes, Wat. I'm home. Wat, do you know where Lufu is?'

'Lufu?' His brow wrinkled.

'Yes, I'm looking for Lufu.' Still holding his hand, she led him, docile as a lamb, back into the deserted cookhouse. 'We need help if anyone is to eat tonight. Where's Lufu?'

Wat shook his head. 'Gone up?'

'Up?'

Wat looked blankly at her, and Cecily sighed. 'Oh, dear—never mind.' She rolled up her sleeves. 'We had best make a start on it ourselves. Wat, please fetch some water—the pail's in that corner.'

Wat pursed his lips.

'Won't you help me, Wat?'

Eagerly, he nodded.

'Then take the bucket—that one, over there.'

Still clinging to her hand, not moving, Wat swung it from side to side. Smiling he repeated, 'Cec home.'

'Yes, Wat, I'm home.'

And then, to her mingled astonishment and horror, Wat fell to his knees, pressed his face into her belly, and burst into tears. He clung like a baby, shaking and sobbing. A pain in her chest, Cecily put her arms around him.

And naturally Adam Wymark chose that moment to walk into the cookhouse.

Adam stood just inside the cookhouse door, blinking at the sight of the beggarly lad in filthy homespun who was sobbing into Cecily's skirts. The lad reeked—Adam could smell him from the doorway—but Cecily was embracing him with no sign of revulsion. Far from it—she was stroking his lank hair back from his brow, hugging his unwashed person to her, and murmuring soft words that he could not understand into the boy's ear. Saxon words. Words that could speak treason and he would never know it until it was too late. But somehow he did not think treason was being spoken here. Fool that he was, he did not *want* it to be treason that was being spoken here…

'Clearly one has to be Saxon to win your favour,' Adam said, forcing a smile.

They sprang apart. The boy edged sideways, sleeving his tears. Cecily's chin came up. 'This is Wat,' she said. 'An old friend.'

Adam leaned against a littered table and folded his arms. His stomach was churning with doubts concerning her loyalties, but he'd be damned before he'd let her see it. But, hell, both Cecily and the boy looked the picture of guilt. He adopted a dry, teasing tone. 'First Edmund—you kiss him. And now Wat. He is embraced. How many other admirers are hiding in the woodwork? Will I have to fight for your hand?'

'No, S… Adam. It's not like that,' she said, biting her lip and flushing.

'No?' Adam tipped his head to one side. The boy Wat was watching them open-mouthed; the tear-tracks had left clean streaks on his face. 'Cecily, come here.' Adam wanted to have it out with her about her little visit to Golde Street, but he could not—must not. The waiting game, he reminded himself. You are playing the waiting game.

Hesitantly, still biting that lip, she took a step towards him. Something was worrying her. She was holding herself in a way that told him she half expected him to hit her. Guilt? Or something else?

'Closer. I have something to tell you.'

She took another step towards him as, behind her, Wat edged past and made a dash for the door. 'What is it?'

'Closer.' Their feet almost touched. Her blue eyes were wide. Innocent. Guileless. Charmingly hesitant, if he could but believe what he was seeing. If only he had never heard her in the gold-smith's house…if only she did not look so afraid…

'Adam, is something amiss?'

Leaning forwards, he took her hands and stared into her eyes. Her pupils were dark, her lashes long. He could see the light from the doorway reflected in them, the shadow of his own self. 'Cecily,' he muttered, and shook his head. Hell, why was it so important that she did not hate him?

'Adam?'

'I've spoken to Father Aelfric. He speaks a little French, and I speak a little Latin, and between us I think we managed to

understand each other. He has agreed to marry us on the morrow.
I gather that if we don't wed then we'll have to wait till after
Christmas—because it will be Advent, and it is bad luck to marry
in Advent.'

'That's true.'

'So.' He gave her a lopsided smile. 'Reasoning that we need all
the luck we can get, tomorrow's our wedding day—if you are still
in agreement?' Jesu, why had he done that? Offered her an escape
route again? He might not trust her, but he damn well wanted her—
he should take her and have done. It wasn't as if he was in love
with the girl that he should be so concerned for her feelings.

Those beautiful blue eyes didn't so much as flicker. 'I have
agreed,' she said. 'Tomorrow will be fine. There is no need to wait
till after Christmas.'

Adam gave what he hoped was an unconcerned nod as a new,
urgent thought relegated Golde Street to the back of his mind. He
wanted—no, he ached for her to give him some physical sign of her
acceptance. A squeeze of her fingers, perhaps. A smile, even. For
a moment she did not move, and then it was as though she had read
his mind. She smiled and reached up to draw his head down to hers.

Her kiss was as light as thistledown and she drew back at
once, crimson.

It was enough. With a murmur, Adam tugged her towards him.
Wrapping his arms about her waist, he buried his face in her neck
and felt the first peace he had known all day.

'Damn this wimple,' he said, drawing back to push it aside. He
kissed her neck, nipping gently at the skin. Fingers on her chin,
he turned her lips to his.

The kiss went on a long time—long enough for his tongue to
trace her lips, for hers to trace his, long enough for his loins to
tighten and for him to want to press himself against her and wish
that tomorrow was already here. Long enough for him to forget
utterly that he had heard her in Golde Street only that morning...

Giving a shaky laugh, he raised his head. 'We'll have to do something about your clothing. I cannot wed you garbed as a novice.'

Nodding, she eased away. Because he wanted to snatch her back, Adam stuck his thumbs into his belt.

'I saw my sister Emma's clothes chest in the Hall. She won't mind if I borrow her gowns.' She tipped her head back to look up at him, and her mouth was sad. 'My mother had some stuff stored away too…'

'All yours now, to dispose of as you will,' Adam said carefully, conscious that she must resent the circumstances in which she had come to inherit her mother's belongings.

'Yes. My thanks.'

He glanced about, seeing the cookhouse for the first time. 'This place is a midden. And it will be dark soon.' Turning from the filthy workbench, he nudged the dead ashes in the hearth with the toe of his boot. 'Shouldn't this be fired?'

'Yes.'

That wary, haunted expression was back in her eyes. *Was* she afraid of him? A moment ago that had not seemed possible, but… 'Where's the cook?'

'Lord knows—run off and hidden somewhere. I was trying to hunt something out for supper.'

'It's a good thought—the men are starving. But I don't expect *you* to cook for us.'

'Someone has to…' She was the picture of anxiety. 'I have to tell you that the stocks are shamefully low…'

He smiled. 'We've not eaten a decent meal in weeks. Another day more or less wouldn't kill us. But *you* should not be cooking.'

'I don't mind. Just till I find Lufu.'

'No, it's not your place—but you will need to order the help. I saw a couple of lads lurking in the stables…'

'That would be Harold and Carl, the miller's boys.'

He was pleased to see the worry leaving her eyes. It was replaced with a look of puzzlement, as though she wanted to fathom him but could not. Well, that was hardly surprising. She was a mystery to him too.

'I'll get young Herfu to haul them over. They can earn their keep,' he said. 'Herfu can help too.'

'Brian?'

'Aye—he cooked for the troop before, and no one died.'

She smiled. 'That's a mercy. I can't promise much tonight—unless we can lay our hands on some meat. There is no time to slaughter a pig or a lamb, and in any case their meat is best hung before eating—there are chickens, though, will they do?'

'A feast. I've been longing for chicken ever since Mother Aethelflaeda tantalised us at the convent.' Adam leaned forwards as a force that was beyond his strength to resist had him dropping a kiss on her nose. *Fool, fool, wait until you know where her loyalties lie.* 'I'll send Herfu over immediately. Once you've instructed him and the miller's boys, come back to the Hall, would you?'

'As you wish. Why?'

'Because we're going to search out the reeve—what was his name?'

'Godwin.'

'Godwin—aye. Maybe Godwin will know where the cook has gone, and I want you with me. It was heavy going, getting the message across to Father Aelfric.'

'Of course. I understand.'

Dusk was falling by the time Cecily walked back into to the Hall.

Sir Richard was ensconced on a bench by the trestle, a cup of wine at his elbow, a lute in his hand. She broke her stride. A lute? Of course there was no reason why a Norman should not play the lute. But it gave her pause to see one of Duke William's knights with a delicate musical instrument. His squire, Geoffrey, and a couple of the troopers sat with him, deep in murmured conversation. Adam was nowhere to be seen. Neither was Gudrun. But Adam's squire, Maurice, was dandling a cooing Agatha on his knee, and Philip…

Her brother's basket lay in the sleeping area, but from her standpoint it wasn't possible to see inside. Was Philip with Gudrun or was he asleep? She didn't care to think that he might have been left alone in the Hall with not a Saxon in sight. True, with Agatha crowing and waving her chubby fists at him so gleefully, Maurice did not look capable of harming a baby, but if Adam and his men discovered that Philip was the rightful heir to Fulford how would they react? Would they kill him? No, surely a man like Adam Wymark—apparently a considerate man—would not countenance infanticide?

Masking her concern, and mindful of Adam's comments about not wishing to marry her in her habit, she stole a glance across the rushes to where Emma kept her clothes chest. It wasn't there.

Nevertheless, Philip's basket was. Casually, she wandered across. Her brother was asleep on his side, with only his face and one tiny fist visible above the coverlet. So sweet. So small. Her throat ached.

Adjusting his covers, she straightened. 'Sir Richard?'

'My lady?'

'There was a small chest here earlier, under the window. Did anyone move it?'

'Was it painted red?'

'That's it.'

'Adam had it hauled up to the loft chamber.'

The loft room to one side of her father's mead hall had been built at about the time of Thane Edgar's marriage to her mother. Being Norman, Thane Edgar's bride had not liked to sleep with the rest of the household. She had expected the Thane of Fulford and his lady to have some private space. The loft room had served Cecily's parents as bedchamber, and also as meeting room for the immediate family.

Murmuring her thanks, Cecily hooked up her skirts and started up the ladder.

At the top, the landing was large enough for two people and the linen press, no more. She paused by the press, steeling herself—she had not entered this room since she had been forced into her novice's habit.

Taking a deep breath, she lifted the latch. Facing her, at the gable end, was her parents' bed—now Adam's. Light slanted down from a wind-eye above it, lighting up a tumble of untidy bedding, a man's green tunic, a crumpled white linen chainse or shirt. A brazier, unlit, stood at her right hand, another on her left...

A movement on the left caught her attention.

Adam! Stripped to the waist, standing before a ewer of water on a stand, washcloth in hand.

He turned.

'Oh!' In the moment before she lowered her eyes Cecily glimpsed a broad, well-muscled chest with dark hair arrowing down towards the tie of his hose. He seemed larger half naked, and most disconcerting. The effect of her years in the convent, she supposed. Curiosity warred with shyness. Shamefully, she wanted to continue looking at him. But shyness won, and she stared fixedly at a bedpost, hoping he could not see her blushes. 'I...I'm sorry. Sir Richard said you'd had Emma's belongings sent up here. I didn't think you...' Her voice trailed off.

'I'll be gone in a moment,' Adam said, his voice amused. 'If you'd pass me that towel?'

A square of white linen was lying in the rumpled mess on the bed. She thrust it in his general direction.

Swiftly drying himself, Adam dragged a clean linen shirt from a travelling chest that sat against the wall between Emma's red one and her father's strongbox. Out of the corner of her eye she saw that he had to duck his head to avoid hitting it on the low angled roof.

Only when he was safely inside his tunic did she risk meeting his gaze. 'This was my parents' room,' she said softly, unable to analyse her feelings on seeing Adam Wymark standing in the same space where so often she had seen her father.

Should she hate this stranger from Brittany? She did not hate him—she did not think she could, for so far he had not shown himself to be a cruel man—yet to see him here, sword propped against the side of the bed in exactly the same way that her father had propped his sword...

Adam buckled his belt, his face unreadable. 'I know, and I'm sorry if it offends you, but I used this room before chasing to the convent after your sister.' He shrugged. 'Tonight it's yours. But tomorrow...' He came to stand close, so close she could smell the soapwort he had been using. 'Tomorrow it will be *our* room.'

Her pulse quickened, her mouth opened, but no words emerged. He stood looking down at her: tall, slender, dark. A Breton knight. *Her* knight. Her mouth felt dry. Would he bring kindness to their marriage? Part of her was beginning to think it possible. But, no, how could that be when he was Duke William's man, and she was marrying him for convenience? She was marrying him for Philip; for the villagers; for the sake of peace...

And for you? Does not a small part of you marry him for yourself? asked an insidious voice. No! Never! I marry him to... As Cecily looked up at Adam, her mouth went dry and she lost track of her thoughts. It was extraordinary how compelling she found the shape of his lips...

'Beautiful...' she murmured.

'Hmm?'

'Oh! N-nothing. I...I...nothing!' she stuttered, her thoughts utterly scrambled.

Theoretically, Cecily knew what happened in the marriage bed—how had Emma phrased it? 'You've seen the stallion put to our mares'—but how did that translate into human terms? She was largely ignorant of what actually went on between a man and a woman. Some men forced women, this she knew. One of the novices at the convent had been raped and sent there in shame when she had become pregnant, even though it had not been her fault. Cecily could still hear the poor girl's cries echo round the chapel when she realised she would never return to her village. Would Adam force her? Once they were married he would have the right...*tomorrow* he would have the right...and no one called it rape when a man forced his wife.

Mother Aethelflaeda had told the nuns that carnal love, as she called it, was only acceptable if the couple were married and were intent on begetting children. They were to take no pleasure in their union, for then it became sinful. 'Carnal love distracts one from the love of God,' Mother Aethelflaeda had stressed, many times. 'It is a woman's duty to give her husband children, yet it is a sin when she takes pleasure in it.'

Confused, Cecily gazed at the man she would marry on the morrow, the man who pleased her eyes, and butterflies fluttered in her belly. If only it were darker in here. He must know he has this strange effect on me. He is laughing at me. He is...

Would he please her body too? Kissing Adam was *already* a pleasure, which must mean she was a sinner. And as for the rest... Well, tomorrow would tell whether she would find doing her duty a pleasure or no. Her legs felt weak. She did not think he would have to force her...

Adam's gaze had lightened. 'You've come to change your gown?'

'Aye—it will feel strange to wear colours after so long.'

He smiled and gently stroked her cheek, warm fingers sliding underneath her wimple. She wanted to lean into the caress like a cat, and rub her cheek against his fingertips. Sensual longings took shape in her mind—forbidden, sinful longings.

'I won't be sorry to see the back of this,' he said, and with his other hand he twitched at her skirts. 'Not to mention this grey apology for a habit that the convent saw fit to clothe you in.'

Taking up his sword, he turned to the door. 'I'll send Gudrun up with more hot water.'

The latch clicked quietly behind him.

Alone in her parents' room, Cecily sank onto the rumpled bed and put her head in her hands. What was the matter with her? If Mother Aethelflaeda had but a glimpse at the turmoil in her mind she would have her doing penance till her life's end.

Downstairs in his basket lay her baby brother, an orphan, an innocent. It was up to her to protect him, and to do that she must marry Adam. Honesty compelled her to admit that she had found his dark looks achingly attractive from the first, and against all odds she was learning to like him personally as well. In other circumstances she might have been happy to wed him, might have been able to make a good marriage with him. But—reaching up, she snatched off her veil and wimple—how could they possibly make a good marriage when of necessity she must keep so much hidden from him?

She twisted the veil into a tight bundle. Adam must not discover that Philip was her brother; he must not discover that one of her father's housecarls, Judhael, was likely determined to overthrow his Duke's regime; he must not discover that Emma was consorting with Judhael; he must not…

The latch rattled, and a young girl pushed open the door. She was on the verge of womanhood, her thick dark hair bound in two glossy braids which hung over her shoulders, her blue eyes were wide, and when they met hers, her lips curved into a welcoming smile. She hovered on the threshold with a jug of steaming water. 'Lady Cecily?'

'Matty?' Matty was the miller's daughter—a child when Cecily had last seen her. Now she was growing into an attractive young woman.

Matty came into the room, clutching the jug to her breast. 'My lady.'

She made to curtsey, but Cecily was up trying to hug her before she had the chance. 'Oh, Matty, it is good to see you.'

Setting the jug down, Matty hugged her back, her smile warm. 'We're glad to see you too, my lady. We need you.' She lowered her voice. 'These Franks frighten me—they frighten us all.'

'There's no need to fear them,' Cecily said, with a confidence that surprised even herself. 'They won't harm you.'

Hastily, Matty crossed herself. 'I pray you are right. But with our men gone…'

'They will not hurt you. Sir Adam will not permit it. We are his people now, and it is his duty to protect us.'

'Truly?'

Cecily nodded reassurance. 'I am sure of it.'

Matty bit her lip. 'If you say so, my lady.' She glanced at the washstand. 'Sir Adam asked me to fetch you hot water.' Unexpectedly, she grinned, and her eyes sparkled. 'At least I guessed that was what he wanted. His English is not very good, is it?'

'That's kind of you—my thanks. And, no, his English is weak, but he is learning.'

Matty went to the washstand, slid open the wall shutter and tipped Adam's water out, regardless of any hapless soul who might be walking under the eaves. She refilled the ewer from the jug, chattering nineteen to the dozen. 'He tried to get Marie to come out of the church to help him translate, but Marie won't budge. She's asked for an escort to go the convent—says she'll take your place. Even though she's a Frank herself, she refuses to speak to them. That's one of the reasons I was afraid. I thought if Marie wouldn't have anything to do with them, they must be evil.'

'Fear is contagious,' Cecily murmured.

Matty paused for a moment, head tilted to one side. 'Aye, maybe it is, an' all.' She shrugged. 'Anyhow, Wilf came back with the mended cart, and Sir Adam and that friend of his—the other knight…' She coloured and gave Cecily a coy look.

'Sir Richard?'

'Aye—him. They're talking to Wilf.' Matty giggled. 'Or rather, they are trying to. They sound right funny when you come to think of it.'

Listening with half an ear, refraining from pointing out that were Matty to attempt to speak Norman French or Breton she would probably sound just as amusing, Cecily randomly pulled a gown out of her sister's clothes chest. It was periwinkle-blue, of fine worsted, with silken side lacings and cream embroidery at the neck and hem. A length of cream and blue braid lying under the gown was evidently intended for a matching girdle. She also unearthed a linen undergown, and a new pair of hose. New hose—what luxury. Heavens, Emma's clothes were so beautiful they were positively immoral…

'You'll need a maid,' Matty said eagerly, moving to the bed and beginning to strip it, efficiently separating dirty linens from woollen blankets. '*He* said you would need one. At least that's what I think he was trying to say. May I be your maid, Lady Cecily. May I?'

'Mmm?' Absently, Cecily shook out the blue gown, and though she knew it was vanity—yet another sin to chalk up on her account—she couldn't help but notice how well it draped. After the harshness of her convent habit, the fabric was soft as thistledown. Would he like her in it? Would he think her pretty? Not that that mattered, of course.

The scent of lavender filled the air, and with it the realisation that Emma must have put bunches of dried flowers amongst her things. Emma. Tears pricked at the back of her eyes. Where was Emma? Could she find happiness with Judhael? Would he look after her? Overwhelmed by conflicting emotions, Cecily covered her face with her hands. She wanted to scream. Was she hysterical? One moment she was hoping Sir Adam thought her pretty—how trivial!—and in the next breath she was fighting back tears. Was that what hysteria was?

Matty was clattering out onto the landing to the linen closet, still talking, and by the time she returned with an armful of fresh linen Cecily had herself in hand. 'Gudrun said to change the sheets,' Matty said. 'Oh, *do* say I can be your maid, my lady. Marie's entering the convent, so she won't do. And Gudrun's got too much to do with running the Hall and with the babies.'

'I'm not sure I'd know what to do with a maid.'

Matty's face fell. 'Oh, but you must have one—you're to be lady here! I know I'm only the miller's daughter, and there's much I don't know about being a lady's maid, but I can learn. I *want* to learn. Oh, please, Lady Cecily—let me be your maid.' Her blue eyes met Cecily's, clear and quite without guile. 'I'd like to do more than hoist sacks of grain for my father my whole life.'

'That's honest,' Cecily said, smiling. 'And, since I happen to think hoisting sacks of grain is not a job for a girl, I agree—you can be my maid. It would seem that neither of us knows exactly what that might entail, so we shall learn together.'

Matty gave a little skip. 'Thank you, my lady, you won't regret it.'

'I trust not. First, let me help you with that bed, and this mess that Sir Adam has created, and then you can help me change. It's time I went back to the cookhouse to see whether either of your brothers has the makings of a cook.'

Chapter Twelve

Cecily had not forgotten her promise to look at Edmund's broken leg. When she came down from changing into Emma's gown, she sent for him and asked that he should wait for her outside the Hall, on the bench facing the village green. That way she could take advantage of the last of the daylight and examine him properly.

The air was icy, and on her way out Cecily snatched up the blue cloak Adam had lent her and wound it round her shoulders. She was glad to put it on—not only on account of the cold, but also because Emma's blue gown revealed far more of her shape than her novice's habit had done, and she felt very self-conscious.

Outside, Adam's men were toing and froing from the Hall to the armoury and stables, a constant flow of traffic. And, late though it was, a clanging from the smithy down the road told her that the armourer had been put to work.

As Cecily took her seat next to Edmund on the bench by the Hall wall, a swirl of gold leaves blew past the pillory and came to rest in a drift by the stocks. Adam emerged from the armoury with Sir Richard and started walking back to the Hall.

'Bloody fiends,' Edmund muttered, glowering sullenly at the

two knights. 'They took my weapons—even my seax, for God's sake. A housecarl without a seax. I feel naked, unmanned.'

'You are alive, Edmund, and that is surely a blessing,' Cecily murmured. Lightly, she touched his leg, and lifted it onto her knee to begin unwrapping the splint bindings. 'How long since you broke it?'

Edmund shrugged, and his silver bracelets jingled. 'Can't remember, exactly.'

'Sometime before Hastings, I think you said?'

Another shrug. 'Must have been—otherwise I would have accompanied your father and Cenwulf.'

'It should be healing by now.' Setting aside the splint and bandages, Cecily probed Edmund's calf. 'This bone?'

'Aye.' He winced.

'Does it hurt when you bend the knee?'

A scowl between his brows, Edmund nodded.

Puzzled, Cecily watched as Edmund flexed his leg. The bone seemed to have knitted together cleanly enough, there was no scarring, the skin had not been broken, and as far as she could see his movement was not restricted.

Adam and Richard had reached the Hall door, and though she was concentrating on Edmund, Cecily's sixth sense told her that Adam had paused on the threshold to look her way before following Richard inside. *Always he watches me. Always. I must be wary.*

Tentatively, Edmund put his foot on the ground. Cecily stood and offered him her arm. 'Here—try and put your weight on it.'

Edmund's gaze met hers. 'Must I?'

'Yes. I need to see how you do—how otherwise can I help you?'

Biting his lip, Edmund rose and, clutching at her for support, gingerly put the weight on his injured leg. 'Ah, Sweet Christ, Cecily—it's agony!' He fell back onto the bench.

Cecily frowned. Something was not right here. A clean break, as this had been, and well knit together…

'It shouldn't be this painful, Edmund. Not after all this time. I cannot think what is wrong. Perhaps you need to rest it awhile longer?'

Retrieving the bandages and splints, she set about rebinding Edmund's leg. At least he hadn't gone pale when he'd tried to stand, and there had been no sweat on his brow—a sure sign of trouble. Nor had Edmund complained of feeling sick when he put his weight on his leg, as sometimes happened if breaks did not heal well. The continued pain was a mystery.

'Best not take any chances. We'll keep these on,' she said. 'Use your crutches, but test it with your weight now and then, and I'll look at it again in another week.' She smiled. 'Perhaps the odd prayer to Saint Swithun might help?'

'My thanks,' Edmund said, but he did not smile back.

She made to rise but, bracelets chinking, Edmund stayed her with his hand. 'Don't go—not yet,' he said, in a swift undertone. 'There's something we must settle, and quickly, while those bastards are out of earshot.'

'Edmund?'

'We must get Philip away from here.'

Cecily raised a brow, and would have responded, but Edmund silenced her with a swift headshake.

'He should not be at Fulford,' he said urgently. 'Not with the place crawling with the bastard's men. We must get him away.'

Heart sinking, Cecily shook her head. 'Away? No, Edmund. He's so small. He must stay here, with Gudrun.'

Edmund's gaze was wintry. 'You think him safe here?'

'Yes… No…I don't know.' Cecily gripped Edmund's hand. 'But he needs his wet nurse. And I don't think Sir Adam would hurt him, if that's what you mean.'

Her hand was flung aside. 'Not hurt him? You think a man come here to win lands for himself would spare the real heir? How can you say that when half of southern England is laid waste?'

'Half of southern England?' A shiver ran down her spine. 'What do you mean?'

Edmund flung her a scornful glance. 'Don't pretend you don't know.'

'Edmund, I *don't* know. I have been stuck in a convent these past four years, Mother Aethelflaeda kept us in ignorance. Please explain.'

'After Hastings, Duke William thought to march to London unopposed. But he thought wrong.'

'There was resistance?'

'Yes.' Edmund's eyes were bleak. 'And in retaliation the bastard cut a bloody swathe through the south. Every town and village he came across was fired and put to the sword. Women were raped, children killed—'

Cecily's hand was at her mouth. 'No! *No*, Edmund.'

'Yes!' Face tight with hatred, he leaned closer. 'I am telling the truth! It was not like Winchester. Around London the bastard's men even burnt the grain in the storehouses, and they killed the animals, ensuring that even if some poor souls did manage to escape they'd starve to death later. Cecily, William of Normandy won't be happy until every Saxon in England is food for crows.'

Catching Edmund's arm, Cecily forced herself to speak with calm and conviction. 'Adam is not like that.'

Edmund snorted.

'He is not. Use your brain, Edmund. He didn't kill you, he merely disarmed you! You would have done the same in his place. Adam has hurt no one at Fulford—not even Father's hounds when they went for him. And he wouldn't hurt Philip. This I know.'

'You fool! You blind, stupid… You…*woman*.' He gave her a little shake. 'Adam Wymark wants the land. Philip is your father's heir. Think, Cecily, *think*! Face the truth—bloody as it is. The man is a Frank. He killed to get here, and he'll kill to stay.'

'He won't kill Philip—not a baby! A baby couldn't inherit anyway. Not for years. He would have to be made ward of court or some such.'

Edmund's expression changed to one of sudden enlightenment. 'You're in love with him!'

'I am not. I hardly know him!'

'Yes, you are. You *want* to marry him. I should have known when you rode in like his whore, smiling at him, speaking his language—'

'It's my language too. My mother was Norman, or have you forgotten?'

'You are naught but a collaborator!' Ignoring Cecily's gasp of horror, Edmund flicked at the fur-lined cloak. 'He gave you this, didn't he?'

'Yes, but—' Appalled by Edmund's venom, Cecily shook her head. 'Edmund, please don't. This is not the way forward.'

Edmund brought his face close to hers. His pupils, despite the fading light, were small and dark. Angry. 'You're wrong. It *is* the way. Philip should not be living among murdering Franks.'

Maurice Espinay and Geoffrey of Leon stepped into the yard and Edmund fell silent. His chest heaved, but he held his peace until they had vanished into the stables.

'I'll get Philip out of here,' he muttered.

'No! Edmund, you have not the right.'

'I am loyal to the house of Wessex,' Edmund said. 'As you father was.'

'Wessex is a spent force.' Cecily sighed. 'Edmund, I have seen the Norman garrison at Winchester, and it would be folly to pit yourself against such might—especially now King Harold is dead and his family have been scattered to the four winds. You are not being realistic.'

'I am glad your father is gone that he cannot hear you speak such treachery.' Edmund's eyes filled with scorn. 'And I am glad that Judhael cannot hear you. He is fighting hard for the Saxon cause, trying to raise money, trying to rally the troops for one final battle.'

'Edmund, I do not want to argue with you, but you and Judhael are *wrong*. The cause is *already* lost. We would do better to become allies with these men. Can you not see? If resistance around London and the south has been dealt with so ruthlessly, fighting here can only bring more pain, more death, more hardship. Is that what you want for the people of Wessex? That *their* land should be laid waste too?'

Edmund reached for his crutches. 'Perhaps the cause is not as lost as you imagine.'

'What do you mean?'

'You'll see.'

The hairs rose on the nape of her neck. 'There's something else, isn't there? You know something else. Edmund, what—?'

Edmund's lips formed a smile, but there was little warmth in it. 'You'll find out soon enough.'

'Tell me!'

'I have said too much already. You are but a woman, and a blind one at that. You have been out of the world so long you cannot possibly understand.'

Cecily clenched her fists, but Edmund's face was rigid. For the sake of peace, she held her tongue.

Thus it was that that evening yet another worry was louring like a thundercloud over Cecily's thoughts. Was Edmund about to attempt something rash? Were others involved? She went to the cookhouse to help Brian Herfu get Harold and Carl in hand and the cloud was large in her mind. It did not shift when she went to the stables to feed her father's wolfhounds, and even her delight in the fact that Lightning and Greedy knew her and nuzzled her did not dislodge it. It hung over her still just before supper when, back in her father's mead hall, she had the trestles put up for the evening meal.

But most of all the cloud shadowed her mood when she stood at Adam's elbow for the saying of Grace. It was awkward, being next to the man who had taken her father's place, but her fears concerning Edmund pushed the awkwardness aside, as they pushed aside everything else. By now she had quite forgotten that this was the first time that Adam had seen her in secular clothing, and thus missed the swift appraisal he gave her, and the accompanying nod of satisfaction.

Around the board, faces from Cecily's childhood glowed in the firelight. At the other end Father Aelfric stood next to Sigrida—the boy and girl whose heads barely reached the trestle must be their children. There was the old reeve Godwin and his wife Aella, whose poor hands were gnarled and twisted with arthritis. There was Gudrun and Wilf and Wat; there was the miller and his wife with Matty…even Edmund swayed in on his crutches at the last moment. True, Edmund was wearing an expression belligerent enough to cramp every muscle in her stomach, but he was there. Everyone was present save Lufu and her mother's maid, Marie. The riddle of Lufu's whereabouts had yet to be solved, and Marie had been escorted to the convent.

Cecily looked at the familiar faces and blinked away a mist of tears. So it had been on feast days in her father's time, with all welcome in the Hall. True, there was clear division at the table, with Cecily being the only Saxon at the top. Flanked by Adam and Sir Richard and surrounded by troopers, she was cut off from her fellow countrymen, who sat further down the board, near the door. It would hardly be a relaxing meal, with Adam's men having their swords to hand, but at least Saxons and Franks were under one roof, breaking bread together. It was a start. The beginning of peace? She hoped so.

'How did you do it?' she whispered to Adam, as Father Aelfric coughed and signalled quiet for Grace.

'Mmm?'

'Get the villagers in here.'

'Father Aelfric told them of our betrothal. They have come to see you, my lady.' Adam's eyes met hers, a slight frown between his brows. 'They honour you, and will take their lead from you.'

Cecily bowed her head for Grace. Would that that were so, she thought, bitterly aware that it was likely to be a mixture of fear and curiosity that had brought everyone to the Hall that evening. Earlier, she had asked every Saxon she had seen if they knew where Lufu might be, and she had got nowhere. People knew, but now that Cecily was about to ally herself with Adam they had closed ranks against her. Even Gudrun and Matty had not let her winkle anything out of them. And Edmund had called her a collaborator. Did the entire village share his views?

Grace having been said, Adam took her hand. 'My lady,' he said, and with a formal bow saw her seated. As he took his place next to her on the top bench, his thigh brushed hers.

Cecily flicked back her veil. Absurdly conscious of the physical contact with Adam, slight though it was, she made to edge away, but a slight pressure on her wrist brought her eyes up.

He gave his head a slight shake. 'I need you close.' His quiet murmur barely reached her above the scraping of benches and the buzz of conversation. '*They* need you close. If we act in harmony it will go better for everyone's sake.'

Was that a threat? What would Adam do to the villagers if she did *not* openly support him? If it was in their interests that she smile at him, then smile at him she would, trusting that her father's tenants would know her for a peacemaker rather than a collaborator. His watchful eyes ran over her face. She had the distinct sense that he was holding himself in check, that he was waiting for her to make some move. Had he overheard her conversation with Edmund? Was he capable of understanding it?

'That blue becomes you,' he murmured unexpectedly, 'and I'm glad you have shed that wimple at last.'

Startled by his compliment, self-conscious all over again, Cecily dipped her head in acknowledgement and extended her hand to him. She was still wearing her convent boots, but he had obviously not noticed. However, she would play the formal part he had allotted her, even if she could not mask that slight trembling of her fingers. Adam raised her hand to his lips. Butterflies. One small kiss and he had butterflies dancing in her stomach. How did he *do* that?

Breaking eye contact, Cecily realised their interplay had been noted. At the far end of the table Gudrun's face had relaxed. Matty gave a little giggle and dug her mother in the ribs. Wat grinned. She didn't look at Edmund.

Something thudded against the door. Heads turned as Brian Herfu booted it open and carried in the chickens on a huge serving dish. The flames in the hearth rocked like marigolds in a breeze. Brian hefted the dish onto the trestle with a thud and went back out into the dark yard.

Spit-roasted chickens glazed with onions. The chickens were so tender that the meat was falling off the bone. Cecily's mouth watered. By the look of it, Adam had understated Brian's talents in the kitchen. The young man was a miracle-worker.

Sliding a platter into place, so that they could both reach it, Adam dropped a trencher of bread on it, apparently intending to share his food with her. Cecily had never observed this custom herself, but her French mother had taught her that it was part of formal etiquette in France that a knight should share his food and drink with his lady. As an overt statement of their union on the morrow, it couldn't be more clear.

Tonight, Adam's every move was designed to prove their unity. He honoured her because it was in his interests to do so.

The door banged again. Lamps and torches flickered as Harold staggered in with a round of white cheese and a bowl of cobnuts. Moments later Brian returned with a dish of steaming dumplings, which he set on the hearth to keep warm. Apple dumplings. Cecily could smell fruit and cinnamon. Carl carried in mead and ale, the jugs so full their contents slopped over the rims, and flasks of red wine appeared on the trestle.

Sir Richard sighed with pleasure and reached for a flask. 'Adam ordered this in Winchester for you, my lady,' he said. 'He thought you would like to try it—it's sweeter than most.'

'My thanks.' Adam had bought wine with her in mind?

The smell of the glazed chicken mingled with that of the apple dumplings, and after the meagre convent fare Cecily was hard put to it not to fall on the food like a ravening wolf. 'Brian Herfu is more than a good cook,' she observed.

'Aye.' Adam's stomach growled. 'Like most of us, he is more than just a soldier.' He speared a joint of chicken on the end of his knife and eased it onto their trencher. 'Would you have gravy, my lady?'

'Thank you.' Cecily stole a glance at Edmund, sitting at the far end of the trestle, below Adam's men. As Adam spooned gravy onto their meat, Edmund's scowl deepened.

What should she do about Edmund? She could not warn Adam that Edmund had plans for Philip, for not only would that reveal that Philip was no more the housekeeper's child than she was, but it would also betray the fact that Edmund's loyalties still lay with Wessex and put him in danger. And in any case Edmund had not actually told her anything. He had not trusted her with details.

Adam's stomach rumbled a second time. With a grimace, he abandoned formality and, cutting a generous portion of chicken breast, nudged it to her side of the trencher. 'For pity's sake eat, my lady,' he said. 'I'm near fainting for want of real food.'

'It's Friday,' Cecily muttered, assailed by guilt even as she picked up her knife. 'By rights we should be serving fish.'

Reaching for the wine cup, Adam shook his head. 'I thank God for this chicken. In any case, as I recall you should not even be eating fish—didn't Mother Aethelflaeda impose a fast upon you as penance?'

'Aye, bread and water. I feel guilty to be eating so well.'

'Don't—those years are gone.' He leaned close, eyes serious. 'Tell me truthfully…you are glad to be free of the convent?'

Was that doubt she could read in his eyes? Could her wishes be important to him? It did not seem likely, yet he had asked, so she answered honestly. 'Yes, sir, I am glad.'

'For the sake of the food, of course,' he said, his mouth lifting up at one corner.

Forgetting herself, Cecily smiled back. 'Naturally for the sake of the food.'

He set the cup down with a clunk. 'You must test me now.'

'Test you?'

'My English. We will converse in English.'

'As you wish.'

He gestured around the Hall. 'This is Fulford Hall,' he said, in clear but heavily accented English.

'Yes, that is good.'

'My name is Adam Wymark. I am a Breton knight. You are the Lady Cecily of Fulford. You are Saxon and you are my betrothed. We will be married tomorrow before Advent commences.'

'Begins. Yes, very good,' Cecily said, astonished at Adam's swift progress. She lowered her eyes to hide a growing sense of alarm. *Had* he overheard her conversation with Edmund? She prayed not. He had only begun to learn, so his understanding must be poor, mustn't it?

'Wilf and Father Aelfric have been trying to teach me,' Adam said, reverting to Norman French. 'You see, like Herfu, I am not just a soldier, I am also a linguist.'

'I see that.' Saints, the one thing Cecily did *not* need was a husband with a swift turn of mind…

'Now, this is where I will need your help,' he continued. 'How do you say, "I hope our marriage will be a successful one"?'

Successful, she noted, with a ridiculous pang she immediately dismissed. He had said successful. Not happy or loving, but *successful*. Nevertheless, she repeated his phrase for him in English.

Adam repeated the words after her.

'Very good,' she said, genuinely impressed. Heaven help them, Adam *did* indeed have a good brain.

As though she had spoken this last thought aloud, Adam looked meaningfully down the board to where Edmund leaned on his elbow, chewing a drumstick. A dark brow lifted. 'And how do you say, "I will not tolerate disloyalty of any kind from anyone, be they serf, or soldier or…"' his gaze shifted back to her '"…or even my wife."'?

Cecily lifted her chin. He *must* have overheard her conversation with Edmund! He must have understood it! Calm, Cecily, calm. That is *not* possible. Adam had been too far away and Edmund had spoken quietly.

'Well?' he urged. 'How do you say that in your tongue?'

Stumbling over the words, Cecily told him.

And, haltingly but clearly—oh, yes, very clearly—with his green eyes boring into her, Adam repeated the words after her.

He would not tolerate disloyalty. A piece of meat stuck in her throat. Blindly, she reached for the wine cup.

The wine was indeed smooth, but Cecily hardly tasted it. Her head felt as though it would burst, there were so many secrets and so much to hide from him.

Adam was leaning on the table, addressing Sir Richard, but the words flowed over her. Adam had a quick mind, and, as he had just warned her, he was not only a soldier. If she did not tread warily he would be bound to discover at least one of her secrets. He had too much charm—especially for an enemy. It was dangerous. She was not used to dealing with men and she had no defences against charming ones—even, it seemed, when Duke William had sent them. Adam tempted her to lower her guard, and in those unguarded moments her liking for him was growing beyond her wildest imaginings. He pleased her eyes too much. That was part of the trouble. She wanted to smile at him and watch him smile back. And then there were the butterflies.

She took another sip of wine, the wine Sir Richard said he had bought with her in mind, and her head throbbed.

In the wake of Hastings how could Lady Cecily Fulford and Sir Adam Wymark possibly have a successful marriage? How could she ever be his loyal wife?

Adam's warning about disloyalty robbed the chicken of its flavour. He observed her continuously—outwardly content, smiling whenever their glances chanced to meet, the perfect knight, giving his lady the best cuts of meat, ensuring their goblet was filled with the sweet red wine. But unspoken threats hung over her head, and the fear that he was merely biding his time, waiting for her to make a mistake, was fast becoming a certainty.

On the other hand there was the wine…

From Sir Richard's comment she surmised that Adam's taste was for a sharper brew, but in this, as in every *outward* sign, he had deferred to her. It was a sham, though. It must be. A sham he kept up for the sake of the villagers. His quiet warning had been a timely reminder. She would not forget it. She wanted peace as much as he. In that, at least, they shared a common goal.

Adam touched her arm. 'My lady?'

His green eyes softened as he looked down at her, and in the flare of the torchlight they were dark with promise. It is a lie. It is a *lie*. 'Sir?'

'Something is troubling you?'

'Aye,' she admitted, before she could stop herself.

His hand slid gently over hers, and she repressed the urge to cling. Chastising herself for her weakness, Cecily gazed at the long, sword-callused fingers, at the bitten nails, at his warrior's hand. A hand that had raised a sword against her people and yet had only ever touched her with careful, gentle consideration. Adam Wymark had a touch that, were he a Saxon Thane chosen for her by her father, might be called loving. She frowned.

'You are thinking about tomorrow?' he asked, nodding at Brian

Herfu to remove the first course. At the far end of the board Harold and Carl scrambled to their feet. Dishes clattered.

'I…' Cecily racked her brain for a worry that she might give him—one that would not involve betraying anyone's trust. 'I…Wh-where will everyone sleep tonight?'

Adam's brow cleared, and his fingers squeezed hers. 'That is all that concerns you? I thought…' He shook his head. 'No matter.' He waved his arm about the hall. 'Surely they will sleep here?'

'Saxon alongside Frank? They will not like it.'

Stiffening, he released her hand and sat back. Saints, he had thought she was referring to their marriage. She stole a glance at him from under her eyelashes. His expression was remote, but for an instant he had looked…hurt. Surely she had not that power over him? No, it was merely his pride that was injured…

She kept her voice light. 'Tell me, when you first arrived here, how many of my father's people slept in the Hall?'

He shrugged. 'Not many, I own. But I could not say precisely, since I took the loft room.'

On her other side, Richard stirred. He had been gazing at Matty, at the other end of the trestle. Setting his cup down, he smiled and winked in her direction. Matty flushed like a rose. Sir Richard grinned. 'I can see at least one Saxon I wouldn't mind bedding down with.'

'Sir Richard!' Cecily glared. She knew very well what Sir Richard's absence from the Palace hall in Winchester had meant, and she wasn't about to have him treat the womenfolk of Fulford in like manner. She opened her mouth to say as much, but Adam's hand stayed her.

'No, Richard,' he said, firmly. 'That girl is not for you.'

Richard looked down the board at Matty. Matty smiled shyly back. Her fear of the newcomers seemed to have vanished like morning mist.

'No?' Sir Richard said softly, holding Matty's gaze. 'You might have to tell *her* that. The wench has been casting sheep's eyes at me all evening.'

Cecily huffed. Indeed, Sir Richard was not wrong—she could see for herself that Matty was encouraging him. Stupid girl—did she have no sense? Cecily must warn her about the dangers of trying out her wiles on men like Sir Richard Asculf.

'Sir Richard,' she said, 'Matty is very young. She is only fourteen.'

'She is enchanting. My sister Elizabeth was married at thirteen,' he said, utterly unrepentant.

'I do not think it is marriage you have in mind with Matty, Sir Richard. Leave her alone.'

Richard shrugged. 'As you wish.' Putting his hand on his heart, he caught Matty's gaze, and with a ridiculous expression of yearning on his face he shook his head.

Cheeks aflame, Matty tossed her head. Adam gave a snort of laughter.

'It's not funny!' Cecily said, glowering. She caught at his sleeve, and murmured, 'He *will* leave her alone, won't he?'

'Be calm. He said as much. Richard is a man of his word.'

'Good, because otherwise Matty can sleep with me.'

'My lady,' Sir Richard said, his eyes sparkling with good-natured mischief. 'Your maid's virtue is safe. I can see she is inno-cent. I will sleep at this end of the Hall, with our men. Adam can keep his eye on me.'

'Truly?'

'Truly.'

There was no malice in his face, nothing of the marauding con-queror. Cecily nodded. 'My father's people may sleep at the bottom end of the Hall, behind the curtain.'

'Who would you put in charge?' Adam asked. 'Edmund or Wilf?'

'Wilf.'

'Very well. Wilf can see to the sleeping arrangements.'

Chapter Thirteen

Rushlight in hand, Cecily toiled up the stairs to the loft room. It was past midnight by the candle clock in the curtained area below, and she could barely keep her eyes open, but at last the inhabitants of Fulford were settled for the night.

Harold and Carl had elected to sleep in the stables, Edmund and Wat were nowhere to be seen, having melted away as soon as the trestles were put up for the night, and the villagers—Father Aelfric and Sigrida among them—had returned to their cottages. Of the Saxons only the household retainers had chosen to remain in the Hall. Gudrun, Wilf, Matty and the two babies were tucked out of sight behind the sleeping curtain, having surrendered the fire to Adam and his men. The newcomers hugged the flames, murmuring over dregs in wine flasks and mead jugs.

Before going upstairs, Cecily had contrived to rock her brother to sleep. Philip's basket had had to be moved while the bedding was being laid out, and this had disturbed him. Thanks to Gudrun saying, 'Here, my lady, you always did have a way with babies,' she had taken him from Gudrun perfectly naturally, and no one had raised so much as an eyebrow. She was pretty confident none of the Franks dreamed she was his sister. It had been good to hold him—though she had had to swallow down some tears at the thought that Philip would never know either his mother or his father. Vowing to give him as much love as she could, she had finally passed him back to Gudrun and gone to seek her own bed.

As she clambered onto the landing, a sudden draught raised goosebumps on her arms. It was turning bitter. Edmund was more than capable of looking after himself, but Wat's disappearance was a concern. Had he found somewhere warm for the night? His father's cottage was a ruin—she must remember to see to that on the morrow. Hopefully Wat would be in the stables, with Carl and Harold…

In the loft room both braziers glowed a welcome, and a lighted candle stood on the bedside coffer. Blowing out her rushlight, Cecily warmed her hands at one of the braziers before sinking down onto the bed. She had not dreamed of asking for such comfort—had Adam done so on her behalf?

Lord, but she was tired.

Unpinning her veil, she loosened her hair. Her whole body ached from so much riding—she was not used to it. Wanting to do nothing more than melt into the mattress, she kicked off her boots. Forcing herself back onto her feet, she laid her belt carefully on Emma's coffer and removed the blue gown. Shaking it out, she hung it on a hook to keep the creases out of it. Vaguely she noticed rush matting underfoot. It had not been there earlier. New? She was too tired to care. Shrugging, she flipped back the bedcovers and, still clad in her—in Emma's—linen undergown and hose, she slid into bed. Her feet encountered a warm brick. She wriggled her toes. What bliss. Thank you, Matty.

In a few moments Cecily was almost as warm as when she had woken in Adam Wymark's arms. Had that only been this morning?

Was Adam cold, down in the Hall? Was his pallet hard and lumpy?

She yawned, and her thoughts ran into each other. Home at last, free of St. Anne's, but how the faces had changed. No Mother, no

Father, no Cenwulf, no Emma. And Franks at every turn. Adam's green eyes took shape in her mind. Smiling, watchful—Fulford's new lord. Was she really going to marry him? Could tomorrow really be her wedding day?

She woke to a woman's laughter in the hall under the loft room. Gudrun.

Refreshed by a night on what must be the most comfortable mattress in Christendom, relishing the softness of her pillow, Cecily smiled and stretched. Light was creeping round the edges of the shutter above the bed.

Below, Matty was singing a lullaby, interspersing each verse with a giggle.

A baby gurgled in response. It had to be Agatha. Philip was too young to gurgle like that. Happy, homely sounds, floating up through the cracks in the floorboards. What joy to waken to lullabies and laughter after years of wakening to the cold chime of the Matins bell, to the sterile chant of plainsong.

Smiling, Cecily bounced upright, pushed her hair back from her face and surveyed the loft room with guilty delight. This was hers to enjoy—*hers*. The boarded floor with its rush matting, the whitewashed walls, the sloping roof, the pottery washbasin, the two braziers—though admittedly they had burned down to ash some time in the small hours.

She was not going to spend her nights in a dreary cell. She'd spend them here in this large and airy loft. And from tonight—her smile faded and she drew the covers more tightly round her shoulders—from tonight she would share it with Adam Wymark, a Breton who could not even speak her language properly.

His travelling chest was shoved against the wall, where Matty had left it after tidying away his clothes. Only one travelling chest? His hauberk and helmet must be stowed in the armoury, along with his sword and gambeson, or else he had them at his side, for they were not here. What else had Adam Wymark seen fit to bring with him from Brittany?

Clambering to her knees, Cecily reached up to open the overhead shutter. Light poured in. Getting out of bed, she padded across the matting to the travelling chest. The lid was heavy and creaked as it opened. A jumble met her eyes.

A dirty linen shirt, screwed up in a ball; another, frayed at the neck; a pair of braies; two pairs of hose, one with a nasty rent in it and stained with what looked like blood. Shuddering, she set the dirty shirt and bloody hose aside for laundering, thought better of it, and replaced them as she had found them. Near the bottom she found a clean shirt. A tangle of leg-bindings. A crumpled green tunic, a dark blue one. The quality of Adam's clothing was good—serviceable, but not extravagant. A sheathed dagger. A leather purse, rattling with coins. She set the purse aside unopened, and her gaze fell on a ladies' eating knife, its hilt set with pretty blue stones.

Catching her breath, Cecily picked up the knife and turned it over. Had this been Gwenn's? Adam *must* have loved her. Ill-at-ease, she glanced once more into his coffer. There was little else. More clothes. A small, hard object wrapped in cream linen. But seeing the ladies' eating knife had somehow stolen her curiosity. She might be marrying Adam Wymark, but she had not earned the right to root through his belongings.

Shoving the knife back where she had found it, Cecily replaced the rest of the clothing and quietly closed the chest.

After a quick wash, Cecily dragged on Emma's blue gown and hurried downstairs.

Gudrun was changing Philip's linens in the sleeping area, and Matty was no longer blithely singing lullabies. Her newly appointed maidservant was standing in the doorway, Agatha on her hip, scowling at some activity in the yard.

'Matty, what's amiss?'

Matty's blue eyes were troubled. 'It's Lufu, my lady. She came back at dawn, and Sir Adam's had words with her. Right stern he was, if I understood him right. She's been put in the stocks, and that sergeant of his has just told their cook to tip pigswill on her.'

'What? Let me see.'

Matty stood aside, and with a growing sense of disbelief Cecily saw that she spoke no less than the truth. For there, in the middle of the horse-trampled grass of the green, sat Lufu, in the stocks. Cecily clenched her fists. The use of the stocks was a common enough punishment, and humiliating though it was it was mild compared to some punishments. But she had thought, she had hoped...

'Sweet Jesus!'

'My lady!' Matty gasped, turning startled eyes on her.

Normally, Cecily *never* blasphemed. But the truth was that Cecily had hoped that Fulford had been given a more temperate lord, and she was bitterly disappointed. Clenching her fists, wishing her eyes were deceiving her, she stared at Lufu.

The years had hardly changed her, though at present she was far from the carefree girl who lived in Cecily's memory. Her broad face was streaked with grime and tears, and her plaits were unwound. Bedraggled brown strands stuck to her cheeks like rats' tails. Her skirts were hiked up to her knees, enabling her ankles as well as her wrists to be locked in the stocks. Her hose had a hole at one knee, and her veil was nowhere to be seen.

Scattered about Lufu were vegetable peelings, stale ends of bread, rinds of cheese, cabbage stalks, chicken bones, and floor sweepings from the kitchen. Hunched over her imprisoned hands, she was the very image of misery.

Her heart going to the girl, Cecily caught Matty's arm. 'Sir Adam didn't have Lufu beaten, did he?' Anger was a cold ball in the pit of her stomach. To think she had thought him considerate— to think that she had hoped Fulford would be governed by a moderate man who might rule with kindness. How could Adam treat Lufu like this?

Matty shook her head. 'No, but she's to rest there all morning.' Her expression lightened. 'Then she's to wash and help that Brian with your wedding feast.'

Gritting her teeth, Cecily strode outside. The sun was dazzling, but not strong enough to ward off the nip in the air. Sigrida was walking up the lane past the churchyard, hand in hand with one of her children, and young Harold was lounging in a barrow by the stable, idly picking his nose. The door to the armoury was open, and someone was moving about inside. Probably *him*. Further off, down the track, the mill wheel was turning; she could hear the faint rumble of the machinery. Smoke plumed out of the roofs of the Hall and the smithy.

Hall, church stables and armoury were ranged about the green, and the stocks had been deliberately placed at the centre, ensuring that Lufu was on public view, her disgrace and her punishment known to the whole village.

'Lufu?' Cecily said, her nose wrinkling at the stench of pigswill.

Lufu raised a tear-streaked face and sniffed. A piece of eggshell was lodged in her hair. 'L-Lady Cecily? You've grown up.'

'Yes.'

'Are you home for good?'

'Yes.'

'And you are marrying that…that b…Breton lord?'

'Yes, but he's a knight, Lufu. Not a lord.'

'He's lord of Fulford, though.'

'Yes, I suppose he is.'

Another sniff. A hopeful look entered Lufu's eyes. 'Are you come to let me out?'

'No, I'm sorry,' Cecily said, as gently as she could. But she would try—by heaven she would try…

'But my lady!' Lufu's face collapsed and fresh tears spilled down her cheeks. 'That sergeant of his—a foreigner! What right has he—?'

'Right of arms,' Cecily said, tamping down her anger in order to calm the girl—at least until she could get her out of the stocks. 'And since we cannot argue with that, we would be wise to submit to him.' She went down on her haunches, bracing herself against the pungent smell of rotting food, and lowered her voice. 'Listen, Lufu. This may be hard to understand, but I did believe…that is…I did hope that Adam Wymark might be as good a lord as my father was. That may still be true. He may yet be better.'

'B-better?'

'He didn't have you flogged, did he? My father would have done.'

Lufu looked mutinous. 'No, he wouldn't. Not Thane Edgar.'

'Don't delude yourself. He most certainly would! Why, he sent me to the convent when I—' She bit off the rest of her sentence. Though her father had treated her harshly, he had done no worse than most men in his position would have done. She took a deep breath. 'This punishment is not entirely undeserved. You must know you've been neglecting your duties. When I arrived yesterday and went to the cookhouse…Lufu, the state of it! It wasn't fit for pigs to eat food from there, never mind people.' She eyed the malodorous rubbish around them, and flicked at a brown shrivelled apple peeling. 'This has all come from *your* kitchen.'

Lufu flushed, turned her head away, and muttered under her breath.

'I beg your pardon?'

'Nothing. I'm sorry, my lady, but—' Her voice broke on a sob, and she began crying again, in earnest.

Cecily put her hand on Lufu's arm. 'Tell me. Lufu?'

'I can't, my lady! I'm sorry, but I can't!'

A heavy stone lodged in Cecily's belly. Not another secret to hide from Adam? She kept her voice steady. 'Calm yourself. You're already in trouble, why not make a full confession? What is it?'

Lufu gulped. 'Can't. Sergeant Le Blanc would take my hand!'

'Your hand? I think not.' Cecily smiled. 'We need our cook to have both her hands.'

Lufu hung her head and her hair flopped forward, screening her face. Her shoulders were hunched. 'He would, an' all,' she muttered. 'Leastwise Edmund said so.'

Cecily drew back. 'Edmund? What does Edmund know of the Sergeant's mind?'

Lufu blew her hair out of her eyes and gave her a sharp look. 'As much as you know of your betrothed, most like. How long have you known him? A couple of days?'

'Lufu, none of them would take your hand,' she said confidently, hoping to God she was right. Lufu folded her lips together and looked away. 'Lufu, they wouldn't.' Impatiently, Cecily took Lufu by the chin and turned her face to hers, forcing her to meet her gaze. 'I *know* they wouldn't.'

Lufu shuddered, and finally whispered, 'But it's the punishment for stealing.'

'For stealing? Heavens, Lufu, what—?'

'A baconflitch. I hid it. After they—' Lufu jerked her head at the armoury '—rode up the first time. Was going to take it to Gunni's shelter, up on the downs.'

'Gunni?'

'My man. He's a shepherd, my lady. His summer shelter is way up on the downs, near Seven Wells. He took himself off there when these foreigners arrived. I thought Saxon meat should go to Saxon men. But now…' Her voice rose to a wail. 'If Sir Adam really is to be lord here, he'll take my hand!'

'He will *not*.' Cecily spoke with as much emphasis as she could muster. 'He may not even need to know you have taken the bacon, but you must tell *me* where you have hidden it.'

Lufu's expression brightened. 'You will speak for me?'

'I will. Provided, of course, you swear not to neglect your work in future?'

'I won't, my lady, never again! I swear!'

'To say that Thane Edgar's armoury is a disappointment would be to understate the case,' Adam said.

Richard grunted agreement.

Adam eyed the Saxon weaponry that Maurice had laid out on the workbench for his inspection: a rusty hauberk, the links of which were coming apart; a couple of cracked shields; a sword so clumsy that it would have taken a giant to wield it—the list ran on. True, there were a couple of dozen arrows, but they were unfletched, and the two bows were of ashwood and not yew. He picked up one of the bows, weighing it in his hand. Some idiot had left it in the damp—it was warped and would be impossible to sight.

Sighing, Adam met Richard's sympathetic gaze. He thrust the bow at his friend and took up the other, which seemed equally twisted. Without a word, they set about stringing them.

Nocking one of the unfletched arrows, Adam stepped outside the armoury and drew the bow, sighting along the arrow. 'God's blood!' he said, exasperated at the wanton waste of what had once been a reasonable practice weapon.

'No good?' Richard murmured, and, drawing his own bow, pointed it round the edge of the Hall towards the green, where the bedraggled cook was sitting amid her vegetable peelings.

'You'd not hit an ox at five paces with this,' Adam said, unnocking his arrow.

'Hmm.' Testing the drawing power of his bow, Richard sighted it at the mead hall roof ridge.

Cecily hurtled round the corner and stormed straight for them, skirts lifted out of the mud, veil flying. To his great annoyance, Adam's heart lurched just at the sight of her. Hell, had he ever mooned over Gwenn like this? He did not think so. But then he had known Gwenn all his life, and no one, not even the little novice, could ever replace his Gwenn. As she stalked up to him his gaze sharpened. A blind man could sense the fury in her—it was rolling off her in waves. So, Cecily Fulford kept a temper hidden beneath all that golden beauty, did she? Interesting.

Matty hurtled round the corner, running to keep up. The girl took one look at Richard, aiming the bow at the roof-ridge, and squealed.

Richard grinned and lowered the bow. 'My apologies, Mistress Matty.'

'My father never permitted weapons of any sort to be drawn near the Hall unless it was an emergency,' Cecily said stiffly, a pleat in her brow. 'He said accidents happen without our help.'

Adam made a non-committal noise. He couldn't argue with that. She was slightly out of breath, and he had to make a conscious effort to keep his eye on her face, not the enticing shape of her breasts. That blue dress…it revealed so much more of her than her old habit.

Cecily looked directly at him, blue eyes cold as the sky above them. 'The practice field is at the back of the stables, Sir Adam. We walked directly into your line of fire.'

Sir Adam. Had he done anything in particular to incur her wrath? he wondered. Or was she was only now showing the natural anger that she must feel against the Duke's regime? 'It's overrun with sheep,' Adam said, more defensively than he intended. 'But in any case you weren't in our firing line, because we weren't going to fire. The arrows are not fletched and the bows are impossible to sight.' He gestured towards the door. 'I had hoped to find something worth saving in here.'

Huffing out a breath, she stepped past and poked her head into the armoury. Leaning on the doorjamb, bow in hand, Adam watched her look at the piles of his men's arms arranged on the left, and the meagre selection left behind by Thane Edgar on the right. He had dealt gently with her thus far, on account of the grief she must be feeling. He knew that she had had some time to come to terms with the loss of her father and her brother, but the grief she must feel for her mother was fresh, the wound very recent, and he had been trying to respect that. She had such a fragile, delicate appearance. But at this moment, with a muscle jumping in her jaw and her fists clenched, she looked as though she could take on the world and emerge victorious. She was magnificent in her anger. He wondered what she would do if he kissed her. Hit him, most likely.

'My father,' the magnificent girl said, slowly and with great clarity, as though she were a queen talking to peasant, and a simpleton at that, 'will have taken the best weapons with him to support our King Harold.'

Yes, she would definitely hit him.

Behind him in the yard, Richard was talking to Matty in French, his voice light and teasing. Matty muttered something about not understanding him, and then her voice faded as she moved off—probably back to the Hall or to the stables, where her brothers were meant to be mucking out the horses.

Chest still heaving, Cecily picked up a Saxon arrow-head, testing the point with her forefinger. 'I expect Father armed as many of the home guard as he could,' she said, still in that insultingly slow voice, edged with anger.

'Aye.' Adam shifted. He ought to get her out of here. An armoury was no fit place for a bride on her wedding day, and he did not want her dwelling on her father and fighting—not today. 'Did you wish to speak to me, my lady?'

'Yes, about Lufu.'

He tapped the bow against his side. 'The girl Le Blanc put in the stocks?'

She stiffened. 'Your sergeant put her there?'

'Yes.'

'But I thought you—'

'I did try to reason with the girl, but since you were lounging abed and could not interpret for me there was little understanding between us.' He lifted his shoulders. 'I left it to Le Blanc to decide on the actual punishment.'

'So you blame *me* because your man put her in the stocks?'

'Not at all. I merely state what happened.'

She searched his eyes for a moment, and Adam wondered what she saw there. A liar? A hated invader? But there was no telling, and after a moment she looked down and began fiddling with the arrowhead, turning it over in her fingers. The anger, he sensed, was leaving her. She sighed. 'So *you* did not order her put there?'

'No, but I should say that I do not question Le Blanc's decision.' Stepping towards her, Adam put his finger under her chin and lifted her face to his. 'You want me to release her?' he asked softly.

'Please,' she said quietly. 'Lufu is repentant. She wants to make amends.' Moving out from under his hand and past him to the doorway, she checked the position of the sun. 'It's almost noon. If you let her out now, she can help Brian with the supper.'

Cecily Fulford looked delightful in her sister's gown—so delightful that she almost stole his tongue. A Saxon girl—no, *the* Saxon girl, the one he was about to marry. That scattering of freckles across her nose was begging to be kissed. That wayward blonde curl was asking to be tugged. If he leaned forward and... But some of that anger still lingered in her eyes, and it checked him. He fought the impulse to take her hand—for this was neither the time nor the place, not with Richard grinning at him like an ass, not with the miller's boys so close in the stables, the men in the yard...

'...and they can use the baconflitch to add flavour. If, that is, you like smoked bacon, sir?' Cecily finished, looking expectantly up at him.

'Baconflitch? What? What did you say?'

'I found a side of bacon. Lufu wants to use it for our wedding supper, if you agree.'

He could resist no longer. What harm? They were about to be

married. As he took her hand he had the pleasure of watching her cheeks bloom with colour.

Richard snorted. Turning his shoulder on his fellow knight, Adam crowded Cecily back into the armoury and out of sight of prying eyes. She was still clutching the arrowhead. Gently, he removed it and placed it on the workbench. He set down the bow. 'I thought there was no meat, cured or otherwise?' He rubbed his thumb over her fingers.

'Oh. No.' For a moment she would not look his way, but Adam was so intent on watching her lips that he scarcely noticed. Then she smiled as prettily as he could wish. 'So I thought, sir. But this morning it…it came to light.'

'Came to light? Where?'

'It had…been put into safekeeping.'

The light dawned. Lufu. So that was what they had been talking about by the stocks. And Cecily—with her blue eyes no longer cold, but full of pleading—she did not want Lufu punished further. Hell, neither did he. A resentful Saxon would not advance his cause here. 'You may order her release,' he said, keeping hold of her hand. 'As long as you're confident she won't poison my men.'

'She won't do that.' Her brow cleared. 'Lufu used to be a good cook. I don't expect that's changed. If my people learn they can trust you, they will serve you well.'

My people. Here she was, pretty and charming when she wanted to be, and yet always there was this shadow between them, this division. *My people.* Not your people, even though England's new ruler had given them into his charge. Would it always be so? *My people.* Cecily Fulford was about to become Cecily Wymark, but would she ever say *our people* and mean it?

They stood staring at each other by the armoury door, and even as she made to pull away Adam was hunting out an excuse to keep her with him. He had a thousand things to do before their wedding at three o'clock, but he would happily put them off simply for the sake of her company.

'About Edmund…' he opened at random, and then wished he had not, for her face closed. He was instantly on the alert, though he took pains not to appear unduly concerned.

'Edmund? Why, he's just one of my father's housecarls—the most fortunate, since he is alive.'

Adam let her pull free. 'I mistrust the man. I pray you will inform me if he lets fall anything that might work to my—to our—disadvantage.'

Was it his imagination, or had she gone a shade paler? Her fingers had certainly curled into fists. As though she was aware that he had noticed, they slowly uncurled.

'You disarmed him?'

'Indeed.'

'H-has he done anything since then to rouse your suspicions?' she asked.

Adam folded his arms across his chest. 'Not unless you call flirting with one of the village matrons suspicious,' he admitted. 'Though I expect her husband might have his objections.'

A look of puzzlement crossed her face and she looked away. 'A mother with a babe? Not Gudrun, surely?'

'No.'

'Then who?'

'Couldn't say. I've not learned everyone's names yet. She met him when she came to draw water from the river. Lives down beyond the mill, near the tumbledown cottage.'

'Lady Cecily!' Gudrun stepped into view round the corner of the Hall, carrying baby Philip over her shoulder. Matty was trailing after with the other baby, Agatha, on her hip.

Philip. What an odd name for a Saxon housekeeper to choose. It was so very Norman. Adam glanced at Agatha. It was odd, too, how close in age the two babies were…almost as if… He shot a look at his bride-to-be. There was some mystery here, and Cecily was in on it, but…

Cold fingers whispered over the back of his neck. His bride was relieved at the interruption. Yes, something was afoot—but she was not about to take him into her confidence. He sensed no hatred in her—disquiet, yes, mistrust, possibly, but no hatred. Inwardly he smiled. His little novice's heart was too full of charity for hatred. And she disliked lying to him. And sometimes…sometimes…

Bustling over, Gudrun dropped a brief curtsey. 'Lady Cecily, we need you in the Hall.' Her homely face sobered. 'Shall we be using your mother's best linens on the trestle tonight? I…I wasn't sure if you'd think it right, in the circumstances.'

'I shall come at once,' Cecily said, lifting the baby from Gudrun. Lovingly, she stroked his cheek and began to sway to and fro, rocking him.

'And there's the matter of your gown too, dear,' Gudrun continued, a pleat between her brows. 'Which will you wear? That blue one is far too plain, and it's so big it drowns you.' The housekeeper glanced sidelong at Adam and took Cecily's arm. 'You must excuse us, sir, but I need Lady Cecily's help. Lady Philippa would not have wanted—' She flushed. 'I…I'm sorry, my lady, I know it's awkward, but your mother would have wanted to see you gowned as a princess on your wedding day, however unhappy the circumstances.' She flashed an inscrutable look at Adam. 'I need to measure her up, sir, so I can alter her sister's clothes.' Barely taking the time to draw breath, Gudrun tugged at Cecily's arm. 'Will you come? We can't manage without you.'

'I'll take my leave, sir,' Cecily said, hugging the baby to her, rocking, rocking.

Adam nodded a dismissal. 'Till three o'clock, my lady. By the church door.'

Attention fully on the babe, she murmured her assent and followed Gudrun back to the Hall.

Chapter Fourteen

Surrendering to Gudrun's urging, Cecily left Matty in the mead hall in charge of the babies, and accompanied the housekeeper to the loft room. A garnet-coloured gown in a rich damask was laid out on the bedcover, alongside a cream silk undergown with an alarmingly low neckline. Reaching out, she examined the texture of the fabric. Silk, and somehow incongruous against the work-roughened skin of her fingers.

'Oh, no, this is too fine for me.'

'Nonsense!'

Would Adam like the gown on her? she wondered. Was it vanity on her part to hope so? Well, perhaps she might wear it—for if she did manage to please his eyes, and if he did develop a fondness for her, then surely she would be in a better position to speak for the villagers?

Gudrun had also found a gauzy cream veil, a fabric headband that matched the gown, and a pair of black leather shoes—fresh from the cobbler's by the look of them.

Unable to resist the lure of new shoes, Cecily plumped herself down on the edge of the bed, yanked off her workaday boots and slipped them on. 'They fit! Oh, Gudrun, feel how soft the leather is.' These she would definitely wear.

Gudrun's smile was warm. 'Better than you've had in awhile, I'd say.'

'They're so beautiful I won't want to spoil them by walking outside.'

Gudrun took a bobbin out of her workbox and snipped off a length of thread. 'Get you out of that blue dress, my dear, and let's measure you for the garnet damask.'

'Gudrun, I…I'm not sure about the dress—'

'You have to wear something, dear, it might as well be the damask.'

And thus, in no time at all, Cecily was standing self-consciously in nothing but her shift and the new shoes while Gudrun clucked about, oblivious of her embarrassment, slipping the thread round her waist, knotting it to mark her measurement.

'You're as tiny as you were when you left us,' Gudrun said. 'I thought you would grow, but you still have the smallest waist in the family.'

Cecily smiled. 'Emma's taller than me, so she would be bigger.'

Gudrun held the thread out again. 'Now for your bosom…'

As Gudrun wound the thread round her again, Cecily's face grew warm.

Gudrun's eyes sparkled. 'No need to be shy with me, dear,' she said, briskly marking the size with another knot in the thread. 'Who washed your clothes when Cenwulf chased you into the pigsty? Who bathed you when you were little? Who…?' Gudrun gave her a sly look. 'Such modesty is fitting in a convent, no doubt, but in a married woman…' She clucked her tongue and shook her head. '*He* won't like it.'

Thoughtfully, Cecily submitted while Gudrun continued taking her measure…the width of her hips, the length of her arms from wrist to shoulder, the length of her from waist to floor… As each measurement was taken, another knot was added to the string.

'Let me see you in the silk shift,' Gudrun said, reaching into the sewing box for the pin pad. 'It laces at the back, which is a blessing as the seams will be easier to take in. The damask, unfortunately, laces at the side; it will be more tricky to alter that. I pray I can get it done for three o'clock.'

'Thank you for doing this, Gudrun. I appreciate it, but you mustn't worry if it's not finished.'

'It will be,' Gudrun said, as Cecily dragged the cream undergown over her head. 'Another day we can look to the other gowns. There's also some fabric in the linen closet, waiting to be made up. It would do for Sir Adam. There's enough stuff in there for his men too, if you're of a mind to follow your mother's tradition. As Sir Adam's wife, it will be your duty to see your husband and his men well clothed. Your mother gave every man in your father's household a new tunic, hose and braies at Yuletide.'

'Yes, Gudrun, I do remember.' Cecily bit her lip. She might not be the ablest of seamstresses, but she knew which housewifely duties would be expected of her. Today, however, it was the more physical aspects of marriage that concerned her. She wanted to know more about what happened between a husband and wife in the marriage bed, and Gudrun would seem the best person to ask. Gudrun had, as she had pointed out, known her since she was a child. She was a married woman herself, so…

The silk undergown was soft and warm, but the neckline—really, it was shamefully low. She pulled ineffectually at the bodice, trying to hide her exposed flesh.

'Don't do that, dear,' Gudrun said, batting her hands away. 'You spoil the fall of the skirt.'

'Gudrun?'

'Mmm?' Gudrun mumbled through a mouthful of pins. She dropped to her knees and began turning up the hem.

'A-about the marriage bed?'

Gudrun's hands worked swiftly as she pulled at the skirt of the undergown. Tuck, pin. Tuck, pin. Tuck, pin. 'Mmm?'

'Could…?' Cecily twisted her hands together. 'Could you please explain to me what happens, exactly?'

Gudrun rocked back on her heels and turned startled eyes up at her. Removing the pins from her mouth, she stuck them back in the pincushion. 'What happens, child? But surely you know?'

Cecily's face was burning. 'I know what…what animals do, of course. I've seen dogs and…and horses—but what about people? It can't be like that with people. Is it?'

Gudrun rose, took Cecily by the hand and sat down on the bed. 'I don't expect this was a subject ever touched upon by Mother Aethelflaeda?'

'No—not unless you count the time that Novice Ingrid joined us. There was much talk then of sin. Mother Aethelflaeda read out a passage from the Bible and interpreted it for us. She said that women gave birth in pain to pay for the sins they had committed when conceiving their children. She talked constantly about carnal love and the sins of the flesh.'

'You poor love—you are afraid,' Gudrun said gently.

'Afraid? No. I don't think Sir Adam would hurt me. At least… I…I hope not. But does…does it hurt, Gudrun?'

Gudrun patted her hand. 'With some women it does the first time, maybe even the first few times, but not always. Wilf didn't hurt me.' She sighed. 'Don't fret, dear. Sir Adam wants your marriage to succeed.'

'Does he? How can you know that? I'm just one of the means by which he legitimises his claim to my father's lands.'

Gudrun nodded. 'There is something in what you say, I'm sure. But that's not the full story. He likes you, dear. I've seen the way he is with you. Already you're more to him than that. And given time…'

'He was married before,' Cecily blurted out. 'I think he loved his wife.'

'Did he, dear? That's good.'

Cecily wrinkled her brow. 'How so?'

Gudrun's eyes danced. 'If he loved her, she'll have taught him how to pleasure a woman.'

Pleasure? The carnal pleasure that Mother Aethelflaeda insisted was a sin? It sounded interesting, but…

Cecily had opened her mouth to ask Gudrun for chapter and verse on the nature of this pleasure when someone knocked briefly on the door of the bedchamber. Before she had time to answer, the door opened and Edmund stepped swiftly into the room, cracking a crutch on the doorpost.

Flushing, Cecily snatched up the garnet damask and held it in front of her chest.

'Edmund, for shame!' Gudrun jumped to her feet, attempting to shield Cecily from him. 'You should *not* be in here!'

But Edmund had neither eyes nor ears for Gudrun. With a dexterity that was astonishing in a man on crutches, he sidestepped her and towered over Cecily. He was out of breath, doubtless owing to his exertions in climbing the loft ladder with a bad leg.

'Delay this wedding,' he said. His eyes were hard as flints, and there was a tightness about his lips and jaw.

Cecily resisted the urge to shrink into the bed. 'Delay? I cannot.'

'You must.' Moving closer, Edmund rested his weight on one crutch, reached down and dragged her to her feet. 'You *must*!'

'No, Edmund,' Cecily said, squaring her shoulders. 'It's not up to me. Ask Father Aelfric. Today's the last day for wedding before Advent begins. If we don't wed now, we'd have to wait until—'

'If you delay even a day you may not need to marry him,' Edmund said baldly.

Cecily skin crawled. 'What do you mean?'

'I've seen Judhael,' Edmund went on, his voice low. 'Steps are being taken. If you can wait but a day, maybe two…' he brought his nose to within an inch of hers '…you won't need to marry a Norman with Saxon blood on his hands.'

'Adam is *Breton*, and the marriage is fixed. I've told you before,

Edmund, you are fighting a lost cause.' Aware her voice had risen, Cecily moderated it and spoke rapidly. 'For heaven's sake, get a grip. I know you grieve for the past—we all do—but you must accept reality. Life has changed. I don't know what you're planning, but it can only lead to more deaths, more injuries. Think about the consequences for others before you do anything rash.'

Edmund's expression hardened, and he yanked the garnet damask out of Cecily's hands, revealing the low-cut silk undergown. He looked her up and down. 'You whore...'

'Edmund!' Gudrun said, tight-lipped. 'That's more than enough. I think you should leave.'

'I'm going, rest assured,' Edmund said. He tossed the gown back at Cecily and, swinging round on his crutches, lurched to the door. 'And when I've gone you may have cause to regret it. I repeat—marry Adam Wymark this afternoon and you will live to regret that you refused my advice.' Unexpectedly, his face softened. 'But, since you're Cenwulf's baby sister, I'll offer it one last time. Put this marriage off. Delay it, even for a day, and you won't regret it.'

'What are you going to do? Edmund...?'

But Cecily spoke to a closed door, for as swiftly as he had entered, Edmund was gone. His crutches tapped along the landing to the stairs, and she was disinclined to follow him into a public area in a cream undergown.

'Sir Adam?'

Adam tossed the axe with the broken handle onto the armoury bench and looked up. 'Maurice?'

'I thought you should know, sir, that housecarl, Edmund...'

'Yes?'

'He has just paid Lady Cecily a visit up in the loft room, and I do not think she was examining his leg.'

A sinking sensation made itself felt in Adam's stomach. 'Edmund had private counsel with her?'

The kiss Cecily had given Edmund on her arrival jumped into his brain. He tucked his thumbs in his belt and called it to mind in more detail. Cecily had leaned forwards, cutting Edmund's words off mid-sentence. It had been a brief kiss. He would wager it had startled the housecarl as much as it had irritated Adam. He sighed. It might not have been a lover's kiss, but it had roused other suspicions…

'No, sir, not precisely private. Gudrun was with her—I made out something about dress fittings, but my English…' Maurice gave a regretful shrug.

The gable end of the hall was visible through the armoury door. From this angle Adam could see the window slit that was high above the bed. The bed that tonight he was going to share with her. He chewed on his thumbnail. 'Hell—hell and damnation.'

Maurice drew back. 'My apologies, sir, but you did say you wanted to know if I noticed anything untoward.'

Adam clapped his squire on the shoulder. 'Yes, Maurice, you were right to tell me.' He stepped outside. 'I knew a confrontation between Lady Cecily and myself was inevitable. It was just that I had hoped it might keep until after our wedding.'

And why was that? a voice asked. *Surely you did not think you, Duke William's man, could win over the loyalty of a thane's daughter with your prowess between the sheets?* No, Adam thought bleakly, as he strode across the yard, that was *not* what he had thought. But he would have felt happier delaying the confrontation until after the bedding, because there was more chance she would come to him willingly if they were amicable. He did not want to force her. Dear God, all he had wanted was the chance to try and teach Cecily to find some pleasure in his body, so that their marriage might not be completely doomed. They had problems that might divide the most loving of couples, but her response when they kissed had led him to hope that in this one small area they might have a chance…

* * *

In the loft room, Gudrun was tutting and shaking her head. 'Don't pay Edmund any mind, dear. This marriage of yours may not be perfect, but we have to make the best of things.'

'I hoped Edmund would see that.'

'He'll come round. His bark was always worse than his bite. At the moment he grieves for his friends. He is guilty for being alive when so many have died.'

Staring at the closed door, Cecily bit her lip. 'I hope you are right.' She looked down at the gown in her hands. Edmund had crumpled it. He had seen Judhael! Was Emma well? So many questions and no chance to ask them. 'I wish I had your confidence, Gudrun. I fear he may do something rash.'

Gudrun took the garnet damask from her and shook it out with a snap. 'Not that one, dear.' Her voice became confidential. 'All bluster, he. Why, it's my belief he may have hurt his leg on purpose, so he wouldn't have to go and fight when the Normans landed.'

'No!' Cecily stared. 'Edmund was one of my father's most trusted housecarls! Besides, you said just now he feels guilty that he didn't fight…'

Gudrun pursed her lips. 'Well, perhaps you are in the right. Who knows?'

'It is worrying, though. It must have been a battle to get up those stairs with that leg. He wouldn't have done that purely for the sake of picking an argument.'

Gudrun shook her head and refused to be drawn further. She held up the garnet damask, and Cecily was reaching out to take it when the door swung open for the second time.

'*Really*, Edmund!' Cecily swung round, the gown clutched to her bosom, and almost bit off the tip of her tongue. Adam! It was Adam and not Edmund whose broad shoulders filled the doorway. His black brows were drawn together in a frown and his eyes were dark with suspicion. He knew! Adam knew Edmund had been up here to speak with her. Her mind whirled. Did he also know that Edmund was in contact with Judhael and the resistance? Did he suspect her too? She straightened her spine and vowed to guard her tongue; no one would suffer from anything she said.

'My lady.' Adam inclined his head, his gaze running over her from head to toe, taking in the cream undergown with its low neck, the garnet dress held in front of her like a shield, her sister's shoes.

Gudrun, whose jaw had dropped when she had seen who stood there, lurched into movement. 'Sir, you should not be in here! Sir?' With a flurry of skirts, Gudrun rushed at Adam, waving her hands at him as though he were a wayward hen she was shooing back into the henhouse. 'Please, sir, we have not finished,' she went on in shocked tones, in English. 'It is not fitting that you should see her until she is clothed. Go, please.'

Fearful for her, Cecily held her breath. Though Adam probably could not understand every word, Gudrun's meaning was clear as crystal. Surely he would strike her? No man, least of all a Frankish knight, liked to be ordered from his bedchamber by a Saxon wet nurse.

He paused, one foot over the threshold, and she could swear his lips twitched. Laughter? He was laughing?

She caught Gudrun's arm, whispering, 'Gudrun, take care.'

Ignoring Gudrun, Adam came to stand in front of Cecily. No, he was not smiling. His mouth was stern, his eyes cool. 'Please to tell your woman that I would have private speech with you.'

'Gudrun, if you wouldn't mind leaving us? I will call you when we have finished.'

'No, dear, it's most improper.'

'A brave woman,' Adam murmured, his eyes not moving from Cecily's, 'but misguided. Please to tell her that if she doesn't leave on her own two legs I shall toss her out myself.'

His tall, conqueror's body surely had to have been made by some demon, since its shape so pleased her eyes yet at the same

time it frightened her. *He* frightened her, with his calm, quiet as-
surance. He was unlike any man she had ever met. The moment
he had opened the door she had recognised anger in him, but it was
not like the hot, loud, uncontrollable anger that occasionally had
taken over her father. This was, in its way, far more alarming. This
was controlled power, and he was very much in command of it.
Adam shifted slightly, as though to emphasise that his threat to
throw Gudrun out was in earnest.

'Gudrun, *please*!'

Gudrun threw a scowl at them and stomped from the room, muttering under her breath.

He was blocking out the light from the wall windows. A silhouette. A strong, slender young man. A warrior. Cecily crushed
the damask to her breast and wondered if he could hear the
pounding of her heart.

'Is it customary in these parts for Saxon ladies to entertain
housecarls in their chamber while dressing for their wedding?'

'I…I… No.' She put some strength in her voice. 'Of course not.'

Adam smiled. It was not one of his more pleasant smiles. 'I
thought not. So, if you please, my lady, would you mind telling
me what you were talking about?'

So quiet his voice. So calm his tone. She drew in a shaky
breath. *Do not let anyone suffer from what you say to him.* 'I…
We… That is…he…'

'My lady…?'

At a loss, she stared up at him. 'He…he does not wish me to
marry you.' There—she had given him the truth, and it was a truth
that could hurt no one.

'And that is all?'

She stared up at him, but with most of the light behind him, his
expression was hidden. 'Sir?'

'No meetings arranged with what is left of the Saxon nobility?
No plans to oust me from Fulford? No plans to kill me, perhaps?'

Thankful that Edmund had not let her in on any of his schemes, again she could give him the truth. 'To kill you? Not that I know of, sir.'

He stared at her for a long moment. 'Would you tell me if you knew, Cecily? That is what I find myself wondering.' Sighing, he turned his back on her, and his voice became little more than a whisper. 'I find myself wishing I could trust you.'

Something in her tightened, and when after another pause she realised he was gazing down at the matting, tearing at one of his fingernails with his teeth, the tightness turned into pain. He was hurting, and she could feel it. He *did* want to trust her. But surely the great Breton warrior could not be hurting because of her? It could not be… And yet…?

She stared at his back, took a deep breath, and moved to his side. 'Adam?' Greatly daring, her pulse racing at her temerity, she reached up and gently took his hand away from his mouth. 'That is not an attractive habit, sir.'

His fingers tightened on hers. His lips came up at one corner and his gaze softened. 'You think not? Then, since you are to be my bride, I will do my best to break it.' He opened his mouth to say more, but someone rattled the door.

'Gudrun,' Cecily said.

'Is that woman afraid of nothing?'

Cecily laughed. 'I don't think so, sir.'

'She has your interests at heart. She is a woman in a million.' Lifting her hand briefly to his lips, he released her. Somewhat bemusedly, Cecily watched him wave Gudrun in and bow himself out.

'He did not bully you, did he, dear?' Gudrun asked when they were once again alone. For the second time, she took the dress from Cecily and shook out the creases.

'N-no, not at all.'

'That's good. Hurry, dear, slip this on.'

Deep in thought, Cecily stood like a statue while Gudrun pulled the dress over her head and chatted and fussed and cajoled. Ought she to warn Adam if she learned of plans to kill him? Certainly she had no wish for his death. But if it came down to a choice between saving Adam's life or the life of one of her father's people she did not know how she would choose. Dear Lord, do not let it come to that, she prayed.

Gudrun adjusted the seams and hem of the garnet gown and, preoccupied though she was, Cecily managed to find words to admire the cream silk that lined the sleeves; she praised her mother's embroidery on the hem and neckline…

'Yes, Gudrun. No one could best Mother at gold and silver threadwork…Yes, Gudrun, the veil is very fine…Yes, Gudrun, it *is* clever the way the leaves and flowers on the circlet match the leaves and flowers in the weave of the gown…'

And while the surface of her mind was busy with Gudrun, another, deeper part of her was wondering what Edmund had been alluding to when he had said he had spoken to Judhael. *Should* she warn Adam? Or would a warning only make things worse? Was Gudrun right when she maintained that Edmund was all bluster?

Gudrun moved about her: pulling, lacing, checking the fabric was falling just so. And slowly the light from the windows moved across the matting. One thing was certain. At three o' clock, as the winter sun began to fade, she was going to be joined with Adam Wymark in Holy Matrimony. A day she had thought she would never see. Her wedding day.

This garnet gown—the gown her mother had embroidered for her sister—would help to conjure their presence, so she would not be standing alone when she made her vows. A small comfort, perhaps, but one she cherished.

As was the custom in England, the wedding was to be held just outside the wooden church. Word had spread among the villagers, and by the time Adam arrived with Richard and his men a number of Saxons had already gathered to witness it.

The doorposts of Fulford church were garlanded. Ivy, juniper and holly, twisted together with cream satin ribbon. Someone had made a rough arch out of lengths of hazel, and more of the cream ribbon was twined around it, holding the evergreens in place. Done in *her* honour, not his, but he was glad to see it.

The villagers fell silent at his approach. Adam ran his hand through his hair—shorn by Maurice in honour of the occasion—and straightened his dark blue tunic. For the tenth time he checked his cross-gartering. To Richard's disgust, he had again dispensed with his sword.

At his elbow, Richard gave a soft chuckle. 'Anyone would think you've not done this before.'

'I'm not nervous!'

'Of course not. You're hopping from foot to foot like a cat on hot coals just for the exercise.'

Adam scowled and glanced towards the Hall. He had not spoken to Cecily since Gudrun had interrupted them, and he wished they had managed to exchange a few more words in private. He had glimpsed her in the Hall later, but she'd been so wrapped up in ordering the wedding supper and in Gudrun's young son that he'd not won so much as a glance.

'She's late,' he said, rolling his shoulders as her father's remaining housecarl appeared in the Hall entrance. Relying heavily on his crutches, Edmund swung across the green towards them, his face rigid with hostility.

Adam's scowl deepened. 'That man bears watching,' he murmured, for Richard's ears alone, though he doubted that any of the Saxons would understand him. He did not catch Richard's response, for at that moment there was a fluttering in the hall, a soft giggle—Matty—and then there *she* was, framed by the doorway.

Cecily.

His heart pounded. She'd been pretty in a novice's habit, more than pretty in her sister's blue dress, but now—wearing that garnet-coloured gown... It fitted—it actually fitted her like a second skin—and she was a princess. Her golden hair hung in two loose braids over her breasts, and a light veil fluttered behind her as she walked across the grass. A princess.

Matty and Gudrun were at her train, wreathed in smiles: Gudrun was holding her firstborn and Matty was carrying the sleeping baby. Thank God for those smiles, Adam thought, for they prove that not every Saxon in Fulford is set against this marriage.

The garnet gown had been laced to accentuate Cecily's slim waist and the curve of her bosom. That bright fall of hair reached beyond her knees. She was the very image of feminine beauty, delicate, soft. Was she really to be his? Adam's mouth went dry. His Gwenn had been darkly pretty, and he had loved her deeply, but her beauty had never filled him with this desperate, almost frantic longing.

Gwenn had always been his sweetheart—they had loved each other for ever, and he had not been afraid to touch her—but Cecily's fragile beauty, her innocence, her Saxon upbringing—how could he hope to win her heart?

As she came along the gravel path towards him their eyes met. She smiled—a nervous smile, as though uncertain of her reception. Aware that he was gawping like a moonstruck boy, Adam swallowed and held out his hand.

'Lose that frown, man,' Richard muttered. 'It would curdle milk.'

Adam smiled.

And then she was at his side, her fingers warm in his. She peeped up at him from under her lashes and her face lost that nervous look. Rosemary—he caught the scent of rosemary. She was carrying a posy. Rosemary and bay and dried lavender, tied with the same cream ribbon that adorned the wedding arch.

'Sir Adam,' she said, curtseying low before him.

That wayward blonde curl had worked its way loose. His smile deepening, he raised her and kissed the back of her hand. 'Lady Cecily.'

He nodded at Richard, who rapped on the church door with the hilt of his sword.

Father Aelfric stepped out, gold thread glinting on his vestments. 'You are ready, my children?' he asked.

Adam looked at Cecily, and drew comfort and support from the acceptance he read in her eyes. He nodded at Father Aelfric, and as one they stepped under the wedding arch. 'We are. You may proceed.'

Chapter Fifteen

'Gudrun, go away!' Cecily said later that night, as she laughingly tried to evade the housekeeper's hands. 'And you too, Matty. I don't need either of you!'

The three women were in the loft room. Braziers glowed softly through the dark and candles flickered on the nightstands. On one of the coffers a tray had been set, with a jug of mulled wine, two clay goblets, and a plate of almond cakes. The wine steamed gently, filling the room with the exotic scent of imported spices—cinnamon and cloves from the east.

The rhythmic throb of music filled the Hall below, where Harold and Carl were entertaining the company with drums, accompanied at one moment by Wat on his flute and at another by Sir Richard on his lute. As mead jars and wine flasks had emptied, the boys' drumrolls had become wilder. Laughter had become more general, and a couple of times Cecily had seen some of Adam's troopers making efforts to converse with one or other of the villagers without being rebuffed. Peace might not be quite the mad dream that Edmund thought it.

Deciding it was high time she retired, Cecily had excused herself from her husband's side, and had run the gauntlet of so many meaningful winks and sly remarks that her ears had burned. Everyone had seemed determined to embarrass her, villagers and troopers alike.

Now she glared at her two bridesmaids. They were as intent on disrobing her as she was intent on remaining robed. 'Go *away!*' Didn't they understand? Circumstances might have forced her to marry someone who was practically a stranger, but she could not, would not, greet Adam Wymark unclothed—even if it was their wedding night.

As a particularly extravagant drumroll and a shout of laughter reverberated round the mead hall, she nipped behind one of the braziers. 'I'm perfectly capable of undressing myself!' The warmth of the brazier touched her face and neck, and her veil fluttered dangerously close to the glowing embers. She twitched it aside. 'I would like some privacy. Go *away!*'

Deaf to her pleas, Gudrun grinned at Matty. 'You go left, and I'll go right.'

Cecily made a dash for the gap between brazier and bed, but Matty second-guessed her and crashed into her. In the tussle, they both toppled onto the bed.

'Got you!' Matty's breath was honeyed with mead. 'Got you!'

Torn between dismay and laughter, Cecily tried to wriggle free, but by then Gudrun was upon them, and in a trice the three of them were rolling around the bed, crushing dried rose petals into the bedcover. Rose petals? Where had they found rose petals at this time of year? And when had they had time to strew the bedcover with them?

'Get off, Gudrun, for pity's sake,' Cecily got out with a choked laugh. 'It's like having a sack of flour on top of me.'

An unholy light flashed into Gudrun's eyes, and Cecily saw that she was about to be on the receiving end of another lewd comment when the door swung open. Candles guttered and the noise from the Hall seemed to rise.

Adam. He had paused, hand on the door-latch, surveying the three of them with a crooked smile. A dark eyebrow lifted and his smile widened.

Cecily shot into an upright position, fumbling to straighten her veil. Matty and Gudrun jumped off the bed, hastily plumping the pillows, smoothing the covers.

'Sir Adam?' Cecily said, with as much dignity as could be expected from a noble lady caught romping on the bed with her maid and the family housekeeper.

He closed the door, muting the sounds of the revels, and came towards her. 'I thought you were tired.'

'Tired? Oh…y-yes. I was just g-getting ready…'

Matty giggled, Gudrun made a choking sound, and Cecily wished with all her heart that she had insisted on Gudrun explaining the intimate duties of a new bride.

Her mouth was dry. There Adam stood—tall and achingly handsome, with his dark hair gleaming in the candlelight and a smile in those green eyes. If she was to secure her place as his wife and stay near her brother she must ensure that the marriage was consummated. If it was not consummated, she could be set aside. She swallowed. It would help if she knew a little more about the physical aspects of marriage…

Adam tucked his thumbs into his belt, feeling as out of place in his bedroom as it was possible for a man to be on his wedding day. Her face had been alight with laughter, but the moment he'd come into the room the laughter had vanished. And there she was, blinking up at him like an owl from the bed. From *their* bed. Her hands were shaking. Her wedding ring glinted in the candlelight with every tremor.

He smiled pointedly at Matty and Gudrun. 'My thanks,' he said firmly. 'We can manage on our own.'

'But, sir,' Gudrun said, 'we're her bridesmaids. We should disrobe—'

'You have been fine bridesmaids.' Dipping into his pouch, Adam handed them each a silver penny. 'Our thanks to you both.' He sent Gudrun another direct look and searched for the right English words. 'Your babe—Philip—is crying.'

Gudrun opened her mouth to reply, but Matty caught her by the sleeve and gave a swift headshake. She towed Gudrun to the door.

Watching them go, Adam tipped his head to one side and said softly, 'Odd, don't you think, the way she has given that baby a Norman name?'

Cecily scrambled off the bed in a flurry of activity, shaking out the skirts of her gown and yanking at the bedcover. Rose petals fluttered to the floor. Adam narrowed his eyes, wondering whether his question had discomposed her, but then he noticed the rose petals and thought he understood the reason for her sudden burst of activity. He moved towards the bed. He might have his suspicions about young Philip—about her, indeed—but there was no place for them in this room, not tonight. She was innocent, and she deserved a bridegroom who would take care with her.

'Cecily?' Her veil quivered. There were two bright spots of colour on her cheeks. Make light of this, he told himself. She's as nervous as you are. He smiled. 'You look like a child who has been caught stealing sweetmeats.'

'D-do I?'

He caught her hand, tried to pull her close, but she hung back and would not meet his gaze. 'Cecily? Look at me.'

Slowly she raised her head. 'Sir?'

Her eyes were as wide as a doe's. Afraid—yes, she was definitely afraid. Laughing with her bridesmaids had been but a mask. 'I realise we have not known each other long,' he said. 'The marriage need not be consummated tonight.'

Against his instincts, ignoring a most unnerving wave of disappointment, he managed to release her and sat down on the edge of the mattress. Nudging aside the rosemary and lavender posy, he tugged off his boots and tossed them into a corner. In the Hall, someone screeched with laughter, the drums pounded. He had started on his belt when a small hand touched his shoulder.

'But, Adam…' the quiet voice was puzzled '…if we do not complete our marriage with full—physical—union, it will not be a real one. It could be annulled.'

'That is true.'

'Then you…we…we must.'

Her gaze was so earnest that he could not doubt her seriousness. Dropping his belt, he stood up. Even without his boots she only came up to his chest. Little Cecily, his Saxon bride.

'If it is important to you that we consummate this marriage, then we shall,' he said, hoping that the only sign of the surge of excitement her words had given him was a slight huskiness in his tone.

'Yes,' she said steadily. 'It is important. This *must* be a true marriage. Only…'

He found himself staring at her mouth, wondering if it tasted as sweet as he remembered. 'Only…?'

Dark colour swept into her cheeks and her gaze slid past him. 'I…I don't know what to do.'

'Not part of the convent catechism, eh?'

She gave a shaky laugh. 'N-no.'

He reached for her wrist and this time she did not pull away. Raising it, he kissed the finger with his ring on it. 'Let me tell you a secret, Cecily,' he murmured.

'Yes?'

'I'm nervous too.'

Her eyes widened. 'You? But you've been married!'

He lifted his shoulders and ran a hand through his hair. 'Nevertheless, I am.'

'I don't understand.'

Adam had to agree. He didn't understand it either. He didn't love her—how could he after so short a time?—but he had not lied. He *was* nervous.

'Gwenn and I—' He stopped. Perhaps it was not quite tactful to mention one's first wife when one was about to bed one's second.

But her face was turned expectantly towards his. 'Gwenn and you…?'

'I…we…we grew up together, and fell in love as naturally as breathing. With Gwenn the act was…' He hesitated, at a loss to explain his relationship with Gwenn to this innocent who had spent the latter part of her life stuck behind the walls of a convent.

Her large eyes were wistful. 'You loved her,' she said. 'Were you nervous with Gwenn?'

He shook his head. 'She was my first. We learned together.' He gave a wry smile. 'I could never be nervous with Gwenn.'

She shifted closer and laid a tentative, work-worn hand on his chest. 'You were confident she loved you. You knew you wouldn't lose her love, that she'd never hate you.'

'Y-yes.' Nonplussed, and more than a little disturbed, Adam drew back and turned to the wine on the coffer. For a moment he stared blankly at the twist of steam rising from the jug. Cecily had hit the nail on the head. He *had* been confident of Gwenn's love. Whereas now… But, no, if followed to its natural, logical conclusion, her reasoning implied that his present nervousness was due to concern that she, Cecily, should not dislike him. Which was, he thought dismissively, ridiculous. He filled a goblet and passed it to her, the fragrance of the spiced wine rising to his nostrils.

Ridiculous. For him this was a marriage of convenience. He had only admitted to being nervous to set her at ease. Yes, he was strongly attracted to her, but his emotions were *not* involved. Nor did he wish them to be, for emotions were apt to cloud a man's judgement. The only good thing to come out of Gwenn's death was that he had learnt to keep his emotions in hand.

'I won't hate you, Adam.' Goblet in hand, she stood before him, slender and straight, a beautiful Saxon princess in a garnet-coloured damask gown. *His* princess. She raised the goblet to her lips, sipped and offered it to him. 'Truly I won't.'

'I'm glad of that,' he whispered, 'because I'm woefully out of practice.' Setting the goblet aside, he reached for her, positioning her so the warmth of her body was where he wanted it, next to his. Gently, he removed her circlet and veil. 'Gwenn died two years since.'

Her eyes became even larger. Down in the Hall, the drums speeded up.

'Yes, there's only ever been Gwenn. My first and my last.'

'Your last? You mean you only ever…? I mean you… only…only with Gwenn?'

Nodding, he ran his hand down one shining golden braid. That wayward curl—the one that was always escaping—twined round his finger and he felt his loins begin to throb. 'Aye, only ever with Gwenn. Until now.' He bent his attention to unfastening the ribbon on a plait and hoped she wouldn't see the trembling in *his* fingers.

Reaching on her tiptoes, she planted a light kiss on his cheek. 'Thank you for telling me,' she whispered.

Adam grunted and fumbled with the ribbon. She smelt of desire, warm and womanly. She smelt of all he had thought he had lost. He felt a pang in the region of his chest. He thrust it aside. 'What's the English word for this?'

'Ribbon.' Her voice sounded almost affectionate. He felt another distinct pang and frowned. No more wine for him tonight.

'Ribbon,' he repeated, as the ribbon fell away and the thick tress of hair unravelled. Adam began working on her other braid. More glorious hair unravelled; unbound, it almost reached her knees. He wove his fingers into the golden strands. It was soft, and held the fragrance of summer flowers and herbs. It made his head swim.

'The candlelight makes your hair gleam like gold—gold silk.' He had to clear his throat. 'I saw your hair before.'

'Did you?' She was watching him almost tenderly.

'Aye.' He lowered his head and nuzzled her ear through her hair. Surreptitiously he inhaled. Rosemary, and underneath it that particular fragrance that he was beginning to recognise as her own. It was far more intoxicating than the spiced wine they had been drinking. 'I saw it, when you helped that woman in labour. I thought you pretty,' he added with a lop-sided grin. 'Too pretty by far to be a nun.'

'And now I'm your wife,' she said, impulsively catching his hand and bringing it to her cheek. 'But how I wish…I wonder…'

'Mmm?'

She shrugged. 'It is foolish, perhaps, but I wonder how it would have been if we had met otherwise. If you had not come with Duke William. If my parents were still living. If…'

He frowned. 'We cannot change what's done. If I had not accompanied Duke William I would never have come to Fulford, and you would still be in the convent.'

She heaved a sigh, her expression so woebegone that Adam heard himself say, 'We could pretend, though, while we are here in our private room. In our bed. We can make believe matters are otherwise.' He recaptured her wrist. 'Come here, wife.'

'I am here. Where else would I go?'

Where, indeed? There was nowhere he wanted her to be save here. She would have been wasted in the convent—wasted. Adam tilted her chin up and pressed his lips to hers, tasting the spicy sweetness of the mulled wine on her tongue. His heartbeat caught up with the pace of the drums, and he felt her body soften in a surrender that was more welcome than he had dared hope for. She reached up, found his shoulders and clung, and when his hands circled her waist she slid hers round his neck.

'Adam,' she murmured. 'My husband.'

Amazement in her tone. And acceptance? Not yet—but one day, God willing. Planting a series of kisses across her cheek, he nipped gently at her ear. She was such an innocent. An innocent who nipped his neck. But an innocent who heated his blood and was wreaking such havoc with his senses that he almost forgot that very innocence and brought his hips more snugly against her. Her breathing changed. Her cheeks were pink.

'Cecily?'

'Mmm?'

'Your lacings? May I?'

Her shy nod gave him permission, and then his fingers were at the ties on one side of her gown, teasing the garnet fabric open. Underneath the heavy damask her shift was light and silky to the touch, her body warm. He must touch her skin. He must…

Finding the lacings on the other side, he loosened them, and tugged impatiently at the material. Had he felt this desperate with Gwenn? Had he felt this needy? It had been too long. He was like a starving man. 'Lift up your arms.'

Silently, silhouetted in the light of the braziers, cheeks dark with colour, she obeyed him.

The damask whispered and then she was free of it, standing before him like a white lily in a cream undergown with an eye-catching neckline. A white lily who was biting her pretty lips…

He smiled, fighting a losing battle to keep his clasp light as he took her wrist and led her to the bed. Flipping back the covers, he sank down on the mattress, drawing her with him.

'Adam, m-my shoes.'

It was the work of a moment to tug them off and toss them into the corner along with his boots.

'I see I have married a tidy man,' she said with a smile.

'Maurice despairs.' Taking her shoulders, he leaned back into the pillows and she fell onto him, her hair, her glorious hair, flowing over his chest.

'C-can we keep some of our clothes on?'

An objection rose to his lips, but he bit it back because she looked so adorably unsure of herself, gut-wrenchingly innocent—

and anyway she was so near him that all he had to do was wind his hand into her hair and bring her head down to his. He did so, and enjoyed a long, long kiss that he never wanted to end. When it did end, he knew he was as flushed as she.

'Gudrun said I had to be naked,' she said, swallowing hard. 'B-but…oh, Adam, I…I can't.'

He stroked her cheek and looped a length of hair round her ear. 'You're shy…'

'I…I'm sorry. Can we do it if I keep my shift on?'

'Aye, but, sweetheart, I told you—if you're not ready, we can wait. The last thing I want is your unwilling body.'

'No, no—I'm not unwilling,' she said, and small fingers skimmed over his mouth. 'Don't think that. It's just that…'

'The convent?'

'Yes. Lying as we did in the Palace at Winchester, lying as we are now, it seems so…so…intimate. Mother Aethelflaeda…'

'Is not here. And I will not allow that woman into our bedchamber. So, please, Cecily, leave her back at the convent.'

'I'll try.'

'Good.' Running his hand down her back and over her buttocks, he pulled up the hem of her shift and found her stockings. He ached to know her skin, every warm, seductive inch of it, could only think about losing himself in her body, but somehow he kept his voice cool. 'What are these in English?'

'Stockings.'

'Stockings,' he repeated. 'They're next. Of course you can keep some of your clothes on, but these will get in the way.'

'Th-they will?'

'They will.' He slid his hand up her leg and dealt with the fastenings. Ignoring the gasp of breath as his fingers trailed over her stomach, he drew off her stockings. One. Two. 'Me next,' he said, clearing his throat. Taking her hand, he set it against the cross-gartering at his calves. Her lightest touch was a torment. Already

he was hard and ready for her. Praying the eagerness of his body
would not repel her, he swallowed and asked, 'And the English
word for this?'

'Cross-gartering.'

'Cross-gartering,' he said, trying out the words. 'Cecily?'

'Mmm?'

'We don't need cross-gartering either.'

'Oh.' She moved to unwind his leg-bindings, and as she did so
her breasts shifted to peep out of the low-cut shift. Adam groaned,
and leaned forwards to press a swift kiss on the scented warmth
of her breast. She made a small sound, part-gasp, part-sigh. Her
fingers stumbled over his bindings, then resumed.

'That's it, Princess.'

'Princess?'

Adam's cheeks burned. 'That's what you look like out of your
convent habit—a princess, a Saxon princess.' Taking his leg-
bindings from her, he dropped them onto the floor, and reached
for her hips. '*My* princess.'

He kissed her nose and her mouth and her body melted into
his. Pressing closer, he let her feel the desire his body felt for
hers. She moaned. Innocent, yes, but not cold. A maid, but not
an ice maiden.

Taking one small hand, he pushed it under his tunic to the ties
of his hose. 'Help me. We definitely don't need my hose or my
braies.' Her cheeks went scarlet, but she tugged at the ties of his
hose and pushed the fabric of both garments down.

Adam sat up and made a point of lifting the hem of his tunic.

'W-we don't need that?'

'No. Too hot,' he said. 'It is a furnace in here.' He held up his arms,
and after a brief pause she hauled his tunic up and over his head.

She drew back, eyeing his shirt. It was now his only remaining
garment, as the shift was hers. Wrapping her arms across her chest,
she frowned at him. 'Adam, you agreed we'd keep some clothes…'

With a grin, Adam turned away long enough to blow out the candle on the bedside coffer. 'Blow out your candle, if you please.'

Still frowning, she pinched out her candle, and became at once a shadowy figure, vaguely outlined by the soft glow of the braziers. Her hair gleamed pale gold through the dark.

Adam swallowed down a lump, and guided her hands to his shirt. 'Cecily, we really don't need this…'

Her breath came out in a shuddering sigh, and there was another pause during which Adam could hear the drums below, could feel the blood pounding in his veins. His manhood ached.

She tugged off his shirt.

'And now you,' he whispered. 'Let the darkness clothe you, Princess.'

Moving closer, he brought his head to hers, raining kisses on her forehead, her cheeks, her mouth, quickly, quickly, hoping that in her innocence she would be distracted and not notice how his hands were running down over her hips, nor how they were tugging at the silk undergown, lifting…

'There,' he said, a note of triumph in his voice, as finally the silk undergown joined his tunic and shirt on the rush matting. 'That didn't hurt, did it?'

'N-no. But, Adam!' She gave a shaky laugh. 'You promised!'

He silenced her with a kiss, and brought his naked body to hers. As flesh met flesh, both of them gasped. Trembling in his eagerness, Adam eased her onto her back. 'Oh, Cecily, the feel of you— so soft, so…'

In the glow of the braziers Adam could see more of her than she most likely realised. Her skin was creamy, her breasts high and firm. Her eyes looked dark, dazed. She was the most beautiful creature in the world. Burying his face in her neck, he let his hand drift down over her breast. Immediately her nipple peaked under his fingers.

'Adam!'

Her voice contained shock, but no displeasure. And that nipple was a temptation he could not resist. Smiling, he kissed a path down her shoulder and over her breast, so that he could take it deep into his mouth.

'*Adam!*' Her hands were in his hair, stroking, caressing, holding him to her. She *liked* it. She liked it… One small hand was sliding under his armpit, tugging him back up, urging his mouth back to her.

'Adam…'

Her mouth opened under his and she continued to move restively under him. Her scent filled his nostrils, more intoxicating than any wine, and her hands slid down his sides. When she pressed him to her, and thrust her hips instinctively at him, Adam heard himself moan. 'Sweetheart, yes…'

'Show me, Adam. Show me what to do.' Her hand was inching round to his front, but it was too much, too soon. He felt ready to burst. If he was not careful it would be over in seconds. Catching her hand, he eased away and set it back on his waist.

'Adam?'

'Not yet, love,' he muttered, quivering with tension. 'You will spoil it.'

'Adam?' Her breath caught and she turned her head away, her voice small. 'You don't like me touching you?'

Gently he brought her head round and kissed her. 'No—on the contrary, I like it too much. You…you excite me.'

In the dim light of the braziers her eyes went wide. 'I do?'

Clearing his throat, he gave a shaky laugh. 'Too much, I fear. You unman me, Cecily.'

'I…I don't understand.'

'Here.' He kissed her cheek and her collarbone. 'This first time, let us start with me pleasuring you.'

There were questions in her eyes, but he settled his lips at her breast and ran his fingers over the silky skin at her sides and down her thighs. They parted at his lightest touch, and when his fingers found her secret woman's place she made a sound that was part-gasp, part-moan.

'That's… Oh! Adam, that's… Yes, *that*. Adam, don't stop, please…'

She was making tiny incoherent sounds—sounds that made him think he could wait no longer. Gritting his teeth, fighting his own instincts—instincts that were prompting him to roll onto her and push himself deep, deep inside—Adam kissed, he stroked, he teased, he caressed. He kept reminding himself that his bride was innocent, that she was a virgin, but it was hard for him to remember because she was panting, her breath coming in short gasps, and all the while she clung to him.

'Adam—Adam, *please*.'

His innocent wife's nails were gouging holes in his arm and shoulder, and then it happened. Her breath stopped and her whole body went tight as a bow. Under his fingers the warm flesh throbbed.

She let out a sigh and her body went slack. 'Adam, wh…what was *that*?'

'Pleasure, I hope.'

Another soft sigh. 'Pleasure indeed.' She gave his shoulder a gentle bite and licked it.

He groaned, utterly lost. The musky scent of her arousal filled his consciousness. In all the world there was only Cecily and himself. When her hands started to explore his body again, Adam could wait no longer. 'Now?'

'Mmm…*yes*!'

He moved over her, positioning himself carefully, with his weight on his elbows. She writhed. 'Stop, Princess, stop. When you do that—' Gritting his teeth, Adam rested his forehead against hers. 'It is too much. You must hold still—please hold still. I am trying not to hurt you.'

She smiled at him through the dusky light, and as he readied to push she pressed a series of kisses to his mouth, took hold of his hips.

'Careful, love. Steady, or you'll—'

Another smile, and she pulled him to her. *Inside.* He was inside. It felt like coming home. He moved once, twice, before he remembered: innocent, she was innocent. Somehow he froze and managed to lift his head. 'You moved. I hurt you.'

'Only for a moment.' Under him her hips were busy, pressing towards him, moving away, finding her natural rhythm. 'Can we move again? Together?'

Innocent no more. His convent bride. Heart thudding, Adam buried his head in her neck and rocked his body back and forth. Someone moaned—*both* of them moaned. 'No pain?'

'No pain. I think—if you move again—there might be *more* pleasure.'

Heart singing, he kept moving. Back, forth, back, forth, the rhythm already perfect. 'That…pleases?'

'Don't…stop.'

Her breath was coming fast. His matched it. The tension was building. It was building too fast. But it had been a long time for him, and she was…she was not helping him slow down. She was covering his face in kisses, nipping at his ear, moaning. His innocent bride. He could not last very long at this rate. One more push, perhaps two, maybe three…

Beneath him, Cecily went rigid. Her insides gripped him. *'Adam!'*

A heartbeat later her name was torn from him in a rush of joy.

By mid-morning the following day Cecily was in the cookhouse, breaking her fast with a thick wedge of Lufu's latest batch of wholewheat bread. She was sinfully late rising—again.

Still glowing as a result of the carnal love she had discovered with Adam during the previous night, she smeared a wedge of bread with honey and sat on a three-legged stool to warm her toes by the central cooking fire. Who would have thought one of William's knights could be so gentle? He'd made it beautiful for her. Carnal love. The love that Mother Aethelflaeda had railed against. With Adam it was… She sighed, aware that the colour in her cheeks owed as much to the memory of her wedding night as it did to Lufu's cooking fire. Even with so much horror between them Adam had made it beautiful. Recalling how he'd overcome her reluctance and had winkled them out of their clothes, down to the last stitch, she hid a smile behind her bread.

'My lady?'

'Oh! Sorry, Lufu, what did you say?' Really, she must try to give more than half an ear to the girl.

'I was talking about Brian, my lady. He's a miracle-worker. Not bad—for a foreigner…'

The cookhouse was indeed improved beyond recognition. Logs and kindling were stacked high to one side, ready for use. Well-scoured pots and pans hung in neat array on the walls; the work-benches and tables had been scalded; months of dirt had been scrubbed away; the floor was clean.

'I'm glad he was helpful.'

'Aye. He had those useless miller's boys jumping about and no mistake.'

'Where are they this morning?'

'Gone to see to the slaughtering. Brian said it was long overdue.'

Cecily stared. Brian was in the right. The slaughtering *was* long overdue—it was not for nothing that November was known as the month of blood. She had observed as much to Adam upon their arrival back at Fulford. 'Evidently there really is more to Brian than soldiering,' she murmured, recalling something Adam had said.

The rumble of cartwheels sounded on the track outside. Bread in hand, Cecily left the fire to look through the cookhouse door. A moth-eaten mule was drawing a heavily laden cart towards the mead hall, its hooves cutting through the last shreds of mist which clung to the ruts in the road.

Lufu joined her in the doorway, wiping her hands on a cloth.

Saucepans and ladles hung from the sides of the cart, clanging as the cart swayed and rattled over the bumps. 'Tinkers?' Lufu clucked her tongue. 'That poor mule could do with a good feed—just look at its ribs.'

But Cecily only had eyes for the man and the woman hunched into their cloaks on the cart. 'Not tinkers, Lufu. It's Evie and Leofwine!'

'Evie?'

'Judhael's sister, from Winchester.' Dropping her half-eaten bread on the workbench, Cecily hurried out. The cart was filled to breaking point—bedding, a travelling chest, a couple of trestles and a tabletop, stools, several bundles. Whatever could be wrong? It looked as though Evie and Leofwine had brought their entire house with them apart from the four walls. She reached them as they drew up in front of the Hall.

Evie had been crying; her eyelids were puffy and swollen. One hand was clinging to the side of the cart, the other was folded over her belly, as though protecting her unborn child. Her cheeks were pale as parchment, her lips had a blue tinge to them, and she was shuddering with cold.

In his beard, Leofwine's mouth was one grim, taut line. He nodded curtly in her direction. 'Lady Cecily.'

'Evie, Leofwine—be welcome,' Cecily said, damping down her curiosity.

Evie looked mournfully across and let out a little sob as Leofwine swung down from the cart and came to stand directly in front of Cecily. 'Are we welcome, Lady Cecily? Are we?'

'But of course. Why would you not be?'

Evie sniffed and two large tears rolled down her cheeks. 'I told you, Leo. I told you she'd see us right.' She swayed in her seat, her pallor alarming.

'Come inside, both of you,' Cecily said. 'Wilf will see to the mule. Wilf? *Wilf!*'

Chapter Sixteen

It did not take long to get Evie and her husband settled before the fire. Gudrun brought Leofwine a mug of ale. 'I'd offer you the same, Evie,' Cecily said, 'but by your colour I think you'd best take this.' Moving to the hearth, she put a spoonful of herbs in a twist of muslin, dropped the muslin into an earthenware mug and poured boiling water over it from the kettle.

'There you are,' she said, passing the steaming mug to Evie.

'What's in it?'

'Nettle infusion, a drop of honey—it will do you and the babe good. Lufu will bring you both some chicken broth presently.'

Evie wrapped her hands round the mug, hunched over the fire, and stared into the flames. 'My thanks.'

Satisfied that Evie's shivering had stopped, and that her colour was returning, Cecily looked at Leofwine and silently indicated that he should move with her out of earshot. When they reached the other end of the hall, Leofwine rested his foot on a bench. His long hair was straggling out of the tie at the back of his neck; his beard was untrimmed.

'What happened, Leofwine?'

He scowled into his ale cup. 'That day you visited my workshop, did you see the builders at the other end of Golde Street?'

'Yes.'

Leofwine's face darkened. 'Normans—the Duke's men, may they rot in hell. They demolished the workshop.'

'Your workshop? But why should they do that? It could not be a reprisal—not when Winchester surrendered without a fight. D-do you think they suspect…?' Cecily caught her breath. What had Edmund said? That the Saxon cause was *not* lost…that Judhael was continuing to fight. And again—when she was in the loft room with Gudrun—Edmund had hinted that the resistance had plans…

'Sweet Mother—Judhael and Emma went to your house! The Normans must know. They suspect you…'

Leofwine put a heavy, work-scarred hand on Cecily's arm. 'No, my lady, it's none of that,' he said, his voice bitter as January frost. 'It might be easier to bear if it was. A man likes to know he's deserved it when he has his livelihood wrested from him.'

'There must be some mistake….'

'No—no mistake. Those foreign devils have cut the heart out of the city.' He glanced across at Evie, who was rocking Philip in her arms, and his face softened for a moment. 'Two whole streets have gone, my lady. Sixty houses in all. We'll have to start afresh.'

'To what purpose? It makes no sense.'

'Our old palace isn't fine enough for William of Normandy,' he replied with a short laugh. 'No—he must have a fully defendable castle. They are building a timber motte and bailey first—later they're to rebuild in stone. The bastard is afraid of us Saxons, and I expect he's right. After this he'll need more than a castle with a moat around it to keep his hide whole.' He shook his head. 'Our palace was fine enough for King Harold, but this bastard— My workshop…our house…' His voice cracked. 'Gone as though of no account. We merely stood in his way.'

'*Sixty* houses?' Cecily could not imagine it. 'The entire street?'

'Aye.' Leowine's eyes were bleak. 'And with Evie so near her time I thought of you. I know you're to wed one of them, but I thought...I hoped...in honour of the connection between your family and hers...'

'Of course,' Cecily said, and it was her turn to reach out to Leofwine. 'You did the right thing, and I assure you you are both *most* welcome.'

Leofwine gave a heartfelt sigh and looked about the Hall, seeing it, she suspected for the first time. 'And Fulford's new lord? Where is he? Will he bid us welcome?'

Cecily spread her fingers so he could see her ring. 'My husband,' she said firmly. 'Sir Adam will not turn you away.'

Leofwine tugged thoughtfully at his beard. 'I trust you are right. Evie is taking it hard, but we are lucky to have Fulford as a refuge. There are those in far worse case than us. I tell you, my lady, it's enough to make me consider taking up arms for the first time in my life.'

'Well said!' Edmund cut in. His crutches clunked against the table as he lowered himself onto the bench. 'Well said, Leo. Spoken like a true Saxon.'

'Don't, Edmund,' Cecily said, but her protest was swept aside while the two men exchanged greetings and Edmund commiserated with Leofwine on his ill-fortune.

'I have more news, Edmund,' Leofwine continued, when he had brought Edmund up to date. 'News that will gladden your heart. Those Frankish swine didn't have it all their way.'

'No?' Edmund leaned his head on his hand and looked up, his face alight with expectation. 'Pray continue, Leo.'

Glancing at the Hall door, Leofwine leaned forwards confidentially. 'The mint, Edmund. The mint in Winchester has been robbed.'

A slow smile spread across Edmund's face. 'The Winchester mint? You do surprise me.'

Edmund's tone did not match his words. Her heart sinking, Cecily's eyes went from one man to the other, observing their reactions, guessing at the level of their knowledge, wondering at the level of their involvement. Had Judhael been responsible for this robbery? She chewed the inside of her mouth, debating with herself whether she judged it a crime to have robbed the mint at this moment. The Winchester mint was a Saxon mint, and yet with Duke's William's conquest it suddenly belonged to the Normans? Was that just? Those coffers had been filled by Saxons, with Saxon silver, for a Saxon king—King Harold.

'Aye.' Leofwine's eyes gleamed. 'Someone ripped the strong-boxes clean from the floor. Must have used the same method—rope and oxen—that was used to pull down my workshop.'

'Really?'

'Aye, so there's some justice.'

Edmund shifted closer. 'Evie's brother, I'll be bound.'

Leofwine's face became blank. 'Could be. Couldn't say.'

Cecily bit the inside of her mouth so hard the metallic taste of blood burst onto her tongue. Yes, it had to be Judhael. Pray God he had not dragged Emma into this. If they were caught the Duke of Normandy would be merciless. What was it Edmund had told her? That the whole of southern England had been laid waste…

Sick with dread, she held her peace. But dread was not her only emotion. She was frustrated too—frustrated and angry. Before Edmund's arrival, Leofwine had deferred to her, had been content to talk to her. But now that Edmund was here—even though she was lady of the Hall and Edmund had been but one of her father's many housecarls—they were doing what men always did: talking to each other as though she, the woman, was invisible. Her father had treated her mother in like manner. As a child she had resented it every time he had done this, and despite the passing of the years her view of such behaviour had not changed.

'Judhael.' Edmund nodded with satisfaction, but his expression was ugly. 'Good—it's time we had some substance behind us. The tide will turn in our favour, Leo. This is but the beginning.'

Leofwine's face remained closed. 'I don't know what you mean.'

Cecily shifted, uncomfortable with the way Edmund was leading the conversation, but just then Adam strode into the hall and Edmund clamped his mouth shut. An awkward silence gripped the room.

Adam had been helping Brian Herfu with the slaughtering, and he was numb with cold. He made straight for the warmth of the hearth. Newcomers. A pregnant woman was seated to one side of the fire, cradling the baby Philip, and at the other end of the hall Cecily was standing with Edmund and a bearded Saxon. She did not look happy.

Conscious of the grim aspect he presented, with his tunic and hose begrimed with sheeps' blood, Adam nodded briefly to the woman at the fireside. 'The annual winter slaughter,' he murmured.

The woman swallowed and gave a curt little nod, but her eyes widened and fastened on the bloodstains. Adam knew by the way she lost colour that she had to be thinking of Hastings. Thankful that he had at least had the forethought to wash the worst from his hands in the river, he flexed his fingers before the fire and waited for feeling to return.

'Adam, we have guests,' Cecily said, breaking the silence. When she started walking towards him, he left the hearth and met her halfway. He took her hand and she shuddered. 'You're frozen!'

'You can't wear gloves when killing sheep.'

'You've been helping Brian?' she asked, surprise in her tone.

'As you observed yourself yesterday, the practice field needed clearing. Did your father not take part in the cull?'

Slowly she shook her head, quietly observing the blood on his clothes, but she did not withdraw her hand from his. Indeed, she was rubbing her thumb over the back of his hand as though she would impart some warmth to him. 'Never. But I expect Brian was grateful, since we're so behindhand.' She waved at the woman at the fireside. 'Adam, this is Evie Smith, and this...' she led him towards the trestle '…is her husband, Leofwine. He is a goldsmith. They are come from Winchester and are in need of our help.'

Adam's insides were in a trice as cold as his fingers. 'From Winchester?' Golde Street. Hell, he had almost forgotten about Golde Street. These must be the people she had visited. Cursing himself for letting himself be distracted by a soft body and melting blue eyes, he forced himself to listen.

As she gave him her account of what had happened to Leofwine Smith's workshop, his mind seemed to split in two. One part of him was attending to the tale his wife was telling while the other was wondering where her loyalties lay. If it came down to a stark choice between the Saxons—'my people' as she constantly chose to refer to them—and himself, how would she choose?

Duke William's plan to throw up a motte and bailey in the south west of the city was not news to him, but he had had no idea that sixty homes would have to be demolished to accomplish it. He noted the stiffness in Leofwine's posture and found he felt some sympathy for the man. The goldsmith had pride. He resented having to fling himself on Adam's mercy.

'My Hall is yours, Leofwine Smith,' he said, in his stilted English. He wound his arm about Cecily's waist, to endorse the welcome he knew she had given. Under his arm, Cecily held herself like a block of wood. Upset that her friends had been made refugees? Pray God that is all, Adam thought, giving her a slight squeeze. Her eyes met his, and they were dark with apprehension. Suspicion twisted within him like a cold snake. No, he thought. Don't, my princess—don't be thinking of betrayal. But there was more, he'd swear. Something else was eating at her…

'You did not think I'd refuse them?' he muttered in French, for her ears alone.

'No—*no*,' she said, but her expression did not lighten.

Edmund was watching them, those thin lips curling in sardonic amusement. It was he, Adam would swear, who was at the root of

Cecily's tension. Damn the man. Left to his own devices, Adam would have had him banished from the village before he could blink. Yet, since Edmund had not actually made a move against him, he could not act—not without being the unjust boor that Cecily's people no doubt expected him to be.

'Leofwine has more to tell your husband—doesn't he, Lady Wymark?' Edmund said.

She flushed and twisted against his arm, the emphasis placed on her new title apparently discomposing her. Ruthlessly, Adam tightened his grip. 'Yes?'

'Tell him, Leo. Tell him about the mint.'

Adam listened as best he might while Leofwine told him—in English—of a rebel raid on the Winchester mint. Though the cold snake in his belly kept shifting—*don't, my princess, don't betray me*—he kept his comments as neutral as he could.

'I wonder if that happened on Raoul's watch,' he said, grimly aware of the disturbing undercurrents flowing between Cecily and Edmund. They had not looked at each other once during Leofwine Smith's recounting, but Edmund's gaze was simply too innocent, and as for Cecily—her body was taut as a bowstring. It was hard to believe this was the same girl who had woken in his arms that morning, warm and soft, a relaxed and loving bundle.

At that moment Edmund's gaze met his, and he stretched his lips into that sneering smile that Adam was coming to loathe. Adam did not trust Edmund further than he could throw him. But what concerned him was rather this: would he ever be able to trust his wife?

Supper was over, the boards were cleared, and Adam alone remained in his seat at the head of the table, for the moment replete and disinclined to move. After so many months in Duke William's train, living like a nomad, hungry more than half the time, it was bliss to contemplate bed with a full stomach. But being gifted Fulford had more than one benefit, and eating well was not, in his view, the most important one. He glanced down the table, towards another of the benefits of Fulford. Cecily, his wife—his *loyal* wife. Or so he prayed.

As was becoming her habit after each meal, she was sitting on the other side of the fire with Gudrun in the Saxon sleeping area. The newborn was in her lap. It seemed everyone had taken to that side of the Hall. Hoping that was not significant, Adam sipped his wine. The pregnant woman sat near Cecily, talking to her husband. Even Richard had found a stool near the women. Idly strumming his lute, his fellow knight was rolling his eyes at Matty while he sang a Norman love song. Doubtless the girl couldn't understand a word, but that didn't stop her blushes.

Adam's gaze returned to his wife and traced her slight figure as she rocked the baby to sleep. Her features were soft in the fireglow. As ever, that tendril of hair had escaped its braid and gleamed on her breast, a curl of gold. Rock, rock, rock, as she murmured gently to the baby. That baby, he thought. That baby— the way she cossets him. Philip.

He sucked in his breath, gripped by a chilling certainty.

Philip. *Philip!* Hadn't her mother had been called Philippa?

And the child on her lap—perhaps Philippa's babe had survived? This one was the right age. This boy could be Cecily's *brother*—and thus, in Saxon eyes, the rightful heir to Fulford!

Eyes sharpening, Adam continued to watch. How she cosseted him. How the entire household cosseted him. Matty's giggle cut into his thoughts. He tapped a finger on the side of his wine cup. 'Richard! A word, if you please.'

Richard broke off his song, kissed his fingers at a crimson-cheeked Matty, and sauntered over. 'Aye?' The bench creaked as he took his place.

'That child—my wife's maid—you swore you'd leave her alone.'

Richard grinned. 'I like her.'

'That's clear. But you'll remember your promise?'

'I'll remember. She's too young for me. But a man needs some feminine company, and who else is there? Everyone else is married.' Richard ran his fingers caressingly over the lute strings and tried out a chord. 'Ease up, man. I'll be returning to London soon enough. What's eating you?'

Adam tilted his head in the direction of Cecily and Philip.

Richard lifted a brow and tried out a scale. 'You mistrust her? What did you expect?' He paused, and his grin widened. 'If you dally with Saxons... It's no good warning me off while you—'

'Richard, be serious! That baby worries me. The time she spends with it, and his name—had you realised?—a *Norman* name...'

'His mother was Norman? Is that what you're saying?'

'Exactly, and I'd wager her name was Philippa.'

Richard's fingers stilled mid-scale. 'Phillipa of Fulford herself?'

Adam raised an eyebrow and kept his voice down. 'It's entirely possible, wouldn't you say? It would explain why my beautiful wife was so swift to suggest marriage. She wanted to protect that child.'

Richard's eyes rested on Cecily. 'I rather thought she wanted to escape the besom at the convent.'

'No doubt. But she didn't have to marry me to do that. I'd already accepted her as my interpreter.'

'Hell, Adam, what's in your mind? I'm sure she has a fondness for you.' He grinned. 'Don't tell me last night was a disappointment? I could have sworn from the way she was looking at you at supper that all was very well between you—in one quarter, at least.'

Adam grunted, refusing to be drawn. Cecily was changing the baby's napkin, wrapping him tenderly in swaddling bands, ready for the night. 'That infant has to be her brother. Do you think it normal for a young woman to take such an interest in a housekeeper's son?'

Richard raised an eyebrow. 'Could be broody?'

'It's possible. But her interest in that boy concerns me. And then there's Edmund.'

'The lame one? He seems harmless enough.'

'A blind, I assure you. He is far from harmless.'

'Evidence?' Richard asked, plucking randomly at some strings.

'Not a scrap, but I don't trust him. He was Thane Edgar's housecarl before he was maimed.'

'You reckon he knows the mob that broke into the mint?'

'It's possible.' Adam watched Cecily tuck the baby in his basket. 'He's certainly involved in something, and I've a suspicion he's hoping to drag my wife into it.'

Richard's expression sobered. 'You really think she would betray you?'

'God alone knows where her loyalties lie. Think about it. It can't be easy for her.' Adam sighed, and turned his cup in his fingers. 'If only I could get her to confide in me. I've half a mind to clap Edmund in chains, but on what grounds?'

'Best wait awhile,' Richard said quietly, bending over his lute. 'If you're right—and I agree you have reason for suspicion—he'll act soon enough. And if he acts rashly he may lead us to the Saxon encampment. According to Tihell, the rebels are rumoured to have gone to earth somewhere between Winchester and the coast. They could be quite close.'

Adam rubbed his chin. 'You reach the same conclusion as me, my friend. So.' He looked bleakly across the hall at Cecily, who had kissed the baby and was making her way to the loft ladder. 'We wait. Lull them into thinking we are complacent, and then…'

With a flourish, Richard struck a chord. 'We strike.'

'Aye.' Adam rose and stretched. 'And now I go to woo my wife, and pray that before long she will trust me enough to tell me the truth about her relationship with that baby. If she does that…' Catching a cynical gleam in Richard's eyes, he gave a rueful grin. 'I find I want her to trust me.'

Richard shook his head. 'As I've said before, you're a fool with your women, Adam Wymark,' he said softly.

'Not such a fool as you think. By the way, I have arranged to meet Tihell at the Winchester garrison.'

'Oh?'

'He's been watching my lady's sister, and he may have a more precise location for the rebel encampment. I meet him tomorrow. Will you accompany me?'

Richard's lips curved. 'Assuredly—I have business of my own to attend to.'

As Adam made for the loft ladder, Richard's gaze swung back to Matty. Picking up from where he had left off when Adam had called him over, he went back to the next verse of the Norman love song.

The loft ladder creaked, and Adam's footsteps sounded on the landing outside.

Alert for the sound of her husband lifting the latch, Cecily quickly peeled off her gown and underskirt and dragged a cream linen nightgown over her head. The nightgown had miraculously appeared in her mother's clothes chest some time during the day. There had been no trace of it immediately after her wedding. Gudrun, she was sure, must have hidden it. Gripped by a shyness that years of convent life had bred into her, Cecily's fingers became thumbs. She wanted to be safely under the bedclothes when Adam came in. Her heart thudded.

Would he want to do *that* again? She had no idea how often married people did *that*, except… A vague memory surfaced—one of the novices giggling as she recited the list of days when married people were permitted to have carnal relations. There were not very many of them. They could not do…*that*…on Sundays, they could not do it on a Saint's day, they could not do it on Fridays, nor in Lent… In fact, according to Mother Aethelflaeda's calendar there were not many days when carnal relations *were* allowed, so she was probably not going to be called upon to perform her marital duties again tonight. Conscious of a vague sense of disappointment, Cecily frowned.

The latch lifted. She had not finished tying her neck fastenings. With a small squeak she dived into the bed, sat up, and wrestled with the ribbons.

Adam came in with a smile and latched the door. Heeling off his boots, he kicked them into the corner. His hand hovered over the wine jug. 'Wine, Princess?'

'N-no, thank you.'

He waved at the poker propped up against one of the braziers. 'I can mull it, if you'd prefer?'

'No, thank you. I had enough earlier.'

Adam grunted, and started to strip. Cecily sat, loose plait over one shoulder, and watched him out of the corner of her eye, half-curious, half-embarrassed. He did not have a shy bone in his body. His belt followed his boots into the corner, his tunic was tossed onto a hook and then his shirt. The bed shifted as, naked to the waist, he sat to unwind his leg-bindings.

The sight of so much naked male skin had curls of nervous excitement winding in her belly. Her fingers itched to reach out and touch, to see if he felt as warm and smooth as he had last night when, apart from the dim glow of the braziers, they had both been cloaked with darkness.

Throat dry as dust, she swallowed. Might he want her again? Perhaps a cup of mulled wine had not been such a bad idea? she thought, shooting another covert glance at her husband's bare back. The muscles there flexed in the most fascinating manner. His shoulders were so wide, and the way his back narrowed down to his waist…Why, even his back pleases my eyes, she realised, startled. His hair was glossy in the candlelight, dark as a raven's wing. His neck still looked vulnerable to her, used as she was to men who wore their hair long, in the Saxon fashion.

Adam turned, caught her watching him, and a dark eyebrow arched upwards. The scattering of hairs on his chest was dark and ran down—ran down to… What did he look like *there*?

'Cecily?'

Cheeks burning, she wrenched her gaze up and caught the tail-end of a grin. 'Mmm?'

Leaning towards her, he took up her braid and idly began to unplait it. 'I ride for Winchester with Richard in the morning. I'll leave young Brian in charge of the men, and I plan to be back well before nightfall. Are you happy to rest here for the day?'

'Of course.'

He fanned her hair out over her shoulders, warm fingers lingering on her breasts. Her nipples tightened. Oh, no, it looked as though Adam Wymark *was* going to want to do...*that* all over again. How shocking. She swallowed. When he repeated the movement, cupping her breasts through the linen nightgown, a pleasant ache started in her belly. Oh, *yes*! So it had been last night, she thought, holding back a moan. How did he *do* that? Carnal love. He was very skilled at it. And truly Mother Aethelflaeda would be disgusted with her response. So wanton. She felt hot all over. And she was sure today was not a day that was approved for doing...*that*...

'That's good,' Adam said, clearing his throat and continuing with his gentle caresses until her nipples felt as though they were going to burst free of the gown. He was touching her, and her body was straining towards him, greedy for more. 'Very good.'

Fingers under her chin, he brought his head to hers and their lips met in a lingering kiss. The moan escaped her and Adam drew back, his hand going to the tie of his chausses.

'Wait! Adam, you forgot the candles!'

Eyes immediately guarded, he gave her one of his lop-sided smiles. 'The candles—of course. How could I forget?' He pinched out his candle; she pinched out hers. Around the bed the darkness thickened, save for the glowing braziers. 'Better, Princess?' She heard a quiet sigh.

'Y-yes. I'm sorry, Adam.'

His body met hers, warm and welcoming, and Cecily melted. He had the power to turn her bones to water. Carnal love. Why had no one thought to tell her how exquisite it could be? And on a forbidden day too.

'No matter,' he said, skimming his hand down her flank as she fell back into the pillows, helpless with sinful longing and guilty delight. Utterly reprehensible. He twitched at her nightgown. 'But, since you are trying to hide in the dark, this can come off.'

'Yes, Adam.' She raised her arms to help him. 'I did not think you would want me tonight.'

'Not want you?' Hand on her gown, he stilled. 'Why on earth not?'

'It is not one of the approved days. Mother Aethelflaeda had a calendar—'

'A calendar? Dear God! Cecily, I will *not* permit that woman to poison what we have. If we want each other, we will have each other. Do you understand?'

'Yes, Adam.' *If we want each other,* he had said. Not *If I want you,* but *we.* Her heart swelled.

'One day, Princess. One day.'

'Adam?'

The nightgown was being drawn over her head and muffled his answer. 'One day we will make love naked, in broad day. We will hide nothing.'

'Adam…'

'But in the meantime…' Shifting over her, he gently bit her neck. 'In the meantime…'

Chapter Seventeen

'Matty? *Matty!*'

Gudrun, Cecily thought sleepily, has the voice of a trumpet when she chooses. She rolled over, buried her nose in Adam's pillow, and breathed in his scent. Last night, after they had done *that* not just once but twice, Adam had muttered something about not wishing her to catch a chill and pulled her nightgown back over her head. She had fallen asleep in his arms, but this morning he was gone—to Winchester, apparently. She inhaled deeply. Adam. She would get up in a moment, truly she would. She only wanted to doze on his pillow for a couple more minutes, recapturing…

'Not got him!' Down in the hall, Gudrun's voice rose to a wail. 'Saints, where is he? He can't have walked!'

All thoughts of dozing were put to flight by the urgency of Gudrun's tone. Lurching out of bed, Cecily grabbed a shawl and rushed out onto the landing. She peered over the guard-rail. 'Gudrun, whatever's the matter?'

Gudrun's face turned up towards her, white as whey. 'It's Philip, my lady. He's not in his basket!' She turned to Matty, who was calmly eating an apple. 'Are you sure you didn't put him down somewhere?'

Matty lifted her chin. Unlike Gudrun, she didn't look the least bit worried. 'I'm not about to forget Philip, Gudrun. I'm not daft. Maybe one of Sir Adam's men has him?'

Gudrun made an impatient gesture. 'That's not likely.'

'Could be wrong there,' Matty mumbled through a mouthful of apple. 'One or two of them seem quite taken with him.'

Careless of her state of undress, Cecily scrambled down the stairs. 'He can't be far. Matty, are you positive you didn't take him over to your mother and leave him there?'

Matty swallowed down some apple and shook her head. 'Last time I saw him was when he woke to feed in the middle of the night. Gudrun put him back in his basket.'

Cecily eyed Matty's apple. 'You didn't see him in the cook-house when you went to the storeroom?'

'Didn't think to look. Thought he was asleep.'

Cecily's heart began to beat in heavy strokes. Forcing herself to speak calmly, she wound her shawl about her shoulders. 'Gudrun, I take it Sir Adam and Sir Richard have already left?'

'Yes, my lady.'

'I'm going to dress. Please fetch Brian—try the armoury, the stables and failing that the practice field. Whatever he's doing, tell him I need him here *at once*. We must find Philip. He can't be far away. In any case, it must almost be time for his next feed.'

Gudrun pressed a hand to her breasts. 'Past time,' she said, wincing. Her face tight with worry, she hurried out.

Minutes later, wearing Emma's blue wool gown and cream veil, Cecily stood frowning by the pillory in the village square. Everyone was looking for Philip, but no one had seen hide nor hair of him since his last feed in the small hours. Where could he be? Or—worse—who could have taken him?

She oversaw Brian's progress round the village. Harold and Carl were hauled from the stables, knuckling sleep from their eyes. 'No, sir, we've not seen him.' Father Aelfric and Sigrida were prised out of their cottage. From her standpoint Cecily couldn't make out their reply, but the priest and his wife shook their heads and looked towards her with puzzled eyes. Brian pounded on the door of the mill—no joy there either. A couple of men were despatched down the road towards the other houses, and she watched them trudge back, shaking their heads.

Brian's expression was not promising as he returned to her side at the pillory. 'I'm sorry, my lady,' he said. 'No one's seen him.'

The cookhouse door was closed. Some sixth sense prompted Cecily to ask, 'Brian, did you speak to Lufu?'

'Aye, my lady. But she can't help, either.' Brian spread his hands. 'It's a mystery. Maybe little Philip will cry when he's hungry, and then we will hear him.'

Nodding, Cecily turned away. Her heart was heavy as lead. Philip had to be somewhere. A baby so young—a newborn who could not even crawl—could hardly get lost on his own. If only Adam had not gone to Winchester that morning—but, no, what *was* she thinking? Adam must never know the full extent of her concern for Philip...and in this crisis she must remember that, friendly though Brian was, he was Adam's man, not hers. She must conceal her deep concern from Brian. She could allow herself to appear worried, but not frantic...

But someone *must* have seen something. 'Has anyone spoken to Edmund?'

'Not seen him this morning, my lady.'

'I thought not.' Her eyes were drawn back to the cookhouse. Grey smoke was puffing out through the vent in the thatch, blending with a line of dark clouds blowing down from the north. How odd. She had not seen Edmund either. Driven by blind instinct, she picked up her skirts and headed for the cookhouse.

Lufu was on her knees, raking out the bread oven. As Cecily entered she kneeled back on her haunches and wiped her brow with the back of her hand, smearing it with streaks of ash. 'I told that Brian I've not seen Philip,' Lufu said, jaw jutting.

Cecily said nothing, merely held the girl's gaze. Lufu knew something about this, she'd swear…

Dropping the ash rake, Lufu got to her feet. 'I didn't see him, my lady—honest. Not seen him since yesterday evening.' She wiped her hands on her skirts and crossed her arms under her bosom.

'Tell me why I don't believe you.'

Lufu turned to the workbench, muttering.

'I beg your pardon?'

'How can I say why you won't believe me?' Lufu demanded, swinging round. 'I'm telling the truth. I haven't seen that baby since last night!'

'You may not have seen Philip, but you know where he is.' Silence. 'Don't you?' More silence. Cecily hauled in a breath. 'Lufu, this is my *brother* we are talking about. A tiny baby. One who was born early and who needs all the care he can get.'

Silence.

'Edmund has him, hasn't he?'

Lufu put her hand to her brow, drawing another streak of ash across it. She picked up a wooden spoon from the bench; she put it down; she recrossed her arms.

'Lufu, for pity's sake!'

'*All right!* Edmund has him. But he's safe, my lady. Edmund wouldn't hurt your brother. He is the rightful Thane of this place, and that's what they want.'

They? Cecily shut her eyes. Lufu must mean Judhael and the Saxon resistance. 'The rightful Thane,' she muttered, and opened her eyes. 'I am his *sister*, Lufu. Thane Edgar's daughter. What did they think I would do to him?'

Lufu shrugged. 'He's got another sister—one who's loyal.'

Stung, Cecily caught her breath. 'Emma? *Emma's* looking after him?' Lufu mumbled something that sounded like assent. 'That's a mercy, but Philip needs a wet nurse too.'

'They know that. Don't worry, my lady. Philip of Fulford will come to no harm.'

'No harm! My brother is stolen, to be used as a pawn in some power game, and you tell me he'll come to no harm! Would that I had your confidence.'

Lufu hunched a shoulder.

'Tell me where they've taken him.'

A muscle twitching in her jaw, Lufu fiddled with a knife on the workbench. Praying for patience, Cecily waited.

'He'll be fine, my lady. Don't you fret.'

'Lufu, for the love of God! Where *is* he?'

Lufu whirled. Tears gleamed on her lashes, witness to the struggle going on inside her. 'Up on the Downs. Seven Wells Hill. Near the Old Fort.'

Seven Wells Hill. Cecily let her breath out. She had never been there, though Cenwulf had talked about it. Miles from the nearest dwelling, high on the Downs, Seven Wells Hill was the site of an ancient earthworks which had been a ruin even before the time of the Romans. It was a desolate place, apparently—weatherbeaten and abandoned, home to skylarks and buzzards, but not much else.

'Philip will be safe enough with your sister.'

'Judhael is behind this, I take it?'

'Aye.'

'Who took him? Edmund?'

'Aye. What will you do, my lady?'

Cecily thought rapidly. She knew exactly what she was going to do. But she was not about to trust Lufu with that knowledge—not when the girl had stood to one side while her brother had been abducted from the place that offered him the most security. And, yes, Philip *was* far safer in Fulford—even though Fulford had been taken over by Adam's troops. Better that than be carted off to some Godforsaken encampment in the back of beyond, even if

he was with his own countrymen. But this was not the time to dwell
on such ironies.

Cecily shrugged lightly, and kept the panic out of her voice.
'Do? What can I do save wait for my lord to return from Winchester?' *And keep everyone so busy that their heads will spin and they
will have no energy left to wonder what I am really about.*

The stack of fuel by the fire had already dwindled since yesterday. Luckily. She looked pointedly at it. 'Lord knows there's
enough to do to keep the Hall running without me interfering in
the men's affairs. To begin with, the log store by the stables is
almost empty. Harold and Carl can help me replenish it, else this
winter will be miserable indeed. And then...' Cecily slanted a
sidelong glance at Lufu to make sure she was listening 'The
slaughtering is almost done, so you can make a start with the
smoking and salting. Matty and Sigrida will lend you a hand.
Matty's mother too, if the miller can spare her. I'll ask Evie if she'll
help. It might take her mind off her woes. And if that work's too
heavy for her, you can set her to packing the apples in straw. And
when Brian has finished in the practice field he can set the men to
work digging latrines.'

'New ones?'

'Yes. They should have been moved a couple of months since.
We must get them dug before the ground gets too hard.'

Waving an airy hand, Cecily picked up her skirts and sailed out
of the cookhouse to tell Gudrun—the only person here she could
trust—that Philip was with her sister. That done, she would set
everyone to work before riding to Seven Wells Hill. She would fetch
Philip back herself. She had no choice. Wat would accompany her
as her groom. He might be simple, but he would know the way.

Inside, she was in knots.

The trail wound on through a thicket of yew. Cecily turned in
her saddle, but already Fulford was lost to view. She kicked Clou

on, and shot a glance at Wat. Wat smiled happily across at her, blissfully ignorant of the urgency of their mission.

The way got steeper; the path narrowed. Brambles and briars snatched at the ponies' legs. Spiders' webs sparkled in the bushes, dewdrops trembling on their filaments.

'Wat, you are sure this is the right way?' Cecily asked, drawing her cloak—Adam's cloak—more securely about her. Without rousing suspicion, she had not been able to bring much in the way of provisions. Philip's blanket was currently stowed beneath Cloud's saddle, and she'd sneaked a frugal lunch of bread and cheese and a flask of ale into her pack. A couple of russet apples. But that was all. They could not afford to get lost. They could not afford to spend the night in the open.

Wat nodded vigorously. 'Right way. Up hill. Then no wood. Then Gunni's hut. And…and…'

Cecily remembered. Gunni the shepherd was Lufu's sweetheart. His hut on the edge of the Downs marked the halfway point to Seven Wells Hill. Or so Cenwulf had told her, in that other life, before Duke William had brought his army to England. 'And after the hut,' Cecily said, finishing Wat's sentence for him, 'Seven Wells?'

'Aye, Seven Wells.' Wat's expression clouded, and he fingered the dagger at his belt, perhaps not as carefree as Cecily had assumed. 'Cec take care at Seven Wells.'

'I will.'

They emerged from the gloomy woodland into a bright expanse of sheep-grazed turf—the Downs. Here, the wind cut keen as a knife, and the sky was a large blue tapestry with grey clouds building up in the east. Clumps of gorse and broom broke up the broad sweep of green; heather frothed along the trackway.

Wat's pony stumbled on an old anthill. 'Gunni's hut,' he said, pointing.

The hut was nothing more than a roughly thrown together heap of stones with a roof of dried bracken. As a shelter, it was basic,

but Cecily could see it would keep off the worst of the weather
There was no sign of Gunni, but then most of the sheep had jus
been put to slaughter. One or two had escaped their fate and wer
grazing their way over the downland. But no shepherd.

'Not long to the Old Fort then, Wat?'

'Halfway,' Wat said, toying with the hilt of his dagger. 'Halfway

They stumbled across the rebel encampment almost by acciden
It lay hidden in a wooded hollow, just below Seven Wells Hill. On
minute Cecily and Wat were staring up the chalky path that led u
to the Old Fort, apparently the only souls for miles around, and th
next half a dozen armed men had leapt out of nowhere.

A filthy figure dived at Cloud's bridle. Wrenching on the reins
Cecily caught a glimpse of a drawn sword, of two deadly-lookin
daggers stuck into a broad belt, and a pair of savage blue eyes. Th
man's features were obscured, partly by the nasal bar of his helr
and partly by a beard that couldn't have been trimmed in over
month. Every inch of exposed skin was streaked with grime, fro
his half-hidden face to the hand hauling on her pony's bridle. Hi
sheepskin jerkin was no cleaner.

Even though Cecily had known rebels were in the area, and ha
been expecting them to make a move, her breath came fast and sh
struggled not to panic. These men were fellow Saxons. She wa
safe. Wasn't she?

Steel flashed in the winter sun.

Wat made a choking sound, his face white as bone. One ma
was hauling on the reins of Wat's pony while another had hi
sword levelled at Wat's throat.

'No! Stop!' Cecily cried. *Appear calm.* Lifting her chin, she me
her countryman's gaze square on. 'My name is Cecily. I am Than
Edgar of Fulford's youngest daughter, and I am searching for m
father's housecarls—Edmund and Judhael. Would you kindl
direct us to them?'

She tightened her hands on her reins to hide their trembling. She was *not* more afraid than when she had first met Adam and Sir Richard. She couldn't be. These men were Saxons…

She raised her chin another notch. 'And would you do me the courtesy of unhanding my groom?'

They were led deeper into the trees that clustered at the base of Seven Wells Hill. It began to rain—a fine drizzle, more mist than rain, that caught in Cecily's veil and dampened Cloud's neck and mane. Woodsmoke, the smell of it faint but certain, caught in her nostrils.

A couple of hundred yards later they arrived at a natural clearing, with a fire in the middle. The fire was smoking and hissing, and more armed men were crouched round it, huddled in their cloaks. Her breath was still fast; her skin was like ice. Was this fear? Could she be afraid of her own people? *Adam, oh, Adam, help me.*

'Judhael!' The Saxon leading Cloud called out. 'Edmund!'

Two men broke away from the group by the fire. Edmund was walking freely, with no sign of his crutches, his splint, or even a limp—as hale and hearty as could be. He had deceived her. A sickening realisation. The other man was tall, and he had long fair hair that was caught back at his nape with a sheepskin ribbon. His eyes were a cold, dead blue. Judhael. He took Cloud's reins from Cecily's escort.

'I'll take it from here, Gunni,' he said.

'Gunni?' Cecily's jaw dropped as the man in the sheepskin jerkin turned and walked towards the fire. Her father's shepherd. She hadn't recognised him.

'Edmund, where's Philip?' she asked. 'He is safe? And what about Emma?'

'They're both here. Both are quite safe,' Judhael said, in a curt, clipped voice. Far from reassuring her, his words chilled her to the marrow—for they did not fit with the look in his eyes, which was dead and utterly detached. 'What interests me is how you knew where to look for us.'

Involuntarily Cecily's gaze focused on Gunni. Judhael's eyes narrowed. 'Lufu?'

The hairs rose on the back of Cecily's neck. Never had she seen a man look so ruthless. 'No. *No!*'

'Lufu. Damn her for the leaky vessel she is. Here, Edmund.' Judhael thrust Cloud's reins at the other housecarl. 'You take care of this one. I'll not be long.'

Edmund watched him stalk from the clearing, an uneasy expression in his eyes.

'Edmund, what will he do?'

'Am I Judhael's keeper?'

'He wouldn't hurt Lufu…would he?'

Shaking his head, Edmund led the ponies to a low branch and tethered them. 'Cecily, you can't save the world.'

A shelter had been set up under the trees—a tented affair, made out of canvas. Under the awning, several people were sheltering from the rain. Dour-faced warriors with swords at their hips were sitting on split log seats—about two dozen all told. It was hardly the vast rebel army that Cecily had been expecting. Their resources were pitiful: a few stacks of wood; a deer carcase slung between two poles. The bole of a tree was their conference table, and their shelter had no walls to keep out wind or rain. Or wolves. She shuddered.

'You thought Philip would be safe in this place?' Though fear had its grip on her, she was pleased her voice was steady. 'I think not. He was born before his time, and needs more care than you can offer him here.'

Edmund's face closed. 'Your brother is where he belongs. With Saxons. We'll look after him.'

Cecily recognised that set expression. Her father's face had worn just such a look on the day he had announced that she was to go to St Anne's. All her weeping, all her pleading had availed her nothing. She bit her lip. She knew immovable mule-like stubbornness when she saw it.

Briefly, she shifted her attention from Edmund towards the men under the awning, hoping against hope to find a chink in their armour. But the faces that gazed out were equally stony, equally without fellow-feeling. There was no sign of Emma—no one she could appeal to. She hid a sigh. Perhaps an oblique method might succeed where direct confrontation would fail… Perhaps if she adopted an approach she had been too young to try four years ago…

Fixing a light smile to her lips, she looked back at her father's housecarl. 'I suppose your mind is made up?'

'It is.'

She kicked a foot free of its stirrup. 'Then I had best help, hadn't I? Edmund, help me down. I've Philip's swaddling bands in my pack.'

'I'm sorry you do not see eye to eye with us, my lady,' Edmund muttered as he helped Cecily dismount. The silver bracelets that her father had given him jingled on his wrist. He waved at Wat to lift her pack down and, leading her through the rain towards the shelter, added, 'Judhael was insistent Philip should be our figure-head, and you must see that our cause needs a focus.'

Cecily shot him a sharp glance and snorted her scorn before she could stop herself. 'A babe? Your cause is so desperate you needed a *baby?*'

'Aye.' Edmund smiled, but his grey eyes remained sharp and hard as flints. 'The men's spirits were at a low ebb. Your brother— the legitimate heir to one of the largest holdings in Wessex—will act as a banner around which they can rally. More men will join us. We only want a fighting chance to overthrow the bastard before he gets fully entrenched.'

He's entrenched already, Cecily thought. If he's tearing down good folks' houses unopposed in Winchester; if he's throwing up mounds to build *castles*. But she wasn't about to alienate Edmund further by saying as much. 'How are you feeding him?'

'Found him another wet nurse—Joan.'

'Oh?'

'Come and meet her.' Edmund ducked his head under the awning. 'Joan? Joan?'

The people in the shelter—all eyes—fell silent as they entered, and the only sound was the rain drip-dripping on the canvas. A woman in grey homespun stepped forward. She had a baby over her shoulder and was winding him. Her face was careworn and raddled with grief. She was pitifully thin.

'Philip! Oh, let me—please.'

The woman Joan released her brother without protest and watched blank-faced and silent while Cecily reassured herself that he was well. Philip had just been fed, his sleepy, sated expression attested to that, but a dampness about his wrappings told her that his linens hadn't been changed all morning.

'Wat, please pass my bundle...my thanks,' she said, as Wat thrust it into her hands.

'You see, Cecily,' Edmund cut in. 'It is as I said. Your brother thrives.'

Biting back the reply that Philip would have been better off if he had been left in Gudrun's capable hands, and not dragged across the Downs like a sack of meal and left in wet swaddling bands, Cecily bent over the baby and set to work changing his clothing.

Conversation resumed about them. When she had finished, Edmund was seated on a nearby log, honing the edges of his seax on a stone. Was he guarding her?

'Your leg seems to have healed rather miraculously,' she said, speaking softly to mask her anger.

Not only had Edmund kidnapped her brother from Fulford, but in this too her father's housecarl had deceived her. He had lied, and he had called her healing skills into question. It was true that when examining him at the Hall she had wondered at the length of time it was taking his leg to heal, but how foolish to take him at his word when he had said it continued to pain him. Why had she not questioned him further? Certainly she had had other, weightier matters on her mind that day, but her instincts had told her his leg should be fine, and she had ignored them. How stupid. *Adam would see her in her true colours. Lightweight. Naïve. Stupid.*

Edmund had the grace to flush—a sign, she hoped, that he was not completely lost to her. 'I'm sorry I deceived you, Cecily. Judhael thought it best that way. He needed me at the Hall.'

'You were spying!'

'Watching out for your brother.' His jaw tightened. 'It was easier if that foreign brute you bed with thought him harmless…'

'I married Adam so *I* could watch out for Philip! For all of you!' Cecily reminded him tartly. The rush of rage she felt at Edmund naming Adam a 'foreign brute' had her bending over Philip and fussing with his blanket. Adam—what were the rebels intending to do about Adam? The answer was swift in coming. They would kill him if they could.

Hoping Edmund hadn't noticed her sudden intake of breath, Cecily managed to nod. 'Th…this is not a healthy place for Philip,' she said, turning the conversation away from Adam with only the slightest tremor. She did not want Adam dead. The very thought made the blood freeze in her veins. But there was not a hope that Edmund or any of these desperate Saxons would sympathise with her view. As a Saxon who had married one of Duke William's men, she was in this camp on sufferance, thanks only to past allegiances. If she put so much as a toe out of place they'd slit her throat and toss her in a ditch as a collaborator.

'Not healthy for him here?' Edmund was saying in an irritated tone. 'Among his own people? I should think it's the *very* place for him. When I swore to fight for your father, Cecily, I made that vow for life. To a man, King Harold's housecarls died at Hastings; they gave their lives for him, honouring vows like mine. Why should it be any different for me and these men here?' He gestured at the others sheltering with them under the awning, and the jingling of those silver bracelets he had earned from her father underscored his words.

Settling Philip in a basket, Cecily took a place on the log bench next to Edmund. He had sheathed the seax, she noted, breathing a little easier. 'Loyalty is admirable,' she murmured. 'But please, Edmund, take care. What does loyalty become when a cause is lost?'

Edmund scowled and folded his arms. She took heart that he had not stormed away. If she could reach anyone here it would be Edmund, and for pity's sake she had to try…

'Edmund, what does loyalty mean to you?'

Rain dripped on the canvas.

He frowned. 'Why, it's when a warrior swears to uphold his Thane…'

'Why? Why are such oaths necessary?'

He made an impatient movement. 'Hah! That you—a thane's daughter—should ask me that!'

'Tell me, Edmund. I want to understand.'

He shrugged. 'A thane needs his warriors to stand by him through thick and thin. It's the ancient way. Without warriors backing up the law the world would dissolve into anarchy.'

'And if a warrior were to go back on his oath?'

'He would be made *nithing*, an outcast.'

'I am told that King Harold himself swore a solemn oath in Normandy, when he promised to uphold Duke William's claim to the English throne.'

Edmund sprang to his feet. 'That is a lie! Norman propaganda! Harold was tricked.' He brought his face close to Cecily's, and the pupils of his eyes were small as pinpricks. 'If you swallow everything that foreign husband feeds you, you'll choke.'

Cecily folded her hands together to stop them shaking, and sat very straight on the makeshift bench. 'I'm sorry, Edmund,' she said, as meekly as she could. 'I'm trying to understand. Now, do hush—you'll waken Philip.'

To her relief, Edmund subsided at her side, and tentatively she touched his arm. 'I fear that by remaining loyal to my father you and Judhael do these people no good service. Look around—you're living like animals, and the people of Fulford need your strength…'

Edmund glowered. 'The oath I swore to your father was sacred…'

'So sacred it will lead you—and these—' she jerked her head at the others '—to an early grave?'

'If need be.'

Cecily shook her head. It was hopeless. Edmund was as intransigent in defeat as her father would have been, and Judhael was too, no doubt. Was the male mind always so inflexible?

Adam flashed into her brain. He was holding his hand out to her in their bedchamber on their wedding night—she remembered that slight vulnerability in his eyes as he had offered himself as her husband, as he let *her* decide. Adam was something of a riddle. Hadn't he married her at her suggestion, even though he had set out to marry Emma? Her husband's mind was neither fixed nor rigid…

In fact, Adam and his compatriots had shown remarkable openness, considering that they had come to Fulford as conquerors. She could picture Adam and Richard with their heads together, hunched over a wine flask at the trestle; she could see Adam talking with his squire Maurice in like manner, and with Brian Herfu also… At the time the significance had escaped her, but in each of these cases hadn't Adam been *discussing* before he made his decisions and issued commands? He was in the habit of assessing Sir Richard's comments and those of his men, of amending his plans in light of them…

Her father would have deemed it a grave weakness to consult others. Not so Adam. And if any were to ask her, a woman, which of the two—her father or her husband—were the stronger, she would say her husband. Adam's strength was a new kind of strength; his leadership was a new kind of leadership, one which went far beyond the old oaths that led men blinkered to their deaths.

The time for such oaths was past; the world was changing, and unless Edmund and Judhael changed too, they would be left behind.

Adam's way was the way forward, and she loved him for it.

Loved him? She all but choked.

She *loved* him? Certainly she ached for him to help her now.

Swiftly ducking her head, Cecily let her veil drift forward, lest Edmund read her stunned expression. Surely not—surely you could not love someone you had only known for a few short days?

Yes—*yes*, her heart told her. You could if that someone was Adam Wymark. She had warmed to him almost from the very first, and…of course she loved him. Why else would she melt at his touch? She loved Adam, and he—a pang ran through her—he loved his first wife, Gwenn.

Staring blankly down at her brother, asleep in his basket, unaware of the dangerous undercurrents swirling about him, Cecily saw no easy path ahead. But if such a path existed she would find it. And that, Edmund, my friend, she thought fiercely, is an oath that I am making to myself, and it is one that I will fight to *my* last breath to fulfil.

The rain was pooling in the awning above them. Edmund reached up and adjusted the canvas, and the water tipped onto the ground. At once it began seeping into the shelter from the side. Everything was damp—the chalky mud underfoot, the logs they were sitting on, their clothes, even the air they breathed—for they could not light a fire under the awning. It was no fit place for a baby.

Shivering, Cecily undid the neck fastening of Adam's cloak, pulled it more closely about her and refastened it. She lowered her voice. 'Edmund, let me take Philip back to Fulford. If you truly have his best interests at heart, you'll let me take him. What use is a figurehead dead of lung-fever?'

'No.'

'But, Edmund—'

'No!' Edmund jumped to his feet and towered over her. 'Philip

stays here. And, since you have come to visit, you can stay too.'
He held out his hand, palm upwards. 'Give me your eating knife.'

Cecily stiffened. 'Am I your prisoner, Edmund?'

A muscle jumped in Edmund's jaw. 'Your knife, if you please.'

Reluctantly, Cecily took her knife from her belt and passed it
to him. 'You didn't answer me. Am I your prisoner?'

'Ask Judhael when he returns,' Edmund snapped and, whirling
on his heel, strode into the rain.

Chapter Eighteen

Adam stripped off his gloves as he crossed the threshold of Fulford Hall and nodded a greeting at Gudrun, who was sewing in the doorway where the light was strongest. She had her cloak about her shoulders to ward off the draught. Neatly avoiding little Agatha, who was laying in the rushes, Adam gratefully accepted the mug of ale Matty offered him and made a beeline for the fireside. The ride back from Winchester had given him a thirst, and he was damp to his core.

Matty relieved him of his cloak, shook it out, and slung it over a nearby peg. Maurice came in. He was on his own, as Richard and his squire were no longer with them, having remained behind in Winchester. Adam could see no sign of their guests, or his wife. As he unbuckled his sword and took a seat on one of the fireside stools, he wondered where she was. After receiving Félix Tihell's intelligence that some rebels were definitely hiding out near Fulford, he found he needed to see her. Where the devil was she?

Gudrun was bent industriously over some linen, scissors flashing as she cut off a length of thread. Herfu clattered in, looked at Adam, and stopped dead in his tracks. Tutting, Gudrun flapped at the lad to get him out of her light, and as he moved towards Matty and the ale jug he threw Adam an odd look.

'Gudrun, where is Cecily?' Adam asked, in his halting, careful English.

The housekeeper glanced up from threading a needle. 'Went out, sir,' she answered shortly, and bent back over her work.

Adam glanced at the wood basket, and was glad to see that it had been replenished since dawn, when he'd ridden out. He cast a log on the fire. A stool creaked as Maurice joined him. 'Out? Where?'

Gudrun hunched deeper over her sewing. 'I do not know. She didn't say.'

Brian Herfu cleared his throat and pushed himself away from the trestle. 'Sir Adam?'

'You know where she is, Herfu?'

'N-no, sir.'

The lad's leg was jiggling, the way it had when they had faced the Saxon shield wall at Hastings, before the Breton line broke, the way it invariably did when Brian was facing something unpleasant. Cold fingers trailed down Adam's back. 'Herfu?'

'Your lady went out before noon, sir. She led me to believe she was only beating the bounds, setting the miller's boys to work in the woods. I…I thought she would be back within the hour…'

Throat dry, Adam got slowly to his feet. 'And…?'

'After two hours had passed Le Blanc went to look for her, and…and he…he's not returned either.'

Adam stared blankly at Herfu for a moment because his mind, despite all they had learned from Tihell in Winchester, refused to digest what the lad was saying. 'She's gone?' This was what he had feared would happen from the moment Tihell had informed him that Emma of Fulford had been tracked going onto the Downs a few miles south of here. So why should he feel as though the ground had been cut away beneath his feet? Why was there a pain in his chest?

Herfu nodded. 'Yes, sir.'

'You are certain she went willingly?'

'Yes, sir.'

Adam's heart fell to his boots. 'Well, Maurice,' he said, disgusted to hear a distinct tremor in his voice, 'it seems Tihell was in the right. Her sister *is* in the area. Would you care to lay odds on my wife having joined her sister with the Saxon rebels?'

Rising, Maurice stood awkwardly at Adam's side and jerked his head towards Gudrun, who had laid aside her sewing and was openly observing Adam's reaction. 'I'm not so sure, sir. That one knows more, I'm sure.'

Thrusting his ale at Maurice, Adam strode straight to Gudrun. 'Where is my lady?'

Gudrun's eyes met his steadily. 'I do not know.'

Maurice was right. The housekeeper *did* know something. Her gaze was just a little *too* unflinching. If Adam had thought it would do any good he would have hauled the woman to her feet and shaken the truth out of her. Instead, he waved Brian Herfu over. 'Herfu?'

'Sir?'

'What happened after I left for Winchester? Full report. What did my wife do?'

Brian swallowed. 'She...she set us all tasks. The slaughtering being done, Lufu and the women were put in charge of the salting and curing, the troop was to dig new latrines, and Harold and Carl were to gather wood. Lady Cecily led me to believe she left to check up on them.'

'Led you to believe, you say?'

'Yes, sir.'

Briefly closing his eyes, Adam forced himself to face the fact that Cecily had deliberately set out to deceive his man. And, if that was the case, her loyalties were no longer in question. His wife had betrayed them. Had betrayed *him*. Pain sliced through him— the worst kind of pain, a pain that was every bit as keen as the pain he had felt when Gwenn had died. No, *no*.

He hardened his heart. He could not care. He did not care. He had sworn that never again would he care to the point when it hurt.

'It…it was awkward, sir,' Brian was saying. 'After the baby vanished.'

'Baby? What the hell is going on?'

With a sigh, Gudrun shoved the needle into her work and set it aside. 'Philip, sir.' She cleared her throat. 'He was lost this morning.'

'*Lost?*' Adam was utterly at sea. The woman was telling him, as coolly as you please, that the baby she doted on was lost. Why did she not look more concerned? Nothing made any sense.

Except the bald fact that Cecily was not at Fulford.

Had she gone to escape him? Or to join his enemies? But even these questions, important as they were, were lost under an over-riding question: *was Cecily safe?*

And now here was Gudrun, placidly telling him that baby Philip had been lost. He struggled to concentrate. Was she *safe*?

'He was stolen. Abducted,' Gudrun said. 'Your men could not find him, and when they stopped looking Lady Cecily went to search for him herself.'

Adam rubbed his forehead. What was he missing? Gudrun was too calm—far too calm. She had to know where Philip had been taken, which meant that she knew where Cecily had gone. They were *all* in on it. He smothered a curse. 'Did she have a groom with her?'

'Yes, sir. In a manner of speaking,' Herfu chipped in.

'In a manner of speaking?'

'Wat accompanied her.'

'*Wat?* Christ on the cross—that boy's no proper escort!'

Herfu looked at the floor. 'Sir, it was as I said. Lady Cecily implied that she would remain within earshot.'

'Hell's teeth.' Adam glared at the downbent head. 'Sometimes, Herfu, you haven't got the sense you were born with.'

'I'm sorry, sir.' His foot jiggled. 'Th…there's more…'

'Out with it.'

'It's about the cook—Lufu. She's vanished.'

'*Again?*'

'Yes, sir. I've just been to the cookhouse, and Evie says she's not seen her for the past hour or more. She and her husband have been salting meat on their own. The miller's mule has gone too.'

Adam swore, and snatched up his sword. 'Maurice!'

'Sir?'

'Find me a dry cloak, and saddle that grey gelding. And the two blacks.'

'We're going out again, sir?'

'Clever boy.'

'Full arms, sir?'

'Yes to the helm, and no to the mail. I'm not about to draw attention to myself, which is why I'll take the gelding and not Flame.'

Maurice opened his mouth and closed it.

Adam gritted his teeth. 'What?'

'Sir Richard wouldn't approve, sir.'

'Sir Richard isn't here to approve or disapprove. But we will wear leather gambesons—padded ones. *Move*, man.'

'Aye, sir.'

Gudrun reached for Agatha and whipped her out of the doorway as Maurice ran out.

'You, woman,' Adam said in English, before he recalled her previous mistress, Cecily's mother, had been Norman. He reverted with relief to that tongue. 'Come back, please.'

Agatha on her hip, Gudrun approached warily. 'Sir Adam?'

'You know where she went?'

'I...I know where she was headed, sir.'

Some of Adam's tension eased, and he managed a smile. 'Good. Where's your husband?'

'Wilf? Butchering the sheep carcasses behind the cookhouse, sir.'

'Does Wilf ride?'

'Of course, sir.'

'Fetch him. He can be our guide. Herfu, you stay here. Post some guards up on the rise.'

'You're expecting trouble, sir?'

Buckling on his sword belt, Adam strode after his squire. 'When will you learn, lad? Anything is possible.'

Under the canvas shelter, hugging Philip to her breast, Cecily was battling with despair. Not one of these people would meet her gaze. Undeterred, she cleared her throat, 'My sister, Emma, has anyone seen her? Judhael said she was here.'

Outside, someone squelched through the mud. A horse whinnied. And still not a soul would meet Cecily's eyes. She looked directly at the shepherd. 'Gunni, Emma is all right?'

Gunni shrugged, and reluctantly met her gaze. 'Lady Emma's well enough. She went to gather dry kindling as we will be lighting a proper fire this evening.'

Emma? Gathering wood in the rain? But she nodded as though it was her sister's habit to perform menial tasks. 'So I shall see her soon?'

Gunni nodded. 'Aye, lady, soon.'

Not ten minutes later, a woman ducked into the shelter. Even though she was expecting Emma, it was a moment before Cecily recognised her. Her sister's cloak was dark with rain and mud, and when she thrust back her hood Cecily saw that she had dispensed with her veil completely, like a peasant. Her nose was red, her cheeks pale and her hair was thrust back in a single plait that looked as though it had been slept in. Never had she dreamed of seeing Emma so dishevelled.

Cecily jumped to her feet. 'Emma!'

'Cecily!' They embraced, Philip between them. 'They didn't hurt you? I made Judhael swear—' Breaking off, Emma pulled away and stripped off her kid gloves. Cecily noticed they were split at the seams and a greyish brown rather than the cream they had once been, and the boots that peeped out from under Emma's bedraggled skirts were not the beautifully stitched riding boots that Cecily remembered. They had been replaced with heavy workaday ones, similar to those she had worn at the convent. The transformation took her breath away.

'What?' Emma asked, seeing her expression.

'Nothing. It's just…you…you're so changed.'

Emma lost her smile. 'We've all changed.'

'That's true.'

Tossing her gloves aside with an echo of her old arrogance that tugged at Cecily's heartstrings, Emma drew Cecily onto the bench and gazed at the baby in her arms.

'I wondered if he would bring you here. I hoped…' Emma's voice trailed off.

'What? That I would join you?' Firmly, Cecily shook her head. 'This is no place for our brother, Emma, you must see that.'

Unhappily, Emma sighed. She lowered her voice. 'Of course I see that. It's just that Judhael…he…he can be so very persuasive. He always knows he is right, you see.'

Cecily made an impatient noise. 'This is an instance when Judhael is *not* right.' She drew breath to say more, but a warning squeeze on her arm had her glancing towards the opening of the shelter. Judhael was there, watching them.

Emma scrambled to her feet so quickly that Cecily frowned. Was her sister *afraid* of him? After seeing them at Winchester, in the Cathedral, Cecily had assumed they were lovers, but it was beginning to look as though she feared him…

'You got plenty of wood?' Judhael demanded, in a most unloverlike voice. He shoved his thumbs in his belt, and as he did so Cecily noticed that the back of one of his hands was scored with a deep scratch, the blood on it recently congealed.

'Aye.'

'And the beacon? You checked that?'

'Yes. The cover's not been touched, so the wood's quite dry. I put fresh kindling there too, just in case.'

'Come here then, wench, and give me a kiss.'

Wench? Open-mouthed, Cecily watched in astonishment as her prim sister, her butter-wouldn't-melt-in-her-mouth sister, let Evie's brother sweep her into his arms in front of his men, in front of everyone. And she didn't even blush. The world might have changed, but her sister had changed even more.

As Judhael angled Emma's head to him, so she could receive his kiss, Cecily found herself staring at the dried blood on the back of his hand. It looked odd—as though—a shudder ran through her—Judhael had not scratched himself, he had been bitten, and the bite looked very much like a *human* bite!

Wilf took Adam and Maurice directly through the woods to the chalky rise which led to Gunni's hut. With worry about Cecily's welfare a cramp in his guts, Adam thanked God that the man did not waste time with delaying tactics or pointless deviations. He simply pointed through the rain up a slippery track and said, 'There it is, sir. Gunni's hut.'

At the top of the rise Adam saw a rough tumble of stones that had some order to it and was roofed with dried bracken. A man in chainmail had beaten them to it. Le Blanc. He was on his knees by the wall of the shelter, bending over the body of a woman, tucking his cloak around her like a blanket.

Adam stopped breathing. He could scarcely bring himself to look. It couldn't be Cecily, it couldn't…

At his side, Wilf sucked in a breath. 'Lufu!'

The name had Adam breathing again, and his guts griping with guilt. Not for the world would he wish harm on Fulford's cook, but if it had been Cecily… He burned to look into those blue eyes once more, to know that she was safe. The question of whether Cecily had betrayed him or not was a mere trifle compared to that.

These past days the fear of betrayal had occupied his mind, but now that the worst had apparently happened there was room for only one thought: Cecily *must* be safe. The implications of this— hell, he would think about implications later.

Now that he could breathe again, he noticed that Le Blanc's roan and a mule—the miller's?—were tethered by the hut.

'Lufu!' Wilf hurled himself from his horse.

Le Blanc's mouth was a thin, angry line. His helm lay on the ground beside him and he was holding the girl's hand, chafing it. Her lip had been split, she had a nasty discolouration on one cheekbone, and blood in her hair. 'She's alive, sir,' Le Blanc said. 'But she won't waken.'

Tossing his reins at Maurice, Adam hurried over.

Wilf had Lufu's other hand and was stroking it, speaking softly in an English so heavily accented that Adam couldn't catch the full meaning. But any fool could understand the gist of it. Wilf was fond of her. He was telling her that she would be all right now they had found her.

Staring grimly at Lufu, Adam prayed the man was right. Apart from the bruising to her face, her skin was the colour of bleached linen, and her breathing was alarmingly shallow. 'God's Blood, she looks as though she's been through a mangle.'

'I reckon she has.' Le Blanc swallowed and gestured vaguely towards a rocky outcrop. 'She was beaten. I...I saw most of it from behind that. I couldn't do anything, sir, there were too many of them.'

'Them?'

'Saxons. They would have—'

'Take it slower, Le Blanc, so Wilf can follow you.'

'Sir.' Le Blanc's eyes found Wilf's. 'I...I'm sorry she's hurt, but the man moved like lightning—'

'Saxon?'

'Aye. I thought he was bluffing at first, it never occurred to me that he'd hurt one of his own, and by the time I'd realised what he was about it was over. Besides, there were others with him. They would have killed me, and I still wouldn't have been able to prevent it.'

Wilf frowned, trying to follow what had been said. 'You say a Saxon did this?'

'There were several present or I would have intervened, I swear. But only one of them spoke to her, and only one of them did the beating.' Slowly, he shook his head. 'What kind of a man would beat his countrywoman to a pulp like this?'

'We should move her inside,' Adam said. 'She's soaking. She doesn't need a chill on top of a beating.'

'I thought of that,' Le Blanc said. 'But it's possible her ribs are broken, and I was worried about moving her…'

'If we use your shield and a cloak as a stretcher to get her into the hut, she should be all right,' Adam said, hoping to God he was right. 'We have to get her warm. And someone must go for proper help.' Adam turned to Wilf and asked in English, 'Is your wife the best person to deal with this?'

'In Lady Cecily's absence, yes.'

Cecily, Cecily, where are you? 'Fine. Let's get Lufu into the shelter, and make her comfortable, and then Wilf can fetch Gudrun. She'll be a better judge of whether Lufu can be got safely back to Fulford than any of us.'

Together, they eased the unconscious Lufu onto Maurice's cloak and Le Blanc's shield. Inside the hut the light was poor, but to one side there was a low shelf with a mattress stuffed with heather. They placed Lufu on it.

After Wilf had set out for Fulford, and his hoofbeats had died away, Adam made Le Blanc strip off his mailcoat. 'Leave your helmet behind too,' he said. 'I'm leaving mine here.' Saxons did wear conical helmets, but Adam did not want to present too warlike an aspect. If he and Le Blanc were spotted he'd rather they were taken for huntsmen or poachers.

Uneasy about the idea of continuing up Seven Wells Hill so

lightly armed, Le Blanc didn't scruple to say so. 'Wouldn't we be best to wait until Wilf returns?'

A hideous image of Cecily in the hands of the beast who had beaten Lufu flashed into Adam's mind. 'No time,' he said. 'But I'll take Maurice instead of you, if you'd rather stand guard over Lufu.'

Le Blanc bristled, as Adam had known he would. Two years Maurice's senior, Le Blanc had campaigned with Adam in Brittany *and* Normandy, and was not about to cede superiority to a mere squire. 'No, sir. I'm your man.'

'Maurice, stay with the girl.'

'I'll not leave her, sir.'

As the grey and the roan climbed towards the summit of Seven Wells Hill, the rain began to ease and the breeze strengthened. High up, a red kite coasted into view. Uncertain of what he was looking for, but praying they would stumble across something, *anything*, that might lead them to Cecily, Adam found himself envying the big bird its vantagepoint. Perhaps it could see Cecily. Not that the vista was bad from up here, with what must be the whole of Wessex spread out below them on all sides. At the peak, it must be like standing in the middle of a map.

Shivering, grateful for the thick padding in his gambeson, Adam urged the gelding to the summit, and took a moment or two to get his bearings in the hope of seeing something that would tell him what to do next. He was almost at a complete loss, riding on pure instinct—something he never liked to do. At bottom, he was a planner, a strategist who disliked taking unnecessary risks, but today his instincts were screaming at him, telling him that all the planning in the world might not be enough to lead him to Cecily.

Below lay the wooded valley they had ridden through—the one that led to Fulford. Behind him, to the north, lay Winchester, with its acres of cultivated fields. The peasants' strips were clearly visible, brown stripes marked off by ancient hedgerows, by the twisted trunk of a leafless crab-apple or a lichened medlar. To the south the land rose and fell in soft curves as it disappeared into the distant reaches of the South Downs. Today they were blurred by low-lying cloud and dark with the last of the rain, but on a clear day one might see the sea he had crossed.

'Take a look at this, sir!'

Adam wrenched his gaze from the undulating waves of downland that he had been scouring in the vain hope of seeing a diminutive figure in a blue cloak and wheeled his horse round.

'A beacon!' Le Blanc had pulled up in the centre of a flat, grassy area at the top of the hill. Leaning to one side, he drew his sword and flicked at several turves of grass that formed a mound in the middle. As the turves flipped over, Adam saw they were camouflaging an oilcloth, which in its turn had been flung over a squat metal brazier. Clinging to his pommel, Le Blanc lifted the oilcloth with the point of his sword. The brazier was brimful with wood and ready to fire, assuming that the oilcloth had kept off the worst of the weather.

The brazier had probably last seen use when Duke William's fleet had been sighted to the east of the Narrow Sea. It would have called out the fyrd, the local militia. With its commanding position, the Seven Wells beacon would be visible in most of Wessex...

'Do you think it's still in use?' Adam said, his pulse quickening as inspiration struck. 'Le Blanc?'

'Sir?'

'Fire it. Fling damp vegetation on it so it smokes like hell, and then gallop back to Fulford. Fetch Herfu and as many men as you can muster.'

Le Blanc blinked. 'But, sir, Saxon scouts are bound to see the smoke, and every rebel within spitting distance will be on you in a heartbeat.'

'Exactly.' Adam waved an arm to encompass the vast landscape spread out below. 'Look about you, Le Blanc. If we don't fire it we could be searching for their camp till the last trumpet sounds. This will draw them out in no time.'

'I'll fire it, sir, but I'll not leave you. Maurice is bound to see the smoke. He can raise the alarm.'

'They'll outnumber us.'

Le Blanc shrugged. 'Nevertheless, I'll not be leaving you.'

Chapter Nineteen

Cecily pushed back the flap of the awning. Edmund was outside, arguing with Judhael.

'It's impossible, I tell you,' Edmund was saying in exasperated tones. 'So many are dead! And those that are left have fled or have no authority.'

'What about old Morcar of Lewes, and Siward Edwardson—?'

'You've just hit the nail on the head there, Judhael. They're *old*. Both of them doddering, grieving for sons lost in battle. You're mad if you think they carry any authority...' He caught sight of Cecily and lowered his voice, and Cecily could not catch the rest.

Sighing, she wrapped her arms about her middle and went to peer in Philip's basket. The baby was awake, on the point of dozing, a dribble of milk at the corner of his mouth for the wet nurse had just set him down.

'Thank God you found Joan,' Cecily muttered to Emma, who was still watching the men by the campfire. 'Otherwise we'd be in for a sleepless night. I only hope we can keep him out of the draughts.' Impulsively, Cecily gave her sister a hug. 'I love you.'

Emma turned, her eyes awash with tears. 'It was not meant to be like this,' she whispered, in a choked voice. 'I—'

'Judhael!' A lookout cried out. 'Prisoners!'

Cecily was on her feet in an instant, the hairs lifting on the back of her neck. No…*no!*

Four horses were being ridden into the encampment. Thank God, Cecily thought, on registering the riders' flowing hair and beards, Saxons. No sign of Flame. For a moment she was giddy with relief. It was only Judhael's scouts, coming home to roost for the night. There were no prisoners; the lookout had been mistaken…

As the cavalcade rode slowly through the thickening dusk towards the campfire it was possible to make out that two of the horses did in fact bear high-backed chevaliers' saddles, with pommels at the front. Cecily froze. Her countrymen thought horses too valuable to risk in fighting; they only used them for transport. And since Saxons fought on foot they had no use for such saddles…

And then she saw him. *Adam.* Her heart lurched.

Adam and another man were bringing up the rear. They had rope halters around their necks, but that was not the worst of it. Thick branches had been lashed across their arms and shoulders like yokes. With their arms forcibly outstretched, and the weight of their burdens unbalancing them, they were slipping and skidding in the mire. George. The man staggering alongside Adam was George Le Blanc. Their clothes were plastered with mud kicked up by the horses; their heads were bowed; their faces hidden.

With a sob, Cecily gripped Emma's arm and dragged her from the shelter. Gunni followed, close and silent as her shadow. The trees loomed up around the clearing, their trunks tall and dark in the twilight; the fire sputtered; torches flared.

One of the scouts unwound the leash tying Adam and Le Blanc to his pommel and tossed it to Judhael. 'Found a couple of strays by the beacon,' he said, jumping down from his horse with a grin. 'Thought you'd like to put them out of their misery.'

Cecily stumbled nearer, but Emma hung on her arm like an

anchor, and when their eyes met Emma gave her head a quick shake. Ignoring her, Cecily broke free and edged closer. She was not mad enough to think she was a match for Judhael and these men, but she had to get near Adam—she *had* to. There was room for no other thought.

The torchlight flickered on his dark, rain-slicked hair. *Adam, Adam, look at me,* she pleaded silently. *Let me see you're not badly hurt.* And then, while one of the Saxon scouts was busy muttering in Judhael's ear, Adam lifted his head, and the flames from one of the torches flickered across his face.

Her insides turned to water. Adam had been beaten; one of his eyes was swollen and half-closed, and those lean cheekbones were smeared with a dark substance that could either be blood or mud. His arms were stretched out, roped to the branch so roughly there was definitely blood at his wrists. Looking directly at her, he lifted his mouth in a lop-sided smile. He mouthed her name, 'Cecily.'

Edmund muttered at Judhael and drew Adam's gaze. A slight narrowing of the green eyes told her Adam had marked Edmund's unsplinted leg.

'Emma,' Cecily whispered, desperation putting wild ideas into her head. 'Give me your eating knife.'

'Don't be a fool!'

Cecily swallowed a groan. It was hopeless. What could one girl do with an eating knife? But she could not stand by and watch when—

'Edmund tells me that you are Sir Adam Wymark,' Judhael said, speaking in English. 'The "hero" of Hastings and our self-appointed lord and master.' He threw a disparaging glance at George Le Blanc. 'This must be one of your Bretons. Only one? Odd—I'd heard you had a whole troop. Careless of you not to bring the rest with you today—have the others deserted?'

A lock of dark hair flopped across Adam's unhurt eye. He

tossed his head to clear his vision, but the yoke on his shoulders unbalanced him, and he struggled to keep his footing in the mire. Someone laughed. Cecily's nails dug into her palms.

'Lost your tongue?' Judhael asked. 'Or can't you understand me?'

'I understand you,' Adam replied. His English was heavily accented, but his voice was strong.

'My man tells me you ran into his arms like a long-lost lover,' Judhael said, folding his arms. 'Now, why should you do that?'

Adam stood as straight as a man could with his arms strapped to a wooden yoke. 'I came for my lady.'

Tears stung at the back of Cecily's eyes, and the scene blurred. Oh, Adam, you idiot.

'Your lady?' Judhael's voice was harsh, disbelieving. 'You came for Cecily Fulford?'

'Yes.'

'Liar—you think to trick me. The garrison at Winchester put you up to this. We know you were there this morning. You have come to try and discover where I have hidden the silver.'

'No, but tell me where it is and I'll be happy to pass the message on.'

'Gunni!'

'Judhael?'

'Our guest doesn't seem to realise he is in grave trouble. Bring it home to him, will you?'

Rolling up his sleeves, Gunni clenched his fists. Cecily clutched Emma, and when Gunni drew his arm back to strike she flinched and shut her eyes.

'So you're Gunni?' Adam's voice, almost conversational. 'The shepherd?'

The thud of Gunni's fist connecting with Adam's stomach had her eyes flying open in time to see Adam double over with a grunt. As he toppled, one end of the yoke thumped into the mud, bringing him down on his knees. Cecily's heart contracted. He looked weary beyond thought. How much of a beating had he sustained up on the hill?

'You're Lufu's man?' Adam gasped. A trickle of blood ran down from his hairline.

'Lufu?' Gunni froze in the act of aiming a booted foot at Adam's ribs. 'What about Lufu?'

'She'll be all right—' another gasp '—we think.'

Reaching for Adam's gambeson, Gunni hauled him to his feet, yoke and all. 'What do you mean, you *think* she'll be all right?'

Adam swayed under the weight of the yoke. 'Le Blanc there found her.' He paused to search for words. 'By the little...shelter, I think the word is. Your shelter, I was told. She was unconscious.'

'Liar! Filthy liar!'

Adam shook his head. 'She'd been beaten and is in a far worse state than I.'

Abruptly Gunni released Adam and, horror dawning on his face, turned. 'Judhael? Brun said *you* went that way. Did you see anything?'

'No.'

Gunni's gaze sharpened. 'Judhael, you wouldn't...?'

'Of course I wouldn't,' Judhael said, swift as an arrow. 'The bloody Frank did it.'

'No!' Cecily burst out. 'Adam would never do such a thing! But *you*...that bite...that bite on your hand...' Across the clearing, a corner of Adam's mouth lifted. It was the smallest of movements, virtually imperceptible, but Cecily was absurdly alert to everything about him—from the bruising on his face, to his empty sword scabbard, to the mud on his boots...

Judhael stalked across the boggy clearing, elbowed Emma aside and towered over her. 'Soft, is he?'

'Not in the least,' Cecily said. Her skin was like ice, but she refused to quail before him. 'But nor is he cruel. Adam had his man punish Lufu for laziness, but he only put her in the stocks. He wouldn't have her beaten. None of *them* would. But you…your hand testifies to what you have done.'

Emma's breath hitched, and Cecily realised that Gunni was not the only person to be watching Judhael in appalled disbelief. Emma and Edmund wore expressions that must mirror her own. This was her father's housecarl, Judhael, but he was not the honourable man of old. He had become a tyrant.

'Brun? Stigand?' Edmund gestured at two of the men by the campfire. 'You went out with Judhael earlier. What have you got to say?' The two looked uncomfortably at Judhael and clamped their lips together. Surely they would exonerate Judhael if he had had nothing to do with Lufu being hurt? Their silence condemned him. 'Judhael?' Edmund's hand went to his sword hilt.

'Sweet Christ—as if I would! Surely you don't believe his word over mine? The blasted Breton is trying to divide us. Gunni, continue.'

'He did it,' Le Blanc said, his gaze pinned on Judhael. 'I…how do you say?…I watched him.'

Gunni's face suffused. 'You bastard, Judhael!' A large fist slammed into Judhael's face and Judhael went down. Gunni looked at Adam. 'At my hut, you said?'

'Aye.'

Gunni snatched a horse from a scout, flung himself into the saddle, and was off, mud spraying in his wake. A skin-shrivelling silence gripped those who remained. Something cold was thrust into Cecily's palm. Emma's eating knife.

'Emma?' But Emma was not looking her way—she was staring at Judhael as though he'd crawled out of a cesspit.

Not stopping to think, Cecily hurled herself across the clearing to Adam. No one attempted to hold her back. She gave a swift, feather-light caress to his bruised cheekbone and swollen eye, and was rewarded with one of his lop-sided grins. And then she was sawing for all she was worth at the leather ribbons binding him to the yoke.

'Hurry, Princess,' Adam murmured, glancing over her shoulder at someone coming up behind her.

'I know, I know.' But the chill had had turned her fingers into thumbs, and the leather resisted Emma's eating knife, and Cecily was terrified lest she slice through one of the arteries on Adam's wrists, and…

'Let me,' a voice said, directly behind her. Edmund, with Gurth at his side…

Desperately, Cecily gripped Emma's knife.

'Gurth, the yoke,' Edmund said. 'Hold it fast.' Gurth moved behind Adam.

'Edmund, no,' Cecily moaned.

Edmund grinned, and for a second Cecily glimpsed the old Edmund—the Edmund she had known in her childhood, before she had been sent to the convent, before the Normans had crossed the Narrow Sea. Edmund's seax flashed, and the yoke dropped into Gurth's waiting arms. Gurth hurled it to the ground with a thud.

Adam's arms fell, and he blanched as the blood rushed back into them. Taking his hand, Cecily draped it over her shoulder. Adam gripped her to him like a vice, their fingers entwined, and suddenly, despite the mud, despite the damp and the cold, it felt like summer.

Le Blanc too was freed from his yoke. He stood, bemusedly rubbing his wrists, his eyes fixed on Judhael, who sprawled in the mud with Stigand's sword at his throat. One hand over his nose, Judhael attempted to rise, but Stigand's sword, a slim silver line in the firelight, held him down.

Pointedly, Edmund sheathed his seax. 'I've travelled as far as I'm going with you, Judhael. You take roads that I'll not walk on. Lufu…' Wearily, he scrubbed at his face. 'You should not have done that. Lufu is one of us.'

'That trollop has a loose mouth. It needed closing.'

'But to leave her unconscious and bleeding, out in this weather…! No, Judhael, that was ill done.'

Stigand allowed Judhael to struggle up on one elbow. Blood trickled from Judhael's nose, his lip curled. 'So, Edmund, you're allying yourself with the new Lord of Fulford?'

'I didn't say that, but I've done travelling with you.'

'And what about me? Do you hand me to the Frank, so he can dangle me from the nearest gibbet?'

Emma put her hand to her mouth and sucked in a breath. Leaving the shelter of Adam's arm, Cecily started towards her. Faint hoofbeats could be heard in the thickets to the south of the clearing, from the direction of Seven Wells Hill.

'Make your mind up,' Judhael said, wiping the blood from his nose. 'The Breton must have laid a trail for his cavalry—listen, they've tracked us down.'

'Damn it, Judhael, you're a brother to me. I can't see you in your winding sheet.' Edmund waved at Stigand, who sheathed his sword. 'Go on—get out of here.'

The hoofbeats were getting louder. Scrambling to his feet, Judhael dived at a horse and threw himself into the saddle. Wheeling about, he offered Emma his hand. 'Not the life I'd hoped for, love, but will you join me?'

Emma stumbled back. 'I... I...*no*! I'm sorry, Judhael. I...I can't.' Blindly, she fled to the awning, cheeks glistening with tears.

Judhael's jaw dropped and he seemed to age ten years. 'Emma? *Emma?*' He spurred after her, but Edmund snatched at his horse's bridle.

'*Go*, man, if you value your life. They're almost on us!'

Judhael singled out one of the men by the fire with a look, and lifted an eyebrow. 'Azor, are you with me?'

'Aye.' Slapping Gurth on the back in a gesture of farewell, the man grabbed a horse from its tether and vaulted up.

'Eric?'

'I'm with Edmund. When it comes to bludgeoning our womenfolk...' Eric shook his head.

White about the mouth, Judhael directed a last frown after Emma, and clapped his heels to his horse's sides. Mud flew. He and Azor thundered out of the clearing, heading north as the last rays of daylight gilded the tops of the trees.

A heartbeat later, Wilf and Brian Herfu cantered up to the campfire at the head of Adam's troop.

Candles lent the loft room at Fulford a soft glow, and the braziers warmed Adam's skin. Washed and stripped to the waist, he was standing on the rush matting, submitting resignedly to Maurice's ministrations.

Naturally he would rather have had his hurts tended by his wife, but she was below, behind the curtain in the sleeping area of the Hall, caring for Lufu. He was only suffering from a black eye and a few cuts and bruises. True, his eye throbbed like the devil, and it had puffed up so much that seeing out of it had become impossible. However, he had had a black eye before, and in a few days it would be back to normal. He might yearn for his wife to take the place of his squire, but it would be churlish indeed to summon her when Lufu's needs were greater.

'Turn about, sir,' Maurice said. Dipping his fingers into a pot of evil-smelling ointment, he smeared it onto Adam's shoulder, where the yoke had left a colourful bruise.

'I'm not a horse, man,' Adam said, wincing as Maurice worked it in with rather more energy than was comfortable.

'Sorry, sir.'

Adam wrinkled his nose, trying to see over his shoulder into the pot. 'What in the name of all that's holy is in that stuff?'

'Your lady said it would reduce swelling and bruising. It's got…' Maurice paused. 'Arnica in it—yes, I think that was what he said. Arnica.'

'Arnica never smelt like that when my mother used it. What the evil's mixed with it? Rancid fat?'

The door latch clicked and a draught whispered across his skin. Cecily. His mood instantly lifting, he smiled—or rather he hoped he did. The swelling on his face probably made it look more like a grimace.

'It's goose fat, along with a few other things, and it's not rancid,' she said, returning his smile. Advancing into the room, skirts rustling over the matting, she took the pot from Maurice. 'My thanks, Maurice. I can do the rest.'

Taking Adam's chin in gentle fingers, she examined his face, turning it this way and that in the candlelight. Maurice quietly let himself out.

'I hope you're not thinking I'll let you smear that on my face,' Adam said, watching her out of his good eye. Her skin was flawless, and her lips were an invitation to sin—especially when she was smiling at him like that.

'No? You think it will mar your looks?' she said. 'Believe me, sir, you could hardly look worse.'

'I dare say I'll live.'

'That you will, thank the Lord.' She took one of his hands and traced her fingers over his bitten nails before applying the ointment to his wrist with swift, gentle strokes.

Adam looked down at the top of her veiled head, conscious of a tightness in his chest and the beginnings of that familiar stirring in his loins. She had no idea… She was no longer a virgin, but her innocence remained intact. She did not have the slightest idea that a look, a touch, and he was reduced to a quivering mass of wants and needs and… He sighed. He wanted her. He would always want her. But—he grimaced—he wanted more than her body, he wanted her heart; he wanted her soul. He had not intended that this should happen. He had thought to wed her and bed her, and that would be an end to it. No messy emotions. No pain.

But here, staring at her downbent head, with lust making him hard as iron, there was pain. He loved her, and he wanted her to love him back. This was just like Gwenn. This was *worse* than Gwenn. This was not meant to happen. She was here in their bed-chamber, tending him in a loving manner that roused his every sense, and he knew she would not reject him, and yet the pain remained, inextricably entwined with lust, it would seem. He could not fathom it.

She might have rushed to his defence in the rebel encampment, but he had yet to win her complete trust. Was that at the root of it?

No one had confirmed it to his face, but Philip had to be her brother. If Cecily confessed as much to him, he would know he had won her heart and her trust. And, yes, her heart was what he ached for. He had fled Brittany for a new life, hoping to escape old memories. Not for one moment had he believed that he would find a new love in Wessex, one which burned every bit as brightly as his love for Gwenn had done. But it was too soon to burden Cecily with this. She would not welcome a declaration from him for awhile.

Eyes on that rebellious curl, gleaming gold in the candlelight, Adam cleared his throat. He could be patient. 'How is Lufu?'

'Like you, she is black and blue. I suspect she has cracked a rib, so I've strapped her up. She must have fallen and hit her head on a stone, which is why she was concussed, but it's no worse than that.'

'Thank God.'

'Aye. Emma and Gudrun will watch over her tonight.' She lifted her head and grinned. 'And Gunni, of course. He is sticking to her like glue. Everyone's come to see how she is—Father Aelfric, Wat, Harold, Carl—everyone. Our people are pleased to have her back in one piece.'

Our people. Our people. A shiver Adam recognised as hope ran through him. She continued to fuss over the burns the bindings had made on his wrist. Idly, he reached for her curl and wound it loosely round his forefinger. Shifting closer, he inhaled: rosemary, soapwort, *Cecily*. Her scent wrapped round him, befuddling him. His wife.

'And your sister?' he asked, managing to stop himself from hauling her to him. 'What will she do?'

'I'm not sure. Edmund has offered to help Leofwine and Evie build a new house in Winchester. She may go and live there with the three of them for a time.'

'She's welcome to stay here. As is Edmund.'

Cecily shook her head. 'They won't do that. Not at present. Maybe later, when memories have…faded.' She hesitated, doubt in her eyes.

He tipped his head to one side. 'Yes?'

'They'll never tell you where that silver is. They won't even tell me.'

'I realise that. My guess is that Judhael will have taken it. Cecily, I don't care about the silver.'

'Truly?'

'Truly. Judhael's fighting a lost cause. A cask or two of silver won't change that.'

'So you…you really aren't planning to hand Edmund over to the garrison commander?'

Slowly Adam shook his head. He released the curl and watched it spring back into its natural shape. 'As I said, he is welcome here if he is willing to swear fealty to me.'

'In time he may.' Cecily sighed.

'Princess?' He picked up the curl again, threaded it through his fingers.

'I…I was talking to George Le Blanc while I looked at his hurts. He told me how you came to be captured…'

'And?'

'He says you lured the rebels up to the beacon with smoke signals. Why?'

Adam shrugged, freed his hand from the strand of hair, and made to turn away. He did not want her to read what was in his heart. She was not ready. He steeled himself to face the fact that she might *never* be ready.

'Wait, Adam,' she said, catching his other arm and applying ointment to it. 'Why would you lure them like that? Did you think that you and George alone could protect your interests in Wessex?'

Her head remained downbent, she was entirely focused on his wrist, but something about her tone told him that her question was not an idle one. His answer was important to her. He tipped her chin up. A faint flush was staining her cheekbones. 'Cecily, as I told Judhael in the clearing, I came for you.'

A tiny crease appeared between her brows. 'Yes, I remember that is what you said. But surely…? M-me? You put yourself in mortal danger with only one man at your side—for me?'

'I came for you.' Removing the pot from her, he put it on the washstand and slipped his hands round her waist. She would not refuse him. If he could not have her heart, there was comfort to be found in her body—*much* comfort. 'You are the most important of my interests in Wessex,' he said, dropping a kiss on her forehead.

'I…I am?'

She wasn't fishing for compliments. She really didn't believe him. That father of hers—to thrust a loving, lusty girl like Cecily into the clutches of that cold-hearted Prioress…

'Certainly. I'd like to say I had a plan for winning you back, but I'd be lying.' He shook his head, his voice husky as he brought her body next to him. 'When I returned from Winchester and found you gone I thought you had betrayed me.'

'You were angry,' she said softly. Resting her cheek against his chest, she put her arms about him and loosed a storm of lust and longing in him. It was enough to make him forget the aches in his back and shoulders and ribs; enough to make him forget the swelling of his eye…

He cleared his throat. 'I was, but when we stumbled across Lufu I was obsessed by one thought—to get to you before Judhael treated you in the same way. I had no idea what I might do when I reached his camp. I just rushed in like a madman.' He shook his head in self-deprecation. 'Some strategist, huh?' Her head shifted, and when she kissed his chest he nuzzled the top of her head.

'I'm glad you did rush in,' she said. 'It brought home to Emma and Edmund that Judhael was turning into something…monstrous.'

Gently, he raised her chin. 'Am *I* monstrous in your eyes?'

'You know you are not. I…I have grown very fond of you.'

Fond? Disappointment engulfed him, but he strove to hide it. Would he always be the invader here? Would the true identity of her brother stand between them for ever? 'That remark deserves a kiss,' he said lightly. 'I hope you like kissing ugly Bretons with black eyes.'

Her lips curved. 'I do if they go by the name of Adam Wymark.'

'That's lucky,' he said, smiling as their lips met.

It was a long kiss. Adam intended to keep it gentle, but her lips softened and parted, and her tongue met his almost eagerly, it seemed, and her body was warm against him, and her hands had somehow slipped under the waist of his braies and down over his buttocks, holding him to her while she pressed herself against him. A groan escaped him. She had no idea… When she moved like that he wanted to feel her breasts move against his bare flesh. He wanted…

Breathless, he drew back and looked at the bed.

She flushed and gave a shaky laugh. 'Yes, it *is* late, isn't it…?'

Smiling, he manoeuvred her towards the bed, and began pulling out the pins that kept her veil in place. So far there had been no mention of the snuffing out of candles, which was promising. 'It is late indeed. It is time for you to show me how fond you are.'

She drew back, not meeting his eyes. 'Adam, there is one thing…'

'Mmm?'

'A-about Philip.'

Casting aside her veil, he froze. *Yes! Tell me—tell me now.*

'He…he…' Distancing herself from him, she wrung her hands. 'Adam, you say I am important to you—' her voice cracked '—but I have something to say to you that will truly anger you.'

'I doubt that.'

She twisted her head back and forth. 'No, it will. You see, I have lied to you about Philip…'

'I know.'

'He…he's my brother…'

'I know.'

'Not Gudrun's son, but my brother— Wh…what did you say?'

Adam captured her hands, brought them to his lips. 'I know. I know it all. I guessed it some while ago.' Her eyes were wide and dark, her expression puzzled.

'And you're not angry? You're not planning to send him away or…?'

'Kill him?' Adam's lips twisted. 'I hope you'd know I'd not harm a baby.'

Her fingers clung to his. 'I do know that—yes, I do. You are a good man—how else could I love you? It…it's just that—'

His heart pounded and he gripped her by the shoulders. 'Say that again.'

She blinked. 'What?'

'The part about you loving me.'

Shyly, her eyes met his. 'I do love you. But I have already told you—'

'You said *fond*.' Throat dry, he swallowed, stumbling over the words. 'Fondness is not love.'

'I…I know. I…I thought you would prefer to hear that. I realise I can never replace your Gwenn, but—'

Heart swelling, Adam leaned his forehead against hers and gave a shaky laugh. 'Oh, dear girl, of course you can't replace Gwenn. No, don't pull away—listen. Gwenn was Gwenn, and you are you. But don't think I don't love you. I do.' Aware his fingers were boring into her shoulders, he slackened his grip and took a deep breath. 'I love you, Cecily. I will never stop loving Gwenn. She was part of me, but she is in the past. You are my present. You are my future. You have become the wife of my heart. When you are not with me I ache to see you. When you are with me I long…' He grinned. 'You know what I long to do.'

Her blue eyes were fixed on him, soft and warm and loving. 'Truly? It is not just carnal love?'

'Truly. I love you.' The look in her eyes made his bones melt. Cecily, his princess—*his*. Only now was he beginning to believe it.

'Your brother will live here,' he said, while he could still think. 'And when he is older, if he wishes, I will sponsor him to become a squire. After that…' He shrugged. 'The rest is up to him. His life will be his to make of what he wills.'

'Oh, Adam.' She offered him her lips. 'Kiss me.'

Drawing her to him, he took the taste of her deep into his mouth, savoured it, wondered how he had ever lived without it.

'Butterflies again,' she murmured, her tone edged with wonder.

'Butterflies?'

Shifting slightly, she pressed his hand to her belly. 'Here. When you kiss me, butterflies start to dance here—countless butterflies, more than the stars.'

'And that is a good thing?'

Gentle fingertips caressed his cheek, outlined his mouth, left fire in their wake. 'Yes, indeed. And sometimes when you touch me…the merest hint of a touch…' She sighed. 'It is most strange.'

He reached for her girdle, smiled as simultaneously she reached for the tie at his waist. 'It is the same for me.'

'Really? We must be very odd. Adam…?'

'Hmm?'

'Tell me you love me one more time…'

'Cecily, I love you. You are the sun and the moon to me. You are my soul… Will that do?'

Smiling, she fell back onto the bed. A small hand reached up to draw him close. 'It will…for the time being…'

Shivering with delight as her hands ran up and down his back, he gestured at the bedside candle. 'Do you want this out?'

'No, my love. From tonight there will be no more dark secrets.'

Smiling, he caught her to him and brought his lips urgently to hers.

* * * * *

Welcome to cowboy country...

Turn the page for a sneak preview of
TEXAS BABY
by
Kathleen O'Brien
An exciting new title from Harlequin Superromance for
everyone
who loves stories about the West.

Harlequin Superromance—
Where life and love weave together in emotional and unforget-
table ways.

CHAPTER ONE

CHASE TRANSFERRED his gaze to the road and identified a foreign spot on the horizon. A car. Almost half a mile away, where the straight, tree-lined drive met the public road. He could tell it was coming too fast, but judging the speed of a vehicle moving straight toward you was tricky.

It wasn't until it was about two hundred yards away that he realized the driver must be drunk...or crazy. Or both.

The guy was going maybe sixty. On a private drive, out here in ranch country, where kids or horses or tractors or stupid chickens might come darting out any minute, that was criminal. Chase straightened from his comfortable slouch and waved his hands.

"Slow down, you fool," he called out. He took the porch steps quickly and began walking fast down the driveway.

The car veered oddly, from one lane to another, then up onto the slight rise of the thick green spring grass. It just barely missed the fence.

"Slow down, damn it!"

He couldn't see the driver, and he didn't recognize this automobile. It was small and old, and couldn't have cost much even when it was new. It was probably white, but now it needed either a wash or a new paint job or both.

"Damn it, what's wrong with you?"

At the last minute, he had to jump away, because the idiot

behind the wheel clearly wasn't going to turn to avoid a collision. He couldn't believe it. The car kept coming, finally slowing a little, but it was too late.

Still going about thirty miles an hour, it slammed into the large, white-brick pillar that marked the front boundaries of the house. The pillar wasn't going to give an inch, so the car had to. The front end folded up like a paper fan.

It seemed to take forever for the car to settle, as if the trauma happened in slow motion, reverberating from the front to the back of the car in ripples of destruction. The front windshield suddenly seemed to ice over with lethal bits of glassy frost. Then the side windows exploded.

The front driver's door wrenched open, as if the car wanted to expel its contents. Metal buckled hideously. Small pieces, like hubcaps and mirrors, skipped and ricocheted insanely across the oyster-shell driveway.

Finally, everything was still. Into the silence, a plume of steam shot up like a geyser, smelling of rust and heat. Its snake-like hiss almost smothered the low, agonized moan of the driver.

Chase's anger had disappeared. He didn't feel anything but a dull sense of disbelief. Things like this didn't happen in real life. Not in his life. Maybe the sun had actually put him to sleep....

But he was already kneeling beside the car. The driver was a woman. The frosty glass-ice of the windshield was dotted with small flecks of blood. She must have hit it with her head, because just below her hairline a red liquid was seeping out. He touched it. He tried to wipe it away before it reached her eyebrow, though, of course that made no sense at all. Her eyes were shut.

Was she conscious? Did he dare move her? Her dress was covered in glass, and the metal of the car was sticking out lethally in all the wrong places.

Then he remembered, with an intense relief, that every good

medical man in the county was here, just behind the house, drinking his champagne. He found his phone and paged Trent.

The woman moaned again.

Alive, then. Thank God for that.

He saw Trent coming toward him, starting out at a lope, but quickly switching to a full run.

"Get Dr. Marchant," Chase called. "Don't bother with 9-1-1."

Trent didn't take long to assess the situation. A fraction of a second, and he began pulling out his cell phone and running toward the house.

The yelling seemed to have roused the woman. She opened her eyes. They were blue and clouded with pain and confusion.

"Chase," she said.

His breath stalled. His head pulled back. "What?"

Her only answer was another moan, and he wondered if he had imagined the word. He reached around her and put his arm behind her shoulders. She was tiny. Probably petite by nature, but surely way too thin. He could feel her shoulder blades pushing against her skin, as fragile as the wishbone in a turkey.

She seemed to have passed out, so he put his other arm under her knees and lifted her out. He tried to avoid the jagged metal, but her skirt caught on a piece and the tearing sound seemed to wake her again.

"No," she said. "Please."

"I'm just trying to help," he said. "It's going to be all right."

She seemed profoundly distressed. She wriggled in his arms, and she was so weak, like a broken bird. It made him feel too big and brutish. And intrusive. As if touching her this way, his bare hands against the warm skin behind her knees, were somehow a transgression.

He wished he could be more delicate. But he smelled gasoline, and he knew it wasn't safe to leave her here.

Finally he heard the sound of voices, as guests began to run around the side of the house, alerted by Trent. Dr. Marchant was at the front, racing toward them as if he were forty instead of seventy. Susannah was right behind him, her green dress floating around her trim legs.

"Please," the woman in his arms murmured again. She looked at him, the expression in her blue eyes lost and bewildered. He wondered if she might be on drugs. Hitting her head on the windshield might account for this unfocused, glazed look, but it couldn't explain the crazy driving.

"Please, put me down. Susannah… The wedding…"

Chase's arms tightened instinctively, and he froze in his tracks. She whimpered, and he realized he might be hurting her. "Say that again?"

"The wedding. I have to stop it."

* * * * *

Be sure to look for TEXAS BABY,
available September 11, 2007,
as well as other fantastic Superromance titles
available in September.

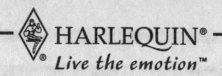

HARLEQUIN®
Live the emotion™

American ROMANCE®

Heart, Home & Happiness

HARLEQUIN® **Blaze**™

Red-hot reads.

HARLEQUIN®

EVERLASTING LOVE™

Every great love has a story to tell™

 Harlequin® Historical
Historical Romantic Adventure!

HARLEQUIN®

HARLEQUIN ROMANCE®

From the Heart, For the Heart

HARLEQUIN®

INTRIGUE

Breathtaking Romantic Suspense

Medical Romance™...
love is just a heartbeat away

Next™

**There's the life you planned.
And there's what comes next.**

HARLEQUIN®
Presents
Seduction and Passion Guaranteed!

HARLEQUIN®
Super Romance®

Exciting, Emotional, Unexpected

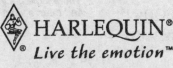

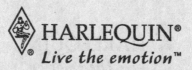

HARLEQUIN®
INTRIGUE®

BREATHTAKING ROMANTIC SUSPENSE

Shared dangers and passions lead to electrifying
romance and heart-stopping suspense!

Every month, you'll meet six new heroes
who are guaranteed to make your spine tingle
and your pulse pound. With them you'll enter
into the exciting world of Harlequin Intrigue—
where your life is on the line
and so is your heart!

THAT'S INTRIGUE—
ROMANTIC SUSPENSE
AT ITS BEST!

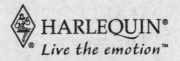

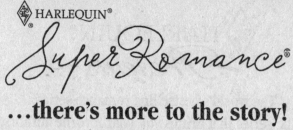

HARLEQUIN®
Super Romance®

...there's more to the story!

Superromance.
A *big* satisfying read about unforgettable characters. Each month we offer *six* very different stories that range from family drama to adventure and mystery, from highly emotional stories to romantic comedies—and much more! Stories about people you'll believe in and care about. Stories too compelling to put down....

Our authors are among today's *best* romance writers. You'll find familiar names and talented newcomers. Many of them are award winners— and you'll see why!

If you want the biggest and best in romance fiction, you'll get it from Superromance!

Exciting, Emotional, Unexpected...

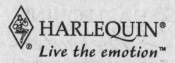

HARLEQUIN®
Live the emotion™

HARLEQUIN®
Presents

The world's bestselling romance series...
The series that brings you your favorite authors,
month after month:

Helen Bianchin...Emma Darcy
Lynne Graham...Penny Jordan
Miranda Lee...Sandra Marton
Anne Mather...Carole Mortimer
Susan Napier...Michelle Reid

and many more uniquely talented authors!

Wealthy, powerful, gorgeous men...
Women who have feelings just like your own...
The stories you love, set in exotic, glamorous locations...

HARLEQUIN®
Presents

Seduction and Passion Guaranteed!